from Tra

# THE
# WOODS

## RONALD LEE GEIGLE

ISBN 978-0-9912713-1-3
First paperback edition: February 2014

Published by Polidais LLC, Washington, DC, in association with:

**WordVirgin**
Seattle  Washington, DC  Edinburgh
www.wordvirgin.com

Dreams are serious business.
Best to run
after
Not sleep
through
*Anonymous*

# Book One: Spring 1937

## Chapter 1

Magnificent.

That was the word, Albert decided. That was the word that described it all. And because he was good with words, Albert knew that he'd found the right one.

Though just ten miles up the valley from Albert's home in Seakomish, the Skybillings Logging Company was a taste of the magic he'd longed for in all of his eighteen years—or at least all of those that he could remember. Repairing the tracks in a logging railway—which carried ancient firs from the high reaches of the Cascade Mountains to the lumber mills along Puget Sound—gave him blisters that bled and arms that hung like cord wood at the end of the day. But the cold air six thousand feet up in the mountains made him feel warm.

Since the day six weeks earlier when he had arrived at Skybillings Logging Company, Albert had worked for Nariff Olben and his crew laying the tracks—they called them "sections"—for the rough-hewn Skybillings railroad line that inched its way up the Cascade Mountains from Seakomish. The Skybillings track climbed the grade along Roosevelt Creek, with its boulders and hard-charging water; wound through the towering Douglas firs that crowded the steep inclines of the Cascade Range; then—miles later and many thousands of feet higher—finally broke into the sunlight along the sharp edge of a deep and wide ravine.

Skybillings Lumber Company wasn't the only one to lay down a logging railroad high in the Cascades, of course. Skybillings was one of hundreds of railroad logging companies—the locals called them logging "shows"—that operated in the Cascades during the late 1930s.

All of them built and maintained their own lines. Some shared the same tracks in the lower part of the valleys around Seakomish. But then, as you rose higher, the tracks quickly splintered into the lines of individual companies, a spider web that disappeared into the dense forest and steep inclines. With no roads, the logging shows couldn't get the timber out any other way, and sometimes even had to log right up to the snowfields. They ran powerful steam locomotives to haul out the old Douglas firs, some 500 or 600 years old—some nearing a thousand years even—and so wide at the base that six men with arms outstretched still couldn't reach around them. The engines that pulled them were Shays and Baldwins and Heislers, all of them with their names emblazoned in silver or embossed white on their flat black noses. Tons of metal to haul tons of wood.

The Skybillings locomotive, a Shay, ten tons of black iron, spouted steam and cinders, and it screamed against the terrible weight of the firs it hauled. But—once loaded—the Shay finally, painfully, crept along the rock ledges, then descended slowly along the mountain shoulders, back down the Roosevelt Creek Valley, through Seakomish, carrying the massive firs to the mills in Everett or Seattle, mills that stripped them clean and sawed them and shaped them into lumber that was rebuilding New Jersey and New York and "the whole East Coast"—it was how they said it—as America began to recover from the ravages of the Great Depression.

Skybillings was part of that. Albert Weissler—proud of his eighteen years, born in Seakomish, of reasonable muscles and a quick mind—liked that he was now part of it, too.

In spring, 1937, of course, families still rode the rails because of the Depression, which everyone said was already in the history books as the worst ever. The jobs still couldn't be found, at least for most people. Everett itself—the smaller, poorer, little brother lying north of Seattle—ached with the unemployed and the hopeless. The labor union tensions in the woods still festered and got bloody at times. But Skybillings—and the railroad logging shows of the Cascade Mountains—felt like they were, inch-by-inch, rebuilding America.

❊　　❊　　❊

Nariff Olben let out a loud grunt, then sucked in another load of damp, mountain air. He let the rough handle of the sledgehammer ease back against his belt buckle and adjusted the black eye patch that had lost its grip—said he'd lost the eye in a fight on a fishing boat off Malta. Then, in a single motion, he once again wrenched the heavy sledge high above his six-foot frame, drove it hard into the head of the metal spike—with a gunshot crack—and let out another loud grunt, followed by the same raspy gasp for air.

All afternoon, now reaching past four o'clock and quickly approaching the windy ride down the mountain behind the old locomotive,

Nariff recited, in alphabetic order, all the forms of currency that he claimed were in use around the world. In his travels as a seaman on a Dutch freighter and earlier as a railway clerk in Marrakesh, he had developed an "appreciation for currency," as he put it, heightened by the ravishes of the Great Depression, which had stranded him and his freighter in Seattle during the early months of 1931.

"Peseta. Pound. Rupee. No, that's outa' order. Ruble—from Russia, sorry—then Rupee." He said he had to repeat them in alphabetical order because that was the only way he could remember them all. After six or seven, he would raise the sledgehammer again, slam it into the railroad spike, let out a wheeze, then go on: "Schilling. Sucre. Tugrik."

By late afternoon, Nariff Olben had almost run out of currencies, despite his worldly travels. The rest of his crew—Charles Walker, Whitey Storm, Barney Harten, Lightning Stevens, Conrad Bruel—had come to ignore him months earlier. But Albert provided a new audience.

"Let's see now"—whump wheeze—"I think there ain't many down here at the end of the alphabet. There's, ah-course, the Yen and the Zloty, that's Poland, but I think that's it."

They had worked on this section of track since morning, first dumping gravel under the existing ties, then packing it tight. Then, to give the rails additional support, they inserted new ties—six-foot-long twelve-by-twelve's, rough and heavy, sturdy foundations for the heavy spikes they drove in to hold the steel rails.

As Whitey Storm and Lightning Stevens slammed sledgehammers into the spikes, securing the final ties, Nariff restarted his commentary: "Zloty, now I never had a Zloty myself," he shouted, over the slamming hammers. "Zloty was special among the boys I was shipping out of Hanover with for the Mediterranean. They was saying that the Zloty would bring you good luck. Maybe I am livin' proof that that is true, 'cause I never got my hands on one, and I never got my hands on much goddamn good luck neither."

Whitey Storm snorted, and Lightning Stevens grinned. Charles Walker's face showed boredom, but couldn't repress the hint of a smile. Everyone else remained silent, as Nariff squatted along the edge of the track that wound in a semi-circle through the clearing. This broad, open expanse was called the "the landing." Though it lay thousands of feet up in the Cascade Range, this was the working base of the land that Skybillings logged. From here, the fir-covered slopes to the west rose steeply upward, another 6,000 feet or more, as did those to the south—these, finally quitting when the rough granite face of Three Sisters Ridge overpowered the massive firs. Three Sisters stretched to the east for perhaps a mile, and at its base, a ravine that itself was a half-mountain long, deep, and wide.

On the distant shore—the far edge of the ravine and butted tight against the granite of Three Sisters Ridge—lay the rest of the Skybillings land. The timber on the far side was rumored to be the best in the Cascades, but was virtually useless because it couldn't be reached—shut off by the treacherous ravine and the granite face of Three Sisters. It was destined to remain such forever—according to most who knew the woods hereabouts—nothing more than a green-blue mat that floated inside the clouds of winter and shimmered far-off during summer's dry heat.

Whitey Storm squatted next to Nariff, eyeing the ties. He slammed his hammer on an occasional spike for good measure.

"What do you think?" asked Whitey.

Nariff stepped onto the closest rail, bouncing his weight up and down. "Christ man, these little babies is perfect. They probably was plenty good even before we started on 'em, never mind dear old fart, Mr. Valentine." John Valentine was the foreman who ordered the work two days earlier. "It don't matter which union a man belongs to—it don't matter if you are an AFL man or a CIO man or you think the both of them should go to hell—everyone will agree that John Valentine is a fart."

Nariff Olben was a man of perfection. Albert saw that from the very first day. Despite his apparent don't-give-a-damn attitude, Nariff insisted on precision in all of his work that few other section chiefs in the Northwest even came close to. He just muffled it in vinegar and bullshit.

"John Valentine must've got a feather up his arse about these rails," said Nariff, now surveying the entire expanse of track, hands on his hips. "Maybe a feather up his arse 'cause he ain't ever touched enough of them Yens and Zlotys and Pounds and Liras in his miserable, God-fearin' life."

"John Valentine is a prick," offered Conrad Bruel—a scowl on his face that made him look older than his twenty-one years.

"A hearty aye to that, mate," snorted Nariff, but with a bellowing laugh that disintegrated into coughing.

Buckers and fallers who had been working on the higher elevations of the Skybillings land came streaming down the hill, some walking, but most trotting alongside the Shay locomotive that was now rumbling slowly down the steep incline. Its two trailing flatcars looked like toys beneath the mass of the Douglas firs they carried, both logs dripping broken twigs and fir boughs and mud goo. The Shay screeched painfully against the dead-weight tons of steel and wood pushing from behind.

Ferguson, the engineer, hung his chubby head out the window to check the rails. The fireman stood on the locomotive's front platform studying them carefully.

"Sonabitch is looking good, Fergie," shouted the fireman in the direction of the cab. The engineer opened the throttle slightly, bringing up the speed of the Shay, which now towered ten feet above Albert and the rest of section crew. Albert's feet tingled from the vibration of the Shay, his nostrils full of the hot aroma of steam and oil and raw wood.

Fergie now added a little more throttle, shouting toward Nariff. "You old shit-ass, Nariff Olben. I didn't think you had enough brains to make those things hold a toy wagon."

Nariff smiled and flipped him the finger. Fergie tipped his hat in response.

Now the Shay passed slowly over the section of rails that had gotten the new ties, which obligingly shifted, but as intended, gently eased back and then re-settled firmly in place.

The buckers and fallers who had been running alongside the Shay swept past, many now breaking into a sprint to the crummy—the old flatbed rail car, equipped with seats and a small gas engine, that took the crew back to the bunkhouse. As soon as the Shay finally passed through the clearing and was on its way to the Everett mills, the crummy would follow close behind, until it reversed course at the railroad fork at Anderson Creek, switching to the side-track that would take them to a slight dip in the mountains where the Skybillings bunkhouse stood.

Albert had heard men talk about Nariff Olben. That he was too old and too full of tall tales to be in charge of the section crew. But Albert wanted to shout as the train passed by without incident.

"What are you so fuckin' happy about, kid?" asked Conrad Bruel with a sneer. Nariff, Charles Walker, Whitey, and the rest of the crew had already started back to the tool sheds, at the distant end of the clearing.

Albert shrugged. "Nothing. Just happy to see that our hard work paid off."

"Your buddy Nariff Olben ain't gonna keep his job long, you know." Conrad shielded his voice slightly so only Albert could hear.

"Why's that?"

Conrad smiled, though the heavy ledge of eyebrows turned the smile into a threat. "John Valentine is gonna kick his ass if he keeps mouthing off. He's asking for trouble. Word to the wise."

"You mouthed off just as much about Valentine."

Conrad sneered and laughed. "Nobody cares what I say, stupid. But that old man runs the section crew. And they'll all think he's just trying to start more union trouble."

Albert could not fully grasp the anger in Conrad. It popped up at odd times. It seemed that everyone on the crew was mad at something or someone. Everyone hated Valentine—he was the foreman after all. Max St. Bride was always looking to fight. But Conrad's anger seemed less even, and often sharper.

Nariff, Lightning, Whitey Storm, and Charles Walker had already loaded most of the shovels and sledgehammers into the tool sheds that stood back from the track. Men were now gathering around the two sheds, wiping off the mud and dirt of the day, getting ready for the ride down the mountain to the bunkhouse. Albert noticed shovels and sledgehammers they had left behind on the other side of the tracks, so set off to retrieve them.

But when he stepped onto the first rail, the earth turned liquid. He stumbled and tried to regain his footing, but the rocks and ties under his feet moved again—everything around him was shifting sideways. He pitched forward, landing hard on his belly across the rock they had just laid. When he got back to his feet, he could see both rails quivering and the spikes bending away from the rails.

He searched for Conrad, who was now running toward a mass of smoke and red flame, far away from him—far toward the end of the landing.

"Albert, grab the shovels." The voice was Bud Cole, Skybillings' owner, who swept past him at a dead sprint. Others followed—the fallers, the Swedes, Valentine's crew, then the rest of the buckers and the riggingslingers. They grabbed shovels and sledgehammers as they ran. Several stopped to hoist-up heavy railroad ties that lay along the tracks. Albert pulled himself out of the mud, grabbed a shovel, and fell in.

The heavy black smoke burned his eyes and the *thumming-thumming* vibrations in the ground took away all other senses for a moment—but then the full scene opened clearly before him: perhaps fifty yards ahead stood the Shay, now leaning sharply forward and to the right—half off the tracks, the massive iron wheels roaring, spewing mud and rock as they churned full-power into the blackened earth. In an instant, the rails under the flatcars sprung outward into awkward bows, then ripped apart with a metallic shriek.

The chaos of metal and steam, the fire spitting from the Shay, the choking smell of burning oil and wood, brought Albert to a dead stop.

"St. Bride, St. Bride," screamed Bud Cole, "restart the winch. Get cables around the Shay. Now! Now!" Max St. Bride was already atop the steam winch at the top of the landing, throttling the machine furiously. Several men guided the thick metal cable as it uncoiled from the greasy winch, backpedaling toward the Shay. Within a minute, they had looped it around the smokestack; they bound another around the cab and the rear wheels.

The winch roared and the cables ground into the Shay, pulling hard against the dead weight, as men scrambled to get out of whiplash range. The cable noose drew tighter—St. Bride's revving brought an angry roar from the engine powering the winch—and the muddy ooze finally gave way. The fuming, wounded locomotive slowly began rising—dripping mud and oil as it did, its wheels still mired, but upright nonetheless—all now tethered by string-tight steel cables to two towering firs and the roaring winch.

※　※　※

It hung there. Perfectly balanced. Enveloped by sound and smell, and smoke that stung the eyes, but no movement. Then a wave of men flowed toward it, to save it, to settle it safely back to earth. Several—Conrad Bruel and Charles Walker in the middle—wound more cables around the body of the locomotive, then winched them to another massive fir standing not far from the track. Others poured gravel into the muck—of mud, oil, and charred wood—that lay below the locomotive, then threw down wooden ties, all laid shoulder to shoulder, to build a wooden platform. Lightning Stevens and Nariff Olben stood in the middle, directing the placement, as the makeshift crisscross foundation began to form just underneath the iron wheels. Bud Cole called out for everyone to stand back, then lowered his arm slowly as St. Bride loosened the winch. Again, the sound of screeching metal as the Shay settled onto the wooden base, which groaned under the growing load. Only a few ties slipped.

Bud signaled for St. Bride to let out more slack, which brought more groans from the wood—then a metallic *pingked, pingked* shot through the air as one of the cables snapped and bullwhipped within killing-reach of several men. The Shay jolted downward, but then stopped, as the others cables held tight. Men from both ends of the locomotive rushed in again to set more ties, others raced to add more cables.

Albert set out for the gravel pile, but before he reached it, the sickening staccato sound—*pingked, pingked*—again echoed through the clearing, followed by metal tearing against metal. He turned just as the Shay lurched forward, then pitched violently sideways, sending men lunging in all directions. For a moment, it seemed to teeter, as if uncertain to stay up or fall over, then finally it slumped hard onto its side. As it did, it up-ended the flatbed cars it had been pulling, unleashing the massive fir logs that now shot down the steep incline toward Albert.

Albert lunged for the ground, landing behind an upturned stump, just as one of the massive firs slammed against it—spraying bullets of bark and broken wood into his back and legs. The taste of the dank, bitter dirt filled his mouth and the hard roots and rocks moved beneath him as the log shot over him and sailed downward with a rumbling roar.

In an instant, all was silent. The ground was still. Albert could hear himself breathe. He lifted his head slowly and peered down the slope to find a broad expanse of smashed stumps and torn branches, and the flat outcropping of rock at the edge of the ravine ripped clean of bushes and scrub pine. The logs had swept down this slope, crushed everything in their path, and then shot outward into a free-fall to the bottom of the ravine.

He heard cries and moans. Men lay scattered between the stumps below him, a few not moving. Up the slope, several more lay on the ground, and just beyond—through the smoke and steam—he could make out ten or maybe twenty men, digging furiously with shovels at the edges of the fallen Shay, its smokestack still belching fire across fifty feet of ground, singeing stumps and loose twigs with cinder fire. The engine itself was on its side, engulfed in a foot of mud.

As he stood up, and stared intently at the front of the engine, blinking hard to focus his eyes, he saw Bud Cole pawing away dirt and muck from underneath the smokestack, shouting the name of Nariff Olben.

## Chapter 2

April is cold high up in the mountains of Washington State. Winter sometimes doesn't go until, in a bad year, as late as May or June. Blue-to-black rain clouds usually swallow the afternoon light, muffling it into a sullen grayness.

Albert's mother had laid out his father's last suit. Gray flannel pin stripe, with vest, frayed at the wrists and thin at the elbows. Beside it, a starched white shirt, red tie. All of them lined up on his bed when he came back from his bath.

"Mother, what are these doing here?" he shouted down the stairs toward the kitchen. Why wouldn't a sweater and a coat do? He picked up the suit, rubbing the worn wool between his finger and thumb. He knew it would itch, especially if it rained. Plus, he'd smell like wet dog.

"Mother!"

No answer from the kitchen. Albert hadn't seen this suit since he last saw his father—on a Sunday, after they had gone to church, many years before. That morning, his father seemed to blaze in Christian zeal. It was his turn to teach the Sunday School lesson, so he wore his best suit. Though only eight years old, Albert couldn't have been prouder of, or more frightened by, his father.

Always a calm, quiet man—a man who laughed easily, a man who was always good for a ride on the shoulders—his father now rocked on his toes in front of the Sunday School, speaking in loud, rolling rhythms, his echoing voice thundering throughout the tiny church. Yet when he was done, the ladies who sat in front of Albert and his mother rushed forward to shake his father's hand.

"So you don't want to wear it." His mother had startled him. She was now leaning against the door, peering in. "Let me guess: Because you don't understand why you should wear his suit and besides you'd rather wear your worn-out sweater and jacket." Lydia smiled, her arms now folded.

Albert continued to study the suit. "I might have been thinking something like that," he finally offered.

As she walked into the bedroom, she pushed back a few strands of blond hair that fell from the bun at the back of her head. She fiddled with it, removed a hairpin, snagged the hair with a finger, then pushed it all back into the bun. "Well, that's a perfectly fine question. But you know, you also left out the part about, 'Why should I wear the suit of a dead man, especially to a funeral?'"

Albert slumped back on the bed, groaning.

"What's wrong?"

"I hadn't thought of that. But thanks for mentioning it."

"You're welcome. Now think of all the reasons why you should consider wearing it." She started with her bun again.

"Mother," said Albert, now with eyes closed. "This is a lecture, isn't it?"

"Lecture? I just made a simple statement."

Albert leaned onto one elbow, creasing the arm of the white shirt. Before he could speak, his mother walked back to the door. "I've got to get ready, but you decide," she said, now into the hallway and down the stairs. "Your decision," she called back. "Whether you think a suit and tie are appropriate for the occasion or you think a sweater and jacket."

He rubbed the worn gray fabric at the elbows, just as he remembered it when his father slung the coat over the back of a chair before sitting down to dinner at the Bratton's house that Sunday. They had been invited for dinner, along with the pastor and his family and the three elders and their families. He remembered thinking how dressed up everyone seemed. He was used to seeing loggers wearing striped shirts, black suspenders, thick black pants chopped off not far below the knee—to avoid getting caught in snags and winches— and logging boots that stunk of oil and dirt. Yet all of them—the pastor, the elders, his father—all looked like they had just stepped out of the pages of a Sears catalogue.

"And I'll look just as damn stupid as they did," he said aloud as he picked up the white shirt.

# Chapter 3

The Seakomish People, who had inhabited the land for hundreds of years, taught that when someone died in the valley, the river cried. Depending upon the length of the person's life or the pain of the person's death, the river's cry was sometimes loud and low, sometimes a whisper. But it was always there.

Albert thought of this as he drove his mother and his sister down the lower Seakomish road toward the Stardale cemetery. Rain blurred the windshield, slapped urgently by the wipers. Wind gusts swept the water across the side windows.

His father's suit itched. The collar rode high on his neck, tightened by the hard knot his mother had tied for him. She hadn't said another word about the suit, or how he looked in it. His sister, Elizabeth, snapped gum in the back seat.

He pulled the Ford behind Bucky Rudman's Studebaker. A group of old Chevy's, Fords, and a few worn-out pick-ups—every one of them showing the hundreds of thousands of miles they had clocked—lined the narrow path around the Stardale cemetery. Set on a flat just above Stardale, next to the Valley highway, the cemetery looked over the Seakomish River, which hugged it in a broad arch. A line of Douglas firs stood along the edge of the cemetery against the highway.

Albert didn't actually remember his father's death. He'd since heard the story many times, but he had no recollection of Bud Cole coming to the door that afternoon, asking for Albert's mother, and his mother sitting motionless in a hard-back chair to listen to the story of the limb that broke loose and crashed over her husband's back. Albert had heard over the years, from folks around town, and even once from a teacher, about his mother's unwillingness to cry, either at her husband's funeral or at any time in public following the death.

"She is one strong woman, your mother," said Mrs. Walther, who ran the Seakomish general store. "Your mother never, ever spoke of the accident. She kept on teaching at the school, strong. Not weeping like I would've done. I never knew how she did that, especially left as she was with two small children."

As families got out of their cars, shaking hands, wrapping arms around shoulders and waists, all huddling underneath umbrellas or draped in green ponchos, the rain abruptly stopped. Overhead, the leaden clouds hurried toward the mountains—late, overdue. Darkness held off momentarily.

This was not a moment that Albert had longed for. His thoughts were still locked in that thin indent behind the stump that had saved his life. He stepped across the muddy tire tracks that ran around the outside of the cemetery, following his mother and sister to the graves, but he only saw the blackness of the mud in front of his face, the roaring fir skimming his head.

"Albert." It was a shout from Bucky Rudman, Skybillings' lead topper. Albert hardly recognized him without his belt and harness and all the paraphernalia that dangled from him as he worked his way up the spar trees to lop off their tops. Bucky finally caught up with him—as his mother and sister continued toward the graves.

"Jesus, kid, I heard you almost got squashed by one of them firs that went flying with the birdies." Bucky smiled broadly and slapped him on the back. "With all the chaos and all afterward, I never seen where you were. Little Boy and I were up to our asses in mud trying to save these three poor bastards." He nodded toward the coffins.

It was no surprise to Albert that Bucky would not avoid such discussions, even at the funeral of those who died. Bucky was a cowboy. He chewed, screwed, cussed, and pissed. That was how he often introduced himself—followed by a cackling laugh. Albert suspected that Bucky felt the need to talk so much because his helper, a thin-faced man with pocked skin who everyone called Little Boy, rarely spoke.

Albert ignored Bucky's comment, but then Bucky leaned in closer. "So could you see the old man get crunched?"

"For Christ's sake, Bucky." Several people turned, but Albert tried to ignore them. Bucky nodded, with a smile.

"Beloved, we are gathered at this final resting place to say goodbye to our wonderful friends and brothers—Curt Schmidt, Charles Walker, and Nariff Olben." Reverend Botcher's voice evaporated into the gusts of wind. "On Wednesday, we all know what tragedy struck in the woods above Seakomish. In an instant, the lives of these beloved men—brothers, fathers, husbands—were taken by our Creator."

Albert could hear muffled sobs. Though the rain had stopped, wind coughed occasionally from the west, fluttering the flowers on the caskets.

Albert didn't know most of the families huddled in chairs near the caskets. He recognized Curt Schmidt's twin daughters from school.

Both wrapped in thick brown coats. One dabbed at her eyes with a hankie; the other motionless, staring at the caskets. Albert noticed his mother sitting with Mrs. Schmidt and the girls in the first row of chairs. Behind them was Charles Walker's family—three teenage boys, a grown daughter, and Walker's wife, a narrow, bony woman, with graying hair.

He saw no one that he could identify as a relative of Nariff Olben. At the thought of Nariff, Albert felt again the burning sensation in his throat. He turned his mind quickly back to the itching suit.

Off to the right, in a loose knot, stood Bucky Rudman and several of the choker crew—Conrad Bruel, Myles Norgren, and Lightning Stevens, along with Delbert McKenna, the cook's helper—all ram-rod straight. Petey Hulst, in an orange-colored poncho, held the same expression as when he was working the steam whistle on the mountain—somewhere far away. Bucky Rudman's assistant, Little Boy, stood next to Petey. He did not move, his eyes closed. Max St. Bride was next, a wad of chewing tobacco thick in his cheek. His head bent occasionally to spit. Just behind them all stood Whitey Storm, his arm about the blond-haired girl from Stardale whom he planned to marry in July.

"We know what suffering this loss has brought. We can feel the pain in every movement, in every thought, in every part of our beings." Botcher's face never flinched. Not a flicker of emotion now, though Curt Schmidt's wife laid her head on Lydia's shoulders, muffling deep sobs. The rain began pelting again, a drumbeat on the roof of the metal canopy.

"But we must not remain tied to their passing, to how they passed, to our loss. We must remember these lives in the way that our Creator intended—in the vigor and energy of these lives, in the dedication and love they brought, in the victory of what they tried to accomplish," said Botcher, now a thin voice engulfed in the noisy rain.

Albert noticed that the flower spray on Nariff's casket slid off, but Petey Hulst got down on one knee, straightened it as he picked it up and placed it again, slightly askew, across the casket.

Botcher continued at a faster pace. Maybe the emotion was troubling him, thought Albert, though he couldn't see it on the face. Maybe the weather was too cold for him. Or maybe this was so familiar it bored him. Botcher mentioned a bit of history about each man—about Schmidt's early years with Skybillings, about Walker's sense of perfection with logging machinery, and about Nariff Olben's sense of humor. Then he read some Bible verses and led a hymn that Albert didn't recognize. All the adults seemed to, however, for they sung it from memory—a deep, dragging melody, with dips and lows that Albert found as discouraging as the dark clouds overhead.

When the hymn was done, Bud Cole stepped forward abruptly to stand beside Botcher. Bud was over six feet tall, with broad shoulders that framed a barrel chest. Because he usually held himself in a straight, upright posture, he seemed to tower over other men—as was the case now with Botcher. His dark complexion, deep-set eyes and prominent, slightly bent nose made him seem, to some at least, unfriendly, while most all agreed that Bud Cole always seemed to be a very serious man. Yet Albert had known Bud as far back as he could remember, and he also knew that Bud could laugh and play catch on Sunday afternoons. It was this Bud Cole who had offered Albert the job with Skybillings a few months earlier.

It had been at a church lunch, on a Sunday afternoon. "Want to go to work for us, Albert?" asked Bud, as he sat down with a plate of food.

"For Skybillings? I've never worked in the woods," answered Albert, unsure what his mother would think. Especially under the circumstances.

"Don't take much. Strong back. Small mind."

At first, Albert didn't get the joke, then laughed loudly, which caught his mother's attention. Balancing a coffee cup in a saucer, she walked over to where they were sitting near the end of the buffet table.

"Anything that causes a belly laugh like that deserves repeating," she said, sitting beside Albert, who glanced at Bud.

"I was just telling this young man of yours, Lydia, that he has a good mind and a strong back," said Bud, smiling. "Asked him if he wanted to go to work for Skybillings."

Lydia sipped carefully from the ceramic cup, focused entirely on not burning her lips. Albert wondered if she had heard. She looked toward the other end of the room, with several children playing and circles of parents, some still eating, others balancing desserts and coffee on their laps.

She directed her answer to Albert, though it wasn't an answer. "So you've been offered a job by the Skybillings Logging Company," she said, peering with her blue eyes, not blinking. This was a sign that Albert recognized. His mother would signal her anger with calm words and motionless eyes.

Bud Cole slid his chair back, scraping the legs across the cement floor. "Of course, you could work down here in Seakomish, at the office. I'll probably be opening one this spring. We need a person with a good business mind to help look after books and things. No need to go into the woods, actually."

With that, Bud excused himself, saying he had to refill his coffee. Lydia said she didn't need more, when he asked to refill hers. But he didn't come back after. Albert couldn't decide which of them—his mother or Bud—had been more rude. Albert remembered, though, that this led to the first discussion he had ever had with his mother— later that night—about his father's death, about how his father had come to be partners in Skybillings with Bud Cole, and about how it started and how it ended.

She explained that starting the Skybillings Logging Company in the first place was his father's idea, not Bud Cole's. That the logging market was shooting up, the Great War was over, the 1920s seemed to bring such prosperity, such good things really, and Fred Weissler, Albert's dad, felt that he and his family and his best friend deserved a chance to get in on it.

So Skybillings was born. At first, a tiny operation. Just the two of them—Fred and Bud. Lydia made a strong third, however, because she had good business sense, a good knowledge of financing and numbers.

"And you don't want me going to work in the woods because you figure I will die just like he did," shot Albert, during a pause in her reminiscing.

Lydia did not answer. She looked out the windows of the paneled living room, past the books she held so dear.

"Mother, I'm about to graduate. And I have to have a job. Jobs are impossible to get now. You know it."

She did know it. The ravages of the Depression had shuttered Seakomish for a time. But by then, 1937 after all, things had improved a bit. That was how Bud Cole was able to restart Skybillings after he had to shut it down in '30. The U.S. economy had recovered a bit. The ports of Washington State were active again. But jobs were still scarce. Hunger lines still stretched around the block in Seattle.

Lydia walked to the window, still looking out into the dark woods behind the house. Lydia did not believe in curtains on the main floor of her house. She wanted the light in. And she wanted to see the darkness of night.

"I cannot decide for you, Albert," she said quietly.

He looked at her from across the room, wanting her to say yes or no. He could fight with no. He could gain support from yes. But from this, there was nothing. And, like so many of the things between him and his mother, it never came up again.

❋    ❋    ❋

As he now stood in front of the coffins, Bud Cole cleared his throat, then adjusted his stance.

Reverend Botcher took a small step backward to offer more room. Rain ran down the gutters of the canopy, and umbrellas shielded the crowd, huddled tight.

"I want to say a word if you don't mind," Bud started. He cleared his throat again.

"Pastor Botcher here has offered us some comforting words, today, but I want to add—to each of these families—that I personally want you to know the deep pain, uhhh...," he cleared his throat again and wiped his hand across this mouth. "Nariff and Charlie and Curt were men that I loved as if they were my own brothers. And while I, we, would have done anything to save these men, we know that we cannot replace them. But, I want all of you to know, that Skybillings Logging Company will fill in, best we can, to help, you know, clear the way in the future."

Bud Cole shifted his stance and started again, now in a hurry. "What I mean is, Skybillings, today, is still a struggling company. And this here economy is a bad one. But Edith and Mrs. Walker, we will provide whatever support we can to help get you through. God bless you."

With that, Bud turned around and stepped out from under the canopy, into the rain, which soaked him quickly. Botcher resumed his position, led the congregation in one more hymn, then adjourned the gathering with a prayer.

As the crowd thinned in the heavy rain, Albert noticed Bud—his thick dark face solemn and hard, still standing in a green army slicker at the edge. Water dripped from his cowboy hat—why did he wear it? It was awful and ugly, thought Albert. Without speaking to anyone, Bud brushed water from his face and walked slowly toward his car.

## Chapter 4

A black car rounded the corner onto Main, coasted for a moment, then lurched forward and roared up to Talbert's Bar, screeching to a halt. All four doors swung wide and poured several dark figures onto the street. Bundled tight against the rain, they raced across the sidewalk, through the pool of flashing light from Talbert's neon sign, and into the doorway.

"Mother Mary of Jesus in Heaven," cursed Bucky Rudman, who was the first through. He slumped against the wall, his green slicker draining onto the wood floor. Petey Hulst, Lightning Stevens, and Delbert McKenna—glistening from the sheets of rain—all hurried in after him. The aroma of liquor followed the Skybillings men into the bar.

"Imagine a bunch of goddarn idiots driving on a night like this," said Bucky, as he plopped two stubby arms onto the bar. The others filled the stools on either side. Lightning, at the end of the row, wrung drops from the black curls that hung over his collar. Petey gently twirled water from the tips of his handlebar mustache. Delbert rapped both sets of knuckles on top of the bar, while Little Boy Whittaker settled onto a stool at the end, facing them all.

The bar felt close and moist, a hothouse of stale beer, caulk boots, raw tobacco, and the mustiness of close bodies. A cloud of smoke shrouded the back room, while overhead bulbs fanned thick light onto a pool table that separated the back room from the bar. Shouts and laughter, and occasional barks of conversation, drifted from a circle of men hunched over the pool table and from what seemed a hundred men or more toward the back. Several women poked in and out of the crowd, adding occasional high-pitched squeals.

Earl Talbert emerged from the smoke—towel over one shoulder, hair dripping wet, and three empty pitchers in one hand, several empty bottles in the other. His shaggy whiskers hung damp from a round face, topped by a thick layer of white hair. With a potbelly and a gait that tipped him forward, Earl swept past the new drinkers without looking up.

"Earl, Earl," shouted Delbert, still rapping his knuckles on the bar. "Beer for this group of lugs. We need some *lu-bri-ca-tion*."

"You'll just damn wait," was all Talbert offered as he splashed the pitchers into a soapy tub and disappeared through a doorway.

"What the hell we gotta do to get some service in this here joint?" shouted Delbert, displaying a grin with no teeth on the bottom. His face folded into creases along the cheeks. At one time, the face might have actually been handsome—a sweep of olive skin set atop a broad, dimpled smile. But now, the dimples suffocated in whiskers, the smile splintered by a row of brown, crooked teeth and, on the bottom, pink gum. Delbert had been with Skybillings even back in the '20s. As the bull cook, his job was the odd jobs—from sweeping the bunkhouse floors to washing dishes, and sometimes, when things were very busy, even lending a hand in the logging. When Bud Cole re-opened Skybillings in '35, he said that one of his first hiring choices was Delbert. "I couldn't think of a man better qualified to do odd jobs than Delbert McKenna," said Bud.

Earl Talbert reappeared in the doorway, pulled several mugs from a cupboard and swung them underneath a silver spigot. After he sloshed the mugs in front of the Skybillings crew, he took them all in with a sweep of his eye.

"By the looks of it, none of you birds need any more to drink. You're more'n half-tanked as it is."

Lightning let out an abrupt belch, Petey smiled his dazzling, toothy grin, and Delbert sucked the beer in a gulp, belched and slammed the empty mug back onto the wood.

But the only one who responded to Earl was Bucky Rudman. "Earl, do you remember a woman by name of Rita Milligan, lived down in Stardale?"

"Rita Milligan, Rita Milligan...," Earl's voice growled as he tapped the bar. "You mean the one with the blond hair? Husband got killed working for Deek Brown? Didn't she have big tits?"

Bucky cackled. "That's her."

"What about her?"

"That little honey was hot as they could be when I got to know her about six months after her old man kicked the bucket." Now Bucky whistled low. "We musta done everything to each other short of hooking up jumper cables."

"What the hell does this have to do with anything?"

"All I was trying to get across, Earl, was that the Widow Milligan and I must've tried every goddang position known to man and woman and in-satiable cattle..."

"And so?"

"And so"—Bucky now smiled sweetly—"before we was done, the only way for a man to finally get his head screwed on straight was to pour a little alcohol into the system to clean the pistons. Similar with a wake after a dang funeral—especially a wake for three poor bastards squarshed by a railroad engine. Only way to finally get your senses hooked back together is to oil 'em, but good, and do it with the finest beverage known to man."

Bucky paused as he leaned across the bar. "That's why we is the way we is, Earlie-Pearlie, and why we need just a taste or two more."

With that, Bucky trimmed down half the mug in front of him, then split into a barking, rolling laugh that began deep in his belly, rolled through his chest with rapid jerks and—as always—ended with Bucky pounding on the object closest to him. In this case, the sticky surface of the bar. Though Bucky Rudman was known as one of the best toppers in the woods, this was a rendition of his true trademark. He'd saw off the tip of a 200-foot fir, climb onto the top of the tree, and pound his chest like Tarzan.

Earl sighed and shook his head. "So how was the wake?"

Bucky smiled broadly. "Speaking for Bucky Rudman, I dealt with it the only way I know how. I sidled up to Charles Walker's wife, took one look at that proud set of jugs on her, and..."

"Christ, Charles ain't even cold in his grave." Earl's face was pure disgust.

"I was just looking, Earl. I did not touch out of respect for the dead."

Petey cut him off. "Cease with the sacrilege Bucky, or I'll put a curse on your pecker."

Bucky looked hurt for a moment—then emptied another mug, followed by a belch.

Earl surveyed the five men. "Any of you guys sober enough to tell me how the wake really was?"

Petey volunteered. "Maybe a hundred people. All kinds of food—and drink." This brought laughter from all. "The mayor—What's his name?—and the chief of police. Every preacher in town. Even a reporter from the Everett Chronicle."

"The Chronicle?" asked Earl, filling more pitchers. "What for?"

Petey shrugged. "Three AFL union boys die when a Shay locomotive tips over in the woods. And what with all the talk in the valley about how the CIO union upstarts is gonna take on the AFL guys... you figure it out."

Earl seemed to have lost interest in the pitchers of beer. "I'll be damned. I hadn't thought of that. This is just the kind of accident that the CIO needed. Proves their point exactly—the good old AFL ain't the union it used to be, and it ain't doing the job of protecting the worker. The AFL spends all its time rabble-rousing on behalf of the sawmill workers, and it tells the loggers to kiss its ass." He paused, as if a new thought hit him. "I'm just glad I ain't Bud Cole. Three dead on your watch, and in the middle of all this."

Several of the men from the back appeared at the end of the bar, near Little Boy.

"Where's the beer, Earl?" demanded the one closest.

"Oh, sorry," said Earl quickly. He carried the three pitchers to the back room, but hurried back to the Skybillings crew at the bar. "I wanted to ask you boys a couple things," he said, pausing for a moment to catch his breath. He looked around quickly, then lowered his voice. "What the hell happened up there anyway?"

"Why don't you let the dead rest in peace?" asked Petey with a slight slur.

"You superstitious or something, Petey?" Earl snorted. "Whole town is talking. You know that. Three men killed just like that. Makes them kinda wonder. Clare Ristall and all his CIO boys must be dancing." Earl's eyes tilted up. "Was he at the wake?"

"No," said Bucky quickly. "Up in Everett giving some kind of union speech." Earl wiped his hands on a towel, then leaned close to Petey. "Any truth to the rumor that Bud Cole was pushing too hard—like back in the '20s—when his partner got killed?" He stopped quickly, as if the question were too direct. "Of course, maybe it was just one of those things, you know? Accidents happen. But the state inspectors are going to be asking, don't you think? I expect that the Skybillings money people are gonna be madder than hell."

"What do you mean—'money people'?" asked Bucky. "Bud Cole owns Skybillings himself. He's his own man."

"Like hell he is," shot Earl. "Bud Cole and his Skybillings Lumber Company is leveraged to the hilt. To some big boys in downtown Seattle. I heard a rumor that they may pull out, and Bud'll have to close again."

Earl snorted, then he started in again. "Which makes that damn speech he gave at the funeral all the stranger. Why the hell did he say that? What's he talking about? My own personal view is that Bud Cole is a little nutty."

But Petey interrupted, twirling his handlebar mustache furiously. "I sure as hell hate funerals. They ain't good for the living nor the dead."

Earl shook his head. "That ain't the question on the floor, Petey. What's going on up there at Skybillings anyhow? Some people say that after Fred Weissler got killed way back when, Bud was never the same. Went a little wacky."

"Best funeral I ever attended was when I was fifteen years old," offered Petey. "I was on a freighter in the Pacific. Off Melbourne. Melbourne as in Melbourne, Australia. Sailor got his head bashed in a fight. The captain had him put into a pine box and dropped overboard. Whooossh!"

Earl shook his head, as he looked down the line of Skybillings men. "You shit-asses are drunker than I thought. There ain't a one of ya that can answer a question half sober."

"I answer questions half sober all the time," offered Delbert.

"I always liked funerals," said Lightning Stevens abruptly, startling the whole group with a voice that rumbled through the noisy bar. "Gives a kind of book-end to a man's life. Like my uncle—just last month. His funeral was nothing but songs. No preaching. No sobbing. Just songs."

"Funerals aren't what I want to know about, Lightning, dang it," snorted Earl. "What I want to find out about is all this talk I'm hearing about Skybillings and such. I bet Clare Ristall's CIO boys slam Skybillings shut in no time. I wouldn't be surprised that this kicks off the strike that Clare's been threatening all along."

Suddenly, Lightning's voice filled the room. "*Blessed are Thou, O Lord*," he sang in a deep, resonant base. His black hair hung across his shoulders. He stood abruptly, gripping the stool as he sang:

*The waters stood above the mountains.*
*Glorious are Thy works, O Lord.*
*The waters flowed through the mountains.*
*Glorious are Thy works, O Lord.*

The voice, though restrained, carried each note precisely. He held the final in a deep vibrato, but then began to pitch forward over the stool. Bucky caught him just in time, and pushed him back up until he stood comfortably next to the stool again. Lightning didn't seem to notice. The deep voice began again, but now he faced the window, washed with rivers of rain from the growing storm.

"What's that goddamn Injun singing?" Delbert asked Earl. "That ain't no Christian hymn, is it?"

"What other kinda hymns are there?"

Delbert frowned at the answer, then crawled from his stool, steadied himself with one hand, and turned toward the pool tables. His suspenders hung near his knees, his pants drifting lower with each movement. In a raspy voice, he began singing:

> *On a hill far away stood an old rugged cross,*
> *The emblem of suffering and shame;*
> *And I love that old cross where the dearest and best*
> *For a world of lost sinners was slain.*

For several stanzas, Delbert's and Lightning's voices collided, but occasionally they landed on similar notes, bringing harmony amid the chaos. As one of these moments faded, Earl slapped his mug on the bar.

"Everybody shut up, goddamn it." But Lightning and Delbert started again, so he stomped his foot repeatedly. This settled Lightning onto his stool with a thud, while Delbert stopped abruptly, with a look of genuine anger at Earl. The laughter and shouting from the back room disappeared quickly as well.

"All this awful yammering has made this place feel more like a fuckin' house of worship than a goddamn saloon," blasted Earl, to make sure all could hear. This brought laughter and several snorts. "If that's so, then Earl Talbert is the Reverend, Pastor, Elder, and High Priest."

A round of applause followed, along with some catcalls and boos. Earl hushed them as he raised his mug of beer into the air.

"Therefore, your humble servant offers this benediction for the three Skybillings men who died." Chairs scraped in the back of the room as the men rose to their feet.

"Here's to three good men, three good loggers, three fellow workers." Earl paused, as his gaze took in the entire room, a gray haze of men in blue-striped shirts, black suspenders, dirty boots, and pants cut high–a family portrait of Seakomish loggers.

"May the souls of those who died in the heat of battle rest in eternal peace. If a man has got to leave this life, he best do it fighting like hell," said Earl to a muffled chorus of "here-here's" and "amen's." Earl slung his head back and drained the mug.

A chorus of belches followed.

* * *

By midnight, the smell in Talbert's grew pungent—stale sweat combined with spilled beer and clouds of smoke swirling into the rafters. The volume of the jukebox rose with every hour.

Earl delivered another round of beer to the Skybillings crew still huddled along the bar: Lightning hummed quietly along with the jukebox, Petey waxed his mustache with drops of beer, Bucky and Delbert leaned against each other as they drank. Sitting next to them, Little Boy nursed his beer—looking into the distance. A woman in a red dress stopped next to him, then leaned into him when he whispered in her ear.

"How about another coupla' pitchers in back?" asked Billy Sammons, a thick man who appeared from the blue haze of the back room. As he thumped his weight onto the edge of the bar—both arms were blue with tattoos—he bumped into Bucky Rudman's shoulder. Bucky turned and cursed, but otherwise ignored him.

"So this here is the Skybillings death squad," laughed Sammons as Earl filled a pitcher for him. "Or maybe these are the ones who're gonna croke next, Earl. What do you think?" Sammons laughed and put his arm around the woman in the red dress.

"I don't want trouble tonight, Sammons," said Earl loudly—enough so that the back room would hear. "Leave all that union shit outside the door."

Sammons laughed heartily. "Don't have nothing to do with unions, Earl." He paused again, to make sure all of the Skybillings men were listening. He leaned against the woman.

Sammons' voice was taut, yet it lilted upward at the end, suggesting laughter. "See, Bud Cole's got no business being in them mountains that high-up in the first place. His AFL union boys ain't got the talent, and they sure as hell ain't got the balls. That's for the big boys; not the snot-noses. Ashford & Southern built that line up Roosevelt Creek ten years ago and decided that land was nothing but a jungle.

So they let it go back to weeds. Ain't no way a cut-rate little operation like Skybillings and Bud Cole is gonna be able to log it. Not in a hundred years."

Bucky's voice broke across Sammons'. "You're full of shit, Sammons. Skybillings has thousands of acres of stumpage up there next to heaven. Skybillings also has got the talent—*and* it's also got the balls. Not like the pussies from Ashford & Southern who gave up."

Sammons laughed. "Skybillings is a washed-up, no-talent outfit—that's the explanation."

Bucky pushed his stool back. "And I'm saying you got your CIO-union head shoved up your CIO-union ass," snapped Bucky. "Skybillings had the best operation in this valley in the '20s. Could've whipped every one of you boys at Ashford & Southern."

"But that was in the '20s, Bucky-boy." Sammons voice rose, now directed at the back room. "Today, Bud Cole is over-the-hill, trying to push a bunch of dead-end slackers and half-wits too hard—isn't that right boys? You can put caulk boots on a bunch of women, but that doesn't mean they're going to have cocks."

Before Bucky could respond, Little Boy shot off his stool, catching Sammons full force. Though Little Boy was much smaller—even slight in comparison—the force and surprise drove Sammons into the heap of wet slickers with a whomp.

Sammons grabbed the bottom rung of an overturned stool, trying to regain his footing. But with the light, swift movements of a cat in full attack, Little Boy lunged onto Sammons' chest, grabbed a suspender with one hand, and pounded his face with fast blows.

The room echoed with the sound of crashing stools as the two men rolled across the floor. Two Swedes from the back room cursed loudly in their mother tongue, though it wasn't clear who they were cursing. Several others began a chant, "Sammons, Sammons, Sammons." Delbert McKenna pounded his stool into the floor as he whooped for Little Boy. As the men rolled across the floor, Sammons recovered slightly and heaved Little Boy into the back-room crowd, which caught him in extended arms, and threw him back onto the open floor. Sammons aimed for a slam to his chest, but Little Boy's boots found Sammons' knees, sending both men onto the floor once more.

Earl Talbert circled the fighters with a pool cue raised high, but a broad circle of men formed a ring that opened and closed as the fighters rolled. For several minutes, they struggled—Sammons landing some hard punches, but still not able to fully peel away the clinging, writhing form that had turned his face blazing red. Suddenly the ring of men opened, giving Earl Talbert a clear shot with the pool cue, which he brought down with a loud crack.

It caught Sammons across the shoulders and Little Boy across his left side, transforming the quick, sudden bursts into slow-motion, then lead. Little Boy slumped, but Sammons was out cold. The crowd shuffled slightly, as some took a look at the fallen fighters, others returned to their seats slowly. But no one spoke.

Bucky bent over Little Boy, carefully lifting him into a sitting position. "Guess Skybillings ain't the shit-ass outfit Sammons thinks it is," said Bucky as he sloshed a mug of beer over Little Boy's head.

## Chapter 5

The double-winged plane dropped low, then tilted sharply upward as it released its payload. The bombs hung for a moment motionless, then dropped straight toward the main trench—thick, black rain, followed by quick thumps that made the ground swim. Bud was already running toward the trench, shouting for the men to dive. But his legs were lead, planted heavy in a muddy earth. His eyes swept around him, looking for the men, but saw only red smoke roaring upward from the trench—and the awful heat, with blinding patches of yellow, that made him shield his eyes.

As his hand hit his face, he jolted upright in his bed, now a jumble of sheets—the brilliant sunlight streaming through a torn shade. France again. He took a breath, blinking hard at the brightness. The dreams had gone on for years after the War—but this was the first time in a long time.

He fell back onto the bed, letting his heart slow. Six men dead. Six. He could hear the rhythm of Mrs. Colloway's washing machine downstairs. His breathing matched the beating of the washer. Not six. Not six. His normal heartbeat returned. Three men. It was only three. Not a dream—the Shay and the fire. The three were dead this time.

The washing machine also told him: This was Sunday. Sunday was washday. Mrs. Colloway only washed on Sundays. He saw her lined face.

Any clothes, Mr. Cole, that you want me to wash are to be in a bag at the door of your room—Bud had two rooms, a kitchen and a bedroom, but she always referred to them in the singular—by 7 a.m. sharp.

But he'd lost track of the day. So he lay there now, thinking. It was Sunday. Normally, he would sleep in. Get up late. Go fishing if the weather was good. But that was then. Now was now, and three men were dead. The Shay deep in mud. How to make sense of it all?

He grabbed the pillow from the floor, and stuffed it under his head. He breathed slowly now, trying to think and not think. Looking at his two rooms. They were enough. A man didn't need much more. He hadn't stayed there for more than a month. He hated leaving his bunkhouse at the camp. Or maybe he just disliked town. Especially now. Men dead; a Shay on its belly; a company, well, who could say?

"Sonofabitch." Bud's rage flamed instantly as he slammed his fist into the wall.

A crackly voice echoed from down the hall: "What in fuckin' hell is wrong with you, mister?" followed by spitting sounds. Old Man Jenkins, who had the only other room on the second floor of the house, must've cut himself shaving. The bathroom they shared—a room with a toilet and another room with a bathtub—stood at the end of the hallway.

"Sorry," Bud shouted back.

Bud liked Old Man Jenkins, who everybody called Old Man to his face. His name might have been Harold or Carl, but nobody that Bud knew ever could say for certain. Old Man had lived in the Colloway rooming house for thirty years at least, moving into Seakomish well before Bud had even heard of the place. He was something of a celebrity. He married younger women—sometimes women with real looks—who then moved into Mrs. Colloway's rooming house with him. But it wouldn't last more than a few months and they'd divorce him, usually ending in a brawl that drew the county sheriff.

As Bud listened to Old Man curse—maybe it was a razor cut, maybe it was just a curse to keep things on course—he smiled because it reminded him of his father. Wilmer Cole. Wilmer never, ever swore of course. He was a committed Christian—stern, to church every Sunday. But the old man would curse in his own way—especially after his wife died, and he was having to take care of himself. "Heaven thundering demon," the old man would say, spitting the words with the intensity to smite the devil himself.

Bud finally sat up. He lifted his legs onto the floor gently. Mrs. Colloway's washer rumbled to a stop. The room was silent. Even Old Man Jenkins couldn't be heard. Bud sat on the edge of the bed, rotating his shoulders, feeling the stiffness from battling the Shay. His fingers still ached from digging. A long gash, now stitched tight, crossed his right thigh where he'd fallen on a spike. Yellow antiseptic that the doctor had dabbed across the wound had spread into a large oval that crept toward his crotch.

For a few minutes, he just sat. Studying the small pine chest of drawers. The worn rug. The walls that needed to be repainted. He wondered how long it had been since they'd last seen a fresh coat.

The muscles in his feet, which he now stretched and rotated, ached from trying to gain a toe-hold in the mud. He noticed scratches on his ankles, several deep. He touched them lightly—where did they come from? As he did, pain shot through his back, which made him cry out.

"Shut-up, goddamn it!" shouted Old Man Jenkins again.

"Shut up yourself, and fuck you!" shouted Bud back, punctuating his point by slamming his hand against the wall again. This time, there was no response.

Bud opened the top bureau drawer, fished around for his toothbrush, and set off for the bathroom as soon as he heard Old Man Jenkins clear out. Moving quietly, so Mrs. Colloway wouldn't come up to greet him, he brushed, washed his face, then focused on breakfast. Nothing in the refrigerator. A jar of milk he'd left in there the last time he was in town—a green mush on the bottom. He lifted it gingerly and dropped it into the paper bag he used for trash, which he quickly folded. The bread he'd picked up the night before would have to do, so he opened the stove, lit the gas, then plopped four pieces onto the rack. He boiled some coffee, bitter and hot.

As he waited for the toast, he couldn't keep the scenes out of his head—just as he couldn't during the night. Standing in the rain looking at those caskets. The damn crazy speech, and the awful wake, with everyone asking questions about the accident and saying sympathetic things that felt mostly like prying. Who could tell what anyone really meant, especially now? All the union nonsense made everybody suspicious from the get-go—whose side were you really on?

Then there was seeing the Shay go over again, then digging with his hands underneath it, discovering that the three of them were dead—very badly dead, at that—and trying to get the others down the mountain to the doctor.

But he willed them all away. This was a path he couldn't allow himself to take, at least not now. In the trenches, during the War, he willed himself to take command of the fear, to focus only on what he had to do—not on how horrible it all was. A cold night in mid-winter, after his platoon had been virtually wiped out, he lay among the dead in thick mud at the bottom of a trench. It came back to him now: barely conscious, his feet numb, his arms and legs throbbing from bullet holes that he figured would drain him of life soon, but his fingers stayed miraculously dry. He wrestled to pull his belt from his pants and cinch it around his arm to stanch the bleeding. But then he heard the German soldiers approaching, so he flipped the belt away, slipping himself in between the dead bodies of a man whose legs were gone and another whose head had twisted awkwardly backward. The Germans came into the trench. Two soldiers stumbled within several feet, poking bodies randomly with bayonets just to be sure they were dead. He made himself stop thinking, stop listening, stop living for a moment, as they drew nearer. When one kicked his leg, it didn't move—the leg of just another dead soldier.

That was what he needed now. He knew this. But he also knew it felt different now. Somehow harder and more alone. So he chose to concentrate on what was in front of him; what he had to do. For now, it was just the walls and the rooms—his home whenever he wasn't in the woods. A kitchen and a bedroom. A table, with four chairs. A counter, with sink, two cupboards above. A plastic picture of Jesus, on his knees in Gethsemane, with a yellow beam of light coming down from the sky, just to the left of the door—a housewarming gift from Mrs. Colloway when he moved in. The other room wasn't much more—a bed, so soft in the middle that Bud felt like his back nearly hit the floor; a four-drawer bureau; a writing desk with a small lamp.

Once Kathryn had left him, he decided to sell everything else and move here. It was all he needed. And he couldn't afford anything more. The Colloway's had agreed to cut the rent because their two sons had worked for him in the '20s—both since killed in sawmill accidents in Everett. So he was grateful. But it was in these rooms that he'd scraped bottom too—in these rooms he'd screamed so loudly that the police came and wondered if someone was being murdered.

Bud finished the coffee and toast, but decided he needed more. How long since he had last eaten? Rather than pulling out the oven rack, he slipped the next bread slices in from the side, and relit the stove.

Not the worst place he'd lived in, by far, but living in the woods was better. His bunkhouse at the camp had no more room, but he felt like he actually lived there. It was where he walled away the rest of the men, where he slept solidly after back-breaking work; where he even allowed himself an occasional shot of brandy after a good day. Crazy, but a man could get a clear head when he was so tired he could barely think. Dangerous—yes, he knew that, given his history.

And then there were his books—that he'd scattered about the bunkhouse. Stacks of books, not in bookcases, but in piles. Without order, without any method of organization. Histories, biographies, political textbooks. His partner, Fred—how many years ago was that?—had said that it was obvious why.

"And that is?" asked Bud.

"You have this deep-down desire to prove that you are more intelligent than anybody else who has an eighth-grade education," answered Fred.

"Sounds like a load of bullshit to me," said Bud. "I've just got a curious mind."

"Well, there may be a lot of things that are curious about you, Bud. And one of them may be your mind. But I can say for a fact that you have a very curious sense of pride and that you can't stand to see anyone get too far ahead of you." Fred said this without a smile, but Bud Cole knew that Fred Weissler spoke to him from the heart and without malice. Bud also knew that Fred was usually right.

Bud jumped when someone knocked loudly on the door. "Mr. Cole, it's me, Mrs. Colloway." For a moment, he thought about not answering, sitting perfectly still until she went away, but then he realized that she would eventually smell the toast.

"I'm afraid I have to get decent, Mrs. Colloway," which he thought would send her away.

"Fine," she answered. "I can wait."

Bud grimaced. But he pulled on a pair of pants—gently, so as not to break the stitches—and hobbled to the door.

Mrs. Colloway had eyes that squinted, even when the sun wasn't shining. "Mr. Cole, it's so good to see you. I just wanted to be sure that you were alright and you had everything you needed."

Bud rocked onto his good leg, opening the door fully. He smiled, pointing at the stove. "Yes, fine, just making a little breakfast."

"That's just wonderful. You need the strength, having to go through something that awful."

Bud knew that Mrs. Colloway was a busybody, but he'd never known her to be this direct.

"Mr. Cole, I just want you to know that I will be happy to bring you some dinner or help in any other way that I can. I just want you to know that. Norbert and I think of you almost as our own son. And we're very protective of family." Her face was horizontal wrinkles, beginning below her curly white hair, and continuing all the way to the folds of skin that entered her blouse.

He smiled weakly, glancing again toward the stove, and explained that he appreciated the interest. "But I don't think I'll be needing anything. I'll be taking off for Seattle this afternoon on some business and then back up to the woods."

She smiled. But before he closed the door, she twisted slightly toward him. "I don't suppose you really have any idea at this point how that all happened. I mean, it's so terrible, isn't it? And all of us worry about those rail lines up alongside those cliffs that way. You know? You just worry—don't you?"

In the hours after the crash, after he had gotten his mind to accept the fact that the Shay was gone—apparently finished—and that three of his crew were dead, he began to wonder how long it would take before the accusations began or before the union boys started making noise. These were the kinds of questions that would start them.

"No ideas, Mrs. Colloway," he said, his voice now sharper. "No ideas, but I'll be sure to let you know when we find out."

She smiled sweetly and left. As soon as Bud closed the door, he ripped open the silverware drawer, grabbed a knife, and stuck it hard into the wood counter. The two pieces of toast were charred by now and blistering hot. Bud decided he would eat them anyway—he opened the refrigerator, scanning the shelves for jelly, but there was none. The same thing for the cupboard next to the refrigerator, and then the one above the sink. But at the back were the bottles—eight of them, some nearly empty, some still full; Johnnie Walker, Jim Beam, Wild Turkey.

This was not a battle worth restarting, he thought as he steadied himself against the sink. A battle that had taken him to the edge and then over. The fact is, he liked alcohol and liked a good part of what it did—how it snorted up his sinuses when he washed it down fast, how it fuzzed the anger and irritation, how it nudged him into sleep.

But he also remembered the feeling of walking alone, on a logging road somewhere near Stardale, totally lost and confused. John Valentine had come out looking for him, and found him near daybreak. And Bud still winced when he looked at the long scar in his arm from when he and Lightning Stevens brawled three of Deek Brown's men over who would get the last drops of a bottle of muscatel. By the time that all happened, of course, they had already begun calling it the Great Depression. He didn't give a damn what they called it. It looked pretty much to him that all hope had been squeezed out of his own life. So the battle over a bottle of booze seemed pretty damn important.

As the shaking from Mrs. Colloway's washer reached his floor again, Bud slammed the cupboard doors shut, took the dry toast, and hobbled into his bedroom to get dressed.

❀   ❀   ❀

Driving fast was freedom. And it always came in the drive from Seakomish, down the valley, into Seattle. For three hours, his mind could float. Just the sun. Or the rain. It didn't matter to Bud. The Seakomish River running right next to the highway—where it ripped through the narrow channel of granite boulders—sprayed froth across the road, especially on windy days. All of that, along with the whine of the engine. Now he revved the old Chevy, shifting hard into fourth gear, until he reached sixty, much faster than it should go—he knew that—then eased off.

In those three-hour drives to pick up parts or plead with the bankers, his mind could sort things out. Something about the hum or the rhythm of the car against the road. The brain uncoupled. The worries slipped into the background for a moment.

He slowed for the curves just below Stardale—here the mountains dropped hard for five miles or so. He'd seen too many cars go over the edge here, from speeding or because their brakes went out. He concentrated in this stretch, but once on the straight-away, he'd open it up. Head-ons never scared him, though this stretch was famous for them.

At the end of it, where the Seakomish River curled back underneath the highway again, was the house that Bud was renting when he and Fred first started talking about creating their own company. He always slowed a bit, to see if it was still in good shape. Somebody had painted the house and hacked back some of the bushes along the driveway, but it looked snug and happy.

Just like all of them, at least at the time, thought Bud. Even Lydia—when she heard about it much later. Why the hell not start a company? Fred had said it first. They could be their own bosses. They would get by okay. The market in the East was picking up. The War was long over. The '20s had opened everything up—things were possible.

They worked for it, though. Bud smiled now, thinking back. From dawn to dark, literally. Both of them standing on wedges eight or ten feet off the ground that they had driven deep into the towering fir trunks. Up high on the trunk, above all the gooey pitch, that was the best place to start cutting. They hauled the massive two-man saw—a wooden handle at either end—back and forth, back and forth, sending geysers of bark chunks and moist wood-shards into the air and often into their faces. They skipped lunches, instead eating their sandwiches with one hand while they kept the saw moving with the other.

Money started coming in. Not a lot at first, but enough. They added a few men—Lightning Stevens, Bucky Rudman, Petey Hulst. Then they brought in several men from British Columbia—many of them Swedes, who took over all the tree felling. Bud and Fred now each headed separate crews: Bud ran the buckers, who cut the trees into manageable lengths; and Fred, the chokers, who hooked the tree sections to cables—connected to a central, towering spar tree—that then dragged them onto a jumbled pile, ready for hauling to the mills.

Bud shook his head as he drove past the turnoff for the sawmill they opened a year or so before the stock market crashed. Fred thought they were nuts to start a mill, but Bud decided that was the way to grow. "Smartest move Skybillings could make, Fred," he remembered saying when he came back to report that he'd gotten a loan to build the thing.

"Why the hell do we want a mill?" Fred always smiled when he argued. Never seemed to get mad—at least until he grabbed an axe or saw and came after you. "Because we'll never build the best damn logging show in these mountains if all we do is cut down trees," answered Bud.

Fred just shook his head. "You were raised wrong, Bud. That's all I got to say."

"Just what do you mean with that?" Bud's dander rose when Fred acted like he had him figured out.

Fred laughed. "Still trying to prove the old man wrong, aren't you?"

But Bud prevailed, and they opened the mill. If only—thought Bud, as a school bus stopped and he waited for a group of children to cross the highway. The driver waved to Bud as she pulled the bus onto a side road.

Fred was like a brother. They fought together in the war, fucked the same whores in Paris, traveled the rails back home, worked alongside each other blasting rock to build a rail line for Deek Brown's outfit. And Fred agreed with most every hair-brained business decision that Bud made—but soon after the mill was up and running, Fred announced he wanted to sell the whole operation, lumber company, sawmill, the whole thing.

"We're making damn good money, Bud. Now's the time to pull out."

"This is just a start, you dumb lug," argued Bud. "Can't you understand that we'll be the size of Deek Brown within a couple years?"

"This ain't gonna hold much longer," insisted Fred.

"What isn't?"

Fred kicked the side of the bunk. "All of this," he shouted. He waved his arms—taking in the bunkhouse, the woods, the world, for all Bud knew. "Look, we're making money. I know that. But a lot of logging shows aren't, and a hell of a lot of 'em are gonna go under. Prices for lumber can't hold much longer. It's nuts—nuts, Bud. Grab hold of yourself, will ya?"

But once again, Bud prevailed. As he roared over the Merritown bridge, he tried to calculate the number of times he wished he hadn't.

He shifted again to give the Chevy a little more speed, along the flat farming land outside Everett. Here, the Seakomish River turned broad and flat, ready to flood at even the hint of summer rain or spring run-off. Farmers worked these fields every spring, plowing in the topsoil from the floods, making it even richer. Sun lit the green fields and warmed the aroma of silage or cow manure as he roared past them.

He might've had a place down here by now, he decided, as he let his eyes drift across the fields. A nice one, on a knoll looking over it all, and he'd be retired—or at least out of the woods. But the Depression stopped such thoughts cold. No sooner had Fred been buried, and the market crashed, than Skybillings was over. While he hung on as long as he could, it wasn't long. Petey Hulst, Lightning Stevens, even Bucky Rudman stayed with him to the end. But finally, he couldn't pay even them.

Bud couldn't remember now, whether that was '30 or '31. Even though he had fallen into the bottle again, and had been given up by his friends as a lost cause, he swore over and over again that he would somehow struggle back—that he would somehow rebuild Skybillings.

A flatbed truck passed him suddenly, cutting in close as it dodged an oncoming truck, its horn blaring. He swerved sharply to avoid being sideswiped and gave the driver a finger. But all he got in return was fifteen men—sitting on the flatbed—giving him the finger back.

He had to laugh. Maybe it was just such faces, finally, that brought him back, he thought, as he settled into the long stretch of road approaching Everett. Instead of faces that gave you the finger and laughed at your bad driving, the faces of the men of Seakomish during the worst of the Depression showed resignation and failure. Very little anger—that was gone within the first year. It was self-doubt that set in—wondering whether they could even do the job again, much less whether they would actually be able to find one. He knew what was going through their minds because he thought the same things about himself.

"I was good," he heard himself say one morning as he made breakfast—two eggs and a shot of vodka. But something made him wonder why—if it was true in the past—why wasn't it still true, true right then, in the present? And while the bottle didn't leave him quickly, neither did the notion. Through the worst of the Depression, in fact, it was that notion that pulled him forward—that made him start asking around among the banks and lenders down the valley when the economy started coming back in 1934.

As he began to slow for a pick-up that was trying to pass him, he heard a pop and felt the wheel shake violently. The Chevy danced back and forth across the lane, whipping into the oncoming lane for a second, then wrenching back to the shoulder. Bud fought to hold the wheel, driving his foot onto the brake.

When he finally got it to the side, he surveyed the damage—a gaping hole in the front right tire. He didn't bother looking for a spare, since this one was the spare.

"Goddamn it," he muttered. What to do now? Cancel the meeting in Seattle? It was already 11:30; he'd never make Seattle by 1:30. In fact, he wasn't sure he'd be able to get the flat fixed and on the road before dark. As he contemplated the options, a pick-up slowed and pulled in behind him. The driver got out—a fat man, wearing a red plaid shirt and suspenders, with his sleeves rolled up.

"You look like a poor sonofabitch who needs a ride mighty bad, Mister," said the man as he eyed the tire.

"And you look like a messenger from God," Bud answered without a smile.

"Been referred to in the same context as the Almighty many times, I must admit—never quite so favorably, though. How 'bout I give you a lift into Everett?"

With that, Bud grabbed his car keys and the flat tire and jumped into the pick-up. The driver's name was Lloyd Kurl. He said he worked for the sawmill in Lowell, just the other side of the fields and the Seakomish River—he pointed off to the left, out his window—and was headed into Everett to pick up a load of saw belts.

Bud explained that he ran a logging company.

"I thought all you small fry loggers were riding the rails with everybody else," said Kurl as he approached the outskirts of town.

Bud laughed. "No, but there's been plenty of days when I thought it'd come to that."

Kurl looked at him now as he drove. "Mind if I ask a personal question?"

Bud shook his head.

"How the hell does a small show get the dough to run at all in this day and age?" Kurl looked at him through heavy red lids and bristly, unshaven cheeks.

"A lick and a promise. Maybe a friendly banker—somebody who knew you in the old days. But things are looking a little better. Things are opening up back East a little. So more folks are buying and building."

Kurl shook his head. "Damn world's all out of control. You union?

"The abrupt shift in direction startled Bud, but he tried to hide it. "Sure. You?"

Kurl looked at him quickly as if he were considering the answer. They slowed briefly for a logging truck that carried a single fir log maybe twelve feet across. Kurl hesitated for a moment, then drove the pedal to the floor, bringing a roar from the pickup, as it swept past the truck and back into its own lane, with no room to spare.

Bud was still thinking about narrowly missing the front of the logging truck, when Kurl finally answered. "We're AFL. We're sawmill guys," said Kurl. "But those bastards from the CIO are creating pure hell for us. It's got nasty at times. They think they should represent us mill workers, but I say to hell with them. They're nothing but a bunch of head-breaking thugs."

Kurl turned the pick-up into the gravel driveway of a small place called "Porter's," with two pumps and a door folded back to show a thick, muscled boy laying underneath a Buick. Bud negotiated the price for fixing the flat, and went back to thank Kurl for the lift.

"My pleasure," said Kurl, slipping the shift into first. "Good luck up there, by the way. Something tells me you're gonna need it." He spun rocks as he pulled out.


## Chapter 6

By the time the kid fixed the flat and Bud hitched a ride back to his car, it was already getting dark.

He had called Seattle to ask about changing the appointment until the next day, which Witstrop's secretary finally did—after pointing out that Mr. Witstrop hated last-minute cancellations. She set the meeting for 7:30 a.m. sharp. Though Bud tried to talk her into something later, she insisted that if Mr. Cole could not arrive at 7:30, she would be happy to inform Mr. Witstrop that Mr. Cole would not be visiting at all.

Bud decided to spend the night in Everett. So he set off for the waterfront, where he knew he could find a place that was cheap.

Since the end of the Great War, Everett had become a port city. Freighters from as far away as Japan and Australia shouldered next to each other like hulking iron sentries guarding the waterfront. They waited for loads of lumber, sawed furiously day and night by the mills that sat along the waterfront or next to the Seakomish River, which wound around the flat-top hill that was home to Everett proper.

In the early 1900s, but even in the 1920s—just after the War ended—Everett drew its share of moneyed folk. Timber owners, railroad executives, shipping magnates. Attracted by the timber—and the riches it promised. Many built Nantucket clapboard or grand colonial homes at the north end of town, sporting wide, trimmed lawns and broad sunrooms looking west, across the open water of Puget Sound, toward the Strait of Juan de Fuca and the Pacific Ocean just beyond. Even then, however, Everett also drew its share of drifters and hotheads—cowboy loggers, stevedores and longshoremen, merchant marines from the Far East and South America, lumbermen, country farmers, and every kind of political radical, union supporter, and left-wing sympathizer.

But that was just the beginning. Starting with the crash of 1929, and driven by the ravages of the Depression of the early '30s, Everett collected another wave—this time men out of work, families, even children who rode the rails. They settled in shanties, underneath railroad bridges, in cardboard hovels near the railroad tracks.

By 1937, with the economy of the U.S., as well as of the Northwest, finally beginning to pick up, the ships were waiting on the waterfront once again, the rail lines rocked with lumber moving south to California, or East to Minneapolis and Chicago. And the magnates and tycoons, together with the homeless families, the longshoremen, the loggers, the hotheads, the radicals, and the drifters—all mingled in an uneasy crossroads that smelled of cooking wood pulp and bitter diesel, capped by a cold fog that gave way only for a few hours in the afternoon.

Bud drove along the waterfront, looking for a place to stay that didn't seem too dangerous or run-down. He pulled past a group of men milling about an open fire in an oil drum. They stared at him, but didn't speak. Across the street—next to several bars, a hotel, and what looked like a whorehouse, whose windows were plastered with union posters—he noticed a small rooming house.

After paying the half dollar for the night, and looking into the tiny cubicle—a mattress on the floor and a wash basin—he stepped into the night chill. He buttoned his jacket high, but it offered no protection; so he dashed quickly across the street, looking for a place to eat. A freighter from Japan lay directly ahead of him, moaning against its moorings.

A group of sailors in boxy blue caps stumbled toward him, speaking a language he didn't recognize. Two had their arms around each other's waists. They stopped briefly to chat with two women, young, yellow-haired, leaning up against a corrugated tin wall, the side of a storage shed at the end of one of the docks. The girls smiled through rose lips, nodded and swiveled, but were quickly forgotten as the group stumbled through a door and into a tavern.

Bud shivered from the cold, focusing intently on the doorways as he passed: Waldo's, Bay Shipping, Everett/Seattle Dry Dock. Just beyond the *Corredor* (Buenos Aires), which yawned against the five-inch hemp that held it tight, he spotted a small reader board straddling the sidewalk. Ernie Dramus' Pub. Two lights lit the doorway just down the pier.

He trotted toward it, ignoring the shouted invitations of the girls, and slipped into the doorway. The warm, moist air inside felt as unwelcome and unfamiliar as the night air had seemed earlier; a sticky odor of tobacco hung in the room, which vibrated from the loud music coming from the rear.

"Help ya?" shouted the bartender.

"Just a beer and something to eat. What you got?" Bud crawled onto a stool, and studied a piece of paper the bartender handed him. The corners were bent back, hiding the price of fish chowder and fried oysters.

"The fish chowder is what you want if you don't want to die."

Bud thought the voice was the bartender's, but when he looked up, he realized it came from the seat next to him—a fellow in maybe his late fifties, a mat of stringy brown hair swept back, who didn't look up, just spooned another mouthful from a thick gray bowl.

Bud shouted to the bartender, "Fish chowder," and expected the man to speak again, but he didn't. The floorboards, the silverware, even the bar itself shook with the beat of the music—men and women jammed together on the tiny dance floor in the middle, swaying, while a crowd of men lined the edges. Large color posters along the wall— once brilliant and beckoning, now softened to pastels and sepia— hawked car parts and the U.S. Army.

"Much obliged for the tip," said Bud once the music had quieted and he'd taken his first bite.

"My pleasure." The voice was gravelly, the face angular, and sharp; creases across the forehead, which rode high above a sloped nose; one eyelid drooped low across the eye. His hair was long, curled behind his ears, and touching the frayed collar of a denim shirt.

"You sound like a regular," offered Bud, not knowing whether the man wanted to talk, but feeling like it himself.

"Regular since 1935." He pushed the empty bowl away, pulled a toothpick out of a shirt pocket, but said no more.

Bud didn't like conversation much himself. He found most people uninteresting, something that he attributed to having spent too long by himself. So he caught himself trying to side-step conversations, especially with strangers. He forced himself to Sunday church dinners to prove that he was not becoming a hermit.

But Bud found this fellow interesting. Maybe it was the cold, maybe it was the bitch who worked for Witstrop, but he felt like talking.

"So is 1935 when you moved to Everett or when you found this place?" he asked, looking directly at the man. He noticed a thick scab running across his far cheek. And the drooping part of his eyelid was a line of light red skin, the obvious home of recent stitches.

"Moved here. From Tulsa." He'd already drained his beer and was now rolling the glass slowly between his hands. "Before that, Nashville. Before that, Milwaukee. And before that, Evanston, near Chicago, in Illinois."

"Doing what?"

"A little of this, a little of that." The man turned to take Bud into his full gaze, as if measuring him, as if deciding whether to answer any more questions. He turned back to the glass, motioning the bartender for a refill. "Started originally in Chicago, a teacher."

The bartender returned, sloshed a full glass onto the bar, and clapped the empty against two others in his hand.

Bud shifted to face the man. "You mean like a high school teacher?"

"I mean like a college teacher. Taught engineering. University of Chicago."

Bud tried to decide if this was the story of another drunk or just a poor son of a bitch tossed across the country by the Depression.

Now the face looked directly at Bud. "Why the hell do you care?"

Bud shrugged, but didn't answer. Both settled into a long silence, drinking their beer. Finally, the man drained the glass and reached into his pocket to pay. He put several coins on the bar.

"Mind if I ask you a question?" he asked, as he pushed the stool back. Bud shook his head.

"What brings the owner of a logging operation to the Everett waterfront?"

Bud laughed loudly. "How the hell do you know I'm an owner of a logging show?"

"Written all over ya. First off, you just called it a show. No longshore-man or county fireman would use that word. Second, you got your fingers all broke up, but none sawed off. That means you got something to do with the woods, but you don't belong to a sawmill. And your clothes are too good to be a logger. That means you must be an owner."

Bud smiled broadly. "But if I got broken fingers, I could be a sailor or a union man or a cop."

"And I know every one of them that crosses these piers and you, sir, are not one." He paused. "Besides, you smell better."

Bud introduced himself and shook the man's hand. He was surprised to find a powerful grip, a steadiness in the eyes as he looked directly into the gray face.

"Harry Bachelder's the name."

"So you really an engineering professor?" asked Bud.

"Are you really a logging boss?"

Bud laughed out loud. "Where do you work now?"

"Haul garbage for the city of Everett, which is getting my pay from FDR. So I like to say that I work for the President of the United States."

Bud paid his tab, and followed Harry out of the bar. As they reached the street, Bud stopped Harry to ask if he could give him a lift home.

"No, I just live around the...Look out!" Harry drove both arms into Bud's chest, knocking him into a coil of rope that lay on the pier. Harry tumbled onto him, just as a beer bottle smashed where they had been standing, spraying a ten-foot circle of flame.

Bud coughed, and rolled over, trying to get his breath, to cry out for air, but Harry pinned him to the ground.

"Shut-up," whispered Harry. "Don't make any noise."

Another bottle exploded in the middle of the street. Followed by another. Flames fanned outward in flat, circular plumes, then leapt skyward at the edge—linking-up where the two circles touched. Behind the flames, a wall of shouting men appeared, figures slipping from between buildings and behind parked cars. Most carried sticks and bottles. Bud couldn't tell if they were coming toward them or headed the other direction.

"What the hell is that all about?" he asked Harry as soon as he got his breath back. Bud was now on his knees beside Harry, who crouched in the shadows.

"Meanest sons of bitches I ever met," whispered Harry, his breath sour and beery. "They'll tear your throat out if you look at 'em crosswise."

Bud could hear a chant, a rumbling low chant, beginning along the edges of the crowd that now must have numbered a hundred or more. "Go-to-hell, A-F-L. Go-to-hell, A-F-L." As the mob surged forward, the chant continued. They now stood directly in front of the building where Bud had rented a room.

"This is a little get-to-know-you meeting of the local unions," whispered Harry, wincing as they squatted behind the door of a tin shed. "These boys are CIO men. They're paying a little call on the AFL meeting there across the street." Harry nodded toward Bud's rooming house.

A rock smashed an upstairs window on the two-story building. Then the street light above shattered, showering Bud's car in a burst of glass.

"Jesus, my car's parked right in the middle of all this," said Bud quickly. "I've got to get it out of there!" But Bachelder grabbed the sleeve of his jacket just as Bud was ready to run.

"You ever been around union thugs?" asked Harry. "They'll beat the living shit out of you and then ask questions later. These boys care about the number of scalps they can get, not which side the scalps are on."

Bud found this talk a bit bloodthirsty, and pretty unlikely. But on the other hand, the crowd in the street seemed to be growing by the minute. Now 150, maybe 200 men milled around in front of the hotel. They looked to Bud like loggers—many wore caulk boots and high-cut pants. But others looked like sailors or farmers—some heavyset, a few small, almost boys, and those around the edges seemed barrel-chested and wearing black armbands.

As Bud knelt on the cold planks, hugging the back of the tin door, he laughed.

"What's so funny?" asked Harry.

"I'm supposed to convince a money man in Seattle tomorrow how goddamn reliable I am and how he can bet another $500,000 on me," said Bud swiftly. "But here I am, kneeling on a goddamn dock, I'm about to get my ass kicked by people I never met, and my car is parked in the middle of a fucking labor war I got nothing to do with. Would you give money to a guy like that?"

"Not if he was so stupid that he got himself killed," snorted Harry. "But if he was smart enough to save his butt under the circumstances, now that I might even consider an act of some intellect."

A roar erupted from the crowd. Bud noticed that a large bald-headed man leaned out a window on the top floor of the building and began shouting into a bullhorn. Though the wind whipped the words away from where he and Harry crouched on the dock, Bud could tell it was a string of curses directed at the CIO men down below. This brought more chants, rocks, and the sound of smashing glass. Bud wondered if that was his Chevy.

Harry suddenly pulled a cigarette lighter from his pocket and held it near the end of the shed door that blocked them from view. The tiny flame illuminated the doorway that went inside. He got onto both feet, in a low crouch, and shuffled through the doorway into the shed, coming back with several empty beer bottles and a short piece of hose.

"What are you doing," asked Bud, watching him slice the hose in lengths of about two feet each.

"You ever siphon gas when you were a kid?" asked Harry, handing one of the bottles and pieces of hose to Bud.

"As a kid? Christ, every logger knows how to siphon gas."

"Well now's the time to put your skills to work." Harry looked around the shed door to the street.

The crowd was still milling, but now another sound appeared—rumbling, more shouts, more breaking glass, coming from the other side of the shed. Bud guessed that perhaps fifty men suddenly emerged from the buildings further down the street—creating two large masses of men facing each other, separated by pavement covered by broken glass and flickering flames.

"I think the meeting of the AFL and the CIO is about to start," said Harry with a chuckle. "This new mob is all AFL boys."

"What the hell is so funny about that?" Bud shuddered as the night chill seemed to invade his bones.

"See those headlights in the distance?"

Bud saw a line of headlights to the left, way down the street, perhaps a hundred yards away. They stretched from one side of the street to the other.

"My guess is that the AFL boys knew that this CIO demonstration was coming. So they got ready." Harry snorted loudly, seemingly getting real joy from the situation. "Those assholes from the CIO are about to get caught in the classic squeeze play—the AFL mob on one side, and a line of AFL cars coming at 'em from the other."

Bud looked to the left and saw the headlights begin moving slowly toward them. Sure enough, it was clear that the CIO mob—which had begun moving toward the AFL men on the right—were about to be run over from the back by the approaching cars. But they seemed so intent on attacking the AFL men that few seemed to notice.

The CIO mob simply surged forward.

Harry motioned Bud to follow him down the pier to several small motorboats that were now riding on the high tide even with the pier.

"Here," said Harry, pointing to the first outboard. "Start siphoning." Harry was already on his knees in front of the next one. Bud unscrewed the gas cap and plunged the hose into the tank. As he began inhaling on the hose, he could hear bullhorns blasting, muffled occasionally by cursing and shouts.

The gas came splashing out of the engine, and filled the beer bottle to the top. Then he filled two others. Harry's bottles were already full.

"Stuff these inside, and make them goddamn tight, so as little spills as possible," said Harry, handing Bud several pieces of rag. Without waiting, Harry started running back toward the street.

"Jesus, Harry, we don't want any part of this," shouted Bud.

"You're dumber than I thought." Harry paused while he surveyed the street.

"These little Molotov's are going to save your meeting and your damn car. Our job is to mingle. Just work your way into the crowd from the shadows and start shouting. Start raising all kinds of hell, and hold these sons of bitches high as possible, so everyone can see them. Just keep moving toward your car. Get there as fast as you can, but don't let 'em suspect we're not part of them."

With that, Harry slipped into the CIO crowd from behind. For a moment, Bud thought about just staying put. But then he grimaced and leapt into the street. Like Harry, he was swept into the flowing crowd—into the sudden heat and confusion, into the hail of stones and curses that grew heavier as the two mobs approached one another. He checked quickly to make sure the line of headlights was still well behind them, but then remembered Harry's warning, and turned back into the crowd.

A tall man with broad shoulders, wearing logging boots, shouted into the bullhorn next to him. Several smaller men to his left lobbed rocks as hard as they could, while a knot of what he guessed were longshoremen tore apart a small shipping crate—each grabbing a broken piece of wood with bent nails near the tips.

Bud spotted Harry, chanting loudly and lifting the Molotov cocktails over his head like a high school cheerleader with pom-poms. As he did, men in plaid shirts and railroad caps, a few wearing cowboy boots, some holding tire irons and clubs, surged forward—smashing into the leading edge of the approaching AFL mob. In an instant, the two mobs of men collapsed into one—a melee of flying rocks, swinging clubs, hand-to-hand battle, and grunts and screams as bodies spilled across the pavement.

Through the chaos, Bud saw Harry drifting across the width of the mob, inching closer to the side of the street on which Bud's car was parked. While Bud tried to do the same, he felt a heavy thud across his back, which sent him to his knees. But his bottles somehow didn't break. Rather than trying to get up, he rolled toward the parked cars, and crawled between them, finally emerging next to his Chevy.

"Start the fucking thing!" Harry's voice exploded from just behind the car, as two large men, with blood on their shirts, raced after him. Harry suddenly fell to his knees and lunged backward, tripping both of his pursuers who sprawled onto their faces.

Bud started the engine, threw it in reverse, and stopped just as Harry lit the rag and tossed the flaming bottle into the path of several other men now racing for the car.

As the car lurched forward, a giant "whoosh" and fireball erupted about twenty feet behind them, scattering men in all directions. By the time Bud had shifted the car into first and was speeding toward the wall of headlights bearing down on them, Harry had already lit the last Molotov and heaved it directly into the path of the headlights. With another "whoosh" the bottle exploded, sending headlights veering away on both sides.

As they did, Bud jammed the pedal to the floor and roared between them. When he looked in his rear view mirror, he could see drivers jumping out, stomping at the flames still scattered across their running boards.

❄    ❄    ❄

In 1937, Seattle was two cities. One a rising metropolis— skyscrapers, broad avenues, a thriving waterfront, ornate theaters, department stores. The other, a shanty town of corrugated tin and cardboard, home to hundreds of desolate men and women, even families. Locals called it Hooverville.

George Bertram Witstrop stood at a broad, rounded window in Seattle's tallest building and looked down across the patchwork roofs of tin, cardboard, and wood planks that spread along the south end of the waterfront. Even in the morning blackness, he could see several men, and it appeared to be several children, carrying planks of lumber from a railway car on a sidetrack. Their hurried movements told him they were not likely the rightful owners.

"Mr. Witstrop? What's your decision?" The man asking the question sat at a mahogany table, two perfect piles of paper in front of him. One a tablet, the other a collection of dog-eared papers. On the bottom lay a leather notebook, neatly closed with a slender red ribbon peeking out at the spine.

"Mr. Witstrop?"

Witstrop turned back, when he heard his name, a look of irritation on his face.

"What?" he asked sharply. Then, just as suddenly, he seemed to recover his concentration, but turned back to the window. In the distance, a small green ferry crossed Puget Sound, still dark in the early morning light. During the time that he had been standing at the window, the horizon swam from its blackness to a murky gray, the color of full dawn still low in the east. A tiny jagged edge in the distance outlined the Olympic Mountains, just west of Puget Sound.

Two brief taps at the door were followed by a slender woman who brought in two cups of coffee, placed one on the mahogany table, the other on the windowsill next to Witstrop. He didn't seem to notice.

The man started speaking again. "As I said, sir, the alternatives here are not very appealing." He moved the tablet carefully to the left as he leafed through the pile of colored papers to the first yellow page. "If my figures are anything close to accurate—and God knows whether the state has any clue about what is real and what is not—it is clear that Great Northern Railway and the Pacific Lumber Company, to say nothing of Ashford & Southern, already own something like eighty-five percent of the available Cascade timber north of the Oregon border."

Witstrop turned away from the window, lifting the saucer and cup gently. He sipped once, to determine temperature, then took a long gulp. He wiped his long mustache, which hung low across his lips, with a fanning motion of thumb and forefinger. Then sat slowly, in a chair at his desk.

The young man looked briefly at his own cup of coffee, but didn't touch it. "As I said also," he continued, "the current statistics say that—at the rate these companies are buying what's left and at the rate they are shipping—it will only be a matter of months, latest by the end of the year, that they will lock down virtually the entire Northwest lumber trade." He looked up, pausing for a response, but got none.

"To continue with the point I noted earlier about the options not being very appealing, here is the other factor we face: The company we are looking at is not...," he paused, searching for the word, and started over. "The company in question is not what we would call a sure bet. Our surveyors remind us that the land they've got is very high, it is hard to get to, and they will use up most of what we have financed so far just to get all their facilities and tracks and so on in place. To do any serious business, they will need a lot more."

He stopped, again appearing to give Witstrop time to speak. Still nothing.

"Plus," he drew the word out as if it had several syllables, "they recently had an accident that killed three men. And, from what we are able to tell, that will set them back two or three weeks in even getting timber moving again. That's to say nothing about how the unions will react to it all." He reached for the coffee, but stopped with one small sip.

Witstrop finally swiveled in the chair, uncovering gold cufflinks set off by brilliant white cuffs, and met the man's eyes. "Young man, I have long accepted the fact that you do not bring me good news," said Witstrop. He ended the sentence with lips pressed together, in a tight flat line. "I ask you to bring me good news, but you always bring me bad news."

The young man blinked quickly and picked up his pen as if to make a note. But he immediately put it back down. Witstrop rubbed a dark, leathery hand across his chin and throat, keeping it for a moment on the thick flesh that rolled in a wave above and over the tight white collar.

"So give me the recommendation," said Witstrop suddenly, impatience rising in his voice.

The young man cleared his throat. And paused, as if waiting, or perhaps rethinking.

"Find another company, sir. These guys are too risky. Forget what we've already put into them and move on to somebody else." The answer came too quickly. The young man seemed to feel it, because he began speaking again in clarification, but he was cut off.

"Jesus man, everything is risky. You just said so yourself. Isn't it the hell just as risky, more risky, to let these other sons of bitches close us out entirely?"

"Yes, it is, but..."

"To eat our lunch? To have us for lunch?"

"Mr. Witstrop, the finances just don't look..."

"Never do. Never do. Haven't seen 'em once that I thought so. So don't give me that excuse."

Witstrop turned to the window again, bouncing out of the chair quicker than the young man thought a man of his age or size could do. The sun was just now rising, peeking over the Cascades, behind them, to the east and pouring bright light through the southern windows of the corner office. Puget Sound was now sparkling blue and green, and lines of gray clouds seemed headed in a direct line toward them.

Witstrop turned now, with a sudden smile. But then pulled it back as quickly.

"So, you are adverse to risks and you do not bring me news I want." His voice was more of a snarl now. "Can you at least tell me when this fellow is supposed to arrive—what's his name again?" He studied the grandfather clock near the wall of bookcases, then pulled out a pocket watch from his vest and began tinkering with it.

"His name is Bud Cole. Actually, he's already here."

"Then get him in here, for Christ's sake."

The young man gathered the two stacks of papers, bundled them into the leather pouch, and hurried to the door. He paused briefly before opening it, as if he expected Witstrop to say something. But Witstrop only looked at him.

The secretary reappeared with another cup of coffee—the steam drifted toward her in curls as she walked toward Witstrop's desk. She put it down, without speaking.

Before she left, she ushered two men into the room. "Mr. Witstrop, let me again introduce Bud Cole and...," she now paused to ask the other name again, "...and Harry Bachelder from Skybillings Logging Company."

As the young man stepped past them, she nodded to Bud and said quietly, "And this is Mr. Witstrop's assistant, Theodore Petrisen."

The young man nodded slightly, but immediately slipped out of the room.

Witstrop looked at Bud Cole intently, not smiling or offering his hand. His eyes fell upon Harry, the scab across his cheek, and the long, dirty hair that hung over his collar. His face showed deep creases at the eyes and vertical furrows that ascended from above his nose. Though Bud Cole looked cleaner, his clothes were just as dirty. Both reeked of gasoline.

"Sit down gentlemen." Witstrop nodded to the conference table.

"Which one of you is Don Quixote and which one of you is Sancho Panza?" asked Witstrop, in a sudden exhale as he settled back in the chair. He stared at them, unflinching, no smile.

Bud responded quickly. "I would probably qualify as the don in the sense that I'm responsible for our being here," said Bud with a broad smile. "But from a purely spiritual level, I suspect both of us would have to plead guilty, sir." Bud continued to smile, but Witstrop ignored the comment.

"My assistant tells me that Skybillings is now seeking a $500,000 loan from Panama Northwest, on top of the money we already invested in you," said Witstrop quickly. "Do I have that right?"

Bud nodded. "That's right. We believe we have put together a good, high-quality logging company. As you know, we had a firm track record in the '20s. Ours was the biggest of the small companies before the stock market crash. And, with this additional investment from you, we can log-out the land that I believe your surveyors took a look at recently."

Bud had no clue what the surveyors recommended, but he guessed it wasn't favorable.

Witstrop thought about the answer for a moment, then stood up suddenly and began pacing. He walked across the expanse of tall windows facing Puget Sound, then those on the far wall facing south.

"Cole, I see nothing but goddamn risk in your operation. Nothing but goddamn risk. I've got a survey report that says you are planning to log land that might be called, even in the best of circumstances, impossible. My surveyors say we are talking about inclines in places of 45 percent and that you have to pull rail lines up grades that are, on average, well above 10 percent."

Bud had expected this. He had rehearsed the answers, along with the questions, for the last week. "We handled inclines of much greater than that during the '20s. That's nothing to put off a good bunch of loggers. We've already hired an experienced section crew with the first funding you gave us. We've already put down the track sections into some of the steepest areas, we're already hauling logs out of there."

Witstrop listened to this, then turned toward the brilliant snow peaks on the Olympics, now glistening against the rising sun. Bud sensed that he had only a few more moments to speak in his defense so he hurried on.

"We all recognize that stumpage in the Cascades is limited these days. The big boys have sewed everything up that's lower or easier or quicker. If we are going to operate in the Cascades in 1937 at all, it doesn't get better than this."

Bud sensed Witstrop about to pronounce a decision. So he pressed on. "And anybody who wants to get any kind of business foothold in the timber industry is going to have to make do with this kind of land. It's either this, or nothing. And if it's nothing, those big boys will own those woods and the rails that run through them for the next hundred years."

Bud realized he'd been punctuating each sentence by tapping his index finger on the table. Witstrop turned abruptly as if startled by the tapping. He smiled slightly. A fatherly, friendly smile, displaying large crooked teeth. Bud realized when Witstrop smiled that he was actually a handsome man.

Harry sat quietly next to Bud, looking occasionally at whomever spoke, but often peering out the window. He had argued strenuously with Bud to not bring him into the meeting. He had nothing to do with Skybillings, also pointing out that he looked like a beaten-up bum and could do nothing but hurt the chances of Skybillings to get the financing it needed to survive. But Bud had sworn that any man with brains enough to get them out of the middle of a labor riot was the kind of man he wanted with him arguing for money.

Witstrop took both of them in—looking intently at Bud, then Harry. "Mr. Cole, even if you can get those logs out, even if you can, I see two other drawbacks," he said, then paused to add, "And by the way, why don't you let me worry about whether or not my company gets a business foothold, as you put it? That aspect of my company's activities is none of your damn business."

Bud smiled but remained silent. Witstrop held him in the gaze of gray eyes in deep-set sockets for a moment before proceeding.

"As I said, even if you can get those logs out, I am told you have a locomotive laying on its side up there right now. I am told that you lost three men underneath it. I am doubtful that the state is going to ignore those deaths, and I doubt that the unions are going to overlook them. I'd be surprised if they even let you open on Monday."

He began pacing in front of the windows facing west. "But I will ignore all of that," said Witstrop, with a snort. "I will assume that this great Skybillings Company that you built up so carefully in the 1920s and which—I might add, was tits-up for five years, or should I say shit-faced down?—can yard-out all those logs. But I don't see how you are ever going to build a railroad trestle to span a ravine that, according to my surveyors, is something like a football field across. Wait, I'm sorry Cole, maybe they said two football fields."

Bud never believed that Witstrop or his surveyors would finally settle on this. He would've staked a case of beer and his first-born—not that he had one—that this deal would either go up or down before any talk of building a trestle to reach the timber across the ravine on the far ridge came up. So his defense was as weak as the reality was harsh—he knew very well that building such a trestle was virtually impossible. Besides, he knew nothing about trestles, at least those of the size that would be required to reach the far ridge. He could feel the heat in his stomach begin to rise into his chest.

Witstrop sensed victory. He stopped pacing and turned to the windows, hands behind his back. "Mr. Cole, have you ever built a trestle of that length before?"

"No I haven't, Mr. Witstrop," answered Bud, "but we may not have to. We might choose to blast the face underneath Three Sisters or we might find a way to go in from the valley floor."

"Let me ask you another question," continued Witstrop, ignoring the answer, still turned toward the windows. "Have you ever built a trestle before?"

Bud had dreaded this. If Witstrop didn't want to pay, then why not just say no? Why the lecture, the arrogance? This was his old man again—pouncing, not just winning, but pouncing.

"No, I have to say, I have not—of that size, at least." Bud said it with more energy than he felt. "But like I said, we may not even need a trestle."

Witstrop started laughing even before Bud finished—a rumbling laugh that seemed centered in his belly. He held Bud in a close, intense gaze now.

"Mr. Cole, if you don't mind me speaking bluntly?" He paused for effect. "That's bullshit." He flexed his jaw downward, as if stretching it or trying to rearrange the skin under the tight collar. His eyes lit with energy.

"You and I know it is bullshit. You and I both know that, don't we?" he asked. "That leaves only one question. The only way I have a chance to recover anything close to that $500,000—to say nothing of the money I've already invested in you, or should I say that I have pissed away on you—is if the Skybillings Logging Company builds that trestle. So just who is going to build your trestle, Mr. Cole?"

Witstrop held the back of the chair with thick hands—a victor about to enjoy the conquest. Bud stared at the table, drawing in a breath, readying an answer.

"I am," said Harry, in an almost inaudible voice.

Harry looked directly at Witstrop, who blinked quickly, slightly uncertain, as if trying to remember who Harry was. Witstrop suddenly quaked with laughter. His eyes opened wide, as if enjoying a good joke that the two of them had played on him.

"That's wonderful, Cole. That's just a fucking wonderful joke. Your hobo friend here is going to build your trestle." He paused for a second between each of the final words, as if to give himself enough air to fuel the waves of laughter. His crooked teeth flashed in the morning sun, his large body silhouetted against the brilliant blue and white of the water and sky.

As he began to recover from the laughter, he bent down across the table, raised his eyebrows, and leaned closer to Harry—as if he was now a co-conspirator in a joke that Bud and Harry had successfully played on him.

"Tell me, my good man, where did you learn to build these railroad trestles?"

Harry did not look at Witstrop. His eyes focused on a line of white clouds floating over the water, moving toward them.

"The University of Chicago."

Witstrop's face, now only a foot or so from Harry's, displayed an instant battle between laughter and confusion. The full, jowly cheeks seemed ready to begin roaring again, and almost filled with air. But the forehead creased, displaying furrows that fell into a sharp V just above the nose. The face seemed caught, as if slapped by a cold gust of wind that slipped through the tall windows behind him. Clearly uncertain of the ground, his next question was more tentative, but still protected by an incredulous, unbelieving smile.

"You want me to believe that you were an engineering student at the University of Chicago?"

"No."

"Then why claim you were?"

"I said I learned to build trestles there. I didn't say I was a student there. I was a professor there."

Witstrop still leaned across the table, unmoving.

"You ever been to Chicago, Witstrop? To the Loop?" Harry's tone was clipped.

"I grew up in Chicago," snorted Witstrop. "I owned my first company in Chicago."

"Then you know where Michigan Avenue crosses the Chicago River," said Harry, not bothering to wait for an answer. "Then you know that is a lift bridge spanning an opening of ninety-two feet, with a leaf weight in the neighborhood of 4,000 tons. What is special about this bridge, I'm sure you know, is that the two bascule type bridge leaves are side-by-side, so traffic can continue on one even if the other is not available. You would further know that the materials in that bridge were made of special alloys from Brazil and Argentina to withstand the expansion of Chicago summers and the contraction of Chicago winters."

Witstrop stared at Harry, his white mustache moved up and down every few seconds.

"I conceived that bridge. I engineered that bridge. I calculated all the torque needed for that bridge. And I developed the alloy that is in that bridge, sir."

Witstrop sank into the chair he'd previously used as a lectern.

Harry continued. "And if you would like other examples of my work, you can go to Paris, Rio de Janiero, and Singapore. All of those municipalities have used aspects of that technique to build bridges that, in at least two cases, span—as I believe you put it—the length of a football field—or two football fields."

Harry stopped and turned to Bud, whose face now seemed to gather more color. All three men sat in silence. When the secretary opened the door to bring in another cup of coffee, Witstrop just looked at her, breathing to himself, "I'll be goddamned."

# Chapter 7

A stiff breeze from the north topped the waves in frothy white, tilting several fishing boats hard into the troughs. Though they seemed destined to be swamped by the deep blue-green water, the vessels always righted quickly—corks in a tub. Cutting through the middle of them—halfway toward the line of mountains that ran along the other shore of Puget Sound—were several large freighters, sending up V's of white water as they pushed into the stiff northerly breeze.

"That's us," said Bud pointing, as he jammed the car into second gear to climb a hill.

"What are you talking about?" Harry's voice seemed to arrive from a great distance.

"That one moving north—there between the fishing boats—a lumber carrier. Look at its deck. That's how Skybillings timber moves." Bud stepped on the brakes quickly to slow at a switchback. Harry grabbed the dashboard.

"You always drive like this, Cole?"

Bud snorted, shifted back into second, and punched the gas pedal. The Seattle to Everett Highway ran directly next to the water.

"Don't like driving this close to the edge?" Bud smiled now, looking at Harry.

"Neither this close to the edge, nor with a fool like you behind the wheel."

Bud laughed. "Wait'll you see where we're going."

"I can't wait."

The ship continued to plow northward, though now closer to the channel at the opposite shore.

"You can even see the wood there on the deck. Probably on the way to the Orient."

Harry peered into the sunshine, but didn't speak. Long strands of brown hair lay just above his eyebrows.

"Probably one of Witstrop's," continued Bud. "Panama Northwest moves something like fifty million board feet out of Seattle a year, and probably that much out of Everett. Mostly to San Francisco and South America. By now, they're trying to move more into the East—New Jersey, New York, Boston—through the Panama Canal."

Harry glanced at Bud, but didn't respond. The trees along the road waved in the afternoon breeze, sprinkling bright sunlight into the car.

"How long you known Witstrop?" asked Harry, after a long silence.

"Three years maybe. Got the first loan about three years ago." Bud shot Harry a side-glance, wondering where the question was going. "Why?"

Bachelder studied the road as if deciding whether to engage in conversation or simply insist that Bud stop the car to let him out.

"Rich, shrewd, arrogant," said Harry. His voice seemed distant again. "Makes decisions only if he thinks them through, only when they're good for him, and only when he feels like it."

Bud turned to Harry, waiting for more. "So he's a good business-man. Nothing unusual about that."

Harry studied the upper reaches of the cedars that now sloped down from a steep hill to their right.

"I think Witstrop is all of that, but there's something else in him. Something you don't see as much these days in businessmen as you used to."

"What's that?"

"Something about how he carried himself, how he parried and blustered."

Harry's voice dribbled away as a car passed, honking its horn and flashing its lights. Harry looked quizzically at Bud, who didn't seem to notice. "Witstrop is a man who operates well beyond his own field of vision."

Bud studied the road intently, mulling this, wondering what Harry had in mind—for that matter, wondering who this Harry Bachelder really was. Bud snorted at the thought that he knew Witstrop a hell of a lot better than he knew Harry; yet now Harry was an ally, had gotten him through the meeting with Witstrop, and saved his skin in Everett.

"You don't agree?" Harry's question carried a hint of irritation.

"Never thought much about it."

Harry's tone was flat. "I just mean that Witstrop assembles his facts carefully, knows where he is going, and decides on a course of action. Nothing unusual in that. But Witstrop doesn't stop with what he knows. He factors into his calculation what he doesn't know—he calculates the uncertainties. Then, within a certain range of error, he sets down the outside boundaries of either what may hit him or what may happen."

Bud smiled. "Is this how an engineer's mind works, by any chance?"

Harry didn't listen. "That conversation with him had two separate pieces, did you see them?"

Bud looked at Harry with a smile. "Why don't I just say I didn't, so you have a chance to tell me?"

"Excellent," replied Harry. "The first part was everything from the time we walked in to the time he referred to his inspectors who paid a visit to your train. Up to that point, he was operating with facts, numbers, bits of information, or at the very least, good senses about what he was dealing with. You a card player, Cole?"

"I've done my share."

"The first part of the conversation was something akin to what an experienced poker player uses up to the point that he asks for more cards. At that point, he knows what he has, he calculates the odds of winning or bluffing with what he holds, he considers the chances of getting more cards as well as the implications of asking for more cards, and then he constructs a strategy—what he will do if good cards show up, what he'll do if bad cards show up, and so on. Everything after that, however, is bluff—facial expressions, how he holds his body, tone of voice, and of course, how much money he is willing to put on the table, and so on. All thin air. All made up. That's what Witstrop did."

"He was bluffing?"

"Not that he was bluffing. That's simply the analogy. What I am trying to get across is that—based on what Witstrop knew and didn't know, and based on what he wanted—he started venturing into a new field of play when he started with the inspectors. All the business about the state, the trestle, building the trestle, closing your shop—all of that, showed a man who knows, down deep in his soul, that to succeed, you have to extrapolate, you have to approximate—the military boys call it triangulating—then you have to rush forward with gusto and precision, so that your opponent is lost in your web of arrogance and brilliance, and all of the bluster you built from a few bits and pieces of information."

For several minutes they drove in silence, now away from the water and headed east, toward the mountains. A freight train pulling tank cars and flatbeds, laden with logs and cut lumber, began rumbling across the highway ahead, quickly bringing traffic to a stop.

"Sounds too complicated," said Bud, as he slowed the car.

"I'm not making it too complicated at all. Being shrewd, being rich, being arrogant—I suppose all of those are factors. What really makes a good businessman—what really lies underneath all those layers of wool and talc and aftershave—is the ability to know where the uncertainty in business transactions begins and knowing how to function effectively and creatively within that. That takes arrogance, yes. Stated more benignly, it takes self-confidence, discipline. You've got to manage all of your faculties so that no part of the equation gets more weight than it deserves."

Bud took a long look at Bachelder, who seemed lost in thought.

The train shook the ground, gently rocking the car. The boxcars flickered past quickly—red, black, orange, interrupted by long flatcars of logs—but then began to slow. As they did, faces became visible inside many of the boxcars—men standing in the open doorways, or sitting with feet dangling down. Several cars carried what looked like families. The train continued to slow, perhaps slipping onto a siding further up, then finally it stopped, still blocking the road.

An open boxcar came to rest directly in front of Bud's car. The door stood wide open, displaying a large pile of bags. Two men reclined on them; two more men stood at the door—one with long gray hair, pants cut off below the knees, wearing boots without laces; the other wore an old yellow shirt, a mackinaw, and stocking cap. Both stared at Bud and Harry as they sat waiting for the train to move.

"They think we're the enemy, you know," said Harry.

"Enemy?"

"Bourgeois, upper-class. We're the ones who crashed the system for them. We're responsible."

Bud shook his head.

"No, listen to me," continued Harry. "You own a car, you've got gas to run it, you've got some kind of business to conduct between Seattle and Everett, otherwise you wouldn't be sitting at this crossing. They think we're the enemy."

Bud studied the men. "C'mon, Harry. It's 1937 for Chrissake. Those guys aren't thinking that. The damn crash was almost ten years ago. All that Marxist and Red Commie talk is all finished."

Harry smiled slightly. "Then I guess you've already forgotten that little riot you decided to park your car in the middle of last night?"

Bud let out a sigh. "I know the unions are nuts. But that revolutionary talk went away when Roosevelt took over." Bud paused. "Those poor bastards on that rail car aren't Communists; they ain't even union crazies, I'll bet. They're just looking for another chance somewhere else."

Harry snorted, as the train began to move. The man with the gray hair nodded slightly as the car moved away.

❀ ❀ ❀

The highway turned sharply east and entered a flat meadow. The broad, fertile flood plain of the Seakomish River spread out before them—fences running zigzag into the distance, squares of green and brown dotting the valley floor, several red silos offering the only altitude in the sunny flatness.

Bud came back to the topic of Witstrop. "So do you think I can trust him?"

Harry considered this for a moment before answering. "I suppose you can trust him as much as you can trust anybody else you do business with," he said finally. "The only thing to not lose sight of is that Witstrop has a portfolio of wishes and goals that are, in no way, apparent to you."

Bud tried to decide if he found Harry's tone condescending, or merely irritating. Accompanying the clear intellect, thought Bud, was arrogance—but then he knew that from the start. Maybe Bachelder was so good at analyzing Witstrop because he was just like him. Or maybe he wasn't—Bud had chosen Harry for his obvious talents. That some obvious shortcomings were attached to those talents was one of the prices he probably had to pay to get his trestle built.

Bud laughed suddenly as he recalled the look on Witstrop's face when Harry said he could build the trestle. "You sure as hell obstructed old Witstrop's field of vision—or however you said it—when you told him you could build the trestle."

For the first time, Harry laughed—a cackling sound, pitted with occasional coughs. "I thought his mustache would twitch right off his goddamn face."

Both laughed, but this time Bud seemed to enjoy it even more, slapping the steering wheel while he drove. "What are the chances that I could stumble into a guy in the middle of a riot that had built the best damn bridge in Chicago?"

"Not great."

Bud passed a tractor, then eased back into his lane. He looked to Harry, who still had a smile on his face. Bud thought about Harry's answer for several miles.

"You did build those bridges didn't you?" Bud's voice carried the warmth of the earlier laughter.

Harry's face was relaxed, the flesh around his neck full of color. He sat now in the seat with an arm plopped onto the edge of the window. His left foot crossed his right knee. He nodded gently.

"I got you through the meeting, didn't I?" Harry smiled, looking at Bud directly.

"That wasn't the question."

"Very attentive, Cole. You're right, that wasn't the spoken question. But the broader question was: Can I do what you need—which is to build your trestle and keep your logging operation afloat? The answer is yes. Yes on all counts."

Bud drove the gas pedal downward again as he roared past a slow truck. The black sedan racing toward them in the opposite lane had to swerve to the right. As Bud returned to his lane, the sound of a horn roared past them. Bud looked to Harry, who was still relaxed, no anxiety in his face.

"For Christsake, answer the question," said Bud sharply.

"You are terribly predictable, Mr. Cole. Do you know that?" asked Harry with a smile. "If you're ever going to win a battle of nerves with George Bertram Witstrop, you have to be just a tad less predictable."

"Goddamn it, Harry. Can you do the work or not?"

"The answer's yes. I already told you I could. I can build any bridges you need."

"But did you build that bridge in Chicago that you told Witstrop about?"

Harry smiled broadly. "Of course I didn't, for God's sake. I made all that up."

"What in the fuck do you mean?"

"I mean just what I said."

"Then how the hell do you know how to build a trestle?"

Harry now shook his head, a friendly tone in his voice. "Bud, you confuse the real questions and then twist them in your mind so that nothing but shreds of confetti come out. You need to correct that."

Bud slammed the brakes, screeching into the gravel at the side of the highway. The truck he'd just passed swerved and blared his horn as it roared by on the left. The car slid sideways across the gravel before it finally came to a halt. Harry looked frozen in his seat, his face drained of color.

"Harry, as far as I'm concerned, you can get your ass out of this car right now."

Harry still held the dash, finally re-settling into his seat, and took a deep breath. He leaned back, holding both bony hands upward, fingers spread flat. Bud noticed a wedding ring on his left hand. "Look, I told you the truth. I was a professor of engineering at the University of Chicago. Structural engineering—stresses, spans, structures, all that shit. But when it comes to building those specific expanses I told him about, those were flat out lies."

"Goddamn it, if he'd figured that out, he would've thrown both of us out of there and my company would be down the shithouse hole."

Harry nodded. "That's right. But if I hadn't said it, your company would've been down the shithouse hole anyway."

Bud shook his head. "Let me tell you one thing, Mr. Harry Bachelder. You better goddamn learn that I run this operation and I make the judgments and calculations and decisions—my employees don't. You could've pissed away everything I've worked for."

"Bud, you're hysterical. It was clear that Witstrop was overshooting his headlights—he had 'bluff' written all over his face. If I hadn't come to your rescue, he would've ground you up so bad, there wouldn't have been anything left."

Bud continued to shake his head. "No. No. Remember one thing, Harry: I'd rather have this infernal company go to hell than let anybody else make the decision for me. Just remember that."

Harry shrugged. Bud started the car again and eased back onto the highway.

## Chapter 8

There was nothing notable about Skybillings Logging Company. It was another railroad logging company in the high mountains of Washington State. Like hundreds of others—in Oregon and northern California and British Columbia.

Skybillings had started, it had stopped, and it had started again—1925, 1930, and 1935, in that order. With the Depression finally loosening its grip, now was the time to make the last start stick. That was Bud Cole's hope. Who knew what the economy might do tomorrow?

He saw how so many men, successful men, some who owned their own logging shows, collapsed on the inside when the economy collapsed around them. A life of hard work—a life with a foundation of a job and a place in the community—created a comfortable order and certainty for a life, even if that life always stood within a whisper of death from a flying cable or a loose limb. In an odd way, sudden death was part of the order. You knew it could happen, and you thought about it—and you prepared for it best you could.

But economic and financial death so massive and widespread as this clawed deep into a man's soul. It came so fast—just a hint of trouble to start, then it blanketed every business and town. Jobs ended. Then companies closed. Families moved to find new chances. But the foundation had been split and scattered. The belief that, with good skills and common sense, with good training and earnest effort, a man could control his life, had vanished.

For some reason unknown to him, Bud had bounced off the bottom sooner than most. He could see all around him what the pain he had felt—and the feeling of total failure—could do. He would fight back somehow. If he was alive, he would fight back.

Which was how Skybillings came upon the land that it now owned. Bud visited every logging company owner and foreman he knew. The idea was to talk, and to find out what they were thinking. How could he get back? The logging business would eventually come back somehow. When it did, where should he be? And what should he do now?

He knew it was crazy thinking for a man who'd so recently scraped the bottom, especially for someone so familiar with the bottom of a bottle. But there it was. Go forward, or stop and die.

During a talk with Deek Brown, who was Bud and Fred's first employer after the war, Bud learned that Ashford & Southern wanted to sell acreage that was high in the Cascades—so high they'd decided to abandon it, even though they'd put in a rail line up Anderson Creek Valley and erected a logging camp next to Thunder Lake.

"Why would they want to get rid of it?" asked Bud.

"Simple: With practically everybody in the industry shut down, there's easier pickin's," said Deek. "They can sew up the rest of this valley by buying out low-lying stuff—easier to log, easier to re-sell— so why bother with timber that high? Ashford & Southern are aiming to be the new timber barons, Bud, didn't you know that? Bad times can make rich people, you know."

Bud knew about Ashford & Southern, about how they were unscrupulous in all manner of activity, how Tuttle Ashford, the president of the company, would stop at nothing to succeed. So many others like him had failed in the Depression—something Bud saw as perhaps the only silver lining. But Ashford hadn't. He'd been just the opposite: even more successful.

So why not benefit from Ashford's largesse? Bud didn't mind having to climb a little further into the Cascades to get logs. He calculated it all out, and the up-front money would be manageable—though he didn't have a penny of it. And Ashford would never view Bud and Skybillings as a threat to his empire-building.

So Bud turned his attention to the money. Actually, to finding the man with the money—no easy task, even when times were good. After many weeks of failures, of trips to Seattle and Portland, twice to Vancouver, it finally came in the form of a loan from Bertram Witstrop, president of the Panama Northwest Shipping Company. Bud had found Witstrop not through the visits he paid to logging owners, sawmill foremen, or past suppliers that he'd used, but by having a beer at Talbert's after a week of visiting prospective lenders in Portland.

"Two guys were in here today who looked either like FBI or big-money men," said Earl Talbert, as he sloshed a beer in front of Bud.

"Why would the FBI visit Seakomish?" asked Bud.

"Well, I wouldn't know that, would I?" sniffed Earl. "I could ask the same question about big-money men—and I wouldn't have an answer for that either, would I?"

Bud just smiled at Earl and let him get it out. Earl liked being in the center of things, knowing what was going on in town. But he wanted to do it his way.

"Anyway, they were just asking funny questions, you know? Like who are the big companies still in business around here, and where do they get their money from. And who they should talk to if they wanted get a foot into the logging business. And whether any of the companies had special connections to any of the railroads—Great Northern, especially. What does that sound like to you, Bud?"

"Sounds positively odd," said Bud. "Did they say where they were from?"

"Something called the Panama Northwest Shipping Company," said Earl. "Sounded like a bunch of hooey, frankly. I never heard of such a thing, and I bet it doesn't even exist."

But it did, and when Bud finally talked his way into a meeting with Bertram Witstrop, the deal was set, though Bud knew the odds of success in timber so high up in the Cascades were against him. Snows set in early at such elevations. And the wear and tear on steam engines was great—with steep inclines of ten or even twenty percent on some ridges. And smack-dab in the middle of the acreage he was buying, running down the middle of it like a big open wound, was a ravine so deep that he couldn't get a switch-back rail line down to its bottom, and so wide that building a trestle over it was impossible. So he couldn't reach the trees on the distant ridge—reported to be among the best remaining stands of old-growth Douglas fir in the Cascades.

But what Skybillings could reach was dazzling: thick stands of towering fir that blotted out the sky when you stood next to them. If Bud could log this land, he would be back in the fight. Skybillings would be whole again.

❊　❊　❊

Bud spit out the words. "Here's what we're looking at, boys." He took in the entire mess hall—trying to find every man among the hundred-or-so faces. "We're gonna put in a railroad trestle running right below Three Sisters Ridge by September."

He paused. He knew that most wouldn't really understand the words for a few seconds. Others wouldn't believe them. "A trestle across the face of Three Sisters will open up the far ridge for the first time. Nobody's ever logged it. Fact is, I doubt anybody has even been over there—ever. Once we've got the trestle up, Skybillings will be shipping the best timber on the market."

Most of the men had stopped eating. Some stared at him. Others smiled, thinking it was a joke.

"Gentlemen, this here is Harry Bachelder," said Bud with a wave of an arm toward Harry. "He's an engineering professor out of Chicago." Bud looked up with a big smile. "Any you rascals ever heard of the University of Chicago?"

No one responded. "Harry's going to be in charge of putting up the trestle. What I'm gonna do is split the crew in two—one will work under Harry; the other will work under John Valentine. Valentine's men will log out everything we can on this side; then we'll cross the trestle and work on the other."

The room was still. Zoe, the camp cook, stood in the doorway to the kitchen, a coffee pot in her hand.

"We'll go right along the face of the ridge—that's where the canyon is narrowest. We'll drive the beams into the rock ledge that runs along the base of Three Sisters. It'll take a lot of blasting. A lot of hauling timbers. We're gonna use the biggest pile driver in the valley—already got it on order. We may need two before it's all over."

Bud stopped. His eyes scanned the faces. Virtually all, blank. Waiting to hear more, which Bud took as a good sign. So he turned quickly to Harry and asked him to introduce himself and say a few words about the trestle.

"Not much to say really," said Harry, standing up slowly and stepping in front of the men. His face hung along its edges. "If you boys thought you worked hard before, you're about to learn otherwise. Building a trestle like Mr. Cole here has in mind is gonna be a hard piece of work. But it can be done."

"How long'll she take?" The question was from the back.

"It'll take roughly a month—assuming that the weather holds," said Harry. "If we get interruptions, two months."

"And how long will it take if three more men get killed?" The voice was that of Gordon Appleseth, a tall man with a narrow face, rimmed by a thin black beard.

Harry smiled. "On my watch, nobody is gonna get killed."

Appleseth laughed. Now Max St. Bride stood up next to him, loudly dropping his fork onto the table. His face swept the crowd. "Three men on this here crew got killed not even two weeks ago. Those bodies ain't cold yet. We got a goddamn Shay locomotive laying on its back. And this outfit is gonna build a goddamn trestle"—he paused for emphasis—"across a rock face that's probably a half-mile long, and we are gonna do that in a month?"

This brought laughter from the men at his table. St. Bride turned to Bud, who leaned against the wall. "Did I hear that right Mr. Cole?"

"You heard right."

St. Bride laughed—a deep, rattling growl. "In that case, this ain't a logging show. It's a goddamn death squad." St. Bride hitched-up his pants over a melon belly. "Where the hell's the union on this? I want to know what my union—my important union that I pay these damn dues to every month—is gonna do to protect us workers?"

St. Bride looked around for the AFL union representative, a man named Herrera, who was sipping the hot coffee Zoe had just poured. "Did you hear that AFL man? You hear what the boss man is gonna do? You gonna let this stand?"

Bud slapped a metal cup onto the table. "Sit down, St. Bride."

St. Bride scowled, but didn't move.

"Sit down or I'll sit you down," said Bud quietly. St. Bride smiled broadly, then winked at the men at his table and sat down slowly.

"Anyone who doesn't like the sound of this can walk out of this show right now—no hard feelings," said Bud. He studied the room. Most men met his gaze. "I don't give a damn what your reasons are. But before you do, think about this—everyone who stays gets a 5 percent raise. And when we're finished with the trestle, everybody gets 5 percent more."

The room erupted in applause. Several men stamped their feet. St. Bride flipped the middle fingers of both hands to the room at large.

※　　※　　※

They called it skyline logging.

It got its name from the intricate cable and pulley systems used for drawing the fallen logs from where they were cut to where they could be loaded onto railroad cars. The cables ran high overhead, strung tight between the top of a centrally located fir tree—called a spar tree, standing alone and naked, stripped of all limbs—and the top of a mirror-image tree well off in the distance. The cables were held to the treetops by thick metal collars.

But that was just the start of the spaghetti-works needed to haul logs. Running along the overhead cables between the two spar trees was a squat metal box—about the size of a suitcase—referred to by most loggers as "the car" or "carriage." One set of cables sent it zipping out to where the trees were cut; a separate set pulled it back. Both were driven by a heavy steam engine usually plunked onto a flat square of ground not far from the main spar.

Albert knew all about skyline logging from his earliest years. Virtually every logging show in the Seakomish Valley ran some version of it because it was fast and efficient. Albert also knew that it was fast in killing loggers, especially the men at the distant end of the operation, the ones who attached the cable to the logs, then scrambled away quickly. They were called "choker men" or "choker setters," because they had to grab the two cables that dangled loosely from the car, then wrench them noose-tight around the log—as if choking it—to make sure that it didn't work loose as the steam engine drew it toward the spar tree.

The reality was that metal cables subjected to such forces of movement and stress often broke. Or pulleys gave out. Anchor trees sometimes broke in half.

Before his father died, and often after as well, Albert and his mother and sister attended the funerals of the men who worked as choker men. In the early years, he'd asked his father what had happened. He usually got very general answers—like "a cable snapped" or "something came loose"—but despite his father's best efforts to shield him, Albert overheard the conversations from the next pew or around the casket at the cemetery. "The cable snapped and took his head clean-off," they would say. Or, "He didn't get out fast enough and the log dropped right on top of him."

Now, Albert was a choker man.

❀　❀　❀

Even after only a short time on the choking crew, the pattern was familiar: The screaming steam whistle, the metal digging into the bark, then the ripping whoosh as the logs shot into the air. And like always—at least in the two weeks he'd been on St. Bride's choking crew—Albert bent low and turned away just as the logs rocketed into the air and showered him in bark, mud, twigs, and rocks. Once they were away, he turned back slowly to watch their crazy dance down the hill, jumping and jolting, drawn by the steel cables, tearing at slash and broken stumps along the way, finally settling in tall piles next to the spar tree at the bottom of the clearing.

"Rowdy-dow! Rowdy-dow!" shouted Max St. Bride, the crew's "riggingslinger"—the one in charge of the choker crew and in charge of deciding which logs went next. "You all were too damn slow on that load." Though St. Bride's stomach hung low on a low frame, he scrambled easily over the matchbox chaos of fallen firs. "You motherfuckers are just too damn slow. We gotta move these logs! Can't be standin' around with our fingers up our arsses."

The logs were now at the bottom of the hill, where two men unhooked the chokers and sent the car back up the hill. "Here she comes, here she comes," shouted St. Bride, snapping his suspenders quickly. Albert stepped back to avoid the swinging cables as the highline drifted above his head, then slung the loose cables down next to his feet.

"Goddamn you, kid," shouted St. Bride. "You afraid of that thing?"

"No, I just don't want to be killed by it."

The job was just as Lightning Stevens explained it on the first day. "It ain't gonna require brains, Albert," said Lightning. "Just balls."

St. Bride pointed to two more logs, with a "rowdy-dow, row-dy-dow." And the two pairs of men grabbed the chokers and swept the steel cables around the logs. Lightning Stevens dipped below a fir as wide as he was tall, while Myles Norgren whipped the cable over the top. Albert grabbed the other cable and dropped onto his chest. With a single motion, he rolled onto his back, pulled the cable hard downward, and slid underneath the log.

"Pull the bell closer, Conrad," shouted Albert. Conrad Bruel wasn't bright, but he was strong and knew choking.

"It won't reach." Conrad kneeled as low as possible, but the nub-end of the cable wouldn't fit into the clasp, called a bell, that moved freely along the cable. When the cable end was inserted into the bell, it became a metal noose and cinched the log tight.

Albert yanked again, but still the cable wouldn't come further. "Go back a couple of feet." Conrad nodded and disappeared, while Albert lay underneath the log and waited. On your back, under two tons of log, he thought. He spit dirt away from his mouth and tried to wipe from his mind the picture of the Shay falling onto Nariff Olben.

"Rowdy-dow! Rowdy-dow!"

Albert felt a sudden rush of heat in his chest as he heard the words. If the other log moved, it would slam into the log above him. Just when he decided to get out from underneath—no matter what St. Bride would say—Conrad slid the bell down just far enough. Albert clicked the nub of the cable inside it and cleared the log just as it swept into the air. As it did, a broken twig slapped him across the face.

"Slow it down, St. Bride," shouted Lightning Stevens, as Albert fell to the ground, clutching his face.

"Slow it down?" St. Bride laughed loudly. "Slow it down? Didn't you boys hear Mr. Bud Cole saying how we was going to speed things up? 'Gotta put in a trestle, boys.' 'Gotta get it in by September, boys.' Did you happen to miss that part of our breakfast conversation this morning, Lightning Stevens?"

Albert got back to his feet, wiping the mud from his face. A patch of hard-slapped red skin emerged.

"I didn't hear nothing about trying to kill the people who worked for him," shot back Lightning.

"You're one of them AFL boys, ain't you Lightning?" asked St. Bride.

"What about it?"

"Your union ain't doing diddly shit to protect you, is it? Old Max St. Bride is only doing what he is told to do. And your union representative man is sitting around playing with himself."

"This don't have nothing to do with unions, St. Bride. You're giving the orders. You're running this show too hot. And you're gonna get one of us killed—or all of us."

St. Bride leapt over a thick stump, spitting tobacco as he hurdled it. He now stood within two feet of Lightning, who towered over him. "And what the hell you gonna do about it, Injun?"

Before Lightning could move, Myles Norgren jumped between the two men. "Both of you shut up, will ya?"

But Lightning tried to push him away. "Already had three men killed this month because of assholes like you, St. Bride," shouted Lightning.

"Like me? What the hell did I do?"

"You goddamn CIO killers did-in Nariff Olben, and you know it."

Now St. Bride lunged for Lightning, but Norgren stuck his foot out, sending St. Bride sprawling into a bed of fir twigs. By the time he'd regained his footing, the highline screamed overhead, as the returning bell and rigging roared toward them.

"Rowdy-dow, rowdy-dow," shouted St. Bride, as if nothing had happened.

"Let's move. Over here." St. Bride had clambered across the fir he'd earlier hurdled. He pointed to the two logs he wanted the men to choke, as if the battle with Lightning had never occurred. As Albert struggled to pull the cable below the log, he noticed out of the corner of his eye that St. Bride seemed to have a smile on his face, though the black stubble and the dribbles from the chewing tobacco made it hard to tell.

❊   ❊   ❊

For the first few days after Bud switched Albert to the choking crew following the accident, Albert couldn't move. The aches were so deep they seemed to reside inside his bones. Getting out of bed in the morning blackness brought shooting pains in his ankles and lower back.

But slowly the pains eased. He could move more easily in the heavy boots, even finding the job of scrambling around the logs to hook the chokers bearable. The air was warm, the leaves and dirt moist and cool. He could move faster than the bigger men, and although his narrow frame meant that he was the one who had to crawl underneath the logs, the danger was balanced by the fact that he felt like he was actually contributing.

Albert also grew more comfortable with the crew. Lightning Stevens was a hothead—ready for a fight—but also patiently explained to Albert how to set the chokers, how to move out of harm's way. Myles Norgren was friendly, though distant—a card-carrying Communist who seemed more interested in the ideas than in doing anything about them. And Conrad Bruel, Albert's choking partner, ran either hot or cold: friendly one moment, angry and alone the next. And he always fidgeted—arms, legs, hands, something was always moving. Albert knew he could count on Conrad when setting the toughest chokers, but that's as far as it went.

But for Max St. Bride, Albert held a special dislike. Albert sensed a true desire to do harm, though he had trouble figuring out how St. Bride chose his enemies. At times, the deep growl and bulging eyes seemed targeted at anybody who was ever a member of the AFL. Other times, he lambasted the Commies and troublemakers in the CIO. He said some that he knew were actually queers. Then he would laugh it all off, as if he were unaware of what he'd just said or whom he'd just attacked. St. Bride had been working in the woods above Seakomish for thirty years, and it appeared to Albert that he had developed an intense hatred of nearly everyone he'd worked with during that time.

By the early part of May, most of the clearing had been logged. The hillside leading down to the edge of the ravine, where Bachelder's crew was assembling the timbers for the trestle, was largely open. Even the tall stumps that loggers usually left—because it was too hard to cut the massive firs close to the ground—had been removed. A new locomotive, operating on a new section of track that was built around the fallen Shay, had ferried most of the timber down the mountain.

While a part of Albert grew more comfortable daily with the job he had to do, another part of him grew more troubled over the death of Nariff Olben. Part of the reason was that, as the slope cleared of firs, the opening at the bottom of the hill where the accident occurred became visible.

Often, waiting for the highline to return for another pair of logs, he found himself staring at the opening, seeing once again the hot cinders spewing across the hillside as the Shay toppled.

"And what in the fuck are you thinking about now, Sleeping Beauty?" St. Bride's face was six inches from his own. "You stand around here and daydream, you'll get your brains splattered even faster kid. You ever seen a man's brains out in the open?"

Before Albert could respond, St. Bride had spun away and started shouting, "Hoa! Hoa! Hoa!" This brought the skyline to a stop.

Albert could see that the last pair of firs that roared down the hillside had snagged on an old stump. St. Bride scampered across several firs on his way to the scene. "Norgren and Stevens—follow me. We gotta untangle this mess." Both men followed, with Conrad Bruel close behind.

"What the fuck you doing?" shouted St. Bride when he noticed Conrad on the way.

"I'm gonna help."

"Like hell you are. You and the kid stay right where you are." St. Bride turned away and disappeared behind several stumps, as he, Lightning, and Myles headed down the slope.

"Let the old shitass work with two old deadbeats," said Conrad. "Fuck him." He thumped down onto a stump, unlaced a boot, pulled off his sock, took a whiff, turned it inside out and shook dirt and leaves to the ground. Conrad's constant movement wasn't really fidgeting exactly. It was more like electricity ranging through his body, electrifying one part, then another, with sudden little jolts.

"Serves you maggot-asses right," shouted Conrad, jumping onto a stump. Albert could see that the three other men, well beyond earshot, were wrestling with the logs—Myles and Lightning were pulling on the choker cable, while St. Bride put all of his weight on a six-foot limb he was using as a lever to loosen the snag.

"Pull it on the right," he shouted at the group, stabbing the air with his hand. All three men must've heard, since they looked up briefly, then went back to their tasks. Conrad thrust the middle fingers of both hands into the air. "What's a drunk Indian and a Commie know about loosening hang-ups?"

"That's not the first time that maggot St. Bride has done it either," he snorted. "St. Bride acts that way, Albert. Don't forget it. And don't turn your back on him either. You don't kiss his pecker like he expects, and he takes the work away. He lets you sit and wait."

Conrad now began to pace—actually to shuffle back and forth between the sapling that he'd previously propped his feet onto and a piece of fir log. "Man could go broke if somebody like that takes the work away. No money on Friday, no pussy Friday night."

Suddenly the hangup and St. Bride didn't seem to bother Conrad as much. "You should see 'em Albert. A logger goes down there on the weekends with a fat pecker and a fat roll of cash and those little babes will spread 'em without even asking your name." Albert watched a hawk circle lazily above. Its red tail flashed brightly in the sun as it tilted to the left, then the right, peering into the slash for rodents.

"You ever thought of killing a man, Albert?" asked Conrad abruptly.

"What?"

Conrad smiled. "I asked you if you ever thought about killing a man."

Albert shook his head and looked back to the hawk. "You mean just because St. Bride told you to stay up here, you want to kill him?"

"Hell, no," snorted Conrad. "Got nothing to do with that snag." He reached into his pocket, unsnapped the lid from a can of chewing tobacco and slipped a lump under his lip. "Just wondered if it ever crossed your mind."

"Can't say as it has."

"It will, just wait." Conrad's voice was not menacing. "Once you get a little experience, take a few knocks. Then it'll cross your mind. Maybe when you're in the mess hall or when you're riding the crummy or you've had a few down at Talbert's or you're ready to jam your dick into some young cunt—then it'll go through your mind."

Albert studied Conrad. His jaw seemed less pronounced than it had. His row of tall, white teeth were hidden.

"You'll get a little flash in your head, and it'll be a picture of a man with a blade in his neck, or you'll hear the sound a man makes when he falls over the edge of a canyon." Conrad laughed, then spit a dark lug of goo at his feet.

Albert felt a cloud darken the warmth of the sun on his neck. The crew down the hill had finally loosened the snag and were headed back. "You don't really mean that stuff, do you?"

Conrad snorted, his thick neck twitching slightly while he tapped his knees with long fingers. "Course I don't. Talk is good for your soul. Remember that."

❀   ❀   ❀

"How's it going on the choking crew?" asked Bud, as Albert jumped off the crummy and started walking toward the bunkhouse. Albert noticed that Bud waited until the others were far enough behind that they couldn't hear.

"Going okay, thanks," said Albert, though he wanted to blurt out that Max St. Bride was a lunatic and trying to kill the crew and blaming Bud Cole for everything and that Conrad Bruel could, very possibly, murder somebody without thinking twice.

"You getting along okay with Lightning and Myles?" Bud picked up Albert's stride, nodding to several of the men who passed. "They're good fellas. Lightning's been with us since '25. Myles joined in March, but I could tell the first week he was a hell of a worker."

"I figure that I've got a lot to learn from both of them," said Albert, not sure what else to say and not sure why they were having the conversation.

Bud stopped and turned to face Albert directly. "You'll let me know if you run into any problems?"

"Sure," said Albert. Then he decided to just be direct. "Did I screw-up or something?"

"No, not at all. Just keep up the good work." Bud nodded, then fell into a conversation with Harry Bachelder, who was walking the other way.

When Albert got to the bunkhouse, Conrad was already taking off his boots. "See that you was sucking the management. That sort of shit can get you into big trouble around here, if you're not careful."

Albert flopped down on his bunk. His back felt like a piece of steel was wrapped around it. "Conrad, you got an imagination the size of Texas. That was Bud Cole making polite conversation. Nothing more."

"You know anything about the strike a couple of years ago that closed down all the logging up and down the Cascades?"

"Course I do. I live in Seakomish. Strikes are hard to miss."

"So you know it had something to do with the unions and the owners battling like cats and dogs?"

Albert remembered the strike well. Seakomish was virtually closed for months because the AFL closed the woods and the owners remained firm. Albert didn't much pay attention. His mother's job was safe. And he was thinking only about girls at the time. But he knew that it got bad in town. His mother gathered food for families at the school. He knew several families who abandoned their houses and just drove away. He didn't know where, or if they would ever return. Union men and strike breakers—brought in by the owners—faced off more than once on Main Street.

Conrad pulled off dirty socks and began fidgeting with his pants. "Owners like Bud Cole caused all of that. Just remember that. How many months did we have to sit around and beg for handouts from the grocery stores and churches for food?"

Albert didn't care. His back ached, and he wanted to just lie flat. But maybe this was an inkling about what went on behind Conrad's buck teeth and constant movement. "I actually didn't take you for being a union man, Conrad," offered Albert, against his better judgment.

"I'm a union man, alright. AFL. The only good union around," snorted Conrad. "Them assholes like St. Bride are nothing but Reds—just like Norgren. All CIO. They just want to bust apart logging companies these days. They want the goddamned Communists to come in and take over everything, just like in Russia."

Several other men swept through the door to the bunkhouse, cursing and laughing. Bucky Rudman slapped Albert's boots. "Didn't your momma tell you not to put your shoes on the bed, kid?"

Little Boy Whittaker followed behind and had half his clothes off before he reached his bunk. Myles Norgren farted as he plopped onto his bed. Whitey Storm took off his boots quickly, then leaned back onto his bed with a loud, "Ahhhhhh." The bunkhouse filled with conversation and the close smell of sweat and dirt. In the confusion, no one paid attention to the conversation between Conrad and Albert.

"So that's why you hate St. Bride so much? Because he's CIO?" Albert propped up on one elbow.

Conrad pulled a gray t-shirt over his head, but he didn't seem to hear the question. He looked at Albert, who continued to wait for an answer. Instead, he grabbed a clean shirt and walked out the door.

Albert was stuffed from Zoe's dinner. But he saved room for an extra piece of pie. Zoe had left several pies, along with a jar of cookies, on the counter after she went to bed. She asked only that anyone helping himself to a piece be sure to use a knife and stack the dirty dishes in the washbasin when he was finished.

The mess hall was filled with conversation—though already past 9 p.m., several men didn't turn in until late. Many logging shows required lights out by 10; but Bud Cole simply asked that men be respectful of those already in their bunks when they decided to turn in and be ready to work a hard eight hours the next day.

With a plate of pie—Albert decided it was blackberry, probably from the bushes along the lake—and a glass of milk, he settled on the floor next to one of the stoves in the mess hall, leaning against the stack of firewood. The crackling fire from the cast-iron belly warmed the oak planks and the stack of wood at his back. Several men were grouped around Petey Hulst near the windows and the other stove—a cloud of blue smoke hung above them. Albert didn't know whether it was poker or tarot—Petey also dabbled in the spirit world—though the laughter that punctuated the proceedings every few minutes suggested poker.

In the far corner, near the door, several more men huddled on benches in a circle. Albert didn't know them all, though he recognized Adam Jost and Wally Nuvill. Jarrett McCallem sat on the far side, facing in Albert's direction, as did Elmer Stubbs and a man with long hair and beard whom Albert knew only as a member of the falling crew. The group—mostly older men—looked cleaner than Petey's group. Maybe it was that most were clean shaven. At the center of the group, bending down on one knee, holding a Bible in one hand and gesturing with the other, was John Valentine. His face seemed lit—a broad smile, flickering eyes, and deep color in both cheeks. Valentine's large frame seemed smaller, now that he kneeled.

Albert finished the pie and the milk. After checking that nobody was watching, he licked the plate clean—the tart blackberry, together with the sweet, flaky crust that Zoe dusted with a glaze of cinnamon, made his throat feel scratchy, yet smooth, as it slid down. Though his mother was a good cook, Zoe was better.

The conversation from both groups reached him at roughly the same volume, allowing him to pick either one, or—sometimes—both. Along with the quiet music from the radio in the corner—Little Boy Whitaker hunched in front of the upright—the sounds felt warm and friendly.

Albert went to the kitchen for a refill. He cut another piece, but this time he added two chocolate chip cookies on the side of his plate. He snapped the lid onto the pie platter, then hauled the tall milk pitcher out of the ice-box.

As he poured, he took in the full view of Zoe's kitchen—perfectly in order, every surface scrubbed clean, even some wildflowers sitting in the middle of the workbench where she chopped vegetables and kneaded dough.

The moon played across the porch, angling through the windows and onto the workbench. Albert sat in a chair alongside it, taking in the feel of quiet and order about him—the blue-and-white checked curtains that skirted the lower halves of the windows; the buckets of flour and macaroni marching in careful order along the shelves just underneath; the wooden crates of tin cans, some marked coffee, the rest marked tomatoes, stacked neatly under the benches that lined the walls. Zoe cooked for a hundred men. She ordered the food, planned the meals, organized the service and delivery, and generally kept order in the mess hall.

As Albert pondered Zoe, he carefully placed the empty plate in the sink and took the two cookies with him into the mess hall.

Several of the men had left, including most of Valentine's group, though Valentine himself was still sitting with one of the men, Bible now open on the wooden table, listening intently and nodding as the man spoke.

The poker game had petered out, though cards were still spread across the table near the window. The stragglers from the poker game were now seated on benches around the far stove which crackled loudly. A pot of hot water stood on top. Petey Hulst sat on a piece of firewood, tipped on end, next to the stove. His red-checkered flannel shirt matched the dark, leathery glow of his face. A curved pipe, gray and white, hung from his mouth—now largely hidden by a jet-black handlebar mustache that twirled into hard, waxy points at either end. Petey's voice danced in a kind of sing-song rhythm that it took on when he told a story.

The rest of the men sat in a semi-circle around Petey and the stove. Lightning Stevens sat on a bench directly in front of Petey, his cowboy boots on the floor next to him, large feet propped on a piece of firewood facing the stove. Conrad Bruel, Myles Norgren, Whitey Storm, Bucky Rudman, and two faces that Albert didn't recognize sat on the other benches.

When Albert walked in, he sensed that a story was underway. Petey nodded, then started speaking again.

"The stories about Olaf Carn may be true, or they may just be the talk of scared loggers," said Petey slowly. "By my reckoning, Olaf Carn would be living around these parts, give or take twenty, thirty miles—that's assuming he's still alive."

Albert had heard about the legend of Olaf Carn since he was a boy. Some suggested he was a lunatic who hid in the woods to kill people; others simply said that Olaf was a logger's yarn that had gotten out of hand.

"Did you ever work with Olaf back then?" asked Myles Norgren.

"Nope, never did. Never even met him. He was up in these woods the whole time. I was working north of San Francisco. It's just that word traveled so fast that I picked it up down there in only a coupla months. Stories had it that Olaf Carn was working somewhere along the Anderson Creek Valley—right in these woods—with Zollock & Sons Logging."

Petey now took a long drag on his pipe, blowing smoke in a thick gray stream toward the log roof overhead.

"See, the IWW, the Wobblies—these were the wild-eyed union guys around 1910—was going to close down Zollock & Sons. The Wobblies said they didn't like the fleas and lice in the bunks. So come one Monday mornin', they shut everything down. They stood three deep across all the roads going into the camp. Zollock comes outa his shack with his boys and says to the foreman, who was standing in the Wobblie strike line, 'Whatze hell ya got goin' on here?' And the foreman says, 'All of us is on strike. The IWW is closing this here camp. This here camp is on strike on behalfa' the Industrial Workers of the World.'"

Petey shook his head and smiled, his gray eyebrows arched in points upward. "So Zollock chews on this a little bit. He talks it over with his boys—but see, Zollock and the boys knew it was coming. That's important to remember. Zollock didn't get to be the biggest, meanest logging operation in these parts before the war by not figgering what might happen. So Zollock pretends to be surprised by all this rigmarole and he mulls this over a little."

Petey's eyes squinted slightly, a wide grin on his face, gaps in his yellow teeth—an actor, on a stage, his bent fingers now rubbing his whiskers, as if Zollock himself sat next to the fire and pondered the challenge of the Wobblies and the foreman: "'Well now', says Zollock. 'You closes us down, do ya?' And the foreman says again, 'IWW closes you down for the Industrial Workers of the World.'"

Petey's voice suddenly shook with emotion, as he again assumed Zollock's character. "'Well, you somebitch, how 'bout you argue wit dis,' shouted Zollock, and out from the brush come fifty pig-faced, sweatin' son-of-a-bitches, carrying rifles and bats and tire irons and pole axes, and they lit into the Wobblies with a fury like these mountains never saw.'"

Petey now paused. The fire crackled.

"Before it was over, nine strikers were dead—some dang near butchered. When the police finally got up there, heads was gashed so deep that you couldn't recognize 'em. The only one who escaped was Olaf Carn. Word had it that he had killed one of Zollock's sons, using the fella's own pole axe on him. But before the rest of them could get Olaf, he slipped into the woods and disappeared. Slick as a whistle."

Petey now tilted back slightly on his piece of firewood, warming his hands next to the stove and taking a long draw from his pipe. He seemed suddenly lost in the black cast-iron moldings that ran below the belly of the stove.

"So did they look for Olaf?" The question came from one of the men Albert didn't know.

"Sure did. The way I heard it, Zollock and his strike breakers hunted the woods for two weeks, sniffing every cave, every miner's tunnel, even walking Anderson Creek for miles to see if he slipped into the water to hide. But they didn't find nothing."

The crackling of the fire now took over again. Albert noted that the moonlight had gone completely. The windows were ink black.

"What did the police say?" The question came from Lightning Stevens.

"Police said that it was a family of cougar that must've got hold of the crew—such was the damage on the bodies."

"Cougars?" Lightning Stevens grunted. "Nobody believed that, did they?"

"Some did. And a lot didn't want to know. I'm telling you boys, the work of this valley back then was wood—still is. You stop the wood, you stop the life hereabouts. Wobblies had some complaints. Had some support. People didn't like the dangerous work of bastards like Zollock. But Wobblies wasn't no good for commerce neither. Close a mill and nobody works—period. So, when it was all done, the cops decided it was best to say that a few dead Wobblies probably got that way from cougars, not from pole axes."

"So what happened to Olaf?"

Petey chuckled, a broad smile again recapturing his face. "Never seen again, except in the stories people tell."

Petey cleared his throat suddenly, breaking into a raspy, rumbling cough that rattled deep in his chest. For several seconds, he drank in air. But just as quickly, his breathing settled.

When he started again, his voice seemed thin, though his face still showed a hint of the excitement of the story. "Ever since, lot of folk talked about Olaf Carn, about how he lives somewhere in these woods, maybe in one of the abandoned mines, about how he takes revenge against the killers—in his mind, the killers was the logging companies, any logging company. After all, it was the logging companies that hired the strike breakers that carried the pole axes that bashed in the faces of the Wobblies—these is the targets of Olaf Carn, or that's how it was told when I first heard about it down in Frisco."

Petey took a long drag on the pipe, then puffed a cloud toward the electric lights that hung above him, dark. "Stories had it that Olaf lived off the land—maybe in a cave, maybe in a hovel, growing his own food or stealing from the logging shows. But every now and then, he'd take potshots—kill a logger, steal a woman from town, set off dynamite on a rail line. He promised that he'd get back at the loggers, one way or another."

The faces around the circle facing the fire did not speak. Jarrett's eyes were on the flames; Lightning Stevens stared into Petey's face. Conrad Bruel and the others sat motionless, as if waiting for more.

A low growl, almost a grunt, came suddenly from the kitchen door: "I worked with Olaf Carn." Max St. Bride leaned against the doorframe, a thick brown stubble across his face, his belly hanging low across dirty work pants. He walked slowly toward the fire, settling onto a bench next to Lightning Stevens. Albert noted that St. Bride tipped leftward slightly when he walked, trailing a hint of alcohol.

But his voice was clear, the words unslurred. "I worked with Olaf Carn for two years at Zollock before all that." He took a drag from a cigarette. As he blew out the first cloud, he started laughing—deep, low, the laugh of a man who is enjoying a joke somewhere inside himself, with little concern over whether anybody else understands.

"Just before I left there—would've been about 1910—just before the Wobblies. Olaf says to me, 'We oughta kill these bastards before they get a chance to kill us.' He says, 'Ya know, Max, you and me oughta organize all these assholes and stop this sufferin' and if they say no, we oughta just knife 'em all.'"

St. Bride chuckled through several more puffs, then got up and left.


## Chapter 9

One month to the day after Nariff Olben and the other men were buried, Bud Cole announced that they would try to upright the Shay. The trestle was far from done, he admitted to the crew, but he decided they needed it ready to help move the timber once it was completed.

This brought a chorus of complaints. The old locie was too heavy. It was tilted almost on its back, mired deep in mud, impossible to lift with a frog—a low-slung mechanical contraption often used to lift locomotives back onto the tracks. But Bud wouldn't accept it. "By the time that trestle is done, we're gonna need more than one Shay," he insisted.

To Albert, the argument seemed thin. The trestle wasn't only far from done, it was barely started. But he was troubled about raising the Shay for a different reason. He was angry that no one ever mentioned Nariff after his death. It was as if he vanished. Now, with Bud's decision about the Shay, the debate focused on whether it could, or should, be done. Two of the men Albert didn't know—two men from the bucking crew—got into a fistfight over whether the Shay could ever be raised. But through it all, still no mention of Nariff. Not even in passing.

That's when he decided he had to do something on his own. He didn't know what. But he decided that he would at least go up to visit the overturned Shay. Something about paying his respects, alone, where Nariff died, seemed right.

The first weekend that promised warm weather, Albert decided to decline the trip down the mountain to Seakomish on Friday afternoon. "What the hell is wrong with you, boy?" shouted Bucky Rudman, as the crummy was almost filled. "Those valley ladies need a young healthy stud like you—ol' Bucky Rudman can't keep all of 'em satisfied."

"Gonna go hiking." This brought a big laugh from the crummy.

"You ain't working him hard enough, St. Bride," shouted Appleseth from the back.

"Last chance," yelled Fergie as he began to let out the brakes. But Albert just waved and headed back into the mess hall for supper. That night, he languished in the joys of the camp without the crew. Supper without elbows jamming you in the side. Sitting with a cup of hot chocolate and watching darkness creep over Thunder Lake. He even soaked in one of the big wash tubs in the bathhouse, before crawling into bed in a bunkhouse that—for the first time that he recalled—was absolutely still.

The next morning, he hurried through Zoe's breakfast—sloshing down eggs and biscuits with a glass of milk. As soon as he finished, he hauled a knapsack from under his bunk, found an old cap, and headed for the tracks that led up to the Shay. But he decided to stop first in the mess hall to ask Zoe for some food to take with him. It was at least a ten-mile walk—half of it at a steep incline from where the track split from the line to Seakomish and began crawling up to the Skybillings logging site.

"It appears to me you're setting out on an expedition, young man," said Zoe as she stopped washing the breakfast dishes to begin a sandwich for him. She didn't ask where he was going, though he knew she wanted to.

Albert looked out the window while Zoe worked. It was almost ten o'clock and the sun had finally unveiled the granite and ice on Crescent Peak across the lake. Albert calculated that he had to hurry if he was to make it back before dark.

"Here is your menu," said Zoe, wiping her hands on a towel. "Three sandwiches, two boiled eggs, an apple, and two pickles. And a piece of pie from last night. Will that hold you?"

"Sure will."

"How long will you be gone?"

"Be back by sunset."

She studied him. Her blue eyes hinted at questions, but none came. "Albert, you ought to know one thing about this camp on weekends. When Mr. Cole is down in Seakomish, I am the one in charge. And when one is in charge, a person needs to be sure that her crew is not going to go out and get lost in the woods or that he is otherwise going to do something foolish and have to make Mr. Cole wonder if he did right by putting her in charge."

Albert smiled and slipped out the door.

❄     ❄     ❄

The air in the woods, especially as the days lengthen in late spring, smells of Christmas—a friendly perfume of moist alder and pine boughs. Once he was on the tracks, walking in the direction of Seakomish, he decided that it wasn't just the Christmas smells that filled the woods. There were other smells, just as sweet—boughs of broken cedar warming in the sun, rhododendron unwrapping from the night dew. As he cleared the first rise from camp, his feet crunching on the hard gravel between the rails, he could feel the wind pick up. For a while, it held steady in the treetops, then was replaced by strong gusts that boxed his ears in a hollow envelope of sound.

Albert shifted the knapsack slightly as he leaned forward into the growing incline. Every morning, Fergie gave the crummy extra steam through this section of track. It rose steady from camp, then leveled off, then rose again. His breath came harder, so he shifted the knapsack again. He knew that if he was going to reach the Shay and return before dark, he'd have to keep a steady pace, especially since the incline only steepened once he got to the main track—one direction headed down the mountain toward Seakomish, the other climbed upward to the Skybillings logging operation. They called it the "Y."

Albert's concentration broke as a jackrabbit scampered across the tracks—darting directly in front of him. The sudden movement sent a flock of blue jays and woodpeckers shrieking into the trees from bushes that ran alongside the tracks. He stopped for a moment, to watch them fly—into a sky that had turned deep blue. Behind him, he could now see the distant edge of Thunder Lake far below, though the Skybillings mess hall was hidden. At the far side of the lake stood Crescent Peak, its white tip glistening in the sunlight.

He studied the peak closely, then swept his eyes downward, finding the rock ledge that Conrad had claimed was the home of Olaf Carn. From this distance, the ledge was no more than the size of Albert's finger, which he knew probably meant that it stood twenty or thirty feet high and ran probably a hundred feet. Could anybody live in there? Not that he could tell from this distance. Directly below, the ledge dropped off, although Albert noticed that blue-green firs crept right to the edge of the ledge on either side.

Albert started climbing again. Never before had he heard so many stories. After supper, after the dishes were cleared and the big potbellied cast iron stove was fully stoked, they sat around in circles telling stories. The best so far had been Olaf Carn. But then there was Lightning Stevens' story of the Indian burial grounds, which he'd heard repeated a few days later by Petey Hulst.

The Seakomish had buried their dead up here—somewhere up high, they said. Trappers in the early days had found the graves, and looted them of trinkets and jewelry, leading the Indians to put a curse on any man who walked the hills again. After Petey told the story, Albert noticed the same effect on the men as the story of Olaf Carn: The faces looked drawn. But these were far from the only stories. There were tales of cougars so powerful that not even the Indians were able to kill them, of coyotes that hunted the early miners, of wind and rain storms that created mudslides that devoured mountains and filled ravines, of snows so deep that men turned into cannibals to survive them.

Damn stupid. He knew that. But still, more believable than he liked. And the crew—well, it was pretty obvious that many of the men believed them. That made all the foolishness harder to close out.

He stopped again to get his breath. He felt like sitting, but the sun was already high. He unzipped his pants, relieved himself onto one of the shiny rails, then began the climb again. The wind had settled, so he pulled his coat off and looped it over his shoulders. The sun gave the warming wooden ties at his feet a hint of the docks, as the creosote filled his nostrils.

Albert wiped the sweat from his neck and laughed. The smell was so familiar. He didn't know how many times he and his mother and father had visited the docks at Mukilteo on Puget Sound. He loved the small lighthouse that stood there. A tiny beach. Boulders that ran along a parking lot. He recalled racing through the waves, trying to reach the gulls that hung motionless in the mist before landing on the creosote pilings and crabbing at him for causing so much trouble.

Most of the trips they took were on Sundays, just after church in the summer. Bud Cole and his wife often came along as well. Albert's mother seemed to enjoy the company of Bud's wife, Kathryn. The women walking for what seemed to Albert like forever along the beach. The men leaning against driftwood logs, stoking a fire in front of them, smoking.

Albert hadn't thought about that in years. He couldn't even remember how old he was then, though he guessed that his dad and Bud had already gone into business together. Nevertheless, the scene came back in sudden brilliance. Earl Talbert, the saloon owner, and his wife were there. Albert's dad and Bud seemed especially happy that day, slapping each other on the back, their big shoes propped on the driftwood. While Earl Talbert kept pointing at Albert and saying, "That boy there'll get it all. He'll be a rich little fellow. If you follow through." Albert sensed that his father was embarrassed, because he then scooped Albert up and nuzzled him with a whiskery chin.

When the women returned, Albert became the center of attention again. Bud's wife fussed over him. She asked him his age and whether he liked school. Did he like to read? She loved to read when she was in school, she said.

"Bud, isn't Albert grand?" she asked, when he recited a poem he'd learned the week before. "He knows poems that I didn't learn until I was well along—practically out of high school." Bud smiled but didn't say anything.

"Come-on you old curmudgeon," she laughed. Now it was Bud's turn to seem embarrassed, so he quickly turned the conversation back to Earl Talbert and Albert's father. Kathryn just shook her head and put an arm around Albert.

As Albert paused again in his climb, this time to drink water, he tried to recall her looks. She was a beautiful woman to a boy of maybe six or seven. Her fingers were like soft white pencils, tapering down to shiny red fingernails. She smelled like flowers he'd never smelled before. This might've led to his mother's comment, said much later of course, that Kathryn's senses weren't at home. Though this didn't mean much at the time, Albert finally pieced it together when, some years later—after his father's death and the end of Skybillings during the Depression—Kathryn had left Bud, moved to Seattle, then went on to Sacramento or some other city in California.

Albert finally approached the "Y" in the tracks, but he didn't let himself stop and rest. From here, he knew the climb would grow even steeper. Already, the sun was past midday, and he still had several miles left—the hardest part, as a matter of fact. This was where

Fergie fought with the crummy every morning. The Shay had plenty of power to make the grade, but the little old gutless crummy would complain and rattle at this stage. No wonder, thought Albert, as he stopped to look back. He was now well above Thunder Lake. In fact, he could see just one corner of the far shore. From here on, he would follow the portion of the track that climbed steeply upward as it, initially, ran back in the very direction that he'd just come from, then began a wide, steep, rightward arch up to Three Sisters and into the landing that served as the base of Skybillings' logging operations.

He continued for another hour. His feet burned. The backs of his legs pulled tight with every step. Though he was worried about the time, he finally allowed himself to rest next to a large stream that rushed under the tracks, then appeared to drop straight over a ledge. Albert found a flat rock and slung the knapsack to the ground. He tilted his cap back, and bent down on hands and knees to slurp the icy water. After leaning back with a mouthful, he dipped the cap into the water and plopped it onto his head. The drizzles had evaporated by the time he'd torn open the sandwiches and began wolfing them down.

Despite several weeks of working on the choking crew, his muscles felt tired from the climb. That was one of the benefits of working in the woods, he decided. He knew that his arms were thickening, his back even felt stronger, and when he lunged in front of moving logs, he sensed that his legs and feet could find stable footing even as the ground shifted dangerously.

Albert rummaged in the knapsack and found the two eggs and pie, which he gulped down. As he did, he again saw Zoe. And her warning about blotching her management record. Nobody crossed Zoe. Maybe it was her looks. Though Zoe was well into her fifties, even Albert found her attractive. Blond hair tied back in a knot, blue eyes inside crinkles of skin that rode outward toward her cheeks. And a slim, delicate build that made more than a few of the loggers secretly long for her. But her sternness, her strict management of the kitchen, kept them far away, and kept her firmly in control.

For the first time, it occurred to him that his mother and Zoe were very similar women. Good looking. The object of men's attention. But both in charge of themselves and beholden to no one. Albert snorted at a new thought: Here he was, caught between the two of them.

❋    ❋    ❋

Albert could feel his heart pounding in his ears. It had been perhaps two hours since lunch, and only now—with his legs aching badly—had he reached the top of the incline. The Shay lay directly ahead of him—its wheels pointed up and outward, at a crazy angle. Though he'd approached the Shay on the crummy every day for the past several weeks, he'd never looked at it from this angle. He could see that, with even a slight push, it could easily plunge into the ravine. A stand of firs just beside the tracks shielded the steep drop.

Albert stood in the tracks, his breathing now settling. He closed his eyes, holding the scene firmly, listening, though he didn't know for what: robins and finches whistled; the firs overhead creaked as they swayed in the breeze; the sound of scampering feet—perhaps a squirrel or a mouse—crackled through dried leaves underfoot.

As Albert stepped gingerly toward the Shay, picking his way carefully between the twisted rails and upended spikes, he peered up at the mighty iron wheels that now hung perhaps fifteen feet in the air. They seemed perfectly balanced, at rest, as if they were intended to hang there, dusted by sunshine that dappled the firs. The smell of oil and grease—and the dankness of hardened dirt mingled with the pungent aroma of creosote—shrouded the broken monster. Albert walked slowly along its length: the gears, the steam lines, the bottom of the fire box. He ran a finger gently along a long metal pipe—he didn't know what it was for—collecting greasy dirt, feeling the cold oil that still dripped.

As he came around the back of the locomotive, past the door, he stepped over cords of firewood that still lay on the ground. Once intended to keep the boiler pounding, they'd been tossed and forgotten. Why hadn't anyone taken them back to camp, to use in the stoves? He peered down the hillside where the logs had rolled after the cars pitched off the track. He studied the stump—and the small impression in the ground behind it—that had saved his life. He hadn't realized how close it was to the edge of the ravine.

Albert took a deep breath. He willed himself to ignore the dirty smell of oil and earth as he leaned forward to look through the door to the cab and the nearly upside-down engineer's compartment. The gears and levers were largely undamaged, though covered with black soot and mud. He bent lower, now looking down at the mud itself. He could make out a smashed lunch box, a clipboard, and two buckets, still bright red.

He took another breath, then dropped the knapsack onto the track. For a moment, he stared intently at the massive engine above him, trying to judge its stability and angle. Then he stepped carefully through the now upside-down doorway into the cab and felt himself sink slightly into the thick mud that covered what had been the ceiling. As he did, he felt the locie shift slightly. A deep groan from the front end, then a thump, but then all movement stopped. Albert thought of the sharp drop of the ravine, perhaps only forty feet away, but he willed it out of his mind. He pushed the lunchbox and clipboard away to give himself a more solid footing.

Why the hell was he here? Why would he be dumb enough to do this? He didn't know the answer, so he decided to ignore it. He looked around, now from inside the cab—looking back at the track where he had stood. Right up there, he thought. Right on that slight rise. When he thought everything was fine. When he thought Nariff's patch job on the tracks was going to hold.

Though little light pierced the cab, Albert peered intently through the opening where the windshield once was. It had broken out completely, leaving a glacier of mud that flowed through the opening. This would've been exactly where Nariff stood, thought Albert—right underneath where I am now. He was pushing against the Shay, to keep it upright, right under here. Just before it collapsed on top of him and the others.

Steadying himself again, Albert absently ran his hand across the mud. This was probably some of the same mud that Nariff stood on, maybe even died on. And he wanted to touch it. To feel it on his skin, to run it between his fingers. As he withdrew his hand, he felt a hard, round object. He dug it out of the muck and then came upon another—this one sharp and heavy.

He pulled out both and stepped out of the cab and onto the rails. Though the locie moved slightly when he crawled out, it resettled quickly. He sat down wearily on the rails and held the two objects up to the light. The first he recognized even through the mud—Nariff Olben's pocket watch. Albert had seen this watch many times since he first joined the crew—the watch that was checked repeatedly during the day to see how many hours, then how many minutes, until quitting time. The last time he'd seen it was when Nariff had tapped it, listened to it, and said, in his Long John growl, "Arrrgh mate, I believe the little timepiece is slowing down on us." That wasn't an hour before he was killed. The other object he'd pulled from the mud was a railroad spike, the bottom portion partly sheared off in the accident.

He held the watch tight for several minutes, looking into the dense underbrush without focusing. He tried to remember the last words Nariff had said to him. Or that he had said to Nariff. But all he could see was the old man, hurrying toward the Shay, just before all of the chaos.

Suddenly, Albert sensed movement in an alder across the tracks. He shot onto his feet and stared into the quilt of green. A squirrel skittered underneath a low pine tree; several robins cheeped nearby, but then flew away quickly, in a flutter of wings and soft wind. Otherwise, not a sound—no rattling bushes or breaking twigs. No voice. He relaxed, wiping a bead of sweat from his face with his oily and muddy shirt.

The light had changed since he arrived. While it had filtered down directly through the fir canopy before, it now shot-in sideways, slipping between and underneath the boughs. This provided greater illumination, but Albert knew that the sun was much lower than it had been. Before long, it would fall behind Crescent Peak, and his trip back to camp would be in growing darkness.

He paused briefly to take in the sweep of the wreckage, then he grabbed the watch and the spike, and slipped them into the knapsack. Before he set out down the tracks, he looked around once more.

"Thank you, Nariff," he said softly. "I was glad to know you." He looked up again. As before, the boughs of pines and the tapestry of green moved gently, but nothing sudden. He took a deep breath, raising his neck to relieve the tension, then set off down the tracks at a full gallop.

As he ran, the breeze cooled the beads of sweat that trickled into the middle of his back. He ran for the better part of an hour, pausing to rest only once. Then he started again. But the combined effect of the uneven track bed, the steep downward incline of the mountain, made his legs rubbery.

The sun had already fallen behind Crescent Peak, with shadows turning the thick woods on either side of the track into a deep gray green. Though the sky overhead still showed blue, the corners were folding.

"Shit," he shouted. The sound of his voice felt good. "Shit, shit, shit, shit." Each word was timed to match each step. The sound was soothing. The first human voice he had heard in hours—even if it was his own. He broke into an old German drinking song that Bucky Rudman was fond of:

*In sex and love there is no rhyme,*
*One, two, screw-em.*
*They know what I do feels so fine,*
*So they ask me to do 'em and do 'em.*

Yet as he ran and sang he began to accept the notion that his race with the sun was not one that he was going to win. Though he couldn't remember how far ahead the track would split so he could turn the corner and head for the camp, he knew he was still far away.

When he came to a small stream, he sat for a few minutes to rest and tried to calculate how long it would take him to reach camp. He guessed well past dark. Christ, maybe not until after midnight. Zoe would raise hell. He bent over and took a drink, and then it occurred to him that this was perhaps the very stream he'd stopped at this morning. If that was the case, it went down the side of the mountain and crossed the tracks just outside of camp. If he followed it down— rather than continuing on the tracks—he calculated that he could be at camp within an hour, certainly in time for dinner.

He sorted out the options: Leave the tracks and he might get lost—but he'd get back fast. Stay on the tracks and he'd be sure to get back—but very late.

"Goddamn it." His voice sounded hoarse. He sat for a few more minutes, thinking, resting his legs. He'd eaten his lunch what seemed like three days earlier. That settled it. He grabbed the knapsack, crossed the tracks, and entered the woods. At first, a small path ran along the edge of the stream. But then it gave way to thick pine and fir needles, pine cones, ferns, grasses, twigs, and downed trees. Albert moved as quickly as he could, given his legs and the fading light, and the increasing angle of decline. A false step could send him tumbling.

Light was virtually gone. A riffle of high white clouds above him glowed orange, then purple, before settling into deep gray. The pace of the stream now quickened, gurgling loudly as it sped down the mountainside. Albert clung close to its side, stepping gingerly, digging fingertips into the ground, using the knapsack to cushion blows when he fell.

At a small clearing, where the trees had slumped down across a small ledge, he stopped to peer out toward the west. He tried to make out Crescent Peak, but it was too dark. Only a faint ridgeline was visible against the horizon.

As he resumed his climb downward, the drop steepened. No longer able to stand upright, he hung onto limbs to ease him downward, then he clutched rocks jutting out of the water—sending gurgling rivers of icy water into his armpits. He realized that he was terribly unprepared. He'd brought matches, but no flashlight, no blankets, not even a change of clothes. Again, the stream curled over a ledge, forcing him to climb downward—digging his hand into the icy water again, stepping down to a rock that caught the icy stream and cast it even farther.

Now he stopped. He turned to face the ravine again, to gather his bearings. He put his right foot down tentatively to find whether the footing was safe. But as he did, his foot slid out from under him, taking his entire weight backwards, in a catapulting, lurching mass of gravel and dirt. He pawed frantically at the ground, clutching for a handgrip, but the avalanche was now a gushing roar. As he slid, he could feel it growing larger, totally engulfing him in rocky liquid. His voice curled into a scream, but he didn't dare open his mouth. Then, with a jarring thud, it all stopped.

For several minutes, Albert lay motionless, as clouds and stars and treetops above him swirled as one. He didn't feel pain, though he saw that both hands were scraped raw. He finally struggled to his feet, and stumbled into a clearing. As he looked up the hill, he realized that he'd stepped into a loose bed of shale. He couldn't tell how far up the mountain it went, because of the darkness. But he was sure he'd slid several hundred feet.

He listened for the gurgling of the stream. But all was silent. Only the call of an owl, preparing to hunt in the moon's brilliant glow, and the rippling wind that moved through the upper boughs.

As Albert got to his feet, brushing his hands to clear away blood and dirt, he stopped. Across the small clearing, he saw movement. Was it a bush that moved? A reflection in the moonlight? He listened. The owl had now stopped, but the wind continued. No other sound. He peered from behind the cedar and studied the patch of ground on the other side of the clearing. The moonlight illuminated the patch clearly.

By God, he did see it. Something moved quickly into the timber behind. Albert started searching for a tree to climb, in case it was a lynx or a bear, or maybe a cougar. But the shape he saw didn't look like an animal. Though it moved swiftly, and crept close to the ground, it had a shape that resembled a man, or even a child—small, wiry. Then he smelled a cigarette.

Albert dropped to his knees. Still no sound, no voices. He could tell that the form was not moving, but stationary—apparently until the cigarette was done. So he crawled into a low spot between several trees that hid him from view, and gathered his breath. He could wait here until morning. It was protected by logs on all sides and if he needed to, he could lay among the fallen logs that dotted the meadow. He felt better. He knew what his plan would be. Wait here, sleep here. Then set out for the camp in the morning.

He dropped the knapsack finally, nestling it against a dead cedar next to him. But he decided to take another look, just to be sure that no one had seen him. As he put his head up slowly, he saw a black form standing only a few feet away, blocking the moonlight, and coming directly toward him. Albert swung to the side to avoid the blow.

"That you, Albert?" A man's voice, deep and gravelly, followed by the blinding beam of a flashlight. "Albert, is that you?"

For several seconds, Albert stared directly into the beam of light—chilled by the human voice, the blinding whiteness, the confusion and contradiction of being alone, being followed, then being found, not by a bear or a killer, but by a voice he knew.

"Albert, it's me, Myles. Myles Norgren. Zoe sent me out to look for you. Are you okay?"

Myles Norgren was the only other member of the crew, besides Petey, to stay the weekend at the camp. The largest logger in the camp and one of the best, with a bushy beard, small round wire-rimmed glasses, and long hair that was slicked back on top, but hung in loose curls around his shoulders.

Still, Albert did not answer. He felt himself shaking from the cold. Suddenly the dampness, and the chill night air, overtook him. Myles slipped off his mackinaw and wrapped it around him.

"Christ almighty, Albert, you're in damn bad shape. Where you been?"

"The Shay."

"Where?" Myles's voice was disbelieving. "You walked to the Shay—the wreck? God almighty, that must be ten miles from here." Then Myles stopped abruptly. "But if you went to see the Shay, how the hell did you end up back here? We must be half a mile behind the camp. The railroad tracks are way over on the other side."

Albert was too cold and tired to lie, especially considering he knew that he needed a friend when he approached Zoe. "I took a short cut."

Norgren burst out laughing. "You took a shortcut? God, kid, remember one thing about these woods, will you? Don't ever take shortcuts."

Albert nodded. He stood up with Myles's help, at first wobbly, but then more stable.

"Can you make it to the camp from here or should I go get Zoe to help?" asked Myles, with a hand under Albert's arm to stabilize him.

"Please, not Zoe, okay?"

Myles understood. So he helped Albert with one hand, while guiding them with the flashlight in the other. After walking several hundred yards, Albert stopped suddenly. He looked directly at Myles, then looked back. He seemed to be confused, or perhaps uncertain of their direction.

"What's wrong?" Myles flashed the light in his direction.

"Why didn't you come and get me when you saw me at the bottom of the rock slide earlier?" His tone carried anger.

"What rock slide?"

"The one where you were in the bushes and you went running into those trees. Remember, I was still ass-deep in shale?"

Myles paused. He looked carefully at Albert, studying his face and his wounds. He could see that Albert's hands were badly scratched, blood was visible at both knees, and it looked like a thick bump was developing just above his left eye.

"Albert, I don't know what you're talking about. I just came out of the camp twenty minutes ago and I sure as hell haven't seen any rock slide."

Albert didn't say anything. He stood still, feeling the throbbing in his fingers, the ache in his back and legs, and hearing the soft ripple of wind in the upper story of the firs above them.

❅    ❅    ❅

It was well past midnight. The fire was already out in the cast iron stove and a chill had set into the mess hall. Zoe had left a plate of roast beef, cheese, and bread for Albert, but had already gone to bed. Albert decided to eat before bothering to wash. Within five minutes, the plate was clean and he had found another half loaf of bread in the kitchen.

Myles laughed as Albert tore chunks off the bread. "By God, Albert, you're finally starting to eat like a logger. No fork, no napkin, no manners." He paused, but Albert chewed in silence. "If Zoe saw this performance, she'd be even madder than she was about you getting lost out there."

Albert's back and legs ached. He looked down at the dried blood on his pants and the scrapes on his hands. He realized that he'd better wash the dirt out of the wounds and get alcohol onto them before he went to bed. But the knowledge that Zoe wasn't waiting for him—with her stern expressions and harsh criticism—made him relax.

"It's because of her that I took the damn shortcut," said Albert.

Myles laughed. "Not because of her... but because you were afraid of getting your ass kicked by her."

Albert shrugged. He returned to a final piece of roast beef and opened a bottle of beer. Though the taste of beer still felt odd to him, the stinging, sudsy cold felt welcome. He downed two big gulps and belched.

"You're starting to sound like a logger, too," snorted Myles.

For several minutes, the two sat in silence. The wind occasionally rattled a window.

"Mind if I ask why the hell you were up at the Shay?" Myles looked at him, no expression.

Albert took another long swig of beer. "Seemed like the right thing to do."

"Albert, we go past that damn Shay every morning. Every night. Nobody pays attention. But you think it's the right thing to do to go up there on a Saturday—ten miles one-way?"

Albert belched again. "That's probably the reason—nobody pays any attention to it anymore. And Bud says they're gonna lift it—and wipe away all the traces of what happened up there." Albert studied the beer bottle. "It just seemed like somebody ought to go up there and, well, look at it. And see it. Not just let it get forgotten and worth no more than the last tree we cut."

Myles took off his glasses and puffed each lens in his mouth, then rubbed it clean on his shirt. When he looked at Albert, he seemed more like a professor or a doctor. Albert wasn't entirely clear about Myles's history. He knew that he was a dedicated Red—a Communist. That he was a card-carrying member of the CIO. And he'd heard something about how he went to work in the woods to get over the death of the woman he was about to marry. But Myles never offered much on his own. These were just stories that Albert had heard from the other men.

"So what did you do once you got up there?" Myles's tone was distant.

"I already told you. I went up to visit the Shay."

"How do you visit a Shay, Albert? Sit on the track and look at it? Wrap your arms around it and hum, 'Goodnight, Irene?'"

"What difference does it make? Why do you care?" Albert was angry. The scrapes on his hands had started to throb and he felt suddenly embarrassed.

"Because I think you were goddamn stupid. And if you're that goddamn stupid, you're gonna get yourself killed in the woods. And maybe if I listen to an explanation of your stupid reasoning, I can help you from getting killed in the future." Albert had never seen Myles angry, but something in the tone still didn't really seem hostile.

"And if I tell you why I went up there, will you promise not to repeat it?"

"Sure. Why not?"

"I dug around underneath the Shay."

Myles took a long swig of his beer. Then he peered at Albert, as if trying to see into the reasoning. He turned to the almost-cool stove, where he plopped his feet. "Jesus. What would make someone climb around an overturned locomotive, hanging pretty damn close to a 500-foot cliff...?" But he didn't finish the sentence.

Albert reached into his pocket and dropped the watch and the spike onto the table. "I found those underneath it." The mud was now dry. Albert could make out the hands of the pocket watch.

Myles leaned forward and picked-up both. As he did, Albert noticed a wedding ring and briefly wondered about the story about the fiancée.

"I found them underneath the engine, just in front of the cab," said Albert. "Where the cab flipped into the mud. I was just standing, looking at the thing, on its back, dripping oil and all. And I just wondered if I might find something inside that was from Nariff. So I got on my knees and crawled in."

Myles studied the spike, then the watch.

"Nariff said he'd bought the watch in South Africa," said Albert.

"I remember."

"He showed it to me the first week I went to work here. He bought it in Pretoria, on a gold shipment for the British. Said that even though the whole world went to hell since, the watch still worked."

Myles chuckled. Then rubbed the glass on his pants. "And where did you find the spike?"

"Same place. Just in front of the windshield of the Shay. Which means it was right about where the locie first went off the track. My guess is that it was one of the spikes in the section of track right where Nariff died."

Myles studied the spike closely, running his finger across it. "This is a pretty piss-poor reason for taking the chance you did, Albert. I hope you know that. Coulda gotten yourself killed."

Albert shrugged. "No worse than working for St. Bride, the way I see it."

Myles snorted.


## Chapter 10

It took a week for the crane to arrive from Everett. When the new locomotive delivered it, and finally settled it in the clearing next to the fallen Shay, Bud was convinced he'd made the right decision. Sitting on the back of a flatbed railroad car, the thing looked like a praying mantis, ready to reach down and scoop up the old locie.

He'd given the order several days before to shut down half the operation just to get ready—a decision he fretted over. The trestle was going slower than he wanted, and Bachelder seemed lost in thought too often. There was still plenty of timber that needed to be moved—that Witstrop insisted be moved quickly—but Bud decided that it would have to wait. Getting the Shay up, getting it hauling again, was critical. That would give him two locomotives. Two would be critical once the trestle was up.

Bud paced around the hulking locie, trying to calculate the angles. Haul it this way, and it falls back. Pull it forward, and it doesn't move. Now he feared that the real problem was that the crane wasn't tall enough. So he came up with an intricate plan of how to set the cables and how quickly to give it steam.

But the first two tries ended with a whoosh and what felt like an earthquake as the Shay fell back to earth. With great straining, the crane could pull the locomotive upright, but it couldn't hold it there.

"It'll never do the job," offered Valentine.

"What was your first clue on that, John?" barked Bud.

Valentine laughed politely. "It wasn't my intention to cause you more trouble, Bud, just offering a suggestion." The crew looked on silently. A sliver of sunshine broke through the heavy clouds.

Bud's eyes took in the setting—the broken Shay, the waiting crane, and the faces of fifty men staring at him, waiting for him to decide what to do next. He turned back to Valentine. "Let's hear it then," he snapped.

"I'd use the good Shay to help pull. Hook cables to the back of it and start pulling as soon as the crane gets the locie upright." Bud knew that the likelihood of that working was small. The crane couldn't raise the Shay high enough for the new locomotive to do any good. But he also knew that he was out of ideas, so he gave the order to give it a try.

Within two hours, the cables had been reset—the steam on the new Shay was up and the crane ready to go. When Bud gave the sign, both started pulling gently. The old Shay shivered, then whined as the cables grabbed tight against its belly. Bud signaled more power, which brought metallic screeches from the wheels of the new locomotive as steel met steel. Slowly, the old Shay came up, first onto its side, then tilted slightly upward. It teetered for a moment, then seemed to stabilize, but then flopped forward with another rumble of the earth. For an instant, Bud thought the momentum might take it over the edge of the ravine.

As the men again began walking around the Shay—ready to rearrange the cables for yet another try—Bud felt the old tightness in his stomach and the heat rising into his chest. He wanted to walk away, to find a job far away. One that he knew he could do and when it was done, he knew he could use it to measure his own value. Instead, the Shay lay there like a dead monster—a ten-ton picture of death and failure.

Harry Bachelder sat down next to him on the tracks. "Want a crazy suggestion?"

Bud didn't answer.

"I recommend you put a new spar tree right over there"—Harry pointed to the clearing on the far side of the new Shay—"and rig it up with all the cables and pulleys and shit that you usually do. Then use it to pull up the locie long enough to get some blocks under it." Harry's face had fully healed, Bud noticed. But he still had the look of a broken, failed bird—narrow, stooped, strands of dirty brown hair creeping over his shirt collar.

"Do you know how much goddamn work is involved in doing what you just said?" Bud's tone was not friendly. The sunshine broke through the clouds once more. Bud shielded his eyes to take in Harry.

Harry shrugged. "You want to get that locomotive out of the mud, that's what you got to do."

Bud thought about it. A spar tree—one of the giant firs, stripped of all limbs, and rigged with cables and pulleys—would have the right angle. He looked around, and spotted a candidate that was probably a hundred feet tall.

"I never heard of anybody building a spar tree to lift a locomotive," said Bud.

"You also never heard of almost getting your ass killed in a labor riot in Everett."

"How long do I have to keep hearing about that?"

"As long as it takes to sink in," smiled Harry. "In your case, that could be quite a while."

Bud stood up and shouted to the men to stop their work. "I have a solution to our predicament, gentlemen. Bucky Rudman is going to turn that Douglas fir right there"—he turned and pointed upward—"he's gonna turn it into a spar tree by tomorrow afternoon. Then what we're gonna do is hook the cable to the middle of the old Shay and pull with the crane and lift with the spar, and Mr. Bachelder here guarantees that that sonofabitch is gonna come back to life."

When he was done speaking, Bud turned to Harry and bowed—a flat, humorless grin on his face.

The crew seemed caught between confusion and laughter. For a moment, no one moved—hands on hips, feet propped on logs, faces covered with sweat and grease. Then they started talking, shaking heads, arguing about the merits. But Bucky Rudman's voice commanded the scene.

"Never in all my born days have I rigged a spar to haul in a locomotive," shouted Bucky. "Not once. But for Mr. Bud Cole and the Skybillings Logging Company, this boy will do his level best." Bucky pranced proudly over to where Bud was standing to get more instructions, happy that he was now the man of the moment.

The spar was ready two days later. Bucky had rigged it, as usual, with flourish. Once he'd sawed-off the upper twenty feet of the towering fir, he climbed onto the flat top, about two-feet wide, and sat down to smoke a cigarette. Then he nailed a woman's brassiere to the top, just below where he was standing, which began flapping in the wind.

"What is that thing up there, Rudman?" asked John Valentine when Bucky finally climbed down.

"What's it look like, John?"

"It looks like a woman's brassiere."

"Well that's damn good, John. Because it actually is a woman's brassiere."

Laughter grew as the others realized what was whipping in the breeze. But Bucky didn't join in. He and Little Boy were organizing cables to finish the rigging.

"You ought to be ashamed of yourself, Rudman," snorted Valentine. "That kind of behavior is disrespectful of womankind."

"Ain't disrespectful at all. In fact, it represents two of the things I respect most about womankind."

Bud Cole didn't say anything about the brassiere. He'd known Bucky Rudman long enough to know that the only time you had to worry about Bucky was when he stopped joking. He'd worked for Skybillings a couple years before the crash. It was Bucky's constant hunt for women—and his willingness to report all his escapades, including his shortcomings—that Bud concluded had kept the men sane as they faced the bleakness of no jobs and no money.

The crew was ready as soon as the spar was rigged. Cable dangled from the top of the spar tree, ran limply over a couple hundred feet of loose soil, and lay across the new track, before enveloping the old Shay. Men scrambled across the locomotive like ants over a dead insect.

Harry Bachelder stood on one of the rails directing them as they secured the Shay. "Around another loop," he shouted, when the crew seemed ready to stop. Then he directed them to drag a cable from the new locomotive and run it through the cabin windows of the old one. After double-checking each one of the cables, Harry gave Bud a nod.

"She's ready."

"Who wants in the pool?" asked Bucky loudly. "I'm giving two-to-one odds. One dollar brings you two." Bucky's smile was broad and good-natured.

"Rudman, for Christ sake, will you do your fucking job and shut up!" Bud Cole dropped the cable he was holding to punctuate the words.

"C'mon Bud. Just joking. Just the boys having a little fun. I figure a little wagerin' will probably perk up spirits around here. Gentlemen, out of respect for Mr. Cole, this is your last chance. One gets you two. Now's your moment to profit from misfortune." Several men handed him money.

"You're a sinful wretch, Rudman. Do you know that?" Bud couldn't believe the voice was his. "All I need is you betting against me."

But Bucky smiled. "Thank you, I do my best."

Bud willed away the heat that was rising in his chest. The only thing to think about now was to use the skills he knew—and he knew they were there. He checked with Fergie to see if he was ready on the new locomotive. Then he checked to make sure the crane was ready. Finally, he gave the signal—and the roar of the steam engines echoed through the canyon as the cables around the old Shay tightened. The spar tree began to shudder as it engaged the massive weight of the Shay, but the old locomotive began to move upward.

Bud gave the signal for more power, then more again. And slowly, the massive Shay rose. The cables from the spar drew it directly upright while the cable drawing sideways from the crane held it there. Bud looked up at the spar tree, which trembled, its guide wires taut against their anchors. For a moment, he thought it might topple. But it held. Lightning Stevens and Myles Norgren were the first men to run toward the Shay, to begin sliding sections of rail underneath it, but Bud called them back. "Give her a chance to fall," he shouted.

For several minutes, they waited and watched. The old Shay was half-standing, half-hanging. The steam engines filled the ravine with clattering as they worked against the Shay's dead weight. A sudden light shower fell from a bank of clouds, washing the mud and dirt from the locie in small rivulets. Finally, Bud gave the signal and Lightning and Myles led a group of men underneath the Shay. Within minutes, the old Shay was settled gently onto the tracks, looking bruised and tired, but—for the first time in two months—showing a hint of life.

Bud looked upward and let out a deep breath. As he did, he noticed the brassiere on the top of the spar whipping smartly in the breeze.

❁   ❁   ❁

For the better part of an hour, Bucky Rudman danced. Around the tables, then on top, then into the kitchen and onto the porch, only to spin around again, and jump back onto one of the tables. "You can't say I'm a sore loser," he shouted as he grabbed Zoe and spun her across the room, suddenly in a constrained minuet, which ended as Bucky bowed and Zoe curtsied.

"Sit down and rest, Rudman," laughed Bud Cole as Bucky swept past with one of the Swedes in his arms.

"No time to rest, gotta celebrate the beauty of how Bucky Rudman's pole once again saved the day."

This brought hoots from the group, and the Swede who had been playing along suddenly spat on the floor and pulled away. "No harm intended," laughed Bucky, who resumed his performance alone. "Just trying to bring pleasure to all of God's little children."

As Bud Cole watched the crowd, he noted that St. Bride, Appleseth, and several others allowed occasional smirks at the revelry but otherwise ignored it. Even Valentine clapped along. Bud took pleasure in the fact that most of the men were doing the same. The Shay had been raised, finally. He knew that the keg of beer that Zoe had brought out after hearing of the successful results had helped a lot. But Bud was more than willing to go along.

As Bud tapped his foot with the clapping hands and stomping feet, he took a deep breath. The stiffness he'd felt in his stomach was, he realized, suddenly gone. The rhythm of the voices and sounds felt welcome. They were still high up in the mountains and the weather still cold and a trestle still unbuilt, but the room was warm, the faces happy and relaxed, and the old dripping Shay was sitting upright.

"I gotta hand it to you, Bud, I never thought there was a chance in hell you'd get that Shay up," said Petey Hulst, sitting down gingerly. "Your Mister Harry knows his stuff."

Harry heard his name and settled on a corner of one of the tables. He nodded at Petey, but didn't say anything.

"But it didn't surprise me," snorted Petey, his eyes wide as he twirled his mustache. "I read it in the cards last week. Told me that the Shay wasn't going to be down forever."

"When are you gonna stop believing those damn cards, Petey?" asked Bud with a smile.

Petey's gray eyebrows twitched. "A man stops believin' and he might's well be dead. I guarantee you that if you believe that those cards are true, they will be true. Want to hear what else they told me?"

But Bud's attention had turned back to the room, which still thumped. Now Bucky was doing a jig on the table. Lightning Stevens had joined him. "If this is what they do sober, what the hell do they do when they're drunk?" offered Bud to no one in particular.

"What else do the cards tell you, Petey?" asked Harry. "Let me guess: That we're going to build the trestle and make a million bucks?"

"They don't talk about logging. At least not right away. They talk about being all confused and such. There is nothing settled in the cards."

"Confusion? Where's the insight in that?" Harry's tone was suddenly sour. "I've been riding rails for two years—and half the rest of the country has too. Jobs are still impossible. Everybody's mad at the money boys—for screwing the country and making a profit on the side. And confusion's written all over those faces."

Petey lit a pipe. "You just proved my point, Mr. Harry."

"How so?"

"If you believe in the cards, the cards tell the truth. Cards say confusion. And that's what we got."

Harry continued to look at Petey, who responded with a smile and a small nod of the head.

Bud stood up and grabbed his slicker. The night had brought a hard rain, which beat down on the roof so loudly that it almost drowned out the revelry.

Most of the celebration was over. Most of the men had left for the bunk houses, and even Bucky Rudman was now sitting next to the stove. Zoe had filled a tall pitcher with cold water that Bucky first poured carefully into a tall glass; then he simply poured the water into his mouth from the pitcher.

## Chapter 11

"Do you have a minute, Bud," asked Myles Norgren, as Bud was saying goodnight to Harry and Petey.

"Sure, what's on your mind?"

"Well, maybe we should talk in private."

Bud studied Myles. He'd always found him to be one of the level-headed members of the crew. Myles's face was stern.

"No need to worry. Hall's almost empty. And Petey and Harry don't mind listening, do you boys?"

Myles looked at the others before he pulled up a chair. "I stayed in camp this weekend. Wanted to get some fishing in. Saturday morning,

Albert Weissler decided he was going to go up to the Shay to pay it a visit. I don't know if Zoe told you, but he ended up getting lost."

Bud frowned.

"He set out about ten in the morning, and about eight that night she sent me out looking for him. I found him huddled underneath a tree about a half mile behind camp."

Myles ran through the rest of the details. Albert was late, so he took a shortcut down the side of the mountain. He stepped onto a shale slide. Landed behind the camp, totally lost.

"So what the hell did he do up there?" asked Bud.

"From what he told me, he looked around, walked around the thing and such. But then the stupid kid decided to crawl around inside it. He actually got down into the mud, dug around inside it and next to it, by the cab—I guess he was looking for a keepsake or something from Nariff Olben."

Harry's voice broke in. "That thing could've gone over the cliff in a split second."

"That's what I told him, but he didn't seem to care much."

Myles reached into his pocket and pulled out the spike that Albert had given him. "He found two keepsakes. An old watch that Olben had bought in South Africa, and a spike." Myles put the spike on the table. "He found it directly under the cab, which means it was one of the spikes holding the section of rail that buckled under the locie." The rain continued to pound hard. The stove crackled.

"Look closely at the spike," said Myles, as the other three men drew near. He pointed to faint ridges along its upper edge. "These here are marks from a hack saw or some kinda file. I figure that when the Shay got close enough to the section of rail that this spike was holding, the pressure got to be too great. The top of the thing came clean off, and the rest of the spikes couldn't hold the train. I told Lightning Stevens about this today, so he and I walked the whole length of track after the Shay was lifted. We thought maybe we could find some more of these things. But not one. All the other spikes were either twisted or almost like new. But we couldn't find another that had been sawed."

Myles paused briefly to clear his throat. "There's one more thing. Like I said, Zoe was getting worried when Albert didn't show up for supper on Saturday. So I walked all over hell looking for him. Finally found him in a hole about a half mile or so toward the mountain. Looked scared as hell, which I 'spose I would've been too if I'd been lost."

Myles leaned forward slightly and dropped his voice, though the room was now empty.

"When we were walking back to the mess hall, Albert asked me if I had seen the guy near the rock slide. I said, 'What guy?' And he said that he saw somebody in the moonlight—a shadow in the moon-light—watching him. That's why he was hiding in the hole."

The only sound in the room was the pelting rain and the groaning wind in the firs. The crackling of the stove had even quieted.

Bud picked up the spike and ran a finger gently over it. "So you're saying that the locie accident wasn't an accident at all. It was sabotage."

"That's what I'm saying."

Harry picked up the spike and studied it closely. Then he tossed it onto the table with a loud thunk. "Maybe the kid got bonked on the head when he went down the rock slide. Maybe just an active imagination."

"But you don't imagine hacksaw marks like that," said Bud.

"It looks like somebody went up there and pried out the good spike, cut a new one almost in half, and jammed it into place," said Myles. "They had one thing in mind: Sending that train over the edge of the cliff."

Bud slumped into his seat, dark circles under his eyes. "So those three men didn't die because of some twist of fate. They died because somebody killed them."

A door slammed in the kitchen. Bud's voice took on a distant, almost wistful air. "Why the hell would anybody want to sabotage Skybillings? And whoever did it knew he was gonna end up killing a lot of people."

❄   ❄   ❄

The rain had stopped. Bud had been walking for an hour, along a trail that ran from the camp all the way around Thunder Lake. He was soaked, but he didn't care. He saw only the scene of six or seven years earlier: the day he called all the men together to tell them that Skybillings was closing. He'd done everything he could. He'd given up his own salary, he'd tried to find new markets, he'd tried to sell the company, he'd even tried to borrow from Deek Brown. But there was nothing left in the bank. And no one wanted to buy the timber.

So he called the men together—they were working just above the Seakomish River. He'd stepped onto one of the big rocks. And he told them that it was all over. Then he divided the cash he had left, and shook their hands. It was the right thing to do. And he did it. And he was proud of it.

And that was it. Within an hour, they'd all left. And he and Bucky Rudman and Petey Hulst were the last to walk out—leaving all the equipment right where it was.

This was the picture he saw as soon as Myles had shown him the spike. As he struggled through the wet brush that lined the path, he saw the faces once more looking up at him—tired, dirty; mouths hung low in despair; fear sewn deep into the puffy eyes. Most with families to feed, now set adrift and wondering where they would go.

Bud stopped walking. The moon broke through the clouds just above Crescent Peak. Shafts of cold blue light illuminated the rock ledges across its face. Maybe Crazy Olaf Carn did live up there. Far up. Away. Forgotten. Oh to be Olaf, thought Bud. To live and hunt and rob and get even. And to slip away into the woods. And be the stuff of legend.

But here he was. Bud Cole. Part businessman, part schoolmaster, part beggar for the crumbs from rich men's tables. A little case of sabotage on his hands. An impossible trestle to build.

Easy. Why should he worry? He couldn't stifle the laugh. How in the fuck could he be here, at the edge of failure all over again? And now with somebody actually trying to do him in? The last time it was just the economy. Just the Wall Street bastards and Hoover who destroyed everything he worked for. Before that, the War. But now, just as he was getting his feet under him, somebody was out to get him.

He sat down on a boulder, near the edge of the lake. He could hear the waves gently lapping the pebbles, and the low moan of an owl, but this time it seemed to stretch out longer. Almost a human tone to it. As he listened, he thought he detected a voice well in the distance, now higher-pitched.

Bud knew the woods and how to manage himself in the woods. But the thought that another person was nearby, another human, this far away from the camp, this late at night, gave him a chill. He crouched low and moved slowly toward the voice, which appeared to be coming from the point of land that stretched into the lake. As he approached, he heard the sing-song rhythm—not the least bit quiet, or restrained, but in full throat.

The moon now disappeared behind clouds, which allowed him to creep much closer. Then the wind shifted, and carried the voice away.

As the moon once again cleared from behind the clouds, Bud could make out the form of Little Boy Whittaker, kneeling on a flat rock, facing the moon and the lake. His voice, in a high-pitched, sing-song rhythm, spoke to the lake:

> *Deliver me from mine enemies, O my God;*
> *defend me from them that rise up against me.*
> *Deliver me from the workers of iniquity,*
> *and save me from bloody men.*

Bud recognized the words, though he didn't know which of the Psalms it was. He recognized it from all the years that his old man made him learn Bible passages. But Little Boy's cadence was easier, and somehow more complex, and made the passages seem more like a song.

Little Boy quickly said the Lord's Prayer, spit in the water, and began walking slowly back toward the camp. Though he passed within inches of Bud, he didn't notice him. Bud waited until the sound of his footsteps disappeared, then looked carefully around the point where Little Boy had been kneeling. But all he saw was a well-thumbed Bible, lying inside a hollow spot of an old, rotten fir, well protected from the rain.

# Book Two: Summer 1937

## Chapter 12

Bertram Witstrop drew in the bittersweet cigar smoke, let it fill his lungs fully, then shot it quickly into the cool night air. The gentle breeze slipping past the yacht devoured the smoke instantly. He leaned onto the railing, took another drag on the cigar—he decided it must've been Havana—and studied the woodwork at his elbows. Was the railing teak? Witstrop bent down, pulled out a monocle, and studied the deep grain closely.

"It's from Java," said a soft voice behind him.

Witstrop looked up to find Tuttle B. Ashford, a drink in hand, standing just outside the door to the captain's quarters. Ashford's smile was warm, his stride confident even on a deck that rolled gently as the yacht nosed into the changing tide. Ashford was easily in his late seventies, but the old man still conveyed a sense of youthfulness, a certain lightness in his movements. Was it his cultured voice, carrying a hint of Groton, wondered Witstrop? Or the smooth manners, or the impeccable European tailoring of his waistcoat and trousers?

"I told the Prince of Whatever, from whom I bought this tub, that if the railings weren't teak from Java, I wouldn't have any part of the goddamn thing," said Ashford, who now stood next to Witstrop. Ashford laughed deeply. "And I'll be goddamned if the bastard didn't tear off all the railings and replace every one of them with teak. So I gave him the $10,000 or whatever he was asking for the thing. And here she is."

Ashford patted the railing as if patting the back of a fine racehorse. "What do you think?" Ashford stood not much more than five feet—his head a bit above shoulder-height of most men. The features were slight—small, precise mouth, gently sloping nose, puppy eyes. But when he smiled, his face became that of a terrier, unwilling to yield whatever his teeth had set upon.

"Of course, beautiful," said Witstrop with as much smile as he could muster. "Nothing like it in Seattle—no question, Tuttle. Probably nothing like it on the whole damned West Coast." Witstrop hated his answer—too effusive; sounded too genuine.

"Couldn't hardly turn down the grand Governor of Washington State when he asked if he could hold his soiree on it," said Ashford quietly, as if conveying a state secret.

Witstrop drew in again on his cigar and held the warm air inside—against the moist evening chill—but mostly to avoid the conversation. He simply nodded at Ashford, who took it as a gesture to resume the discourse about the yacht: Gas lamps from Antwerp. Etched glass from Milan. Door panels hand-carved in Sydney.

"And, of course, the Governor—direct from the state capital," added Ashford, with an innocent, yet wicked, smile.

The handwritten note Witstrop had received ten days earlier had explained that the evening dinner cruise was an informal gathering with the Governor and a few handpicked business leaders to discuss "how they might cooperate." The year 1937 will be a great year, said the note. The nation is finally getting back on its feet. The state of Washington enjoys enormous opportunity. The timber market is strong, mining abundant, the fruit and wheat markets coming back. All the Governor needs is cooperation, added the note obliquely.

"Cooperate, my ass," shouted Witstrop when his assistant brought in the invitation. "What businessman in his right mind would want to cooperate with a Democratic son of a bitch like that? His union buddies and socialist pals are deserting him, and he thinks we can bail him out." Witstrop paced around his desk for half an hour, swearing he wouldn't have any part of such a gathering, especially—especially—on a yacht owned by Tuttle B. Ashford.

"What's your complaint with Ashford?" asked Buchanan, the assistant who had brought in the invitation. "He controls half the timber in the state, so we've got to deal with him. This is a good chance to maybe find some accommodation."

Witstrop had rarely felt the urge to strike a man. But something in the tilt of Buchanan's head and the way he so matter of factly made the statement—to Witstrop it seemed more of a challenge—made him want to slap the young man, then toss him out of the office.

But he overruled the emotion. For a moment, he was even slightly embarrassed by it. "Accommodation," snorted Witstrop, plopping into the chair behind his desk and swiveling toward the window overlooking downtown Seattle and the feathery blue water of Puget Sound. Hell, the word even sounded foreign if you said it a few times, he decided.

After all, he—Bertram Witstrop—controlled Panama Northwest Shipping Company. He controlled its prices; he selected its routes; he decided on its ships, even its captains. That Panama Northwest was one of the fastest growing shipping companies on the West Coast—even amid the worst economic depression that the country had ever seen—was proof of the businessman that Bertram Witstrop was. He didn't have to seek accommodation, with anyone.

Christ, yes, he had problems. He slapped the desk at the thought, causing Buchanan to jump. The biggest problem was Tuttle B. Ashford himself—and the lock grip on timber in the Northwest that he and his cronies in the railroads were developing. As the Depression had deepened in the early '30s, the prices for land had dropped like a rock, prompting the railroads and Ashford & Southern to gobble-up massive tracts—doubling, then tripling, their holdings in the course of a year or two.

Witstrop knew all too well what it meant. If Ashford and his cronies totally controlled lumber—to say nothing of the rail lines that shipped it east—companies like Panama Northwest faced serious danger. Ashford could virtually set his own rates; or he could hand-pick which shipping line survived; or, for that matter, he might even be tempted to start a shipping line of his own, to control the routes to Japan and Australia and South America.

But as much as he tried to ignore it, there was more. Witstrop chuckled about it as he studied the bustling harbor through his office window. How many years had it been—twenty-five, maybe even thirty? Witstrop couldn't remember. But he certainly remembered Ashford's friendly smile—which, at that time, he had actually believed. After all, Witstrop was still a kid fresh out of Harvard. And Ashford was the boss. Why shouldn't he believe him? Why shouldn't he believe that the managing partner of the biggest damn real estate company in Boston was playing square with him?

Witstrop snorted. He couldn't recall the exact details any more. Was their falling out over the contracts Witstrop had drawn up—the partnership agreements involving half the property on Beacon Hill and Back Bay? Witstrop had played fair, he had given each partner the rights they had all agreed upon. But Ashford pulled the rug out at the last minute, inserting new clauses that—without the others knowing it—gave him virtually total control. And when the others finally figured it out, he blamed the "poor legal work by the staff" as the cause.

Imagine that, stabbed in the back by the little bastard that you'd trusted—and worked your ass off for. Even now, Witstrop could hardly hold back from plotting how to do him in—for real, for good. But Witstrop knew there was something more here as well—something hidden in all of those layers of Tuttle Ashford's personality and the deep anger it aroused within him every time he had to deal with it. He couldn't put his finger on it. But he knew it was there. And it told him one thing for certain: Bertram Witstrop would never seek an accommodation with Tuttle B. Ashford.

"But it may be in our best financial interest," said Buchanan sharply, as if reading Witstrop's wandering mind. "We can't go it alone against the likes of Ashford & Southern, especially if they are with the railroads. And we know for a fact that they are. Wouldn't a dinner cruise on Ashford's Harbor Prince be a perfect time for us to strike a deal with Ashford? The old man is hard to get through to. It's impossible for me to get past the damn blockade of supplicants that hang around him."

"I'll think about it," said Witstrop quietly.

Buchanan leaned closer. "Mr. Witstrop, this may be just the opportunity we've been waiting for..."

"Do you understand the words, 'I'll think about it,' Buchanan? Goddamn it!"

"Well, of course." Buchanan stood still in the deep silence. Witstrop studied the distant peaks beyond Puget Sound.

With a soft voice, however, Buchanan ventured forward. "Mr. Witstrop, we are running around with every little flim-flam logging operation trying to get a foothold in the lumber trade in the Pacific Northwest, while Tuttle Ashford's company owns half the damn woods—plus more every day. All I am suggesting is a frontal assault. If Ashford were to work out some agreement with us, it might be just about all we need."

Witstrop's laugh was angry as he swung about. His eyes held Buchanan's firm. "I pay you good money to think clearly," he snapped. "What possible reason would Ashford have for giving a piece of his woods to me—or even making a deal, for that matter? Because he needs the money? Because he wants to be a philanthropist?" The roar in his voice even surprised Witstrop.

"Because it adds to his business," Buchanan shot back quickly, stopping Witstrop as he was about to begin again. "He makes a deal with us and he knows he doesn't have to worry about us ever again. We won't be a threat. We're always there to move his lumber. He doesn't have to horse around with shipping companies that are here today and gone tomorrow. And he doesn't have to worry what we might try if we get desperate. In turn, we get access to the best damn timber in the world and we can kick the ass of any other shipping company, anywhere."

Witstrop didn't answer. He considered the deep blue of the Puget Sound, fanning outward below his office window. Then his gaze fell onto the shanty town of cardboard and corrugated metal that had lined the south end of the Seattle docks ever since the market crashed in '29. Tight ringlets of hazy smoke curled upward from several ugly huts.

"Ashford doesn't want to build a business," said Witstrop finally, the anger suddenly gone from his voice. "He wants to build an empire."

❄   ❄   ❄

The plaintive cry of a seagull, and a sudden chill in the air, brought Witstrop back to the yacht, as several knots of businessmen appeared now on deck, all with drinks and cigars in their hands. Two tall waiters emerged from among them, as the group made its way toward Ashford and Witstrop.

"Tuttle, just a damn impressive piece of machinery you have here," said one with baggy eyes, leaning onto the railing. Witstrop noticed that the eyes seemed to swim in a watery film.

Another with a barrel chest and white hair patted Ashford's shoulder gently. "Rockefeller would sell his grandmother to get a yacht half as nice," he said. Then he leaned close, and in a stage whisper said, "By the way, how the hell did you get a Democrat to host a party on something as grand as this?"

Witstrop watched Ashford bask in the glow of compliments. The old man demurred and gently downplayed the richness of it all, even as he explained the ancestry of the mother of pearl inlays, the rich leather cushions, the Persian carpets, the porcelain urns. Ashford was a master, thought Witstrop. A gentleman, soft and cultured. Perfectly tailored. Unbearably successful. And, if truth be known, how much different from himself, he wondered, when you erased all the history between them and corrected for the hard feelings?

As the waiters re-appeared with silver trays of brandy, the Governor emerged from the captain's quarters—a beaming smile for both Witstrop and Ashford as he found the group.

"Tuttle, I've got to say thank you for this," said the Governor, a narrow man with high cheekbones.

"My pleasure, Governor. Anything I can do to help get the economy of this state moving again. It's an honor."

This restarted the Governor's speech that Witstrop had endured over dinner. The wind-up about how Democrats and Republicans must now work together; that the Democrats in the state capital would do everything they could to help business re-establish itself; that the Democrats could bring the unions to the table and help put the strikes that were snarling the state behind them.

Witstrop had expected the speech. Nothing like a Democrat in trouble, he told Buchanan after he finally decided to accept the invitation. "FDR's abandoned him. Labor's ready to kill him," laughed Witstrop. "He's got no choice. He's got to turn to us."

So when the yacht left Seattle and meandered along the waterfront, then wound its way north, into Everett Harbor, while chubby waiters served stuffed partridge and oysters, Witstrop was more of an observer of what the Governor had to say than he was a listener. Join with me, he said repeatedly, pounding the table so much that the plates clinked. As a Democrat, I can make a peace for business in the face of all this union rabble-rousing that no Republican could ever achieve.

Witstrop had watched the faces around the table. All listening intently. All delighted with the openness and accommodation. Cheever, the fishing boat king. Haverston, the metal and mining tycoon from Tacoma. Warren, the banker and investment broker. Parker, the railroad magnate. And the others—from every business and industry in the Northwest—their faces bright, and happy, and smiling. And, it seemed to Witstrop, believing.

But it was Ashford, Witstrop realized, who was the only other one in the group who was observing the true context. He understood what destination the Governor had in mind. Had Ashford sent him there in the first place? Was all of this Ashford's idea from the get-go? Witstrop didn't know. But he did know that Ashford was already into the second level of the chess game. Closure was written all over his soft face.

As the Governor repeated the message for the third time on the deck, Witstrop studied the black water washing gently against the bow. This was the smell that he loved: damp, cool, a mixture of aromas—fish, rusted metal, soaked wood, and the plaintive cries of the gulls as they arched overhead. As the conversation rose and fell—with rumbles of laughter now from the crowd with the Governor in the middle—Witstrop studied the far shore.

Though he rarely got to Everett, he liked the city. Something in its anger and its lustiness. Seattle was big and crowded and businesslike. But Everett was different. A small, ugly fighter, never standing a chance in the ring, but who slugged fiercely until he either won or was killed in the trying. As Witstrop studied the shore, with its heavy freighters moving gently against the strain of rotting cable, he knew that this, ultimately, was where he would win or lose. In this harbor, on those ships, in this city—now the home of Tuttle B. Ashford—he knew that the fate of the Panama Northwest Shipping Company rested.

"You obviously either need to get laid or to wallop somebody in the mouth." It was the voice of Ashford again. Witstrop had worked his way to the back of the yacht, away from the Governor and his retinue. But Ashford had discovered him once more.

"No, just watching that shore."

Ashford turned to observe the distance. "See the flares on the docks?"

Witstrop pulled out his glasses and studied the shoreline more closely. Flashes of yellow filled the air, then disappeared into a flat glow. "What are they?"

Ashford bit off the tip of another cigar and lit it quickly. "Molotov's. A little meeting of the local unions. Of course, one hates the other. And they both want control of the woods. This is how they work it all out."

Witstrop looked harder. "I'll be goddamned. Are you serious?"

"If I tell my pilot to pull us closer, you could even see the gangs in the street," laughed Ashford. "It happens every other month or so. It isn't quite enough that they beat the shit out of each other in the mills or in the woods. Every now and then, they decide they have to go after each at their union halls. Kind of tickles me, to be truthful. We just stand back and they kill each other." Ashford laughed joyfully.

Witstrop studied the flashes, though they weren't close enough to see whether Ashford was telling the truth or not. The union violence was constant, but this was the first time he'd actually witnessed it—assuming Ashford wasn't bullshitting him. The battle was over which union had jurisdiction over the loggers. Witstrop knew full well that the AFL—the American Federation of Labor—had represented virtually all sawmill and timber workers from the early '30s onward. It led them into a strike that had shut down virtually all lumber and sawmill operations in the Northwest only two years earlier. Witstrop's shipping stopped cold.

But the final settlement negotiated by the union was viewed as inadequate by many, especially the men working in logging camps and cutting the timber. The charge against the AFL was that it had sold out to the employers, settling for a too-low pay increase and failing to secure a uniform contract that would protect all the loggers, regardless of which company they worked for.

In the short time since the strike, many loggers had broken away from the AFL, angry and fed up, casting about for alternatives, finally forming an affiliation that was more aggressive and more militant—and aligned with the anti-AFL labor movement known as the CIO, the Committee for Industrial Organization. The discussions between the upstart group and the old-line union men about which group truly represented the loggers were more often carried out in barroom brawls and face-to-face street battles than over boardroom tables.

"You do recognize this foolishness for the opportunity that it is, don't you Bertram?" asked Ashford softly. He purposely turned away from the Governor's party as he spoke.

"What are you talking about?"

"That little battle you see on the shoreline." Ashford nodded toward the fires as he sucked the cigar greedily, then popped rings of smoke into the damp air. A gull that had been flying closely suddenly swept upward to avoid the smoke. "You haven't gotten so busy with your little shipping concern that you're overlooking the strategic manna from heaven that all this union nonsense presents to us, are you?" continued Ashford, now with a small smile.

"Tuttle, you always spoke in rhyme," snorted Witstrop, adding, as an afterthought, "without the flourish of Mark Twain or the power of Jack London."

"Superb, Bertie," laughed Ashford. "I did deserve that, didn't I?" The soft laughter died slowly—a gentleman enjoying a sound joke. "It's so easy to become a pompous son of a bitch around the likes of them." He nodded toward the group around the Governor.

For several minutes, both men puffed on their cigars without speaking. Witstrop remained silent, unwilling to take Ashford's bait.

"There's no question that he's in our pocket," Ashford finally offered, along with another smoke ring. He nodded again toward the Governor's party when Witstrop looked up. "He's willing to let us tie this state in knots, because we can offer him jobs and economic growth—and that will save his political ass."

Ashford leaned closer now and began speaking quickly, though his voice was still measured, still too soft for anyone else to hear. "You heard him, Bertie. Time for cooperation. Time to stop all this waste with business battling business, unions battling unions. Time to get rid of the Molotov's—and put all this crap about the unions behind us. Time for us to all get in bed together. Good patriots."

Witstrop noted that the last word didn't sound right. It came out as "Patt-riots"—more English than American. Ashford flipped the cigar butt into the water, creating a hissing sound, then silence. Only the sound of the water washing against the bow.

"We can be partners again, Bertie," said Ashford in a rush, as if he finally couldn't contain the excitement. "We can tie up the lumber market, tie up all the rail and shipping. We'll own it all. And that Democratic Do-Gooder Imbecile inside that cabin there will put his blessing on it," said Ashford with a small smile. "In the process, we can fuck the unions to death. All we have to do is put a little bug in the Governor's ear about them taking money from the Commies or something like that, and he'd call the goon squad himself to put 'em in jail."

Ashford paused briefly, but then launched into his plan. "Here's my proposal: You and me—Ashford & Southern Timber and Panama Northwest Shipping—we work out what I'll call a little arrangement—without broadcasting it to the world. I'll give you all the timber you can handle. I will drop all the other shipping companies— just use Panama Northwest. You ship it for me around the world at a deep discount. You know, Australia, Japan, the Philippines. I'll take New Jersey, Baltimore, Philadelphia. Before long, I'm the only timber company, you're the only shipping company, in the whole Northwest. We control who gets what lumber, at what price, for half of the civilized world." Ashford added this as if to ensure that Witstrop got the point. But then he stopped quickly, waiting for an answer. His face now surprisingly open, his expression almost friendly.

The flares of fire on the shoreline had stopped now, the hulking freighters shrouded in the blackness of night. Witstrop could feel the engines rumble through the teak railings as the pilot began revving the motors for the return trip to Seattle. A stiff breeze had sent the Governor and the others into the cabin, where Witstrop could see they were slapping each other on the back.

Ashford didn't seem to notice. He stared at Witstrop. His mouth smiling, but his gaze intent. Witstrop rubbed his hand along the smooth teak railing. "What did that prince say when you told him you wouldn't buy this thing unless it had teak railings?"

Ashford studied him carefully, a puzzled look across his face. He hesitated briefly. "He told me he'd do everything he could to get the wood from Java. Why?"

Witstrop smiled warmly as he pitched his cigar butt over the side. "You know what I would've told you?"

Ashford shook his head.

"How does 'fuck you' sound?"

## Chapter 13

The rain slanted underneath Witstrop's umbrella as he crossed Second Avenue. Two men stepped out from a doorway, with cups outstretched, but he shook his head and dashed into the street. He wove his way through the traffic—sidestepping a delivery truck, whose driver gave him the finger—and hurried into the Cascadian Hotel.

"Afternoon, Mr. Witstrop," said the doorman, whisking away his overcoat and taking the umbrella. "Dreadful rain, isn't it?"

"Goddamn rain. How is it that it always feels like winter around here?" snorted Witstrop, whisking drops of water from his pants.

"Several of the gentlemen have gathered in the Cascade Room on the tenth floor," said the doorman. "Your secretary called to say that the others would arrive in twenty minutes or so."

Witstrop hesitated for a moment.

"Yes sir?"

Witstrop looked blankly at the doorman, as if he'd forgotten why he was there.

"Nothing," said Witstrop, "just thinking." Instead of turning toward the elevator, he walked through two swinging paneled doors, into the dimly lit bar next to the lobby. He ordered a Johnnie Walker and downed it in one swallow, and belched loudly—a sound that echoed in the empty bar. The bartender pretended not to hear.

Witstrop took a deep breath and let it out. Was it that the doorman mentioned his secretary? Or just that he knew what the meeting just ahead held for him? Normally, he would have just walked straight into the meeting and begun with a flourish.

He ordered another. He had actually prepared himself for the board meeting—his board, his bosses. They often treated him like an equal, but they were all arrogant and full of themselves. He also knew what the letter meant the moment it arrived two weeks earlier. In fact, he could have dictated it: "The Panama Northwest Shipping Company Board of Directors requests a meeting at your earliest convenience in light of new developments. Critical, especially given recent market changes. Please see to it that all appropriate books and balance sheets be readily available."

Was it Simon Westrose who was the go-between? Maybe Bishop. For that matter Caulder Skulling—he had gone to Harvard with Ashford. Maybe that's who got the offer. Witstrop checked his watch—fifteen minutes.

But what did it matter who actually got the offer? There was no question that a buy-out proposal had been made to the board. Witstrop snorted, recalling the conversation on the yacht in Everett Harbor. There was also no question that the offer had been made by Tuttle B. Ashford. And now the Panama Northwest board was fidgeting, or perhaps panicking—especially since Wall Street was so unpredictable again.

Accept the terms. That's what they would say. Sell now. Don't wait. Can't beat this kind of offer. Witstrop knew that the offer was, without question, ridiculously high—a foolhardy business decision from Ashford's perspective, at least in the short run. But over the period of a few years, deft as hell. With Panama Northwest out of the way, Ashford & Southern would have the woods and the railroads and the primary shipping lines totally under control. And the goddamn politicians were too blind to see it. Hell, they were helping.

Witstrop felt himself smile, though he hated it. Hand it to that old bastard Tuttle B. Ashford, thought Witstrop. He had promised to retaliate. And so he had.

Witstrop finished the drink and cleared his throat. But he knew it wasn't just the board meeting that was troubling him. It was the personnel business this morning. The death, the aftermath, the paperwork. He'd expected tears when the news had come in the week before—one of his own men, after all, dead, on company business.

Any death is shocking. It ripples through even the best companies. Especially a death of someone in the prime of life. Most of the staff had come to terms with it already—the funeral had been on Saturday.

But only that morning, Witstrop had learned why the grief wouldn't lift—his secretary of twenty years had broken down. She'd been having, in her words, a "relationship" with the man. His wife didn't know. No one did, as far as she knew. But that was the very reason that it all was so terrible, she said through red eyes. She had no one to share her grief with. No one to unburden herself to. She was alone, she sobbed. The man she had loved, albeit behind closed doors and in secret, was dead. She was alone. The words shook her body.

Witstrop had drawn a deep breath and comforted her best he could. Putting his arms around the woman who had brought him coffee and taken memos for twenty years felt more uncomfortable than he expected. But no more uncomfortable than the realization— as she wept—that he had never asked whether she was married or not. God, in twenty years, she could've married and raised children. Lost a husband and started over. Hard to believe that he'd never asked.

As he held her, and struggled to find words of comfort, he realized that the death hadn't just been routine for him either. Not just another death that happens. Witstrop had laid out the work. Witstrop had come up with the plan. Witstrop had given him the orders.

He checked his watch and paid for the drinks.

"Thank you Mr. Witstrop," said the bartender. "Very generous."

❈   ❈   ❈

Witstrop began.

Panama Northwest was perfectly situated. Revenues up, costs down, new shipping lines open, new markets growing. Never mind the latest stock market dip. Panama stock dipped only five percent— nothing in relationship to the growth that the market would soon reward. Beyond that, the Panama Northwest strategy was now paying off. It would soon be an established source of wood and lumber not just on the West Coast, but also on the Eastern Seaboard. Through carefully drawn contracts, it would be positioned soon, perhaps by the beginning of the next fiscal year, to compete—Witstrop paused now, very briefly, to collect eyes from around the room—to compete with Ashford & Southern.

It was like an electric jolt in the room. Half the board shifted uncomfortably at the mention of the name, the others seemed to grow darker. Witstrop thought he detected anger on the face of Caulder Skulling.

"On what basis do you think your strategy will work?" asked Skulling, whose tall frame and good looks made him a caricature of the Boston elite. "I don't see any guarantee of it here—on the balance sheets." Witstrop hated Boston accents.

"Caulder, you and I both know that there are no guarantees today," said Witstrop gently. "What you can see from the materials I've provided, however, is that we're making money. We're growing. And we've got a foothold in the biggest product this country is going to demand when this Depression is over—lumber."

Witstrop paused again, then delivered the line he'd been planning since he'd gotten the letter demanding the board meeting: "And if we stay the course, we can stop Ashford & Southern from creating a virtual monopoly on Northwest lumber and Northwest shipping."

"Why?" The question was from Herbert Bishop. He spoke it with a sneer.

"Why what?" asked Witstrop.

"Why do we care? Why do we care if he creates a monopoly—as long as we get the buy-out price we want?"

Witstrop smiled. He finally felt the cold rain leaving his legs. The warmth of the room seemed to be rising from inside of him. "Because if they have a monopoly, it means we don't." This brought a chuckle around the table. "We can, ourselves, control shipping in the Northwest for the next fifty years with a small foothold into the wood-producing community." Witstrop felt his tone rise, his gestures quicken. He was leaning up against the table, pointing. "Already, gentlemen, we own mills. We operate some of our own logging shows—and plenty more will start soon. We've invested to create a foothold—and Ashford has no idea what we're up to. He thinks this is a rate war. A price war. But he's dead wrong."

Witstrop paused for effect. "And we've got what he doesn't—the shipping routes to the Far East. He can move lumber to the East Coast of the U.S.—and so can we. But we can ship to every nation touching the Pacific, and he can't."

This brought a handful of approving nods, but Skulling and Bishop continued to glower.

"But he's got what we don't, Witstrop," shot Bishop. "Rail lines, for Christ sake. He can get there faster than we can, period. And he will always have an advantage, no matter what we do."

"An advantage perhaps. But not control," said Witstrop sharply. "As long as we don't accede to his wishes, and as long as we let my strategy play out, he will not gain total control."

This led to conversation among several of those around the table, while waiters filed into the room with urns of coffee.

"Bertie, let me make a suggestion," said Russell Dillsworth, one of the founding members of the company—and the man who hired Witstrop. Dillsworth spoke so slowly that most assumed he'd lost his train of thought. Therefore, the room fell into long silences between each sentence.

"You might be able to guess just what kind of money we've been offered—all informal of course, all through informal channels," said Dillsworth, followed by a lengthy pause. "But I, for one, know that the political climate will tolerate monopolies—or the working equivalents of monopolies." He paused again. "And I'd just as soon that we be the one with the monopoly than the one that lets somebody else do the job." Witstrop could tell now that Skulling and Bishop knew they had lost.

Witstrop was about to move to new business, when Dillsworth started again—this time, much faster than Witstrop had ever heard him speak. "But get this straight, Bertie," said Dillsworth. "You better come through on this strategy of yours fast—with some strong results by the end this year. If you don't, you'll be working for Tuttle B. Ashford."

Witstrop again felt the aches deep in his legs. He cursed the rain that beat against the window.


## Chapter 14

Bud Cole liked the rain. Mostly he liked the sound on his bunkhouse roof as he was going to sleep. The steadiness of it usually settled his thoughts. He even enjoyed the complaining that the rains brought in the crew. If they complained about the rain, they didn't complain about each other or, for that matter, him. Plus, they became quieter, looking downward to keep the water out of their eyes, huddling under slickers to keep warm.

He was especially happy that it was raining hard when Witstrop's men finally showed up. The water poured off their rain hats, oozing through the openings in their ponchos. They grumbled as they tried to draw the ponchos tighter—creating new rivulets, which found new openings. So they insisted that Bud hurry in taking them up the mountain, to see the operation, especially the progress on the trestle. The approach was all cleared, new track ran to the edge of the ravine, where a pile driver teetered on a house-size granite boulder. Two bents—the vertical supporting girders for the trestle—had already been sunk into the rock below.

"This is all you've got done?" asked the one who called himself Bolt and said he was the chief engineer of Panama Northwest Shipping. A heavyset man with a thin mustache. He carried a floppy briefcase, which he didn't open.

"Actually, this is a hell of a lot," said Bud sharply. "We've cleared the approach, we've got the first two bents in place, and the pile driver is ready to start the next two." Bud had taken Bolt and his assistant, a thin man who smiled, but did not speak, to a slight rise above where the trestle was going in. This gave them a view of the ravine, as well as the men working directly below them who were readying a long fir as the next bent.

"And when will it be done?" Bolt's words were a challenge, not a question.

"It'll be done in time to move all the logs that Mr. Witstrop needs to have hauled," answered Bud.

Bolt looked at him coldly. "I don't need wise answers, Cole. I would only ask you to keep in mind who owns this operation. I want a firm date. Mr. Witstrop is adamant."

"Well, if the rains stop for a while, and if we start getting a little sunshine, I'd say by the first of September."

Bolt's voice erupted like a shot. "September?"

"That's what I said."

"So how many weeks of logging can you get in after the first week of September?"

"It depends." Bud knew where this was going. "A month. Maybe six weeks." Both were lies.

"How the hell do you expect Panama Northwest to make any money if you can't get this thing up by then? You think Mr. Witstrop is a philanthropist? He needs logs, Cole. He needs those logs that lie across this ravine that you see over there"—he pointed, as if sharing information with Bud that he had never heard—"not just these you own on this side. Do you understand that?"

Harry Bachelder had climbed up the rise. He now stood next to Bud. Water ran down both sides of his face because he refused to wear a rain hat. "It's impossible to get this trestle up any sooner," he said quietly, still gathering his breath. "Early August if we're lucky." Harry hocked and spit loudly, off to the side. Then cleared his throat, loudly again.

Bolt studied Harry as if he were going to start a separate conversation about what Harry had just done. But then he turned back to Bud. "I am going to tell Mr. Witstrop that I spoke to you two gentlemen and that you assured me—without any question at all—that the trestle will be up and running not a day after July 15—of this year, I mean. I'm going to spare you the embarrassment of having to shut this operation down and going back onto the dole." Bolt held up his briefcase as if to say that something was in it that reinforced his point, but he didn't offer anything. The assistant shot harsh looks at Bud and Harry.

Bud looked off at the ravine, while Bolt waited for an answer. A sudden squall of rain hid the far edge from view; then turned suddenly and began racing toward them. "Mr. Bolt, you can tell Witstrop that we'll meet his date—July 15," said Bud.

"Jesus, Bud," whispered Harry. "That's goddamn impossible."

Bud held up his hand to Harry, and continued talking to Bolt. "Like I said, tell him July 15 is fine." Bud finished with a quick smile that he hoped looked genuine.

Bolt nodded and looked at Harry. "Damn rain feels like snow," he grumbled, as he nodded to his assistant to follow him down the hill. He walked past Harry and Bud without further word, but just as he started down the incline, he slipped in the muck and fell backwards.

"Goddamn hell," he shouted, as his assistant and Bud both rushed to help him up. Once upright, he shook away Bud's arm, then stepped gingerly past where he'd fallen, and made his way downward, his assistant's hand under his arm the whole way. With a sneer back toward Bud and Harry, he carefully stepped onto the crummy.

"It's hell making a pact with the devil, isn't it?" said Bachelder as the crummy rounded the corner and disappeared from sight.

"You think we can get this thing built by the middle of July?" asked Bud.

"No. But on the positive side, I've never built one of these things in my life, remember?" Harry turned to Bud quickly with a broad grin, as he slapped his shoulder. "C'mon for Chrissake. Can't you take a joke? I'll have that trestle carrying tons of wood way before then."


## Chapter 15

Washington State was packed with Reds—at least that was the claim in the East. One of the Democratic Party bigwigs in Washington, DC, was reported as saying—referring to the forty-eight states—that there were actually forty-seven states in the country, plus "the Soviet of Washington." That may have been overstated, but it wasn't that far from the truth, especially on the west side of the state—west of the Cascade Mountains.

Maybe it was the frontier spirit that still hung-on that fueled the radical streak; or all the drifters that ended up there looking for another chance; or maybe it was just that people who had fled the hard times of the Midwest or the South turned militant when things turned worse.

Whatever it was, when it came to politics, and especially when it came to unions, Washington State was jumpy and radical—and hard-fisted to boot.

Many believed that the Washington brand of radicalism started with the Wobblies. Around the turn of the century, the Wobblies brought woodworkers together into a left-wing union called the IWW—for Industrial Workers of the World. They called them Wobblies for short, nobody knew exactly why. And they were fed-up with the working conditions in the lumber camps—bad food, long hours, straw beds filled with bugs, all for little pay. The IWW often brought work to a halt in sawmills and lumber operations up and down the coast.

The radical spirit settled down during the Great War and even after, as the people and economy of Washington State enjoyed the surprisingly good times that followed. But 1929 and the concussions from the stock market crash hit the West Coast hard, reawakening the unions and re-arming the radical spirit. The AFL—which was the biggest national union by far—grew fast in the lumber and sawmill trades in the Northwest, including the Seakomish Valley. Union men far outnumbered non-union men in Stardale, Merritown, and Seakomish. Men were willing to pay dues to the AFL, and they were willing to go on strike when the union decided that the workers' voices needed to be heard.

So they did when the union asked them to do so in 1935. Led by a former logger by the name of Clarence Ristall—people called him "Clare"—the loggers of the Seakomish Valley walked off their jobs. Clare Ristall's actual title was Official Representative of the Seakomish Local of the United Carpenters and Sawmill Workers of the American Federation of Labor. The union included carpenters, sawmill workers, and loggers. What it meant in the real world was that Clare argued, cajoled, glad-handed, and speechified his way up and down the Seakomish Valley to show the men that he was one of them and that they should stick together against the logging companies. He argued in every camp that this was the only chance they had of gaining recognition and adequate pay in the woods.

When the strike approached in '35, he held the loggers of the valley together. And they stood firm—manning picket lines for days around most of the logging shows in the Seakomish Valley—until employers finally agreed to settle with the union.

The AFL bigwigs in Washington, DC, hailed the agreement. The leaders of the AFL in the Pacific Northwest congratulated one another on their success. The picket lines came down and the men went back to their jobs. The New York Times, which had a reporter wandering around the lumber camps in the region, reported that the logs of the Great Pacific Northwest would finally begin moving again.

That was about the time that Clare Ristall decided that the AFL, its leaders, its dues, its management, and everything else associated with the union had sold the workers down the river and that they all could go to hell.

❋　　❋　　❋

Clare was late. He jammed the pickup into third gear and swept past a bus on the Stardale Curve, barely slipping back into his lane before two logging trucks roared by. He hoped that Sammons hadn't left already, but the lunch he'd had in Stardale was important.

Lonnie Harrison's comment was still with him—that Clare was probably the only person he knew west of the Cascades who could announce that he was running for Congress and be elected without even campaigning. Clare snorted at the hyperbole, but was flattered by it nonetheless. Even if it wasn't Congress that Harrison wanted him to run for—but rather, the seat in the Washington State legislature from the Seakomish Valley—the notion of it all made Clare feel that the hard work was paying off.

Lonnie Harrison wouldn't have made the trip all the way from the state capital in Olympia to lunch in Stardale if the State Democratic Campaign Committee wasn't already sold on Clare and his chances of winning. Harrison also hinted broadly about "a bright future," which is how the talk about Congress had even come up. Clare laughed gently when he remembered that the whole conversation had actually aroused him. Something very stimulating about politics, he decided, though not so good if it happens when you are standing in front of a room of Masons or the local women's club.

Clare checked his watch and decided that Sammons was probably still waiting, so he increased the speed slightly to make a serious effort to catch him before he gave up. Sammons knew that without Clare he was just another thug. With Clare, however, he was a union organizer.

With the thought firmly in his head that Sammons would wait— and the traffic clearing nicely so he had an almost open road ahead— Clare went back to the lunch conversation. Harrison had spoken candidly. The Democrats needed to fill the seat since the long-time occupant had finally expired—gratefully, according to Harrison— after months in a nursing home. So there would be a special election in November. But he warned Clare that the Republicans were enjoying a renewed surge since Washington's Democratic Governor was in so much trouble and FDR was cutting back the funds to the states. The New Deal was running out of steam, was how Harrison put it. "We need some new blood to keep it running," said the old man, halfway through a second whiskey on the rocks. "You're just the kind of new blood we need, Clare."

Clare pointed out to him that his job these days—and it was taking most of the hours of each day—was getting the Seakomish Valley Local of the CIO organized enough to toss the ass-kissing AFL out on its ear. And Clare pointed out the trouble that could come up—including a strike up and down the valley. But Harrison waved it away.

"Yeah, yeah, I know," snorted Harrison. "That's one of the reasons we want you, my boy. People know who you are. People know you've got balls." With this, the old man slugged back the final mouthful of whiskey.

But what would Lydia think? That thought rolled around in Clare's mind throughout the conversation. As Harrison described the campaign, the meetings in Seattle and Olympia, and then the two-month session in Olympia, Clare wondered what it would mean to the relationship that was developing between them. Lydia Weissler was closer now. In recent weeks especially, he felt the bond growing stronger. Did she finally have the death of her husband out of her mind? Was she finally settled over the fact that her son Albert had gone to work in the woods for the very company her husband had once owned with Bud Cole?

As Harrison had rattled on about the niceties of party organization and paperwork and filing deadlines, Clare assured himself that Lydia's love—or maybe it was just affection—would not wander by his spending two months in Olympia.

Harrison had ordered another drink, which was why Clare was so late. But Clare couldn't hurry the old man. This was part of paying his dues, Clare decided. An early payment. So he ordered another cup of coffee, and spent the time thinking through how Lydia might react to this turn of events.

She had often said she was pleased that he was finally getting the recognition he deserved. So she certainly shouldn't mind that he would be away more often. She seemed genuinely pleased to accompany him to official functions, to be associated in the minds of her students and their parents with Clare Ristall. And Clare also knew that she was enjoying the relationship, even the physical side. He had gotten her to stay all night several times.

As Clare slowed to turn off Highway 4, he checked the rail crossing both ways before jamming his foot again to the floor and bouncing across the tracks. In recalling the dinners with Lydia lately, their visit to the state convention in Everett, even the growing physical bond between them, Clare reminded himself that, surprisingly, the real reward of the relationship was that he felt—for the first time since his wife Anne died—that he was part of a family. His daughter, Shelley—though her mother had died only a few years before—clearly loved Lydia, and was willing to join them on picnics and dinners. Clare Ristall felt his family being reborn, and it was all thanks to Lydia Weissler.

Clare pulled the pickup into the parking place on Main and ran up the stairs. He met Sammons, who was on his way down.

"Thought you was dead in a ditch somewhere," said Sammons, now following Clare back into the office.

"Just a long lunch," said Clare, settling into the chair behind a wide desk. "Whaddya got?"

Sammons was an ugly man. That was what Clare decided as he watched him unpack his satchel once more and spread papers onto the table. Sammons' face had a puffy look, the look of a person who had some kind of disease in his glands. His hair was straight and greasy, and his facial features matched the rest of his body—thick, flat and thick. But Sammons moved lightly on his feet and, though his hands and fingers seemed club-like, he moved them delicately. When he handed Clare a paper, he held it like a feather that gently wafted out of his hand and onto the table.

"I figure that for the CIO to have any real effect, we need about fifty men, maybe a hundred," said Sammons, as Clare eyed the paper. "Need to transport 'em, put 'em up for a while, feed 'em, maybe a little beer to make 'em happy. Probably could use a change or two of clothes, since it'll probably get messy here and there."

Clare studied the sheet carefully, running a pencil lightly over the columns and the dollar amount associated with each one.

"And this will let us do exactly what?" asked Clare.

"Close down five shows—Brown, Ashford & Southern, Zollock, Cascade County Logging, and Index-Townsend."

"Close down. Explain what you mean."

Sammons let out a sigh, studying Clare carefully to make sure the question didn't carry more meaning than it seemed. When he was satisfied that it didn't, he continued. "Close the place up for a day, maybe two, maybe three. In most cases, we put up a picket line. A couple of the bigger shows we send a double line—arm them with axe handles, shovels, that sort of thing."

Sammons walked around the edge of the table and looked out the window before he spoke. Sunshine now bathed the street in an afternoon glow, as the sun inched closer to Roosevelt Peak. "Course, they'll make some noise. Cuss a little. Maybe even take a whack at a steam engine or two, but nothing serious—unless, of course, some of those AFL thugs is there or management gets in the way."

Clare listened while Sammons elaborated on his plan—who would be struck first, where the strikers would stay, how they would get out of the woods, what would happen if they got into serious troubles at any of the sites. Sammons' abilities were deceiving, decided Clare. And that was one of his great strengths. Most people wrote him off as another meaty logger, uneducated and coarse. And Sammons was all of those things. But he choreographed union violence with a hand as delicate as he used to handle the paper he had placed in front of Clare. In that sense, Sammons was especially useful. No one truly respected his talent, and everyone underestimated him, which gave him freer rein to do Clare's bidding.

Clare chuckled as Sammons wrapped up the presentation.

"What's wrong?" Sammons now leaned close to Clare, straining to see if there was an error in the calculations on the page.

"Nothing, nothing at all," said Clare. "I was just struck by the interesting picture you present to the world, Sammons. I like that."

With this, Sammons grinned, displaying crooked teeth. Clare realized suddenly that he'd never seen Sammons grin, much less smile. But now the crooked row of teeth across the bottom stood fully exposed.

In some ways, Sammons sickened Clare because he enjoyed all of this too much. He worked for little more than a pat on the head. Clare had continued to raise his salary, though he had never asked for more, just to make sure that he wasn't tempted to join the AFL fold—or, God forbid, one of the companies. As he watched Sammons, Clare knew that his plans could never survive if Sammons joined forces with the other side.

"We'll close the Seakomish woods to those AFL scabs for good," said Sammons as the smile slowly faded. His head was so close to Clare that Clare could feel the heat of his breath when he spoke. "We don't go for any of that shit the AFL is pulling down in Grays Harbor and in the Willamette Valley. Those bastards' days is over."

Clare cut it short. "I'll write you a check to cover the costs," said Clare, pulling out a key from his vest pocket and rattling with the drawer on his desk. As he did, Sammons stared out the window again, watching the schoolchildren wander along Main Street. He checked his watch. He knew that Lydia Weissler would likely drop by Clare's office soon and that Clare would want him gone.

Clare ripped the check out of the book and handed it to him. Sammons took it, folded it neatly and placed it in his shirt pocket, and cleared his throat. But he did not make a move for the door.

"Yes?" asked Clare, looking up from the desk.

"I was just wanting to know about Skybillings Logging Company. Bud Cole's operation."

Clare glanced at the clock. "What about them?"

"Should I make them the sixth company?"

"Sammons, we've covered this already." Clare's tone was gruff. "I've got other work to get to."

Sammons moved slowly toward the door. "Workers ever get a sense you're going easy on Skybillings and you can kiss it goodbye..."

"Goddamn it, Sammons. I've told you a hundred times that operations that small aren't worth the powder to blow 'em up. Do you disagree?"

"No."

"Well then, what is your complaint?"

Sammons nodded. "Just that you don't want any of our boys to think you're playing favorites because her kid is working there."

"Whose kid?"

Sammons struggled for words.

"Whose kid, Sammons?"

"The schoolteacher, you know. Lydia Weissler," he blurted out finally.

Clare wondered if this was a prelude to Sammons demanding more money. Or was this how Sammons' take on blackmail got started? Clare stared at Sammons without expression, then spoke quietly. "The schoolteacher's son, Albert, does indeed work for Skybillings. But that has nothing to do with whom I choose to strike and whom I choose not to strike. And it's none of anyone's goddamn business since it is my money—not their goddamn dues—that is paying for all this bullshit anyway. You got a problem with that?"

Sammons stepped back several paces as Clare spoke. "Just asking," he said as he slipped out the door. "No problem at all."

## Chapter 16

A puff of powdery white engulfed the soft petals, then settled lazily upon the leaves below. Lydia set the flour jar on the brick ledge and inspected the leaves closely. Tiny red specks scattered, then dropped to the ground. Once again, she raised the jar, dipped a tablespoon, and blew it across the rose. She bent low over the flower, holding back strands of blond hair that nearly brushed the leaves. But this time, the green-white leaf remained motionless.

With each flower, she repeated the steps, working her way slowly across the bed—a Sunday ritual that she performed faithfully, unless the rain kept her indoors.

The roses stood in a semicircle below the steps to the front porch. Their stalks, thick and knotty near the ground, rose in delicate green canes, barbed with brown-tipped thorns. Yet the whispery pastels of the flowers—peach, lavender, pink, and yellow-white—hung low across the thorny stalks, shrouding their danger in innocent beauty.

The roses were her husband's idea. At the time, they had just moved into the house, their furniture nothing more than apple crates and three dining room chairs that his mother had given him when he moved to Seakomish before the War. When they walked across the pine floors—burnished to deep gold with layers of varnish—the narrow living room echoed.

"Think we'll ever fill it?" Lydia remembered asking after they had unpacked all their boxes and rearranged the crates near the fireplace. She sat on the floor cross-legged, attaching a cord to a claw-foot lamp, a wedding present from the aunt who raised her. The fireplace, deep and wide, seemed to swallow her.

"You mean the refrigerator or the house?" Fred's voice always had a laugh buried in it.

"I meant the house, but I'm not sure we have enough money left to do either."

Lydia had moved to Seakomish several years earlier from Sioux City, direct from Iowa Teacher's College, a Presbyterian school for girls. Though her father had paid for her schooling, she had used all of her savings to move—a move suggested by a former teacher, now the Everett school superintendent, who said a job teaching English and history at Seakomish was waiting for her. Because she had failed at every try to land a job in Sioux City or Ames or even in Rochester, across the border, she decided to pack her things, board the train for Seattle, and bid a painful goodbye to her father and her aunt, her mother having died in childbirth.

Fred had put money down on the house when he was working for Deek Brown & Sons. This was even before the Great War—something that struck Lydia. To be that young and still make a down payment on a house, rather than spending the extra income on women or alcohol, was only one of the things that Lydia decided set Fred Weissler apart from the other loggers she had come to know in her time in Seakomish.

Fred Weissler's life always had a focus. He was going toward a particular spot, though—even in his own mind—it may not have been clear about where or what exactly that was. His work, his spending, his choices all aimed in the same direction—sometimes with intensity, but usually with a boyish enthusiasm, an innocence, that Lydia always found as contradictory as she found appealing. When she first met him—at a bake sale on a Saturday night to raise money for the widows of men killed in France and Belgium—she noticed him looking at her from across the school gymnasium. He didn't smile at first, just glanced quickly, then turned away. She worried that she must've seemed forward because her eyes caught the glances, and he looked away before she did. But she liked his eyes. When he laughed, his forehead seemed to slip down a little, the cheeks rode high, and the eyes crinkled.

Fred wasn't a large man, perhaps a little under six feet; she was only a few inches shorter. But his gait, the way he held himself when he walked, made him seem much taller: an open, friendly walk, ready to clasp someone around the shoulders, ready to wave exuberantly at a friend in a passing car. And he liked to run—he ran upstairs two at a time, sometimes leaving her on the second step while he waited at the top; he ran to Walther's for the Sunday paper; he even ran while setting chokers in the woods, which—when she heard this the first time—made her worry, but then decide, just as quickly, to simply not think about it.

When he finally spoke to her that night, she remembered the conscious effort she made not to show too much interest. "Jar of dill pickles says you're the teacher from the high school," he said, one hand in his pocket, the other holding the jar, and smiling through a beard that she decided needed to be shaved.

"I'm sorry?"

"I said, 'I bet this jar of pickles that you're the teacher at the high school.'"

"Actually, there are a number of teachers at the high school." Her tone was purposely cool.

He just smiled and held up a quart jar, jammed with pickles, dill, and red and white spices that floated downward.

She broke into a thin smile, looking at the pickles without answering directly. "Your pickles? You put them up?"

"As a matter of fact, I did," he said, holding the jar now at arm's length, as if studying them for the first time. She noticed dimples above the broad strands of beard, which danced when he spoke. "I, myself, Fred Weissler, drove down to Tillard's place at Stardale, bought two flats of the tiniest cucumbers they had—wouldn't take one bigger than my little finger—and spent a whole weekend putting them up."

"Why?" She knew instantly that the question was wrong. It sounded harsh, judgmental, a city girl frowning on country manners.

Fred slowly brought the pickles back to his chest, looking at her with a smile, but now he was shaking his head.

"By golly, I was right," he said as he settled in a folding wooden chair next to her, sending Melba Mastery and her two children—who had been speaking with Lydia on and off for the entire evening—turning back to the conversation on her other side. The auctioneer continued to rattle in the background—holding three loaves of bread in one hand, the microphone in the other.

"What do you mean, you were right?" asked Lydia, finally giving in.

"Who other than a schoolteacher would ask that kind of question?" said Fred, putting the jar at his feet. "I never ever looked at it that way: 'Why?' Always put them up myself after I left home because I like eating them, like slicing them onto a piece of white bread, squashing it together, and eating it. The hotter, spicier, the better." He paused now, looking at her, still with the smile. "But I never got to the question of 'Why.'"

"What I meant was, it's surprising for a man to do his own canning. Don't most men just eat what they can buy at the store?" Again, she was surprised with herself. She liked this man. She liked his good looks. But her tone seemed clipped.

Fred's denim shirt was rolled in loose cuffs above his elbows. Through the shirt, she could see the thick arms and shoulders, the wide neck, and—from this angle—she noticed that the beard didn't meet up with sideburns: a bare patch in front of his ear separated his brown curly hair from the top corner of his whiskers.

"I reckon that's pretty well right, alright," he said, after studying the auctioneer who now tossed the three loaves to the successful bidder, standing just below the stage. When the elderly man caught them all, the crowd cheered, then applauded.

"But that's not quite true of a man, even a logger, who really, seriously, down deep in his soul decides that he needs a jar of dill pickles. That kind of man has himself some choices. He can give up his hankering and go without pickles. That's not acceptable, in my book. He can move close to his momma and hope she'll make some, but it's a little awkward for a twenty-four-year-old man to move home just for ma's cooking. He can marry and hope his wife is interested in putting some up, but I haven't stumbled onto the young lady who has such low standards as to accept the likes of yours truly. Or he can learn to make them himself. I decided on the last one."

Lydia nodded slowly as he finished. She sensed that this was an "aw-shucks" act that made them swoon down the valley whenever it was turned on. She wondered how many valley girls had given in instantly, only to be left the next day or the next week for someone fairer or younger. Nevertheless, she enjoyed the attention and the charm, to say nothing of the looks—through the polish and puckish wit, she sensed, was a warmth that she had not seen in most of the loggers she'd met.

From there, it was—as her aunt wrote her after learning of their decision to get married—a "whirlwind" romance, something she had never expected of Lydia: the reserved teenager, who never asked to go out with a boy until her senior year; the careful, diligent student who refused to travel with the glee club to see Iowa State football games because of her studies. This was the Lydia who now wrote home about a "wonderful, charming, breathtaking man whom I love from the bottom of my soul."

❋     ❋     ❋

Lydia accidentally nudged the flour bowl and grabbed it just before it fell from the ledge. She glanced up quickly to see if anyone down the street had noticed, but the block was still. The Methodist Church wouldn't let out for at least another hour, and the Presbyterians were holding a camp meeting in Lowell. Across the street, the Holby house was quiet—its porch vacant, though Mrs. Holby usually sat outside on warm mornings. Even the Switzer boarding house, next to Holby's but towering above it with its two stories, showed no sign of activity.

Lydia set the bowl carefully on the first step going up to the porch and stepped out to the sidewalk, hands propped on her hips, peering at the roses. They survived the winter well, she thought, even though roses had no business in such unforgiving soil. An act of faith, truly. But they brightened the house so well: The dahlias and geraniums to the left of the steps erupted in a rainbow of color this time of year, and the wisteria hung low with purple clusters, framing the open porch where she and Fred used to sit. But the roses lent the entry a richness, a defining presence, that she believed made their house stand out from the others on either side of the block.

Though the sidewalk stood several feet away from the roses, she could pick up hints of raspberry perfume from this distance. That was what had made Fred buy them, he had said the day they moved in. From the old backyard woodshed that was already standing when they bought the house, he brought out five bundles, the bottoms wrapped in stringy burlap. She was still sitting in front of the fireplace, trying to bolt together one of the chairs that was loose, when he plopped the whole batch next to her, dirt spraying across the hardwood floor.

"Fred, no! You're going to scratch the floor," she said quickly, leaning to avoid the fan of dirt. "What are you doing?"

"It's called character," he said, dropping onto his knees as he unwrapped one of the objects. He carefully opened the burlap, as if unwrapping a precious gem, and held it up for her to see clearly: Craggy, twisted roots ran toward each other, then away suddenly; a delicate green stalk with thorns above. "We got no furniture. We got no money, except for what's in this house. I figured we needed some color, a bright spot, a little class to tell the neighbors: 'Sure, we're broke, but we're proud—and maybe stupid.'"

But for several years, the plants struggled—thorny beanpoles, really, suffering from powdery mildew, black spot, leaf miners, and spider mites. They tried everything on them—soap and water, flour, even some chemicals from Walther's. Yet it wasn't until '27 or '28 that the roses took off: throwing off disease with only the minimal amount of help, mostly flour. Now the bushes stood tall and broad, covering the lower part of the porch fully, shedding a soft-colored hue on the spaded soil below. An occasional dusting was all Lydia needed to do.

As she stood on the sidewalk, she noticed a slight morning breeze— so unusual in Seakomish—that moved the bushes softly, ruffling the wisteria that dropped its petals on top of the roses. This was Lydia's addition: a memory of her aunt, who died soon after Lydia and Fred were married. For as far back as Lydia could remember, her aunt coddled an aging wisteria bush that climbed along the barge board, constantly winding into the gutters and onto the roof. This led Lydia's father to threaten cutting it down, but her aunt held firm: It dated back further than either of them, having been planted, by her aunt's estimation, in the late 1800s. So when her aunt died, and her father refused to move out to Seakomish—preferring to stay in the town where he was born—he shipped a piece of the old wisteria to Lydia.

Unlike the roses, it welcomed its new home instantly, swirling through a trellis that Fred built, and winding quickly along the eave above the porch. Lydia studied this, noting with pride the way the sun displayed the color and detail of her home: the high-pitched gable roof, the casement windows, framed by dark-gray shutters, the broad porch with its easy chairs, and the flowers which punctuated the sunny face of the house.

She knew that the church crowd would soon start coming around the corner, so she gathered the flour jar, her rose clippers, the spoon, and nudged the side gate open with her leg on the way to the back of the house. A tall row of rhododendrons reached toward her, but because she hated pruning, she ignored them as much as possible. She would have to remind Albert when he got home that the rhodies needed some attention.

Peonia, an old, nearly blind black cat, hopped off the bench in the work shed when she stepped inside, but idled next to her when he recognized who it was. "You need a little attention, don't you old boy?" she said in a sing-song voice that reminded her of rocking the children. Spreading the tools in front of her, Lydia wiped strands of hair that had fallen forward, slinging her upper body to the side to send more toward her back. The cat reasserted his place on the bench, with a blind upward leap, as Lydia straightened the work bench: scissors, watering jug, hand spade, weed fork, and fertilizer lined up neatly, along a shelf she had nailed together from leftover pieces of wood from the bookcase. Below that, pruners, shears, hedge clippers, and thumbtacks.

The cat now entered a prolonged, rolling purr, enhanced by Lydia's scratching his neck. Though he couldn't be trusted out at night, he knew the yard and back of the house well enough to cover the territory as quickly and efficiently as a youngster. Peonia kept the yard, the slate patio, the beds of azalea, fern, and juniper clean of rodents or, for that matter, any other cats—for which he was rewarded with careful combing, frequent feedings, and general pampering by Lydia, as well as the two children.

As she scratched Peonia, talking to him gently, she studied the thumbtacks, first looking at them absently, as she thought about nothing in particular, but then thinking about them more intently, wondering why thumbtacks were in the wood shed. What had she used them for? She couldn't remember bringing them out.

A car door slammed in front, followed by the door to the house. The car backfired twice as it disappeared around the corner by the church. She wondered how Reverend Rawson would appreciate two backfires as he wrapped up his closing prayer.

"Mother, where are you?"

"In the shed." Peonia lunged for the door in one movement to greet Liz's legs with a carefully choreographed, high-backed purring dance that said hello and begged for attention. Liz swept him into her arms and carried him into the shed like a baby, in a thick black blanket of fine cat hair.

"Whatcha doing?" Liz was pretty—a girl of sixteen, but who looked older. Lydia began noticing that, even at twelve or thirteen, Liz had developed the body of a woman—slim legs, rounded hips, and breasts. And she had the face to match—Lydia knew it to be a smaller version of her own, thin and long, with arching light-brown eyebrows, but with her father's dark complexion.

"Who dropped you off?" asked Lydia as she moved several small pots from under the bench.

"Mother, you just answered a question with a question," smiled Liz, rocking Peonia. "You always say not to do that. I asked you first: What are you doing?"

Lydia smiled, knowing the game. "For a little while, I was chasing spider mites off the roses. Then I came back here and started tidying things."

"What are you going to do with the thumbtacks?"

Lydia looked down and realized that the thumbtacks were firmly in the grip of her left hand. "I don't know. Just picked them up as I tidied." She placed them near the rose clippers. "Who dropped you off?"

Liz sung a piece of a lullaby to Peonia, who now arched his back, trying to escape. Liz dropped him to the floor, where he landed on all four feet. She brushed black hairs off her sweater. "A boy. It was a boy I know."

Lydia turned and leaned against the bench. The afternoon sun warmed the shed, giving it the comfortable smell of wood, dried grass, and flowers. Open bags of fertilizer, all along the shelf next to the bench, added a slight chemical sense, but even this fit in comfortably. To Lydia, this was the smell of peace, the smell of a workshop, a garden; the smell of standing alone, quietly, with one's thoughts, in a garden of hyacinth and rose and honeysuckle—though she hadn't been able to grow honeysuckle successfully since she left Iowa. But the warmth also kindled a tiny anger at the conversation.

"Liz. Let us do ourselves a favor here. Rather than my asking you ten questions and you giving me ten evasive answers, why don't you just tell me right out who gave you a lift from Jenny's house? I know that Mrs. Caldwell's car—last I heard, which was yesterday when she came to pick you up—does not backfire."

Liz seemed to ponder this, but didn't answer. She smiled at her mother, as if measuring the dangers either way. "He is a boy that works with Albert. His name is Conrad."

"He works for Skybillings up in the woods?"

"Yes."

"Conrad what?"

"Conrad Bruel. He's really nice. I know him from some school things that he's been to—dances and football games."

"How old is he?"

"I don't know. Maybe eighteen."

"From around here?"

"Mmm-humh."

"And how did you end up getting a ride from him?"

"I was coming out of Caldwell's. Jenny and I were going to walk over, but he drove by and he asked if I needed a lift."

"Liz, you know what I think...," said Lydia, but stopped when she heard the gate scrape.

"Lydia? You back here?" Clare Ristall's voice drifted into the shed from along the side of the house, and Peonia shot out the door to greet him.

"I'll be in the house," said Liz, rolling her eyes and slipping out the door. "Hi, Mr. Ristall. How's Shelley?"

"She's fine, Liz. How are you?" Clare's voice was warm and light.

"Just fine."

"Where's your mom?"

Lydia didn't hear a response, but Clare suddenly appeared at the door of the woodshed—smiling, looking somewhat starched in his white shirt and tie, a man just out of church and happy to be so.

His voice was always friendly. In fact, Lydia long ago decided that Clare's popularity was, to no small degree, due to his voice. Nothing in it sounded anything but warm, it wrapped a smile around even the most routine comment or greeting. Union members, shopkeepers, even company owners liked him—some less than others, of course.

"Sweetheart, you look wonderful," he leaned through the doorway and gave her a peck, then stepped back to look at her again. "This is truly an American portrait." He surveyed her in the woodshed—leaning against the bench, long blond hair falling across the shoulders of her denim shirt, a red bandana pulled tight across her forehead, and framed by stacks of flower pots and two rusty saws hanging directly behind her.

She smiled, but only slowly. She thought about mentioning the conversation with Liz, but changed her mind.

"We missed you in church." Clare loosened his collar and tie, leaning against the doorframe.

"Careful, you'll get dust all over you." She nodded at the frame, but he shrugged.

"Old man Hillsdale wanted to know where his favorite English teacher was today," said Clare. "I figure he's got a serious crush on you." His smiled flicked quickly. "The old lady elbowed him as soon as he asked."

Clare settled against the doorjamb now, as Lydia again began shifting several pots from underneath the bench to the top. As she bent down to open a bag of fertilizer, Clare watched her bend, then straighten. "You know, from what I can tell, the old man's got pretty good taste in women."

She tried to ignore the comment, but had to laugh. "I didn't feel like going this morning. I decided that the roses needed attention, especially if I don't have time this afternoon."

Clare slapped his hands together quickly, as if closing a deal. "So you're going?"

"Clare, I told you yesterday I was going." She shook her head and sighed. She didn't want to be teased.

"But when you weren't in church, I thought you'd changed your mind."

He stepped through the door and nestled softly behind her, his arms slipping around her waist. She felt herself tense for a moment, but then lean back into his arms. "Sorry, I was just afraid you'd decided you had better things to do than go with me to the picnic. I didn't mean to give you a bad time. I'm just glad you're going."

Clare squeezed her as he pushed her hair to the side with his cheek and kissed her on her neck. Then he settled his chin on her shoulder. She could feel his crisp shirt crackle as their bodies met; a hint of aftershave mixed with the woodshed warmth.

"You know what?" he now spun her around to face him, his hands on her shoulders. "I'll pick you up at, say, two o'clock. We'll drive over together and we'll have one hell of a time. We'll drink beer and say hello to the old farts and we'll wolf down some of Mrs. Prager's wurst and we'll be the best damn good-looking couple in town."

She didn't smile. But he kept staring at her, twitching his eyebrows like Groucho Marx, until it became a contest: Would she smile first or would he finally give up twitching? She finally broke into a laugh. "Stop it, Clare. You look like a damn fool."

With that, he gave her a peck on the cheek. "Damn fool or not, I'm gonna look like a million dollars with you by my side." He turned toward the door, adding a loud stage whisper. "'Old man Hillsdale, eat your heart out.'" He clapped and turned around once more, this time with a wink. "Two o'clock then?"

She nodded, with an exasperated grin, as he dashed out the door. This was Clare Ristall—friendly, happy, entertaining, social. Though she had known Clare ever since she had moved to Seakomish, even before she married Fred, she was never sure whether, at any given time, she was seeing the business side or the social side of Clare. Or were the two the same? Though he started in the sawmills and then worked in the woods for years, he had been working for the unions ever since the early '30s. First the AFL—then the strike, which he deemed a total failure. Now he was organizing the CIO in the Seakomish woods and down the valley.

Though labor troubles had wracked other cities in Washington, the mood in Seakomish was different, mostly. Clare was widely respected, especially among the older residents. He built his support not with threats, but with reason, good humor, friendship, even with a degree of gentility—not one to argue or let his emotion get out of hand. The loggers liked him. They decided somewhere along the line that he knew the business and understood what they faced. But also the owners generally approved of him—though that was shaken by the length of the AFL strike a couple of years earlier. They still greeted him by his first name; most of them had apparently decided that his intentions were good, even if his politics and business sense were not. Though he was a strong and vocal union organizer, he was known more as just another person who lived in Seakomish—who sang in the church choir and was a member of the school board for several years.

Lydia swept her hair back again with a nod of the head, then dug into a rusty metal bin of black dirt. She sprinkled several handfuls into each one of the pots, then found a large bag of crushed leaves and pine needles behind the door. She dragged it to the bench, plopped in a spade and extracted a heaping scoop, which she also scattered among the pots.

The fact was she hadn't planned to go, despite what she had promised Clare the day before. She'd woken up feeling alone; no, wanting to be alone. That's why she hadn't gone to church. That's why she decided she wouldn't go to the picnic. But the conversation with Liz, plus the difficulty of saying no to Clare to his face—who clearly longed for the companionship—made her change her mind. Maybe a Lodge picnic was just what she needed. It would force her to chat, to listen to gossip, make small talk, ask people she hardly knew how they were feeling. That was good. That was what she needed. Besides school would start in another couple of months. This would be good practice for the parent-teacher meetings.

She quickly closed the bag of soil, pushing it under the bench, doing the same with the fertilizer. She shoved the flowerpots all to the end of the bench, then replaced the spade on a hook along the wall. As she did, she noticed the thumbtacks leaning against the back wall— the thumbtacks Liz had asked about—and she suddenly remembered: the scene suddenly became brilliant with detail.

She had been in the backyard, about this time of year, she was tacking string to the outside of the shed so sweet peas could climb freely from the ground, and she had heard the gate scrape. When she looked up she saw Fred first—his big smile glowing broadly—followed by Bud Cole, who looked just as happy. As they approached, she heard the logger boots scraping and she picked up the musty smell of loggers—a mixture of oil, grease, dirt, sweat, mixed with the perfume of recently cut wood and sawdust. Something about the smell suggested masculinity that brought up a warmth inside her that she found enjoyable, if a bit embarrassing.

"Lydia, we've got great news," said Fred, with almost a shout as they hurried in and sat down beside her—Fred on the grass, Bud on a small bench beside the woodshed. "We've got the money to open our own company. Me and Bud. We just got the word from the people in Vancouver."

As she looked at the thumbtacks, she could still feel the conflicting emotion she felt back then—pride that her husband could convince an international lumber company from Canada to invest in two loggers from Seakomish, but anger that he had not come to her first to tell her what he was planning. She also recalled—as she reached out to hold the thumbtacks, all now carefully punched back into a piece of cardboard—the fear of that day, the fear that the danger and risk would increase for one of the only persons in the world who she had ever loved.

Yet, in looking at him, sitting cross-legged on the grass, she also saw the exuberance and devotion that had so drawn her even that first time at the auction sale. She could still see him standing there, jar of pickles thrust out in front of him. Now it was a new company, a dream he'd talked about for years, with a friend who was like a brother to him. They both sat there, excited and jabbering—both handsome, happy, willing to take on the world; hands blackened by mud and grease, no object or force or circumstance nearly big enough to stand in their way. They practically stumbled over one another as they explained the details: Starting in a month, $20,000 loan, used equipment from Deek Brown, contracts with Ashford & Southern, and rail equipment from Everett. They told and retold the story of why this was a smart decision, how the market was booming, how they would make their fortune. Fred laughed and slapped Bud on the knee, Bud paced in a circle explaining to Lydia who they would hire, and why she should be excited.

Even at the time, she thought they seemed almost like children—in their dreams, unfazed by even a hint of adversity, willing to make their way without much considering the odds. Lydia didn't like the plan, even from the start, but never really tried to talk them out of it. She couldn't stand in the way of such faith; she could only observe it and pray that it would work.

But as she looked down at the workbench now and the piece of cardboard stuck full with thumbtacks, she realized that she had not used them since; she hadn't even noticed them until today.

# Chapter 17

*A ribbon of thundering white. A blue serpent, angry and wet. A place to go with a girl on a hot summer afternoon.*

Lydia had found the descriptions as surprising as she found them charming.

For the final creative writing assignment of the term, she had asked the senior English class to describe some aspect of their town that they would want a person from another country to know about. They could pick anything, but they had to write about it in a creative, inventive way that would evoke the mood they felt or convey the scene vividly to the reader.

Several had chosen logging, a few the rain, one or two described the trains that passed along the north edge of town. But most had described the river: how it roars over the banks during the spring run-off; the mist that it spits into the cool mountain air; its color in brilliant spring sunshine; its whirling speed and the slick, mossy rocks of its shoulders that will swallow you in a breath.

That the river would be so prominent in the minds of her students didn't surprise her. It gave the town its name, after all, to say nothing of its northern boundary and its orientation to much of the world. It roared along the edge of town, dropping perhaps a hundred feet from where it appeared in the east from a grove of heavy fir to where it rumbled out of sight in the west, around a hill that seemed to consume it. More important, the Seakomish River formed the axis around which the town was laid out—the houses and businesses and school and hospital to the south, the railroad, the depot, and the highway that snaked between towering peaks to Everett lay immediately to its north.

But the power of the Seakomish reached well beyond town. Its white-water anger at the upper elevations churned clouds of pine needles, water-logged chips of bark, and rich, brown silt, depositing them gently in widening fans of fertile, farming soil near the long meadows approaching Puget Sound. In that sense, the river had been the economic lifeblood of the valley for thousands of years, accounting for why towns all the way to Everett were considered part of the Seakomish Valley, not linked by name to the many other valleys and ravines and secondary rivers that crisscrossed the region.

Despite this, Lydia found the students' focus on the river surprising—surprising that it would dominate their thinking to the exclusion of the woods, which in many ways ruled their lives; or the rain, which Lydia found ever-present, even on the sunny days; or the mountains, which wrapped the town in a manger of green shadows most of the year. Was it the nature of her assignment to them perhaps? She had asked them to describe something about which they wanted to tell the outside world. Perhaps logging was too routine, too everyday—unlike a river, which always seemed new and mysterious. Perhaps the rain or even the mountains seemed like too much of a fixture to them, present but distant, or perhaps constant and unchanging. But then again, she decided, it may just have been coincidence: One of those things that, when you really sort it out, doesn't mean anything beyond what it is.

Clare had picked her up earlier than she expected. She'd hurried to gather a scarf and the potato salad and a jug of lemonade, all of which she had settled carefully into the bed of his old pickup. She now hung onto the scarf against the cool breeze as Clare turned the corner and cruised down the steep hill toward town.

From here, the buildings on Main Street seemed to hover at her knees. Seakomish was built on a hillside, starting in the early days just above the banks of the river, but then spread up the hill as business picked up with the War. Since then, most of the houses and even the high school were built in the Heights—as they were called— where the foothills began to gain the stature of real mountains.

From the stop sign, where the road entered Main Street and continued to angle downward toward town, she could see the river appear out of the green haze in the distance, shooting toward the white rapids in the front of the city park. From this distance, she could see several people standing next to the river, and others moving about in the sunlight that filled the park. A gray and green banner was draped over the iron gates at the front; perhaps ten or fifteen cars nestled along the edge of Main Street. A thumping sound drifted their way, though Clare's Ford rumbled so badly she wasn't sure if it was a band at the picnic or the undercarriage ready to drop.

Lydia often walked this way after school, on her way to Walther's on Main Street. When the afternoons were cold or damp, she would wrap tight in a long gray coat, and set out down the hill, fighting to hold her weight against the slope, and dreading the climb back with a bag of groceries.

Where the hill turned onto Main Street, Lydia usually would stop and take in the full view of Seakomish lying low below her; Main Street, with Walther's, the filling station, the low slung roof of Harris' barber shop, with its red-white-and-blue pole turning slowly. Farther east lay the diner, bedecked in a checkered-red awning and a flag, the valley bus line office, with the two attorneys' offices on the second floor, the bank, and the police station. But even more, she could actually see—from this height—the "Crossroads" which she had first heard talked about on the train when she came from Iowa.

After transferring in Portland, she was seated next to a man who said he was a foreman in a sawmill in Aberdeen, a small logging community on the Pacific Ocean halfway to Seattle. When he found that she was on her way to Seakomish to teach, he asked her if she had ever heard of "The Crossroads."

"I've never. Other than the main intersection in Sioux City."

He snorted, suggesting that most Iowans would be lost if they ever encountered this particular set of crossroads. Students in the Pacific Northwest, he explained, were taught for years about the mountains, and the majestic stands of fir that grew on them, the raging torrents that ran off them and carved deep valleys through them, and the battles waged by settlers, farmers, loggers, and before that, Indians, to tame them. The most prominent of them, certainly in Washington and British Columbia, was the Cascade Range—rising in white, granite spikes 9,000 and 10,000 feet, and dotted with volcanic cones, called Rainier, Baker, and Adams, that soared much higher. He called the Cascades the Great Divide of Washington, icy peaks and thick forests that ran down the middle of the state from the Canadian border almost to the Columbia River, 250 miles to the south.

On her way to Washington, Lydia had little understanding of where she was going. She had gone to the library, looked in the encyclopedia, even wrote letters to the Chamber of Commerce. None had been answered. And the professor who got her the job only knew that Seakomish was "in the mountains." So the old man with a broken gait and a raspy voice, but with a scholar's knowledge of Northwest geography and geology, finally painted for her the first true picture of her new home.

The night train clattered through blackness, an occasional light sweeping past as the remnants of train whistle filtered through the car. As he spoke, the images began taking form: Seakomish, lying just to the north of the center point of the Cascade Range, stood as the junction—the crossroads—of perhaps the best valleys of the entire range, as far as logging was concerned. The Jaster Creek Valley uncoiled for almost ten miles north, he said, covered with dense stands of fir, framed by ragged peaks that never lost their whitecaps. A gentle stream that could grow violent in springtime dimpled its floor. Running due south from Seakomish, the Anderson Valley jogged twice before straightening out, five or six miles in all. Running east and west, of course, was the Seakomish Valley itself—a phrase that was used by locals to describe the entire set of towns from the tip of the Cascades all the way to Everett.

But off to the southwest stood another deep ravine that was long and rugged, the most spectacular terrain in the region. Now her seatmate shook his head, slowly, displaying white strands from underneath his stocking cap. This valley was called Roosevelt Creek Valley, as in Teddy Roosevelt, whose name was given it by a Republican Governor who wanted a job in Washington, DC. Though he never got one, he had named the creek and the valley well, said the man.

"I traveled up there once, surveying," he rocked toward her occasionally, though she realized that she felt no awkwardness or irritation. It almost felt welcome. The comfort of a father, telling a daughter a story—a story of a mystical new world of green and ice and raging waters and towering firs, many of which were only seedlings when the Magna Carta was signed. She thought of that for a moment, losing his words as he continued to describe the valley: She would soon live in a community that gained its livelihood and built its very existence on trees that were already growing 500 years before Columbus set sail, trees that originated at a time which was almost closer to the time of Christ than to her own.

"Roosevelt offers man the most beautiful example of God's work this child has ever witnessed," said the man, smiling. "Steep. Hard pull. Man gotta be in good shape for it go right straight up." His hand gnarled near the finger, the skin a splotchy brown, as he showed the incline. "Maybe this day-and-age they got roads or rails running up there. We was cruising the timber to decide if we ought to buy. We got up there and we decided no man have any right there. Lakes at the top, straight-up rock, clouds race over maybe only a few hours a day, the ravines so steep winter leaves only on the summer wind. Best left for lynx and coyote."

His voice stopped often. Lydia didn't know if he was done or resetting the scene in his own mind. "We went in there, up Roosevelt, walking right in the creek, must've been in April or May. Would've been probably 1910. Walked for must have been days, three or four. We got to thinking that we could put a rail along the creek there. But before we got time to even really start planning, a terrible snow came up. We was way up, near the top of the creek, not far from something called Three Sisters Ridge. But that snow roared into those mountains and just stayed there. Stayed for a week—snow, heavy, blocking our chance to get out. We was blind—all of us out there. We huddled against each other, sparing the matches, you know."

Lydia knew that the stop for Aberdeen was near, but she had more questions. Yet she didn't feel she could interrupt.

He lilted sideways slightly as the train slowed, perhaps to sidetrack. Lydia could feel the seat in front move as his hand grabbed it tighter. "The cold felt like an ache inside you. Didn't even hurt that bad on the fingers. All of us, just felt this want to throw-up. You get the pain, the freeze, deep in your bones. Finally, it let up, and the sun was—the next morning—maybe fifty degrees and the wind warm, blowing off the peaks. So we hurried down the stream, afraid that if we didn't get out, the melt woulda drowned us."

He stopped almost as the train did—idling next to a platform filled with several children, and two adults, and a long cart topped with mounds of brown and gray luggage. The man smiled as he got up and shook her hand.

"May I ask your name?" His broken teeth matched the rough, hard skin of his fingers and palm which he offered to Lydia.

"Lydia Malford."

"And why did you say you are going up there?"

"To teach. History and English."

At this the man stopped, his leather case, which he had stowed under his seat, now firmly gripped in both hands in front of him. He looked at her, seeming to take in her face and shoulders, then glancing downward at the rest of her—not in the way many men looked at her, thought Lydia, but as if measuring her physical presence, her capacity as a physical entity.

"You stay in the town, near the school, and you will be fine," he said, his cap on his head, and turning toward the door. "Roughnecks gotta have flowers, they do. Otherwise they always stay roughnecks." He smiled and disappeared through the door.

❊    ❊    ❊

On occasion, if the weather was warm enough, Lydia would rest at the bend in the road, trying to absorb the view of the crossroads, thinking of the old man on the train and the time in her life when she couldn't even imagine what Seakomish would be like. As she stood there, drinking in the image—seeing the ribbon, the serpent, even the summery day that her students saw—she remembered the compliment of his final comment, at least that's how she took it. And she wondered what, truly, she had brought here: Did she change them at all, these logging people? Or had they changed her more? A silly question, one of those without answers but plenty of clouds and hidden bursts of pain, sometimes joy—a bit of foolish thinking she decided, for a woman who had already lived there some twenty years, borne two children, and buried one husband.

"Lydia, the pretty smile," said Clare, as the Ford settled near to the other cars next to the park. She looked at him absently, in time to see him point at his mouth. "Where's the gorgeous smile?"

Lydia laughed, embarrassed at the silence that she must have made him endure. But silences were part of her upbringing and part of her life. Though Clare teased her about them, he endured them gracefully—perhaps even finding a bit of his infatuation in them.

The park tilted toward the water on the far side. Picnic tables dotted the grounds, sheltered occasionally by large groves of Douglas fir. The park opened onto Main Street through a two-piece iron gate, large enough for a car when both sides were swung open.

Lydia enjoyed picnics, in part, because it was a chance to see the parents of her students in settings that were much more natural than across the conference table in the teacher's lounge. She could never have guessed, when riding the train from Portland with her friend from Aberdeen, that logging families would take such an interest in school matters and the welfare of their students. But they had—meetings to assess the progress of a student were virtually never missed. Though fathers could rarely attend during the spring and fall, they were in attendance with their wives during the winter, when heavy snows closed logging operations until March at the earliest.

The school, in fact, played a vital role in the affairs of Seakomish, she learned quickly. She didn't know if the churches were too rigid for men whose youth was spent chasing women and alcohol. Then again, she wondered if perhaps loggers and their wives did not want to hear the incantations of hellfire and death and burning punishment that the Methodists and Brethren of God meted out every Sunday, though she found Reverend Ramsey at the Presbyterian church a good bit more tolerable. Perhaps they found in the school a note of opti- mism—a vote for a future that was less threatening and more lucra- tive for their children than the present was for themselves. But this was only guesswork. She'd never spoken about it with anyone.

As she tried to move through the crowd toward the tables where the wives and teenage girls had already begun laying out fried chicken and rolls and were stirring large containers of bright red liquid, she also noted the brilliant colors of a picnic versus the muted tones of school time. Men who normally wore striped shirts, thick black suspenders, and black canvass pants now dressed brightly in plaid shirts or sweater-vests over starched white shirts. Likewise, the women reflected the sunshine in cotton dresses of pink or green that fluttered in the breeze.

Lydia knew these were people who were not rich. Many, in fact, were very poor. The Depression had ripped through Seakomish with a fierceness rivaled only by that experienced in the largest cities. The reason was simple: The lumber market fell as if dropped from the tallest peak above the river. As it fell, families and lives fell with it: Cars repossessed, businesses shuttered, men traveling to Everett and then Seattle to find even the most basic jobs. But the market contin- ued to fall: Lydia had cried herself to sleep many nights, hoping that the school would not close; wondering how to help her neighbors and friends, but without depleting the hard-earned assets she knew that she and her children might need. By 1932, Main Street was largely empty stores and plywood. Walther's stayed open, often granting families credit that she knew many were still paying back. The bank, of course, closed—as did the depot, the movie theater, and the diner.

Yet there remained a spirit of unity that she had not expected. Logging operations closed rapidly, soon after the crash of '29. Deek Brown was one of the first to go, laying off all 300 workers. Ashford & Southern and Zollock & Sons tried short work weeks, then three-day weeks. By '31, no one remained in business.

The churches pooled food. Reverend Ramsey drove to Seattle every week to ask companies for financial assistance in paying for food for the people of Seakomish, though companies of every kind—freight firms, shippers, builders, iron and mill works, canning companies— all were closing their doors against the ravages of low pay, dropping prices, and failure of confidence.

During the worst of it, with the school hobbling along with half-staff, fathers and mothers would accompany their children to school, sitting in the gym or the cafeteria, talking with one another rather than facing the silent imprisonment of sitting at home, with no money, no opportunity for a job, and little hope that anything would change.

Though Lydia never considered herself to be any type of social worker, she and the other teachers began evening counseling sessions. The school principal, Terrence Stubbs, canvassed the valley— all the way into Everett—for news of job openings, largely public works jobs created by the federal government. Every Tuesday and Wednesday night, he would open the school and, together with Lydia, Morris Baxter the math teacher, and Nelson Purdy the fifth-grade teacher, describe the jobs, where to go to sign up, the pay, and how long they would last. They also suggested how people could grow certain types of fruits and vegetables in the cold Seakomish climate— something that loggers rarely did during good times—and they circulated among the attendees to lend encouragement, to hold a wavering hand, to draw togetherness and community from the shared fear and economic ill.

Yet it was the sense of worthlessness that accompanied the free fall that Lydia found so hard to wrestle with. Strong, muscled loggers— men who had worked the most dangerous jobs, had formed companies, had built railroads across ravines—looked red-eyed and beaten. Some who had worked with Skybillings in the early days had developed nervous tics and stutters, more than one was found hanging from rafters in their garages. Deek Brown's foreman—noted for his elegance in rigging spar trees—hung himself in the garage next door. A man she didn't know on the next street killed himself with his hunting rifle.

None of that was visible in the sea of color or its rising waves of conversation and laughter that she smiled her way through today. The jobs had begun to return. Roosevelt's New Deal had put many men back to work, often building trails in the woods or parks along the coast. Many logging companies had regained their footing.

"Mrs. Weissler, here, give me that." Joel Quinn reached from around a picnic table crowded with food to take the lemonade. "No sense you lugging it halfway across China." His arms were tattooed green, with a mat of thick black hair. Lydia thought he worked for Zollock, though she wasn't sure. He had graduated four, maybe five years before.

"Joel, thanks." She hefted the jug toward him and he headed toward the ladies laying out food. For a moment she paused, noting how unusual this scene would have been only a few years ago, when this much food didn't exist in most of the towns down the entire valley.

"Lydia, over here." She could see Clare wave toward her from near the first row of tables, surrounded by a group of several women and a tall man she didn't recognize. As she began to slip past several couples in a semicircle near the gate, she felt a hand on her arm. Myrna Valentine said something and laughed, but Lydia couldn't make it out in the loud conversation and the music—the high school jazz combo had begun playing again, this time some kind of Dixieland music, with a loud trombone.

"I'm sorry?" Lydia spoke loudly, pointing to her ear. Lydia knew Myrna Valentine from the bank. Myrna now stood close to her, jostled by the group still near the gate. "I said, 'John told me that your son, Albert, is working on the Skybillings crew,'" she said, her smile breaking across a pretty, if prematurely sagging, face. Hints of jowls rounded both jaws.

"Yes. That's right. Started in March."

"John says he is such a good worker. In fact, he helped John and his men just last week on something or other, and John said that he was a real delight to have around." John Valentine was one of the first men that Fred and Bud had hired at Skybillings.

"How is John? I haven't seen him for so long." Lydia knew that Myrna found only one thing more interesting than town gossip: herself or her husband. She made a movement to slip away, but realized that Myrna's hand gently held her arm.

"He has been just working so hard. After the accident that killed all those men, you know, he felt that he really needed to pitch-in and help Bud Cole hold the men together. Something like that is so hard, you know." Myrna's jowls wobbled slightly because she turned rapidly to see who else was moving past them. "You know, younger men have so much to upset them at times like this. It's easy to lose their, well, their presence of mind, I suppose you could say."

The band was now silent, so the sound of conversation and laughter rose and fell. The crowd moved slightly, making room for Earl Talbert and his wife. Lydia noticed that, for the first time since she could recall, Earl had shaved. Emma Jean, ablaze in a yellow hat and white dress, must have decided that he needed to look presentable.

Myrna now leaned close, sharing a confidence, as the crowd again shifted to let the mayor and his wife pass. "As much as I like Bud Cole, sometimes—and I know that you know this from your own experience—he needs a little guidance about how to manage these things. And now he has this Harry Bachelder working with him." She smiled, as if embarrassed. "John is willing to help. It's not that he has the extra time. Goodness knows, he has his hands full with some of those fellows they hire—like this Bachelder fellow. He hardly knows what a choker is, you know. But it's just something he feels he should do."

The music started again—this time thumping into some type of march—drawing the knot of people into even louder conversation. Lydia smiled to Myrna, who now held the elbow of the Mayor's wife, as she stepped around the back of the tables. Harriet Devatt and Mildred Conner, both of the Presbyterian ladies group, smiled and shouted hello.

"Lydia, you're just lovely today," said Mildred, a floppy chin under a painted smile. "But we missed you at church."

Harriet's voice reached above the clarinet and trumpet. "We thought you might've been sick, but so good to see you."

Lydia smiled graciously, explaining that she had other "chores," but then decided that she'd chosen the wrong word. By the time she tried to correct herself, Terrence Stubbs, the school principal who worked for Skybillings during the summer, had moved into the circle.

"Lydia, not that long before we start school again," he said, his face a bulb of smiles and shiny scalp, punctuated by a beak nose that erupted from fat cheeks. He leaned close to her, being certain that the other women heard. "And I know I'll be a lot damn happier pushing papers than setting chokers." He held his hands up—scraped raw along the sides, palms furrowed with thick rows of calluses, brown and yellow.

The sun was now in full force across the park, lighting the crowd's brilliant colors against the green and blue of grass and sky. Lydia detected fried chicken and what smelled like bacon, drifting from the serving table across the park.

As Lydia stepped past the tables, she saw Clare's thirteen-year-old daughter Shelley unfolding a blanket on the grass. Lydia nodded to several smiling faces as she walked to Shelley.

"A pretty girl on a beautiful day," said Lydia as she settled on her knees next to the blanket.

"Hi, Mrs. Weissler." Shelley's blond curls glowed in the light. "Liz is getting food for both of us. Want to eat with us?" Then she looked around and planted a large, sly smile on her face. "Or are you eating with Daddy again?"

Lydia laughed. Shelley was one of the reasons she'd met Clare in the first place. She was in Lydia's class when she taught sixth grade. Shelley was a precocious girl—more advanced than the rest of the class, even including Lydia's own daughter. Lydia found Shelley's matter of factness and her surprising insights about the other children remarkable. And because Shelley's mother had died several years earlier, she developed a special attachment to Lydia.

Perhaps that's why Lydia paid special attention when Clare came in for their first parent-teacher conference. She thought the entire discussion was focused on Shelley, and her progress, but within two weeks Clare had invited Lydia to a church picnic, much like this one.

"I'm afraid that I am going to eat with your Daddy," laughed Lydia. "Assuming, of course, I can find him in this crowd." Lydia looked over the heads, but couldn't spot Clare.

"Just look for the big group with the loud voices. He'll be in the middle of it." The girl's voice was not unhappy, just matter-of-fact. Lydia sat down and explained, once more, that he was busy and had lots of people he was trying to help. "But Shelley, I want you to know that even if he is busy, you can talk to me. I will listen." She was going to say more, but her daughter Liz came bounding up with two plates of food. When Shelley saw them, she showed no sign that she was interested in more talk.

"Please, ladies and gentlemen, we have plenty of food over here," shouted the town's Mayor, Adam Newman. "Please just come on over and line up. Don't let these pretty ladies wait all day"—he nodded to the women who were ready with ladles and spoons along the serving line.

Lydia looked for Clare, but saw him now in a conversation with several women, still near the gate. So she made sure the girls were settled and slipped into the line, just behind John and Myrna Valentine.

"Good to see you, Lydia." Valentine reached past her for a plate and spoon, then handed both to her. "Myrna says you had a good visit."

"Yes, it was good to see her again," said Lydia, shaking the hand that he turned to offer. "Myrna seems to be enjoying this grand day." Lydia smiled and motioned upward, with a sweep of her hand.

"God's wonderful creation," he said, with a thick, broad smile. When he looked at her, his glass eye stared toward the left, while the other moved quickly to find his utensils. Valentine tilted toward her, exposing his whole head to Lydia. She noticed that the chunky face, despite the bulbous features and the errant eye, still carried a degree of handsomeness—a jaw that was set low and sharp to large ears, tan hair, perhaps blond. But it was how he carried himself, more than how he looked. John Valentine had the large, stooped, but powerful stature of a monument, thought Lydia. A monument of a hero who had gone off to the war, and who had come home weary and damaged, but still strong and confident. Lydia suspected that this was how Valentine saw himself too.

"I see Mr. Valentine has discovered the two prettiest ladies at the picnic," said Clare, who suddenly appeared next to Lydia. He hugged her and winked at Myrna.

"Clare, we've been looking for you. Where have you been?" asked Lydia.

"Just over there with Matt Wilson, trying to talk some sense into him about FDR. Thinks the president is going the wrong direction this year..."

Valentine's voice brushed across Clare's. "FDR oughta go home, in my book." The line shuffled forward, with the smell of beans, chicken, and bacon enveloping them. Mrs. Colloway spotted Lydia and smiled. Because the serving line was only a few feet from the river—which rushed swiftly just below them—the conversation was even more difficult.

"Come on, John, that's not the spirit," said Clare, with a slight pat on Valentine's broad shoulder. "Better than who we had before, don't you think?"

"Not in the least. Hoover got attacked with all kind of criticism and unfair complaints. He just made the mistake of telling people that they got to pick themselves up by the bootstraps instead of waiting for a government handout and the people didn't like to hear that."

The mayor appeared behind Clare, whispering into his ear. "Sorry, folks, gotta ask this man here to come over and meet some of the

Ashford people," said the mayor, pulling Clare by the arm. Clare winced as he smiled an apology to Lydia, then hurried with the mayor back to the gate.

Lydia heard Oscar Eusik calling for more people to fill in the gaps along the food line. So Lydia seized the opportunity to excuse herself and move forward to where Oscar was serving chicken. As soon as he saw Lydia, he jabbed his fork into the brown pot and produced two chicken breasts, oozing with sauce. "Mrs. and I been cooking since last night. I tell her, 'Needs more pepper. More hot sauce.' She calls me an old fool, says it don't. So I get up after she's asleep and I fix it."

His face beamed in a broad smile, filtered by a walrus mustache that yellowed along the bottom edge. The afternoon breeze tossed his white hair softly. "Polish chicken don't taste right unless it has plenty of Carolina lightning in it."

With a belly laugh, Oscar plopped the two pieces onto Lydia's plate, though she asked for only one.

"You're just too thin for a girl who has to work so hard." Now it was Mrs. Colloway, whose soft chiffon dress and choker of bright blue caught a glint in her hair. She held a soup ladle of green beans over Lydia's plate, but then dipped the ladle back into the pot for a larger helping.

"No, Mrs. Colloway, I'm fine...." Before Lydia could get the sentence out, another spoonful had landed. Lydia smiled weakly and shifted the plate gently away from Mrs. Colloway's reach. As she did, Beatrice Woolsey, the school librarian, plopped two butter rolls onto the plate.

"Lydia, don't protest." Beatrice clucked through teeth that seemed too large for her face. "I made them myself and I'd be ashamed terribly if I thought you didn't want any." A tiny lady, partial to dark colors and heavy shoes, her face reminded Lydia of her Aunt Milda in Sioux City—something in the teeth and how she formed her words.

Lydia held both hands under the plate as she slipped to a picnic table several steps away from the end of the serving line. From this angle, she could see most of the crowd—half or so still in line, waiting to be served; the other half scattered across picnic tables and brightly colored blankets.

As Lydia bit into one of Beatrice's rolls—surprised that they seemed flat, as if Beatrice had forgotten the salt—she noticed that Clare had spotted her. He waved from halfway through the line. His shirt still had the crisp, starchy look that it always had on Sundays. His suspenders, wide and brilliant red, crisscrossed halfway up his back. As she watched him, she realized that she had never really observed Clare from such a distance before—as he talked and smiled and shook hands. Now he was listening to Fuzzy Bernard as one of the serving ladies ladled something onto his plate.

How well she knew Clare's public manner. She was accustomed to his quick stops, his movements to the side or even back, to shake a hand. Though she often got angry over the fact that they could never get anywhere on time, she liked his natural friendliness. At the start, she found it off-putting. First, the smile, then a handshake or hug, then lots of nodding and laughter, followed by a gut-laugh, then slightly bent torso, chin on hand, propped by arm on hip, furrowed brow, hug, handshake, and wave. But the more she was with him, the more she knew it to be genuine.

When Lydia first met Clare, she had not expected to find him of interest. An ex-logger. Before that, a sawmill man. Now a union business representative—in effect, a political functionary. A social creature who swam through the thick of Seakomish life—even down the valley, Stardale, and sometimes Everett. These were not characteristics that would normally interest her.

But Clare surprised Lydia. He enjoyed art and could detail the comings and goings of European Impressionists. He knew jazz and classical music—he was a charter member on the Board of the Pacific Northwest Symphony in the '20s—but he also could recite the current recordings of Gene Autry and Roy Acuff.

During Sunday drives and picnics beside the river, they argued literature. She loved Edna St. Vincent Millay; he was partial to Archibald MacLeish. They both read Dos Passos and disagreed—incredible insight, was Clare's view; too self-absorbed was hers. They debated whether Hoover tried hard enough, whether the fascists offered any kind of solution for the US, whether another world war would emerge from the chaos in Europe, and they came to different views on FDR—Lydia voted for Hoover, a fact that Clare razzed her about for months.

But Lydia's greatest surprise came when Clare had invited her to dinner for the first time at his house. Clare and his daughter lived in what might be called a bungalow—low roof, sweeping from a sharp peak to eaves that seemed to scrape the holly bushes that surrounded the house. It sat with pride on the corner opposite the Methodist church. Its paint was sharp white, unblistered like its neighbors. But otherwise it melted into the patchwork of wood frame one and two stories, dotted occasionally by a Cape Cod.

But the inside was unlike any house Lydia had ever seen. Clare not only enjoyed art, he also collected it. He was not just a connoisseur of antique furniture, but he decorated his home with it—dining chairs and a buffet and easy chairs that he said were Louis XIV from France. Arranged with an eye toward design, in colors that blended with the paintings and framed the style of furniture with precision, the house and its furniture seemed more curated than arranged.

When Lydia asked him—straight out—how he could afford such things, Clare explained that his wife had inherited money from an uncle in the East who had made his fortune in textiles soon after the Civil War. The uncle had died, without other relatives, leaving her his life savings.

"So you're rich." Lydia's tone was matter-of-fact.

"I suppose you could say that."

They were sitting on a porch in the back of his house after dinner when Lydia brought up the subject. Though it was too cold to use the porch in the winter, he installed a wood stove in the corner and equipped the back wall with glass louvers so he could enjoy the backyard and its vista of green in the fall. Clare was hunched into an overstuffed chair, a thick sweater wrapped around him.

"But the Depression," said Lydia. "It wiped out millionaires."

"Like I said, the old man was rich." Clare smiled and shrugged. "So rich that Hoover and the Wall Street boys only picked around the edges."

Lydia considered this, a furrow of skin bunching slightly between her eyes. Clare had taken her through the house, room by room, identifying the paintings, including one by Whistler. Though she was no expert on art or antiques, she knew the collection was worth a substantial amount.

"But you worked in the sawmills and in the woods, Clare," said Lydia. Her voice seemed to drift—tossed in opposite directions, but then settling softly. "You are union, Clare, and I always thought that union people..."

"That union people were poor."

That wasn't what she wanted to say, but what she had thought. She nodded slowly, watching the smile slowly disappear from his face, though he displayed no hint of anger. Clare's face was an open face: broad near the eyes, rounded cheeks, narrowing to a gentle chin.

Hunched into the chair, with the sweater nudging at his throat, he looked boyish—blond and soft, a face that never lost what must have been a kind of cuteness that it commanded in its youth.

The fire in the stove snapped several times, then hissed—a wet-wood protest against the searing heat. Lydia reached out to touch his arm.

"Clare, I just have some trouble understanding all of this." She pointed toward the living room and paused. He seemed to settle deeper into the chair. "You have money, which wasn't yours, but your wife's. We still aren't out of the Depression, but you are buying artwork of James Whistler. You are organizing men who work in one of the most dangerous professions known to humans, and you have more money than probably all of them put together. And you blister with missionary zeal about socialism and unionism and the rights of the downtrodden while you serve expensive wine from France."

Her eyes studied his reaction, as if searching for something specific, but she saw only his faint smile, the sandy hair swept to the side, his chin—almost delicate in this light—swimming in the dark wool.

For several minutes they sat in silence. The evening light blackened the glass louvers quickly, creating reflections that were chopped into horizontal slices. The only sound was the crackling wood in the stove, accompanied by the hint of wood smoke.

When Clare spoke, his voice was faint, almost peaceful, a stream gently seeking a passage to lower ground. "What's wrong with contradictions, Lydia?" He stopped, looking toward her slowly. "We are animals of intense contradiction, aren't we—both you and I? I am a man, who was borne by a woman. You are a woman, whose origin, in part, lay inside a man."

He paused, but did not look up this time. "We put our money into banks to protect it, yet the bankers run to Mexico and leave us desolate. We hear from preachers about the love of Jesus, yet they demonize and frighten even the most innocent among us. We live in the most beautiful forest in the world, yet we spend our lives tearing it into shreds so we can ship it to Australia or New Jersey."

Now Clare recovered his zeal, leaning forward, gesturing with his hands, as if molding a sculpture that would make his points plain for Lydia to see. "Lydia, we operate in a capitalist economy that is designed to generate wealth and we have only poverty around us. We elect politicians because they promise a better world and we receive only the swift kick of their boots. We educate our children to give them better lives and what do they do? They go into the woods like their fathers and their fathers' fathers and we carry them out in pine boxes just like we have for how many generations before us."

Clare's face reflected the dancing red of the flames now; the rest of the porch was swept by night. "Is it really so contradictory that I enjoy the things that I can afford and that give me pleasure? Is it so inconsistent that, with the time and the resources that my financial good-luck affords me, that I use it in some meager way to better the lot of those around me? Lydia, how does that contradict? How do those directions run opposite from one another?"

He paused as he uncrossed his legs. "I see them only as different channels of the same stream."

Lydia felt a chill; the fire had begun to die. Clare stood up slowly, pulled a cigarette from a pack on a table near the woodstove and lit it, drawing in the smoke, as if tasting the flavor for the first time. He rolled the smoke around in his mouth, then shot a stream of blue toward the ceiling. "There's another way of looking at it, I suppose. Or that's at least worth considering as you make your judgment about me," he said, as he leaned against the doorframe. His face was now shadowed, engulfed by the darkness behind him, but his silhouette reflected the orange glow of the fire.

"Clare, I didn't mean to suggest judgment." Lydia slid forward quickly in her chair, preparing to protest further, but Clare waved his hand toward her, then withdrew the cigarette again from his lips.

"I don't object, Lydia. These are important questions. You should ask them. You should be sure of who I am. Actually, I find it rather pleasant." He smiled and took another drag.

"Without that little nest egg that Anne's uncle left us, I could not finance any kind of union organizing in these woods. The AFL is too strong in Seattle. The CIO boys are a bunch of upstarts, ruffians. No members to speak of, though enough thugs to actually get people's attention. These boys with their week-old stubble and their cheeks plugged with tobacco and their muscles that split their dirty shirts—these boys don't pay dues, Lydia. And the ones in town—the churchgoers and the family men, the body politic—most of them got no use for unions, at least until a few of them go over the edge in a crummy or a trestle collapses. Then they come running. But even after all that, they got no money—not enough for a man to live on and to organize 'em."

Clare's voice grew reedy now, a hint of its thinness when he became excited. Lydia actually enjoyed the sound. It stood out from others. It held a unique place in the church choir. Even in the softest, most moving passages, Clare's voice rang clear and precise at the center of the unified sound.

Clare was now throwing wood into the stove, clanging it shut with a foot. Again, the wood smoke filled the room, but then slipped away when Clare propped open an upper slat in the glass.

"Call me a philanthropist," said Clare as he sat again, blinking from the smoke of the fire. He filled both glasses again, setting the bottle gently on a side table. "Sounds a little arrogant, doesn't it? But what I mean is: I fund what I believe to be good things. I buy art because it brings me enjoyment. I buy antiques because they bring me beauty. And I fund a new, fledgling union because the bastards from the old one are corrupt, because these men need some protection from companies that would let them die for a few measly dollars, and because the thought that I can use some old-world textile money to make life better for a few hundred or thousand men and their families in another corner of the country and in another century brings me some degree of contentment."

One of the early lessons Lydia learned from her aunt was to maintain a healthy skepticism—not cynicism, or constant doubt—but a healthy skepticism about most things: the claims of salesmen, the loyalties of politicians, and the promises of suitors. With Fred—now dead nearly ten years—Lydia knew that she had violated that principle from the start. But ever since—in the frequent invitations and social engagements she had enjoyed with a number of men—she had clung intensely to that principle. And it was this that bounced hard against the image of Clare Ristall.

As Clare finally reached Oscar Eusik's station in the food line, Lydia could hear the laughter—punctuated by Oscar's booming voice—that retold the story about his wife and the seasoning for the chicken. Clare said something to Oscar about the best food at the picnic, to which Oscar bowed. Then, with plate cradled in both hands, Clare turned toward the picnic table, flashing a warm, summery smile toward Lydia as the soft breeze rippled through his white shirt. And he began making his way up the hill toward her table.

# Chapter 18

The dry heat of summer arrived the first week of June—much too early, completely out of place. Most years, the damp, gray clouds and frequent rains of springtime hung on well into June. But this was different. One minute, it seemed, the air was cool and mossy damp. The next, arid and crackling, with swirling eddies of dust around Thunder Lake.

Who could like such heat? Albert hated it when he lived in town. But now, despite the fact that he was so much higher into the mountains, it was even worse—largely because it seemed so impossible. The icy peaks overhead seemed to define the contours of the world, since most of the year the weather hung low and cool over the woods. But such heat—so obviously in contradiction to the glaciers overhead—felt like an affront to the senses.

That Bud Cole switched the crew to a hoot-owl shift, to avoid the heat of the day as much as possible, didn't make it any easier. Getting up at three-thirty made Albert queasy—he wasn't hungry when Zoe and Delbert served breakfast at four. He certainly wasn't in any mood to begin work when first light cast a dim gray overhead. He rode the crummy with his eyes closed, his mind set elsewhere, only to be jolted when Ferguson slammed the brake, and the crew slowly made its way up the hill or onto the trestle to begin the day.

Talk about the filed spike and who was behind it occupied most of the crew's free time. Too much, thought Albert. He didn't mind the talk about whether it was CIO, or maybe even the AFL trying to make it look like the CIO, or, for that matter, crazy old Olaf Carn. He almost enjoyed Petey Hulst's chatter about how it must have involved, in some way, the spirits of the dead Seakomish People whose graves were robbed by generations of miners and loggers long gone. But when the talk turned to who in the crew might have been involved—and these discussions were always spoken quietly, only in small groups—he felt nervous. Sabotage. Traitor. Those words went together easily. But they were never associated with a specific person—at least not that he was able to tell.

The sheriff, Charlie Deets, visited the camp the day that the heat set-in, and talked to Bud for an hour, then rode the next load of logs back to Seakomish. Conrad Bruel said that Deets and two deputies were coming in on a special Shay later the same day to take away two or three members of the crew. But no one came. No Shay showed up. And no deputies.

Bucky Rudman claimed that the sheriff had come up to warn Bud that Skybillings could expect some kind of CIO attack within a week, but he offered no evidence.

"What in the hell would we do if we was attacked?" asked Bucky, between bites of sweet potato the night after the sheriff visited. "You boys all heard that story Petey told about the Wobblies. Said it was cougar. That's how bad it got back then. What would we do? Huh?"

When Bucky decided to stop kidding, he generally turned to scaring people—and himself.

"Nobody is going to attack us, Bucky," said Myles Norgren. "Nobody cares enough to bother. You're making up ghosts."

Lightning Stevens nodded agreement, then added: "Who in their right mind would climb all the way up here to do anything—much less attack this sorry bunch?" This brought laughter.

"But let's just say they did. That they'd sit right up behind us here on the ridge and start shooting at us, like turkeys. Or blow the rails coming down the mountain. Or start a burn—a real good burn in the face of a north wind. That baby would come right over the side of Three Sisters and right down here. What the hell would we do? We'd sizzle like bacon."

The room quieted as he spoke. Men who were laughing shifted in their seats. Forks stopped.

Bucky sensed the attention shifting his direction, filling his sails. "Man o' livin', we're nothing but sittin' ducks here," he continued. The red in his cheeks seemed brighter than the bushy red on his head. "I figure they could take about half of us with gunfire, maybe a third with dynamite, and they could kill the whole kit-and-caboodle of us with a burn. Hell, where would we run to?"

Bucky now turned to the whole room. "Where would we run? Huh? Only one direction. Into the water. But then the fire sucks all the oxygen off the lake and—*whoosh*—we're gone. No air to breathe. We try to swim out further, but the air is gone. And we're all dead. BOOM!" He slapped his hands together with a loud clap, which made several men flinch. This set Bucky roaring with laughter.

Though several of the men scowled and cursed him, Bucky's rolling laughter became infectious, setting one, then another to laughter. Even St. Bride had to join in.

"It's not a laughing matter," said Valentine sharply. This stilled the room once more. "The fact is, any of those union troublemakers could come in here and do any of those things. We're sitting in a bowl down here, gentlemen. And when we're working at the top of the mountain, we are perched precariously on the edge of a ravine—in case any of you haven't noticed. Either way, unless we prepare ourselves, we could get caught by surprise."

Bud Cole, who had been listening without comment, shoved back his chair. "I don't see any reason for this kind of speculation." His voice was firm. "I did speak with the sheriff. He did not say one word about any attack or about any danger. We all know that violence is all over the woods—Auburn, Grays Harbor, Aberdeen, Puyallup. It doesn't matter. CIO is after the AFL. AFL is fighting back. And together, they hate the companies. So we never know—but the chances are pretty damn small this high up. And you all know that."

Bud tossed his napkin onto his plate and stood up. "This seems like as good a time as any to tell you that I am not just troubled by all this idle talk about who may attack us, but I'm also troubled by what I've seen around here in the past few days."

Most faces turned toward him now. Coffee cups settled onto the tables.

"I will be the first to admit that the goings-on of the last five or six weeks are pretty unusual. And, like most of you already know, there isn't any question any more that the wreck of the Shay was an act of sabotage. That makes the death of Nariff and the others murder."

Though no one in the room doubted those facts, this was the first time anyone actually said the words. As such, they seemed to sink deeper. Union violence was one thing. This was a tradition, something that came with the widow-makers and the rain. But actual murder— sabotage targeted in such a way that men would likely be killed— crossed the line, at least in the Seakomish Valley.

"I'm also familiar with what happens in situations like this where we can't pinpoint just who is to blame or why all of this is happening," continued Bud. "Men start eyeing each other suspiciously. It becomes a guessing game about whether somebody inside might have been involved—or who might be behind the whole thing. Then you start bending unrelated facts or off-hand comments to fit the notion that somebody is guilty. So I want to say this, lest any of that kind of thinking gets out of hand. I have got no evidence that suggests there is some kind of traitor here, alright? So thinking along those lines only does harm."

"But somebody did this to us," said John Valentine loudly. "Whether it is someone on the outside or on the inside, we need to find out the facts. Otherwise, Rudman isn't that off the mark, we are sitting ducks."

Bud shook his head. "Look, the first step was to call the sheriff. He's going to investigate and tell us what he finds."

"When's that?" asked Lightning Stevens.

Bud felt the heat rising in his belly, but he over-ruled it.

"He said that inside of a week, he might have some information." Bud paused. "But he also cautioned us that it was very unlikely that he would turn up anything."

Several of the men in the back of the room began to talk. Bud spoke over them. "Look, goddamn it, this crew has got a choice. Either we eat ourselves up with speculation and finger pointing—or we put our minds to getting our job done and doing what we can to protect ourselves."

He surveyed the room and sensed he still had it under control. His voice lightened slightly.

"I am posting sentries on the tracks from town—along Roosevelt Creek. You all know how narrow it is through there. That canyon is the only way into this camp and up to the mountain."

"Are they gonna stand watch twenty-four hours?" Valentine's voice carried the scowl that covered his face.

"Yes. Starting tonight." Bud paused and surveyed the crew. "Look, if anybody has got a better idea, I'm willing to hear it."

The clock on Zoe's stove clicked loudly, echoing throughout the room. Several men coughed. No one spoke.

"Remember: My door is always open." Bud grabbed his jacket from the wall, then left without saying anything more.

❊   ❊   ❊

The heat did not start all the turmoil, of course. Albert was never sure how much backbiting and finger-pointing would have existed without the heat, but he was sure that the heat made it worse. Sleeping was terrible. Albert slept without covers, but still the air felt like a hot blanket on his skin. Olaf Torslon, the foreman of the falling crew, said the heat kept the crew from breathing, so they all moved their bedrolls onto the ground outside. This seemed like a reasonable solution, until one of his crew—a fellow who spoke no English—complained that Delbert McKenna had relieved himself out his bunkhouse window in the middle of the night, all over the Swede. This led to a shoving match between the Swede and Delbert before breakfast the next day.

The hot air also brought new creatures. Yellow-jackets, mosquitoes, ants, even an occasional bull snake that, while harmless, slithered threateningly enough to alarm even the most intrepid logger. But it was the gnats, the loggers called them "no-see-ums," that arrived in swarms, clogging the eyes and ear canals, zipping into the nose and threatening to swarm into the mouth when a logger got fed up enough to curse.

This led to home remedies. Petey Hulst and Myles Norgren rubbed talcum powder and lemon juice onto themselves. Valentine insisted on garlic juice. The Swedes mixed paprika—which they obtained from Zoe—with urine, which they manufactured themselves. This meant that the irritation in the camp was only made worse by the awful stench. This was compounded by the fact that several men—led by Bucky Rudman—wore extra shirts and sweaters during the summer so that the breeze would feel cool when they stripped them off at lunchtime or at the end of the day.

"Smells like a goddamn zoo in here," announced Bud Cole one morning in the mess hall. "I figure the only reason somebody's trying to do this outfit in is the pure stench of it all." This brought a surprising bit of laughter, especially among the Swedes.

"But I'm afraid you gentlemen need to hear a bit of an announcement about all of this." Bud cleared his throat, then introduced Zoe, who walked quickly up to the front of the mess hall, as the laughter disappeared. Her heels clicked loudly.

"This aroma, gentlemen, is no laughing matter." Zoe's voice was confident, her gaze stern. "It is uncivilized and un-gentlemanly to appear at table in such a state. Therefore, as of this afternoon, new rules will apply. No one will be served in this dining room until he has either bathed or, in some other capacity, removed inappropriate odors from himself or his attire."

A round of dull "ohhhs" filled the room, but she held up her hand, palm flat. "This is not a voting matter, I assure you. I have told Mr. Cole the following: Either this stench is removed from this dining hall, or this cook shall remove herself from this company permanently."

The room was silent. No "ohh's." No sliding chairs. Several men cast glances toward each other, but steadfastly avoided Zoe's gaze. Bud Cole stood against the door, looking at his boots, arms folded.

Zoe's ultimatum led to the altogether not unpleasant tradition—at least in Albert's view—of swims in the lake before supper. Since hoot-owl shift meant that the crew got back to camp by 3 p.m., there was plenty of time for a swim before supper went on the table at 5:30. If you had to take a bath, why not strip yourself completely?

Albert had never witnessed such a blizzard of naked skin in his life. Bachelder rigged a rope on a bent fir that hung over a deep section of the lake. After the crummy deposited the crew back in camp in the afternoon, most dropped lunch buckets, peeled off clothes as they ran, and finally exited most of their underwear by the time they neared the lake. Zoe recognized that this was a price to pay for cleanliness in the mess hall, so she purposely kept herself away from the north side of the mess hall until after supper.

Albert thought he actually detected spirits in the camp rise for several days following Zoe's announcement. He knew that this was, in part, due to relief. Zoe might be stern, but she created unbeliev-able food: sausages, torts, sauces, and buckets of ice cream—quality that most of the men had never experienced in their lives. And though few would actually admit it, most enjoyed looking at her. It was awfully nice to have a woman with soft skin, deep blue eyes, and still-golden hair amongst a crew of lugs, even if she was older than most of them.

Therefore, the fact that she was staying, in its own way, gave them cause to lift the dark mood, born of heat and anxiety and the uncer-tainty of who had it in for Skybillings.

❈    ❈    ❈

Even in the few weeks that Albert had worked on St. Bride's crew, the hillside immediately above the trestle had undergone a complete change—from the majestic stand of towering Douglas firs when he began with Nariff; then, to a jumble of fallen logs, cast haphazardly at awkward angles, waiting to be hauled to the spar tree; and now, finally, to broken slash and emptiness, punctuated by tall stumps, shredded limbs, and a thick mat of underbrush and oily dirt. The breeze carried a dryness that choked eyes and noses, made all the worse by the brown silt swept up from the furrows torn into the soil by the highline and choking bells.

On the hillside just above the trestle, most of the cold decks—the piles of logs that were ready to be hauled out—had already been loaded and shipped to the mills. But those at the higher elevations remained. So the crew had laid a long section of railroad track straight up the steep incline. From the bottom to the top, it stretched more than a hundred yards. Though the slope was much too steep for a locomotive to climb, the massive firs could be laid on top of a heavy rail flatcar, then inched slowly down the grade with the help of a steam-powered winch and thick cables.

Squat and heavy, the steam engine that drove the winch was called a "donkey." It sat squarely atop two large sections of log, and was positioned at the top end of the track. With a tall, central boiler that built up the steam, the donkey drove two large drums of cable, hanging like six-guns on either side. One was connected to the skyline rigging system on the spar tree just behind; the other to the flatcar under the fallen fir.

Max St. Bride sat at the levers that ran both.

❋   ❋   ❋

Albert had been watching two red-tail hawks lazily float above the slash, hunting for mice. But two toots from the steam whistle brought him back to the task at hand—guiding the logs onto the rail car and securing them with cables so St. Bride could then ease them down the incline. At the bottom, they would be attached to the Shay for the trip to the mill.

The toots signaled that Valentine's crew had finished hooking logs to the skyline at the far end of the clearing. Albert and the rest of the crew—Lightning Stevens, Myles Norgren, and Conrad Bruel—stood just to the side of the flatcar, waiting. St. Bride throttled the donkey, drawing the logs straight upward from the distant pile, bringing a whine from the cables; then, once the logs slowed their swinging, he began reeling them rapidly toward the spar tree, finally drawing them directly above the rail flatcar that stood in wait.

Albert and Conrad waited for them to stop swinging, then guided the front ends of the two logs onto the flatcar, while Lightning Stevens and Myles Norgren did the same at the other end. As the skyline released, the logs dropped with a crash that shook the ground. The men then began looping cables around the logs to keep them from shifting on the steep descent to the bottom of the slope.

Albert bent low and wiggled underneath the logs at the front of the flatcar. "Tighter," he shouted to Conrad. The sharp gravel between the tracks dug into his back, shreds of bark dangled in his face. Once again, he lay spread-eagled two feet below a ton of wood.

Conrad heaved his weight downward on the cable, loosening some slack, and whipping it underneath the logs. Albert grabbed the slack, tightened the clasp, and swiveled himself out from under the load—a crabwalk across the gravel and the rail.

The flatcar began to move slowly. The donkey revved harder and louder as the cables on the second drum now engaged the full weight of the flatcar and the logs. Albert hated the awful screeching: Whether it was the rails under the massive weight or the whine of the cable against the steam engine drum, or something in the engine itself, he was never sure. He plugged his ears, but it found its way in nonetheless.

"You're getting good at that, young man," shouted Myles Norgren, smiling through his thick beard.

"I hate it."

"Well, I guess that means you got a brain, too."

"Then why the hell did I take this job?"

Now Conrad's voice appeared, just above the sound of the whining cables and the rumble of heavy train wheels. "In the three years I been helping load these monsters onto flatcars, I never seen nobody squashed. Saw a few close calls. But never seen 'em ever drop on a man."

Albert watched the load inch down the incline. The scrub pine dotting the edge of the track bed bent low, then sprang back, as the two logs passed over them. From his angle, all he could see was the massive end-slices of the loaded firs—and the orange concentric rings that dripped goo in the white, noontime heat.

As Albert watched the load strain against the cables—the screeching now rising to a pitch—the thought hit him that it was time for him to quit. To walk out. To say thank you to Bud Cole, but tell him that the woods wasn't the right place for him. His mind wandered, and he lost concentration too often—way too much for woods work. And laying underneath tons of timber as it began to move down a hill wasn't a way to live long.

Besides, why would anyone whose father died in the woods, and whose only true friend on the Skybillings crew died under a Shay, be dumb enough to stay?

❅   ❅   ❅

By lunchtime, they had moved most of the remaining logs, with one jumbled cold deck pile left for the afternoon. They grabbed their lunch pails and scattered underneath a small stand of pine left by the fallers. Directly in front of them, the steam engine—its black boiler still bubbling, but its gears and cables now at rest—perched against a backdrop of three ridgelines wandering westward, white peaks in lenses of white clouds, against brilliant blue.

"Uglier than sin, ain't it?" said Lightning Stevens as he snapped a piece of celery and put the biggest piece in his mouth.

"What?" asked St. Bride.

"That donkey against those mountains. Just look at that scene, will ya?" Lightning smiled at St. Bride as he spoke. "I'll bet just the other side of that far ridge is Vancouver." The men all looked up from their food for a moment. "That ugly contraption spoils the view."

"Loggers don't look at views," said St. Bride.

"Hell they don't. At least as far as this one is concerned. Ain't there something in that scene that moves you, Max? You're sitting right on top of some of the tallest creatures God ever made." Lightning pointed toward the distant ridgelines. "They're like ripples in a big ocean. Waves of granite and ice. They got froze into place thousands of years ago."

Petey Hulst took up the conversation when no one responded. "You're from the Seakomish Tribe, aren't you Lightning?"

"Mmm-hunh." His mouth was full of sandwich.

"Then that's the direction your people arrived from—up north. Just beyond that far ridge." He pointed at the distant line of peaks, so far away that Albert thought they could just as easily have been a line of clouds. "They settled in the eastern part of British Columbia, the Frasier River. Lived there for hundreds of years. Legend has it that they then migrated through that opening there to the left."

All the men again looked into the distance. Most had trouble seeing past the steam engine. Conrad stood up and looked around it. "Where?"

Petey explained that the dip at the end of the ridgeline was a valley. That the Seakomish People had fished for generations in the rivers of British Columbia. But that the fish had mysteriously stopped for several years, forcing the Seakomish to begin a trek southward, working their way through the valley, then toward the coast, until they eventually settled in the Seakomish Valley.

"I guess I can see a little dip there, alright," said Conrad. He settled again with his sandwich, then let out a long belch. "The two mountains on both sides look like a woman's nipples."

The conversation fell away again, replaced by the sound of eating. Lightning tossed little balls of bread to several blue jays that swept down from the pines. The birds snapped up the bread, soared into the trees, and squawked loudly for more.

"You'll spoil the hell out of 'em," warned Myles Norgren.

Lightning laughed loudly. "We just tore the shit out of their home and a few balls of bread are going to spoil 'em?"

Norgren just shrugged. "It isn't natural for birds to eat bread, that's all. They should eat seeds and what not. Berries."

"A little late to worry about that, isn't it?" asked Lightning, but without waiting for an answer he turned back to Petey, whose eyes were now closed. He reclined on a patch of brown grass that hadn't been torn by the mainline. "Petey, I got a question."

"Then I got an answer." Petey's eyes remained closed.

"How do you know so much about Indians?"

Petey still didn't open his eyes, but adjusted himself sideways to find a softer patch of grass. "Studied 'em ."

"But why? Hell, I don't know anything about Indians. And I am one."

"I don't know nothing about Germans, and I'm one of those."

"But that still doesn't answer the question."

Petey opened his eyes finally, then stroked his black and gray mustache. "Probably just from walking these here hills. I did that for many a year, down in California, before that back East. In between, hopped the freights across the plains. Something about black nights, sitting in the grass along the Southern Pacific tracks, or wandering Vancouver Island with nothing but a bedroll."

Petey was sitting now—apparently finally interested in the question. "I don't know," he continued. "Something makes me wonder who was here before me. In most cases, it wasn't my people—or few of them. It was yours." Petey leaned back again. "So I decided to read."

Lightning Stevens now pointed to the far ridge. "And that's where my people lived 500 years ago?"

Petey nodded. "Five-hundred, a thousand—somewhere in that range."

"Never knew that. My father never said anything about it."

Petey shrugged.

"Fathers are shits," announced St. Bride suddenly. This brought snorts from most of the others, but no comments. "My old man left when I wasn't born yet."

Lightning ignored St. Bride. "Is that why you talk to the spirits, Petey—because of the Indians I mean?"

Petey shook his head. "That has nothing to do with the Indians. I talk to the spirits because they're there. Always knew that. Even as a little shaver. My mother told me my great granduncle visited regularly—and she was right. Every Saturday night. And her own father, and her two brothers—usually on Sundays or Fridays. Not until I was going to grade school did I learn that all of 'em had been dead for years."

This was the subject that Petey truly loved. The spirit world awakened him, brought out the brilliance in his leathery cheeks and intensity in his blue eyes. "So when I grew up, I talked to them myself."

"You ever talked to the spirits in this valley?" Lightning's tone hinted at greater interest.

"Once or twice." But Petey didn't say more.

"What do they say?"

Petey studied Lightning for a long time before answering. "They are just trying to understand."

Lightning did not answer.

"It's the devil," snorted St. Bride. "You're talking to the fucking devil, Petey Hulst. One of these days, one of those devil creatures will pick you up by their devil hands and fling you around the room like a rag doll, and you'll be nothing but red ooze all over the walls."

Conrad belched, drawing out the crackling sound for several seconds. Then he reclined, with his hands behind his head. "Why the hell does this subject keep coming up? If Petey wants to talk to the goddamn devil, then let him."

St. Bride now sat up fully. "Because it ain't right to talk to the devil. Man was born to talk to God. And besides, what the fuck does a snot-nosed kid like you know about heaven and hell anyway?"

Now Conrad sat up. "And what the hell does a foul old fart like you know about heaven and hell, St. Bride? When was the last time you was in church anyway?"

St. Bride stumbled. The question surprised him so much that, rather than being angry with Conrad, he struggled to remember.

"Don't worry about it, Max," said Myles Norgren. "It doesn't matter." St. Bride's face eased slightly, apparently comforted by the words. "There isn't any God anyway, so you don't have to worry."

St. Bride's eyes grew. "Goddamn it! There sure as hell is a God. I grew up with a God. My momma taught me about God and the disciples and the Israelites. So I don't have any doubt about any of it." He paused, as if reloading to take aim again at Norgren, but all that came out was: "There sure as hell is a God or my name ain't Maximillian St. Bride."

Norgren's eyebrows shot up. "Maximillian? Your name is Maximillian?" asked Norgren, whose smile exposed brilliant white teeth through black whiskers.

"Yeah. Why?"

"Pretty damn aristocratic name for a logger."

St. Bride studied Norgren closely, judging the derivation of the word. Since Norgren still had a smile on his face, St. Bride decided that the word couldn't be too bad and turned back to the original subject.

"Are you telling me, Norgren, that you don't believe in God at all?"

"That's what I'm telling you."

"So what do you believe in?"

Norgren scratched his beard as he thought about it. "Myself mostly. Those mountains Petey just pointed to. Rainbow trout. The dregs at the bottom of a keg of beer. And a good fuck when I get to town." Several of the men laughed. Lightning Stevens crossed himself.

Conrad finally found an opportunity. "Why doesn't this crew talk more about pussy than God and Indians, for Christ sake?"

But St. Bride continued. "I never heard such blasphemy in my life. You're sure as hell gonna rot in hell, Norgren."

"Ain't no hell neither, Max. No hell. No heaven. No God. No devil."

St. Bride belched. "I always figgered you for a smart Commie, Norgren. Thought you made some sense bitching and moaning about Hoover and those Wall Street buggers. But all this God-talk means you're going to burn in hell with Petey Hulst."

Norgren smiled as he stood up. "Did it ever occur to you, Max, that you share the same religious philosophy with John Valentine? Both Christian. Both God-fearing. Both quote scripture. That ever occur to you, Max?"

St. Bride didn't respond, his face still furled into an angry frown. Norgren gave up. For several minutes, no one spoke. The warm breeze of midday slid down the barren hillside in puffy waves. Petey Hulst was asleep. Lightning and Conrad seemed to be dozing as well. Norgren walked over to the steam engine and plopped onto one of the log runners. Though Bud Cole had forbidden smoking, he lit a cigarette, cupping the ash in his hand. Albert, once again, searched for the hawks, but in the middle of the hot day, even they had sought shelter.

"Still think that talking about pussy is a lot healthier for a logger," said Conrad softly, as if he was speaking to the wind.

※ ※ ※

Albert studied St. Bride as he operated the steam engine, jamming gears and levers, giving the drums more power. What could make a man so sour? Albert concluded that it probably had nothing to do with the job, but with the basic nature of the man. And did he actually understand that the others were making fun of him? Did he care?

"Look bright there," shouted Lightning, as two logs swung above the flatcar, narrowly missing Conrad's head. Conrad bent down calmly, then reached up with one hand to guide them gently over the front wheels. With the other arm held high in the air—in plenty of view so St. Bride could see it—he rotated his hand until the logs settled onto the car. Then he clenched his fist quickly, the sign that St. Bride could drop them.

Albert quickly crawled underneath the load, but the clasp wouldn't connect. He reset it. But again it wouldn't go.

"What's the problem?" shouted Conrad.

"Give me more slack."

Just as he had done earlier, Conrad whipped the cable upward across the logs, then pulled downward with the weight of his body, giving Albert another few inches of cable. With a straining upward motion, and both legs driving hard against the closest rail, Albert snapped the clasp. But before he could slip out from underneath the load, the massive wheels of the flatcar began turning. Albert's only option was to roll into a tight ball between the two tracks and let the massive load pass over him.

By the time he had gotten to his feet, the load was already moving down the steep incline. St. Bride shot him a wicked smile. "Better be faster next time, fella," shouted St. Bride. All Albert could feel was heat in his belly and pulsing in his eyes. Then he noticed that St. Bride was giving him the finger—but only in response to the narrow, middle finger that Albert himself now held high toward St. Bride. For what seemed an eternity, Albert held his finger in place, and only dropped it when St. Bride erupted in laughter.

Albert walked to his post behind the steam engine. St. Bride was now focused entirely on easing the loaded car down the steep hill. As Albert settled onto his stump, still breathing hard with anger, he had the dim sense that the screeching from the straining cables was growing louder. It echoed across the rock face of Three Sisters Ridge.

"You're learning," said Conrad.

"What do you mean?" asked Albert.

Before Conrad could answer, an explosion rocked the steam engine, shooting steam, oil, and flames in all directions. Albert lunged for the ground, slamming into Conrad as he landed. In an instant, flames ignited a broad circle of oil between them and the steam engine. St. Bride jumped from the machine just as another explosion tore apart the boiler.

Albert struggled to his feet as the ground around him erupted in flames. Within seconds, the fire jumped to the dry slash nearby and started swiftly up the hillside—in a direct line toward Three Sisters Ridge. He turned away, hands covering nose and eyes, trying to escape the expanding wall of smoke and fire. He vaulted two split firs, landed hard in deep slash, then pulled himself onto a stump to get his bearings. Up the hill—only flames, gray smoke, and now the sound of trees exploding from the intense heat. Downward, down the steep incline that once carried the logs, he could see men running toward him. Way at the bottom, the flatcar laid on its side, torn-up rail beneath it, and the massive firs splayed catty-whumpus against one another—all lying just short of the edge of the ravine.

"Look alive, everyone!" Albert turned to see Lightning Stevens standing on a stump perhaps fifty feet away, waving his arms.

Men were now arriving at the top of the incline, many running toward Lightning—others already beginning to pull apart the mat of twigs and broken limbs to create an opening between the flames and the ready source of new fuel. Others pried open large barrels of water that Bud Cole had directed be placed near all the steam engines, just for such emergencies.

"We need a fire line on the front side," shouted Lightning. "Across the whole face of the fire. We've gotta stop it from coming down on us. Petey—we need some help. Get the trestle crew up here."

Petey let out three staccato blasts from the steam whistle that echoed through the valley, bringing the thumping pile driver at the trestle to a stop.

"All the rest of you, go around the right side and start building a fire line alongside of this sucker—up and down the hill. All the slash needs to come out."

Albert jumped into the line of men tearing at the branches, underbrush, and broken stumps that lay between them and the blaze. He squinted tight against the stinging smoke and tried not to breathe. The men nearest the steam engine passed buckets along two lines from the large kegs, while several men rushed to a creek—far to the right of the flames—with a pump and hoses.

For more than an hour, they battled to establish a line that would hold. But every time they came close, an exploding log or a whirlwind of cinders and flame pushed them back. The wind continued to draw power from the deep ravine and, with its sudden gusts, drove waves of fire upward.

Albert could feel the pain in his lungs, his eyes stung and his skin felt raw. The hill above him danced in brilliant orange, its freight-train roar rumbling the ground. From the intense heat and sound, and direction of the wind, he knew what was next. The upper reaches of timber near Three Sisters Ridge would soon be consumed. Then, if the wind continued much longer, the fire would rage around the side of Three Sisters, then race full-throat down the other side and toward Thunder Lake and the Skybillings Camp.

"Get out, get out now!" It was the voice of Bud Cole. He was running behind the line of men at the face of the fire, cupping his hands to be heard. "It's gone. Head for the Shays and crummy. We've got to reach the camp before the fire does."

The message took a while to sink in. They were facing an inferno, fighting for their lives. And now, they were supposed to run? Had they heard him right? Men turned to each other with questioning expressions. But then the reality began sinking in, and a few men, then suddenly the entire line, started down the hill.

Heavy smoke swallowed them as they did. Where once there was just searing heat, dust, and cinders, was now a hard, black veil—suffocating, closing-in tight, shutting out everything beyond just a few inches.

Though men were running past him, they were only splotches of movement to Albert's burning eyes. He felt lead at his feet as he stutter-stepped down the steep incline, trying to avoid the deep holes from ripped-out stumps.

Was he running for his life? Was that it? Or was he running to help save the camp? Somewhere inside his labored breathing, inside the heavy fatigue and ache in his legs, was the growing awareness that he could die here. Not at some unknown, far-off time in the future, but on this hill, from this inferno. The explosion, the fire, the chaos of trying to battle the flames had closed out all thought. Now his brain was catching up.

He sidestepped two deep holes, then leapt several cables still attached to the up-ended roots of a large stump. He landed on both feet, but the momentum and the steep slope sent him stumbling forward in a somersault that stuck him legs-down in a deep tangle of slash. He kicked at the brush and vines and twigs, but he couldn't kick and cough at the same time. So the painful coughing left him in a ball, digging his fingernails into the slash for a hold.

Albert couldn't see through the smoke. He couldn't hear himself shout against the roar. And the vines and underbrush held him tight.

He pulled his jack knife from his pocket. Because he couldn't see, he focused his attention on opening the blade slowly, then inching it along his leg until it slid underneath each vine. After several tries, his legs were able to move, giving them enough momentum to kick freely. Within a few seconds, Albert was able to gain his footing and leap out of the hole.

What he found shocked him. Half the crew now stood in several groups further down the slope, looking in his direction. Bud Cole, Harry Bachelder, Myles Norgren, and Little Boy were closest to him, their faces blackened by smoke, and etched by long white lines of sweat and tears that had erased the blackness. For a moment, he thought they were staring at him.

But then Albert realized they were looking past him, up the hillside. When he turned around, he saw why: The fire now burned only about halfway up the hill. The ground between them and the fire—though heavily blackened and smoldering—showed no sign of flames. Even the fire further up seemed to have lost its energy. It had obviously gotten close to the top of the mountain, but then—was it wind, was it something else?—had driven it back downward upon itself. And with all the available fuel already consumed, it was burning itself out.

He turned back to the men, and noticed that the wind had stopped. "It's stopped itself," said Valentine loudly. "It stopped itself. By the grace of God. Praise the Lord!"

"Praise our goddamn good luck," said Bud quietly.

Albert's breath still came hard, his eyes burned as he took in the scene. Within the course of two hours, an explosion, then a firestorm that raged through the stand above them, then—with no real interference from the men themselves—just a small burn that even Albert recognized as no threat.

For many minutes, the men stood motionless, surveying the scene. The only sound was the occasional crash of a tree or stump that collapsed into itself—the sound of an ending, not a new threat. The faces stared at the charred and blackened hillside, as a hundred ribbons of smoke curled lazily into the deep-gray shroud that covered the peaks.


## Chapter 19

Sammons knew he couldn't afford her. She charged $20 a night. Usually worked the Savoy in Seattle. Or the Karlston out in Ballard. But whenever he got to Seattle, he scraped together the money.

Now he watched her dress. Yellow curls hung halfway down her back. Then a sweep of white skin, and legs that tapered down to black high heels. He made her wear them when they had sex. The thought of her heels pointed at the ceiling made him hard again, but he knew that he didn't have any more time. Plus, it was morning. She'd probably demand another $20, which he didn't have.

"So how does a union man compare?" asked Sammons as he finished the last half bottle of beer from the night before.

"Compare to what?" she asked. She smiled as she let a soft yellow dress slip over her head. When it settled, she flung her hair forward, working a thick brush through it.

"C'mon, Carla. Everybody knows that you got half the businessmen in Seattle by the balls. I want to know if a businessman can fuck half as good as a union boy."

"What difference does it make?" She slipped a garter belt underneath the dress, hitched it up to her waist, then let the hem slip back over her knees. She took a cigarette from her purse and lit it absently, blowing a jet of smoke directly upward. "You really want to know?"

"I wouldn't have asked otherwise."

"Union men grunt more."

Sammons burst into laughter.

"I'm serious. I can tell when they're ready to let go because they start grunting, like pigs. Businessmen are quieter—and can usually hold it longer."

Sammons studied her face closely, as if trying to judge the answer. But she turned away quickly and began painting her lips with a tube of pink lipstick. "And union boys talk more."

Sammons knew that he would be late, but the conversation was interesting. It had never come up before. Not in the—what was it?—ten or twelve times he'd paid for her services. Sammons decided that Fitzgerald could wait. Besides, the fucking hobos and drifters weren't going anywhere.

"You mean, when we're screwing, right?"

"No, after. Most men can't screw and talk at the same time. Not big enough brains." She smiled sweetly as she smacked her lips to test the lipstick. "I mean after. After you're done. That's when union men want to talk things out. You know, tell me about the other women. Tell me about their wives. Tell me how they wanted to fuck their sisters."

Sammons was not a modest man, but the last comment made him draw in his breath. He waited for more, but that was it. Carla took a quick look in the mirror and bent down toward him, planting a soft peck on his forehead. "Of course, you do know, don't you, that you're the only union man I've ever let do me?"

She smiled as she drew on the cigarette, but he didn't seem to notice.

He had walked to the window and opened the shade, a burst of brilliant sunshine flooding the room. He looked down at the docks, at the ships moving gently against their moorings, then further south, to the camp of shanties and shacks nestled along the south edge of the port. "Later on, you'll be glad that you bedded Billy Sammons, Carla," said Sammons absently. "You'll be damn glad. Cause those scum businessmen who are screwing you are going to understand, some-day soon, that it's the union boys who are in the driver's seat."

Carla studied Sammons—his thick hands and face, his stomach that hung low. He stood in his shorts, without socks. But she didn't speak. She simply watched his silhouette against the sun.

"I'll tell you, Carla." Sammons now stretched, then grabbed his pants from the chair. "When we are done organizing the woods, then we're gonna work with the boys down there on the docks." He pointed toward the window. "We can close down this port in two hours. And those businessmen can't do a thing—other than what we want. This whole picture'll be different within a year or two."

Carla laughed.

"What?"

"The talk never changes. Only the details."

"What do you mean?"

Carla checked herself in the mirror again and adjusted a clip above her ear. "Whether it's closing the port or closing the logging compa-nies. Whether it's strangling the longshoremen's union or stopping the CIO— you're all the same." She paused now and looked at him directly. "I sort of thought that once a man got rid of his load that he could think straight. You know, he'd feel more relaxed; it'd help keep his senses straight and what not. But the more I do this job, the more I come to the conclusion that a man's brain stays harder a lot longer than his dick."

Sammons studied her—the blond hair, the lipstick, now the smile. For a moment, he felt like hitting her, like ripping the sweet smile off her face, and maybe forcing her to do him again, without paying. But then he began to laugh. This was what he liked about Carla. This was what made him keep coming back.

❄    ❄    ❄

Perry Ostrand was the mayor. You always did business with the mayor when you did business in the shanty city at the south end of the Seattle docks. Hooverville by name.

Sammons hurried to the largest shack, at the end of the last pier at the far end. Several blasts from a tugboat made him jump. The warmth of the sun cooked a pile of garbage that ran along the edge. Sammons knocked on the door, but saw Fitzgerald already sitting inside.

"Where the hell you been?" asked Fitzgerald, his Irish accent thicker than usual.

"Had business."

"Had to get himself a high-priced fuck," said Fitzgerald derisively to Perry, who laughed heartily.

"Good for my complexion." Sammons held out his hand to Ostrand, who crushed it as he shook.

"I haven't seen the Seakomish CIO boys for a while," said Perry with a thunderous laugh. Sammons noted that Perry was so fat that his belly actually jiggled when he laughed. A pinpoint goatee split his jowls.

"How the hell does somebody get as fat as you, Perry, living in a hellhole like this?" asked Fitzgerald.

"Hellhole?" Perry stood up suddenly, pointing at a picture that was taped to a tin wall. "We got, here, a picture of the State Capitol. I got myself a radio. I even got a new icebox." Ostrand shuffled to the icebox and pulled out a thick steak. "Got this the other night by trading cigarettes to one of the cooks at the Savoy. So my question to you boys is this: Who's better off, me or you?" Perry laughed again violently—a happy, bubbling laugh, which made Sammons and Fitzgerald smile.

Nobody elected Perry. He simply gave himself the job. In a "city" of three or four thousand, somebody ought to do it, said Perry. Keep some order. Make sure somebody is there to make decisions. Most of the residents of Hooverville—drifters, hobos, unemployed sailors, even a few families—along the south side of Seattle's docks welcomed his presence. As the Depression deepened in the early '30s and more people lost homes and jobs, the shanties on the south end grew. As did the confusion and disorder. Claims of thievery arose among the inhabitants; someone had to decide who would get the best spots for their shanties. And Perry became that person.

"So why are you two here?" asked Perry lightly. "Social call, perhaps? Come down to see old Perry Ostrand to make sure he's well and alive?"

Sammons spit tobacco juice onto the floor. "Wipe that up," hissed Perry in an instant, catching Sammons off-guard.

"What?"

"Did you spit on the floor of the Savoy when you had your high-priced whore?"

"No, but..."

Fitzgerald looked coldly at Sammons, who quickly pulled out a dirty hanky and wiped up the brown goo. "Sorry."

Perry's face immediately lightened. The broad smile returned. Sammons decided that Perry looked like childish drawings of the sun—full smile, turned up brightly at each end, bracketed by two orbs for cheeks.

"We're here to do some recruiting," said Fitzgerald. "A few high-quality personnel. Experienced in union matters. Maybe law enforcement. Security." He paused. "Heavy lifting."

Perry chuckled. "Men who can break some heads, in other words. Mind if I ask where these boys will be working, exactly?"

"As a matter of fact, we do mind, Perry," Sammons broke in. "Not meaning any disrespect, of course. We just want you to handle the resume gathering, if you will, and we'll take it from there."

Perry leaned back in his chair and took in the towering buildings just above him on the Seattle skyline. The breakfast fires in the shanties were now just diminishing, as men and women settled in front of their tin and cardboard shacks. "Once upon a time, I fashioned myself as an accountant," said Perry. He smiled quickly as he turned back to Fitzgerald and Sammons. "Ran the tightest set of books that the University of California ever saw. Nothing slipped through Perry's green eye shade."

Sammons and Fitzgerald waited for Perry to continue. But he stopped and stared absently out the window.

"I want tough men, Perry," said Sammons quickly. "Men who can handle themselves and, preferably, men who'll keep their mouths shut."

Perry nodded. "Thugs—I understand. You don't need to paint a picture. The only questions that count are when and how much."

"We'll pay 'em three bucks a day, plus food and keep."

"I didn't mean them. I meant me."

"Your usual, I figured."

Perry now laughed heartily. "If you've got ugly work in mind, Sammons, then old Perry's got to find some ugly workers. That takes time, that takes energy..."

"So how much?"

"Double."

Sammons felt like spitting again on the floor, but he caught Fitzgerald's glance and he drew in a deep breath. "Fine. We'll pay you when you've got 'em together."

Sammons was excited. He could see just what they needed to do. Keep the men ready for action by putting them to work at one of the CIO shows in the Seakomish Valley. That would keep them close to town, close to rail lines. As soon as Clare Ristall gave him the signal, Sammons could have the men on the move.

Sammons kept going over the details, but Fitzgerald didn't seem to hear. He was elbow deep in crabmeat and butter. He shielded his face from the sun occasionally, as Sammons spoke, but quickly returned to his lunch. "Why don't you eat your crab, Sammons? A man don't get crab but once in a blue moon. We can talk details once Perry's got our men."

The crab was Fitzgerald's idea. He said that if Sammons got to have a high-priced fuck every time he got to Seattle, he—Fitzgerald—deserved steamed crab, with butter, on the docks, in the sunshine. As soon as they'd left Perry's, they'd found their way past hundreds of shanties and what seemed like hundreds of men who asked about work, and found an outdoor eatery on a dock between two freighters. The pots shot steam upward every time the owner dug out another crab.

"I don't understand you, Seamus," said Sammons suddenly.

"What's there not to understand?"

Sammons let out a long breath. "This is like a goddamn business to you."

Fitzgerald stopped eating for a moment and wiped his mouth on his sleeve. Was he fifty, thought Sammons? Maybe older? Something in the white hair, in the freckles still across the narrow nose, reminded him of his older brother, long dead in the War. But Fitzgerald's voice was what set him apart—not just the Irish accent, which was deep and rolled heavily, but the high-pitched tone and the quick way of speaking. Everything came out fast. "It sure the hell is a business, Sammons. That's why a man needs to use his brains and his senses." With this, Fitzgerald tapped a buttery finger to his temple and went back to his crab.

Sammons sighed. He decided there was no talking any sense to Fitzgerald until he was done eating. So Sammons turned to the crab on his plate, smashing the body with a small wooden mallet. He didn't like crab because it was hard to eat. Crack a claw and you'd get a taste. But the rest, hell, a man could starve. Voices from the ships on either side of the pier drifted down, mingling with the traffic noise and the frequent screeches from tugs and passing ships. The air was all creosote and garbage. For perhaps fifteen minutes, the two men ate silently.

"How long you reckon before we put our new men to work?" asked Fitzgerald after he finished his crab.

Sammons mouth was full so he just shook his head.

"I figure between a couple of weeks and a month," continued Fitzgerald, now picking his teeth with a tiny piece of crab claw. "Just enough time to get our men in place, let them get used to the woods a little. That's when I figure the strike hits."

Sammons listened without speaking, then spent several minutes finishing the crab. When he wiped his hands on his pants, he slid the bench back from the table and peered closely at Fitzgerald. "Can I ask you a question, confidentially?"

Fitzgerald shrugged. "Sure. What's the big secret?"

"No secret. Just wanted this between you and me."

"Promise on the grave of my dead mother in Dublin."

Sammons spat onto the pier. "You figure we'll ever use these men?"

"Depends on whether the owners see things our way. If they do..."

"No, no, that's not it. I didn't mean it that way. I meant more general." Sammons seemed lost for words. "What I'm saying, I guess, is that I'm not so sure Clare Ristall has what it takes to finish this job." Sammons stared at Fitzgerald without moving, waiting. But Fitzgerald continued to pick at his teeth.

"So I guess that's the confidential part, right?" Fitzgerald now smiled broadly. "You're wondering whether our leader has what it takes to be a leader. And you don't want me betraying you?"

Sammons laughed and spit over the pier, but ignored Fitzgerald's comment. "Here's my thinking. You and me understand the working-man. We are workingmen. We're not part of this city life, like Clare—with his funny furniture and all those crazy paintings he collects. The only way we're gonna get the CIO to the place it needs to be in the woods is to put that goon squad that Perry is drumming up to work as soon as possible. And then probably get two or three more."

Fitzgerald cut him off. "For the love of Christ, man, why the hell do you think we're down here?"

"Sure, we're getting one squad put together. But we need more. And faster. But I'm not sure Clare's got the backbone to do what it takes, to actually use 'em." Sammons paused, as if refocusing the thought. "I'm not sure Clare has what it takes to lead CIO loggers in Seakomish," he added quickly.

Fitzgerald whistled, then looked off in the distance without speaking. Finally, he said, "So that's why you want this conversation to remain confidential. Would you be talkin' about insurrection, me boy?"

Sammons studied the face, then the big smile that broke across it. He suddenly laughed along with Fitzgerald. "No, I'm not talking insurrection, but I am saying that Clare has got some soft spots that don't make me comfortable. He's got too many other things that are important to him, too many other interests—and I'm not sure I know 'em all. I got a gut sense that we should begin doing things our way. Stop worrying about what high society thinks."

Fitzgerald studied Sammons for a long time, then got up from the bench. He tossed the crab shell into the water. "I got two answers, Sammons. The first is: I don't much trust anyone in these woods—or on these docks, for that matter—but myself. So the fact that I don't know what's going on in Clare Ristall's mind don't set him apart from anybody else I do business with—including you." Fitzgerald smiled, but Sammons' face did not move.

"Second, as long as Clare Ristall is running this operation, we can count on one thing—money. Money to hire thugs. Money to pay loggers who go on strike. Money to"—he pointed to the floating shells—"to eat crab and get a good fuck when we come to Seattle. This union needs one hell of a lot more of that money, before we start talking about"— Fitzgerald paused—"the order of succession, shall we say?"

The sun now stood directly overhead. Sammons felt the perspiration on his forehead and wished he'd not said anything. But then Fitzgerald leaned close. "But when we've got all the money we need, me boy, we definitely do need to talk about succession." Fitzgerald smiled.

Sammons nodded as Fitzgerald slapped him on the back.


## Chapter 20

The water rushed across flat boulders, then shot outward—a crescent of white plumes, suddenly set free. It slammed into Thunder Lake, twenty feet below, with the rapid-fire explosions of a string of Fourth-of-July firecrackers. Bucky Rudman and John Valentine ignored it, as well as the cold rushing water they stood in, as they pulled in unison on the end of a metal pipe. Delbert McKenna, who stood at the bottom of a slope that tilted gently toward the lake, shoved hard on the other end. But a thick stand of huckleberry had snared it, keeping the pipe from moving either direction.

"Why the hell does Zoe need fresh water piped into the kitchen, anyway?" complained Bucky Rudman. His fingers were slightly blue.

"She says I don't fetch it fast enough with a bucket, that's why," shouted Delbert, above the sound of the rushing water. Delbert was angry. Exasperated. They had laid the water pipe all the way from Zoe's kitchen—threaded it through an opening behind the sink, then settled it across a hundred feet of low brush, then pulled it up next to the creek itself. But not one step of the project was completed without Bucky griping, which made Delbert mad.

"Why the hell can't you just do the job that's gotta get done and shaddap your ugly mouth?" shouted Delbert finally.

Bucky dropped his end of the pipe, standing up fully, as if he were ready to pounce on Delbert. "If you wasn't such an ugly old bastard, Delbert, I'd come on down there and smack the daylights out of you," shouted Bucky.

John Valentine let loose a shrill whistle that stopped them both. "Will the two of you stop snorting at each other and try to get this job done?" Valentine had picked up the end of the pipe that Bucky had just dropped. "I figure if one of us hacks out that huckleberry stand there, this pipe will come right up here real nice. We can put the end in that pool there, put in a few spikes, and we can be done with all this foolishness."

Fresh water had always been plentiful at the Skybillings Camp. Thunder Lake, which lay directly in front of the camp, was clear and brilliant blue. The steep rise behind the camp produced numerous creeks and waterfalls. And Ashford & Southern—for some unknown reason—had even sunk a well. All produced water.

The only problem was that Delbert McKenna struggled with the water buckets, which meant that Zoe had to enlist the help of several of the crew members to bring in enough water to prepare the meals and wash the dishes. Harry Bachelder, who some thought was growing sweeter on Zoe by the day, had suggested an easier method: Why not run a pipe from the closest stream directly into the kitchen? It could be set on small wooden platforms and would run by gravity. When Zoe needed water, all she had to do was turn a spigot that would divert the water flow into the kitchen sink. When she was done, she could close it, and the water would once again run directly into the lake.

Harry had worked several evenings sorting through just where the pipe should run. But the actual work of putting the water line in place had fallen to Bucky Rudman and John Valentine through a coincidence of conversation. They had shown too much interest in the project. So Zoe simply asked them to do the work. Neither one had the courage to say no.

Valentine sent Delbert off to find a machete to hack away the huckleberry bushes, leaving him and Bucky with time on their hands.

"How far you think that fire would have gone if the wind hadn't shifted," asked Bucky, as Delbert headed for the tool shed. Both settled on rocks near the rushing water.

"My guess is that it would've come all the way over that ridge there," said Valentine, tilting a thumb over his shoulder. "After that, who knows? Most likely would've come straight down to the lake. And everything around here would have been gone."

Bucky smiled a happy smile. "Now didn't I predict just that very thing at breakfast a while back, John? I said a good burn could whoosh right down here and suck all the oxygen right off that lake."

"You do know that we all could be dead right now if that thing had taken off, don't you? It could've wiped out all of us—all of Skybillings. And it could've turned into a burn that took ten or twenty thousand acres of timber. How can you turn everything into some kind of joke?"

Bucky noticed Delbert now walking toward them with the machete. "Well, John, there's two kinds of people in this world," said Bucky, standing up when he heard Delbert hacking at the huckleberry. "The kind that figure hell is ready to swallow 'em up 'round every corner—so they worry about it and yammer about it and cause all kinda commotion. And then there's the type that say, 'Hell will get to us when it pleases, and there ain't a damn thing I can do about it. So I'm gonna just enjoy the ride.'"

"Can you answer a serious question, Rudman?" Valentine's large head was turned at an angle to suggest that he didn't want Delbert to hear.

"I'm a serious person, John. You know that. I treat all issues with the seriousness they deserve."

Valentine looked at Bucky as if he'd had enough and was about to walk away. But he continued.

"Do you think there is any chance that the donkey explosion was sabotage?"

Bucky didn't answer. He studied Valentine as if trying to decide whether the question was serious or Valentine was now trying to reel Bucky into some kind of trick question.

When he didn't speak, Valentine continued. "Think about it— St. Bride has been running donkeys for thirty years. He knew how to ease that load down the hill. There is no reason that thing should've blown."

Bucky scratched his beard, then looked at Valentine. "How about we send Albert up there to see if he can find another filed spike?" He paused. Valentine stared at him without expression. "John, I have heard some dumb ideas in my life, but this may be the dumbest. People around here have sabotage on the brain. How old was that damn cable holding the logs? Probably fifty years old. And St. Bride only has half a brain, to boot. This is no more a case of sabotage..."

Valentine interrupted. "Rudman, men are talking. You've heard it too." He lowered his voice, with Delbert just down the incline. "Some are asking questions about your helper—where he came from, you know? He behaves in an odd kinda way, sometimes. Don't get me wrong, I am not accusing him. I'm just saying."

Bucky's face was flat, his mouth set. "You can tell those guys who say that, John, that Little Boy Whittaker is no traitor, and that I personally will vouch for him, and that if anyone touches a hair on his head, I will personally slice off the balls of the bastard..."

A piercing howl from Delbert cut him short. Delbert stood in the middle of the thicket of huckleberry bushes, his back to Bucky and Valentine, a machete in his right hand. Bucky could see blood dripping from the branches laying near his feet. "He must have hacked a leg."

But when Bucky and Valentine got to him, they saw the true cause of his howling: Two small animals lay at the bottom of the last bush, their bodies covered in blood. The heads were missing from both.

"Holy Christ, what's that?" asked Bucky, as Delbert sobbed and shook.

"I found 'em. They was just laying there like that."

Valentine picked one up. As he did, blood oozed from the body cavity. The animal's long tail hung straight between the hind legs, hardened from the dried blood, but now dripping fresh as well.

"Cats," said Valentine. "Didn't Zoe say they had been missing? I figure that one of the coyotes got to 'em." Zoe kept two cats—a white one named Oscar and a calico named Spark.

He picked up the other cat as well and held it toward Bucky, who now patted Delbert's back. "It's okay Delbert. Just some coyotes."

But Delbert continued to sob. His voice burbled through the tears. "No coyotes. Look at where the heads were. No coyote does that."

The two men studied the carcasses more closely. Something had not just torn the heads off, but had scooped down deep into the carcass—as if a small sharp shovel had dug the heads out.

Valentine whistled softly. "Look here, fellas. You can see the finger marks where somebody held the poor critter just before he scooped the head off. Must've used a spade or some kinda claw-type tool."

For the next hour, the three men worked silently. Delbert finally controlled himself enough to hack away the final mound of huckle-berry, while Valentine and Bucky shoved the pipe into place and covered it with dirt. Bucky placed the opening in a deep pool, just above where the stream shot outward into Thunder Lake.

"Pretty soon, Zoe'll want flush toilets," said Bucky, as he placed the pipe in the pool. He laughed loudly, but neither Delbert nor Valentine responded.

❀ ❀ ❀

The three men agreed to keep the matter quiet until they could meet with Bud Cole, who had gone to Seakomish for supplies. Delbert went about helping Zoe prepare supper, while Valentine and Bucky made the final adjustments on the water-pipe fitting where it entered the wall of the kitchen.

"Gentlemen, may I speak with you?" Zoe appeared at the door of the kitchen, wiping her hands on her apron. Valentine and Bucky both caught the stern tone in the voice. When they looked up, they could tell that Delbert hadn't been able to keep the secret.

"Delbert tells me that you found my cats," she said softly.

"That's right, we did," said Bucky. "But we had planned to wait until Bud Cole was available before we said anything."

Zoe nodded, considering this for a moment, as Delbert came around the corner of the building carrying an armload of firewood.

"Goddamn it, Delbert, can't you keep a secret?" snapped Bucky.

"Sorry. It upset me so bad that I had to tell somebody." Delbert's jowls waggled when he was upset. Now they seemed to dance.

Harry Bachelder and Conrad Bruel suddenly appeared, both still wiping themselves dry with towels. Several others followed.

"So how many more did you tell, Delbert?" asked Bucky sharply.

"Gentlemen, just get the facts out—and dispense with chastising Delbert," said Zoe sharply. "I want to understand exactly what is going on here."

Valentine looked at Bucky, who shrugged, so Valentine described how they found the cats in the bushes near the end of the water line. He explained how Delbert came upon them as he slashed the huckleberry bushes.

As Valentine told the story, more men gathered. Several carried towels and soap; others had already taken their swim and were ready for supper. But preparations for supper had ceased. Zoe stood at the bottom of the steps to the porch, arms crossed, as the sun fell further behind Crescent Peak. For the first time in days, the evening air carried a hint of coolness.

"So was it a man or an animal that did it?" asked Zoe.

Neither Valentine nor Bucky answered. They looked at one another, then at Delbert, before Valentine finally spoke. "Could've been a cougar. Or maybe a coyote." The word cougar brought uncomfortable looks around the group.

"This close to camp?" asked a bucker named Parsons. He was one of the new hires that Bud Cole had brought to camp when work began on the trestle.

"Cougars come down this close sometimes," said Valentine, "when they're hungry. Coulda been the weather. Down here for the fish or the water."

This brought silence. Zoe hadn't changed her posture. "So you're saying then that the animals were eaten by a cougar?"

"Not that they were eaten. Just that their heads were missing." Valentine spoke the words slowly.

"Why wouldn't a cougar eat all of them? Why would it leave the carcass?" asked Parsons, who stepped to the front of the group and stood near Zoe.

Valentine didn't speak. He cast a quick glance at Bucky.

"Well, it might have been that they weren't hungry enough, so they weren't interested in the whole thing." Bucky's voice crept up slightly in pitch.

"I'd suggest we organize a shoot," said Parsons, looking around the group. "I've seen cougars that'll go after a man when they get hungry enough. Saw one come right through a wood door once."

The faces seemed uncertain, though this suggestion brought flickers of movement in some.

"I've got a shotgun," said a man with thick stubble—one of Valentine's choking crew. "We can start tonight."

"Just relax a minute," insisted Valentine. "You're going off half-cocked. You're ready to start some kind of cougar hunt, and you don't have a dang clue whether this was a cougar or not." Valentine's face was flushed. His large hands jammed the air at Parsons and the man with the stubble.

"It weren't no cougar." Delbert's voice was soft. "It was a man who done it. You could see just by looking at 'em."

Valentine and Bucky looked at the group as these words came out, but remained silent. Parsons' face turned into a scowl, while the man with the stubble spat onto the ground. "I'll use my shotgun alright, but I won't be hunting any cougar," he snorted.

Bucky sighed, then turned to Zoe. "Let me explain this to get everybody calmed down, Ma'am."

"I wish you had done so from the start." Her arms were still folded, but now she seemed angry.

As he began the explanation, the group grew larger. Men came to the mess hall expecting supper but found, instead, the gathering on the porch—men now scattered on rocks, leaning against the deck railing, some squatting in the dirt to hear all the details. When Bucky got to the point about how the heads had been taken off, several in the group gasped.

"Why do you think anyone would do something like this?" asked Zoe.

Bucky shrugged. "Maybe they wanted to scare the hell out of us. Leave us a little warning sign."

Zoe's forehead furrowed. "But you said the carcasses were found under one of the huckleberry bushes way off in the distance."

"That's right."

"But if they wanted to scare us, why wouldn't they leave them in a place where we would be sure to find them? Why would they ever think we would find them way over there?"

Valentine kicked the dust, before he spoke. "Well, I suppose one explanation, Ma'am, would be that they knew we'd be digging over there in that spot. What I mean is, they might have purposely put those butchered animals over there because they knew that's where we would be putting the water line. And they knew that by leaving them there that we'd discover 'em eventually. Maybe they thought it would scare us more."

Zoe frowned. "You're saying that..."

"I'm saying that maybe they put the critters over there because they knew we were going to build that line."

"I understand that Mr. Valentine," snapped Zoe. "But how would they know that? How would they even know we were going to put in a water line at all?"

Low conversation passed through the group, accompanied by the sound of muffled curse words; then Parsons' booming voice again. "I think what he's saying, Ma'am, is that they'd know where that water line was going to be put in if somebody in this outfit told 'em." Parsons now turned to the group. "Or, for that matter, if somebody in this outfit actually did it."

This brought silence as the men sorted through what was being said and what it meant.

"What in hell?" shouted a muscular Swede who had been kneeling in the front. "You mean we got a fuckin' traitor on this crew? Somebody who did this on purpose?"

The man turned to the broader circle—his arms rising slowly as if he were going to slam fists into the whole group. "Who? Who did this? Which one of you bastards is a traitor?"

But Conrad Bruel now stepped forward and turned to the group. "This is just like the Shay. See? The same person who filed that spike is the same person who killed these critters." Then he paused. "Or he's the one who told somebody on the outside—and then they did it. It's all the same."

His face twisted into a sneer. "So which of you guys knew where that water line was going to go? Time to 'fess up."

The eyes of the men around the group switched quickly from Conrad, to Bucky and Valentine, then around the circle. The only sound was a breeze wafting off the lake.

"Yeah, which of you guys knew where it was going to go?" asked Parsons with growing strength in his voice. "If we know that, we know who's behind this."

The voices of the group rose again, as the men broke into individual conversations. Heads shook violently, saying they hadn't known.

Several suggested that they form a posse. "The point is to start as soon as we can," said Parsons. "We need to start combing the woods. Whoever did it could still be nearby."

Zoe's voice broke across the group like thunder. "This is nothing but idle speculation, gentlemen," she said. "Can you hear yourselves speak? Do you know what you are saying?" She paused slightly, as the voices stopped.

"You have turned into something that is sounding perilously close to a lynching mob. In the course of five minutes, you have shifted from organizing a party to hunt cougar, to a posse to hunt killers, to a mob to find a traitor amongst yourselves."

Some of the men toward the back spoke quietly, but otherwise the crew turned silent.

"Did it ever occur to you that you are doing exactly what this person—or persons or thing or whatever —wants you to do? You're turning against one another, with no facts and no details, just fear and anger and rage."

She paused again, as if she had more to say. But her speech was finished. She swept through the circle and stepped onto the porch. "Delbert, it is time to go to work. Supper is later than it should be already."


## Chapter 21

Bud Cole hated the plan, but he knew he couldn't avoid it. The pressure from Witstrop was too intense. Witstrop had again sent his man Bolt to Seakomish to get an update on progress. But it wasn't really an update he wanted. Witstrop sent him to give Skybillings another kick in the ass—to get going faster.

Bud knew that he had little choice: The trestle had to go up faster. Which only left one option. Skybillings would have to start building the trestle from the far side of the ravine as well. Bud knew he couldn't just add more workers to the section already under construction because there was only so much room for men and equipment.

So the plan was simple. Send a crew down the ravine and up the other side. Cut a trail to move equipment. Rig a spar tree on the opposite edge. And start taking down firs to begin building the trestle from the far side as well. Bud knew the dangers and difficulties—more men, more supplies, more money, but it would give them a chance to meet Witstrop's expectations.

Bucky Rudman groaned loudly about the assignment when Bud told him, but Bud also knew that Bucky relished being the center of attention.

"You want me to hike down that god-forsaken, overgrown, straight-up-and-down, mother-fuckin' ravine and then back up the other side—and I am supposed to set up a spar after that?" asked Bucky when Bud broke him the news after dinner one night. Bud had decided the heavy rains were likely over for the summer, so this was the time to start.

"That is what I would like, yes," Bud answered.

Bucky spent a moment thinking about it, before taking a forkful of pie that Zoe had just put on the table. "I'll need some mules to help me haul all that heavy shit down."

"Men we have. Mules we don't."

"Okay. I'll take at least twelve. That's the number Jesus Christ needed to help him. So that's good enough for me."

"I'll see what I can do," said Bud.

"You ever been down there—in that ravine?" asked Bucky, suddenly looking concerned.

"Walked around a bit, sure. An old miner's trail runs down this side and crosses a couple of streams. Then up the other side—though it's a little steep." Bud paused. "Bucky, if I didn't know better, I'd say that you look a little worried."

Bucky chewed quickly. He'd finished one piece, and was now starting the second. For a reason that Bud couldn't comprehend, Bucky didn't eat the pie from the point, but from the crust-end inward. "Well, Christ, you know all those damn stories. Maybe that old buzzard Olaf Carn lives down there and is waiting for us with a shotgun and a stick of dynamite. You never know."

Bud didn't know if Bucky was serious or was playing to the crowd. The rest of the men at the table listened.

"Like I said, there is a trail," answered Bud. "You get Little Boy and two others to help you pack gear. And you leave tomorrow at first light. I need a spar up in no less than one week."

Now there was no mistaking Bucky's intent. He stood up and stared at Bud, then spoke in a low voice. "One week?"

"You heard me." Bud returned the glare.

"You may just be the crazy son of a bitch they say you are down-town," said Bucky. "There won't even be enough cable on the far coast of that ravine within a week from now—much less a spar. A man can't make the impossible happen, Mr. Cole."

❊    ❊    ❊

Albert wasn't sure if it had gotten cooler. Some said it had.

All he knew was that it still felt hot. The wool socks inside his boots itched so bad that he wanted to rake his fingernails across his ankles until they bled. Streams of sweat dribbled between his shoulder blades, soaking his denim shirt. When he wasn't mopping sweat from his forehead, he swung wildly at the gnats that dove for his eyes. A forty-pound coil of cable rode on one shoulder, a wooden pulley dug into the other.

But the heat didn't make any difference to Little Boy Whittaker. Nor did the itching or the sweat or the weight of the load. Little Boy's pace down the ravine still didn't slow, except for occasional stops for water from the trickles that ran nearby. The prospect of having to lug cables and pulleys down and across this very terrain for the next week depressed Albert even more. But he tried to close out the thought. So he concentrated on the rocks at his feet—Little Boy was leading them down a dry streambed, dug deep from spring runoff, crosshatched with jagged boulders. The descent was so steep that Albert suspected even a slight slip would take him straight to the ravine bottom. So he placed his feet exactly on the edges of the boulders that were available, avoiding the shale and pebbles that lay dead center in the stream bed.

"Sheee-it," shouted Bucky, as the sound of tumbling rocks and a loud thump filled the air. Albert stopped to find him sitting on his rump in the middle of the stream. "Fuck-ing pebbles. Fuck-ing pebbles. Fuck all them fuck-ing pebbles."

Now Bucky turned his attention to Little Boy, well below them and still moving quickly. "Will you goddamn slow down for a minute?" shouted Bucky. "Your supervisor has had an accident, goddamn it."

Little Boy turned, then stopped—looking upward only briefly. Bucky struggled back to his feet, hoisting the spool of cable and his equipment onto his shoulders, and regaining his footing, gingerly.

Conrad Bruel, who followed Bucky, gave him a hoist upward with a free hand. "I got one question, Rudman," said Conrad as Bucky again started down the trail. "How the hell can you cut off the top of a 200-foot fir, but you can't walk down a trail without falling on your ass?"

"You know the only two people that count in this goddamn outfit, Conrad?" asked Bucky in return, now beginning to breathe heavily again as he resumed the trek downward.

"No."

"Me and the cook. You get rid of either one of us and this show closes."

"What's that got to do with falling on your ass on a trail?"

"Just that if I asked Bud Cole to have a little panty-waist like you carry me down this here ravine, he'd have no choice—especially with all his other problems," wheezed Bucky. "So I'd suggest you shut your ugly trap and attend to your own business."

For more than an hour, they traveled in silence—the sound of their breathing growing with the fatigue of each man. The firs were now smaller, crowded by pine and alder. As they descended, the air cooled slightly. The sun's rays crept into the valley only at midday. Though the pile driver continued to rifle the air with short, puffy blasts, the noise muffled slightly, as the thick forest enveloped the four men.

This was the route, then, Albert thought. This was the route that he and Conrad would use to haul all of the gear to the new spar tree that Bucky and Little Boy were going to rig on "the other coast," which is what Bucky now called it. Albert studied the path, his heart dropping further with each uneven step, with each foothold that broke loose and threatened to send him onto his rear, just like Bucky.

He slowed slightly, firming his footing on a jutting rock, to hoist the coil higher onto his shoulder, then the pulley on the other side. A damn burro. He had become a damn burro—and had volunteered for it to boot. He drew in a breath, then started down the path again.

Bud Cole had given him an option, of course. Did he want to go to work for Bachelder, on the trestle, to fill the job of one of the men who had quit abruptly after he nearly fell over the side? Bud was willing to boost his pay, but Albert didn't want it. It wasn't the height that stopped him, he knew that. Or even standing on top of the twelve-by-twelve's, while the pile driver rammed the firs into the ravine floor, causing the trestle to shudder.

Only after he had already volunteered, instead, to help Little Boy and Bucky rig a new spar on the far side of the ravine, did it come to him: He wanted to be away from the rest of the crew. Away from the feeling that finally boiled to the surface when Bucky and Valentine found the animals.

Even the men he had grown close to—and had begun to trust—had begun to change. Myles Norgren spoke less, perhaps fearful that they might finger him because he was a Red. Petey Hulst abandoned his tarot circles immediately, though pressure started mounting for him to restart them. But the real changes, the clearest changes, were in much smaller things. Lightning Stevens didn't slap Albert on the shoulder quite as often. Bucky Rudman tossed fewer jokes across the mess hall at suppertime. The Swedes clustered even more by themselves, and the dedicated union men moved to a different table.

Others took a completely different tack. It was clear to Albert that Conrad—now trailing the group, even further behind than Bucky Rudman—and even St. Bride to some extent, seemed to revel in the rumors and anger. Something in Conrad's face showed excitement, a sense of theater in it all, which made Albert begin wondering whether the rumors about Conrad being behind it all might have some truth in them. St. Bride, on the other hand, seemed strangely content—as if his responsibility for instigating trouble could take a rest, at least for a short time, since the crew was doing a decent enough job of its own.

But down deep, Albert knew that the speculation was in him, too. He watched men more closely now, even in small ways. He listened to the conversation more carefully. He found himself avoiding union talk. He didn't want to be in clusters that griped about Bud Cole. Nor did he feel comfortable near Bud himself. Skybillings was quickly developing a no-man's land—you needed to belong to one group or another. And the more the talk increased, the more dangerous it was to float out there all alone.

So when Bud asked Albert what his choice was going to be, several days of hauling gear across the floor of the ravine, in the shadow of Three Sisters Ridge, sounded ideal, even if it meant sleeping on the ground and living without Zoe's cooking. He didn't want to hear the talk, to look at the eyes. Better to work like a pack animal.

Now, he was wondering if that was such a smart decision.

As they continued to descend into the deep valley, Bucky Rudman shouted again to Little Boy. "Goddamn it, Whitaker, will you slow down? A man my age needs a rest now and again."

With this, Little Boy stopped. He did not look back, did not acknowledge Bucky's request, just sat down on a boulder that lay between two firs. A small stream wound around its base. He bent down on hands and knees and drank deeply from the icy water. But still, he did not acknowledge the others, though Albert had settled against one of the firs and Bucky and Conrad had finally dropped their cables and were cupping water right next to him.

Albert took Conrad's place next to the stream. The icy water seemed to rush into every corner of his body, so fast that a stabbing pain sliced across the back of his head.

As he tried to close out the dirty joke that Conrad was telling Bucky, he settled onto a rock, working his legs and feet outward. The muscles felt like they wouldn't uncoil. He closed his eyes, rolled his head backward from side to side, which momentarily relieved the ache that ran across his upper back.

A wrenching pain suddenly shot up his right leg. "Anybody ever show you how the horse bites?"

Albert tried to pull his leg away. But Bucky's grip intensified.

"See, he puts his teeth in and just digs," laughed Bucky, as his fingers dug deeper. Albert now jammed both hands under Bucky's hand, but the fingers only locked tighter, sending sharp pains up and down the leg.

"Damn it, Bucky. Stop!" Albert's pain etched through each word.

"Only if you wipe that whipped dog look off your face," snorted Bucky. "Life ain't half as bad as you think. In fact, it's all pretty damn good, if you give it a chance."

"Okay, Okay."

"Promise?"

"Jesus, Bucky!" The pain seared upward into his back, as Bucky finally let go, let out a deep roar, and slapped him on the back. Little Boy was already far down the trail, having reshuffled the coil onto his back and begun walking without saying a word to anyone.

"Odd little son of a bitch, ain't he?" said Bucky, though Albert didn't know if he was talking to him or about him. He looked up to see Bucky nodding in the direction of Little Boy. "He works his ass off. Knows what the hell he's doing. Never complains. But he's one queer character—has kind of an absent look in his face. You sort of think he's off in the Sahara or on Mars or something."

Conrad agreed hardily, saying how he had heard how Little Boy had nearly killed the guy at Talbert's bar after Nariff's funeral. This sent Bucky into a laughing fit, but Albert ignored it again. The pounding from the pile driver was back, now in synchronous rhythm with the pains in Albert's legs as he again began down the steep incline.

He'd heard plenty of rumors about Little Boy. None were friendly. Albert had never tried to ask him a question. But as he thought about it, it occurred to him that he had never heard anybody ask Little Boy a question—or speak to him much, for that matter. The rumors about him, Albert guessed, had started with St. Bride, something about what Little Boy did in Victoria.

But because a man was a Red, what did that mean? The woods were full of them, even in Seakomish, the mayor was a Communist. Myles Norgren was a Red. So why was Little Boy's political affiliation so suspicious? Albert decided that it was convenience, more than anything else, which encouraged St. Bride to whisper about Little Boy.

If anybody was guilty of sabotage on the crew it was probably St. Bride, Albert decided as he caught up with Little Boy, who was stepping gingerly into the rushing stream at the bottom of the ravine. Bucky and Conrad were still fifty yards up the hill.

"She'll freeze your dick off," said Little Boy.

"What?" Albert didn't expect a voice.

"That water comes from those peaks up there. Probably two degrees above freezing. I'd guess that if it takes longer than sixty seconds for you to get across this thing, hypothermia will wrap your legs like death." Little Boy smiled without looking at Albert. The soft, curly lashes stood out well in front of his eyes.

Before Bucky or Conrad reached the stream, Little Boy was halfway across, the water reaching his waist. He held one hand on a rotting log that stretched most of the way across.

"What in the hell is he doing?" Bucky finally arrived.

"What's it look like?" asked Albert.

Bucky turned to Albert and smiled. "I see the whipped dog has become the smart ass."

"Sorry."

"No need. I'm only your elder by fifteen years. I got ten years more experience, and I am king shit of the Skybillings operations," said Bucky, with another slap across Albert's shoulder. "But no need to show a little respect. That'd be too much to ask." Albert finally laughed. Bucky Rudman's ability to play multiple characters in a constantly running vaudeville routine finally broke through Albert's haze.

Bucky wandered a hundred feet or so in both directions alongside the stream, but came back looking unhappy. His lips were squeezed together in a tight circle—like he'd just sucked a lemon. "Guess that bastard is right," he said, with dejection in his voice. "I thought it might've been shallower up there. But it's worse. God how I hate ice water on my balls. The very definition of numb-nuts."

Little Boy was leaning against a fallen fir on the other side, smoking a cigarette. His face was turned upward, facing the hot sun. From a distance, he looked like an Indian or Mexican. Albert decided he could be a writer who'd just left a cafe in Paris. But he didn't look like a logger.

Taking a deep breath, Albert rushed into the water, guiding himself along the log. For several seconds, he thought that Little Boy had exaggerated. It was cold like any other mountain stream. But then the deep pain hit—an ache that seemed to bore through his bones. He ignored the shouts of Bucky Rudman behind him until he finally waded to the other side. Little Boy was already running back toward the water, wading into a deep pool just below where Albert had crossed the stream.

The searing pain clouded Albert's understanding until he looked back and saw Conrad and Little Boy hauling Bucky out of the stream. Bucky's face was white, his lips a hint of blue. Little Boy laid him on two flat rocks next to the shore, tearing off his own shirt and wrapping it around Bucky. Conrad grabbed blankets from the bedrolls and wrapped Bucky's legs and arms.

For several minutes, Little Boy rubbed Bucky's right arm and hand, while Conrad worked on the other. Albert laid Bucky's wet clothes onto the warm rocks nearby.

While Bucky was recovering, Little Boy directed Albert and Conrad to haul another piece of log into the stream and connect it with rope to the one already there. "If you're ever going to get across that son of a bitch with all that cable, you're gonna have to hang onto something," he said.

Every time Albert crossed the icy, boiling stream during the next several days, he thought of Bucky. He'd taken two hours to truly recover. By that time, he was already telling dirty stories, but until then, he looked to Albert as much like death as any living person could ever look.

His face was ghostly white, his lips splotchy blue, prompting Conrad to observe that, with the bright red hair, Bucky's face resembled the US flag. Could Bucky have died from so little exposure to an icy stream, Albert wondered.

"How long was he in—a minute maybe?" Albert surprised himself at the sound of his own voice. It wavered slightly, before he could steady the last two words.

Little Boy shrugged. His attention was focused on rubbing Bucky's arms and legs. So Albert sat on the rocks, waiting for Bucky to recover, noting that in the woods, a man could freeze to death on one of the hottest days of the year.

❊   ❊   ❊

Once the four of them found their way up the opposite ridge—a steep climb up a rutted deer trail—Bucky and Little Boy quickly picked what they decided was the best spar tree. A ramrod-straight Douglas fir that towered well above those nearby, set slightly apart, which meant that, once it was fully rigged, it would be able to haul-in logs more easily from the surrounding area and serve as the center-piece of trestle-building. Standing at its base, Albert could easily see the outline of the trestle in the distance—two rows of spindly poles marching side-by-side from the opposite shore.

After he and Conrad had hauled what seemed like several tons of gear through the ravine—cables, pulleys, choking bells, metal con-traptions with spools and gears that Albert couldn't identify, rusty chains and hooks—Bucky and Little Boy started preparing the spar tree. Bucky referred to the work as, "Strip it, top it, rig it, run it."

"You know what that means, Conrad?" asked Bucky, as he readied his climbing spurs, hung two razor-sharp axes from the thick black strap that circled his belly, and thumbed a wad of chewing tobacco into a cheek.

Conrad looked bored. "Take off all the limbs, cut off the top, hook all the cables and pulleys, and start dragging-in the logs," said Conrad. Albert was as surprised as Bucky at the response.

"I will be darned, Mr. Conrad Bruel," said Bucky with vigor. "You are actually beginning to learn something. Now, give me the version about women."

Conrad looked at Bucky blankly. Albert prepared for the worst.

Bucky smiled again. "Well, you use the same process in dealing with a lovely member of the feminine species," offered Bucky as Little

Boy finished stringing the long leather climbing strap around the tree and hooking it back to Bucky's belt—tight enough that it would hold him, loose enough that he could easily flop it upward on the trunk, as he used his sharp climbing spurs to work his way up the tree.

"Strip it, lick it, fuck it, and then run for it."

Bucky's cackling flushed a flock of sparrows from the tall stand of alder nearby. Little Boy crossed himself and mumbled something, then directed Albert and Conrad to begin clearing away the scrub brush and small trees that lay between the spar tree and the edge of the ravine.

Bucky worked his way slowly up the fir, sawing off limbs that were—at least near the bottom—often a foot or more thick. After they had fallen, Little Boy wrestled them away from the trunk. So Albert and Conrad not only had to slash pine and small maples from the slope below the tree, they had to be looking up constantly to watch for falling limbs. After the first few hours, Bucky was too far up for his voice to be heard.

For some reason, none of this bothered Albert. Something in the smells on the cliff, or the freedom from the rest of the crew. Even the flying limbs—dangerous as they were—didn't trouble him much. He lopped off the scrub pine with his machete, though the thicker alder required several whacks with his axe. With each new shrub came a new smell—sweet, succulent oils bleeding from the wounds, some like perfumes, some almost bitter. Occasionally, he would stop to look across the ravine, taking in the distant trestle, or the icy expanse of Three Sisters Ridge towering above them. Or he would survey Bucky's work overhead—ropes and cables stretching down from his belt, as he clung to the stripped tree, working his way always higher.

As he watched Bucky work, Albert decided that Bucky's smart-aleck comments to Conrad a few days earlier were really true. From this far below, Bucky was little more than a large bump at the top of the tree, especially with the green peak at the tip still towering above him. Bucky moved left and right, then around, then up slightly, and back down a few feet as he hacked and sawed. Despite a stiff breeze that swayed the tall fir to the left, then gently back to the right, Bucky—held to the tree by the thick strap of rubber—paused only when a limb was about to drop.

"You know, it does take guts," said Albert to Conrad as he hauled a mass of torn rhododendron brush to the edge of the ravine and pushed it over. Conrad looked at him with a confused expression, until he followed Albert's eyes upward to Bucky Rudman.

"Hell, we're out here on a ledge that drops off a couple hundred feet, and he's at least that much further up the tree," continued Albert, not caring if Conrad answered. "Imagine what it must feel like up there."

They both studied Bucky for several minutes as he sawed a particularly thick branch. The tree continued to sway. Bucky shuffled his feet several times, then wound his way around the back of the trunk—Albert and Conrad could only see the sharp blows from his axe now. Little Boy adjusted ropes and cables to give him the equipment he needed.

"It ain't that damn hard. Swingin' an axe is all he's doing." Conrad looked at Albert with a smirk. "Sounds like you're sceered of heights, Weissler."

"Heads up," shouted Little Boy. A limb instantly slammed into the rock and slash nearby, splitting into several pieces and tumbling over the edge.

"Jesus Christ!" whispered Conrad, standing only a few feet from where it hit. "That's what you call a widow-maker." He now looked upward, more lost than scared.

"I know," answered Albert. "It's how my mom got to be one."

"One what?"

"A widow."

Conrad studied him for a moment, then nodded. He wiped the bark, leaves, and twigs off both arms—then peered upward. Albert couldn't tell if he was just watching out for the next limb, or deciding whether he should quit.

"Goddamn it, Little Boy! You need to give us an earlier warning." Conrad shouted the words half-heartedly, knowing that Little Boy would ignore him. Which he did.

For several more hours they continued to work, with the brush and saplings between the new spar and the cliff's edge slowly disappearing.

Albert could see far down into the ravine now and thought he detected the Swedes beginning from the other side. Bud Cole's plan was in full operation, thought Albert. First, find the spar. Then begin rigging. Then start the Swedes falling the timber around it. And then rig a skyline cable system across the ravine, to speed the work of the trestle on the other side. Bud even claimed that they could use the skyline to hoist the pile driver clean across the ravine—to start the trestle from this side; then get another to continue the work on the section already built.

"Look alive!" shouted Little Boy. Albert had tossed the last of the underbrush over the side and was scrambling up the hill when he saw Bucky begin sawing the last thirty feet at the tip of the spar. This was why they called it "topping," thought Albert. The very tip, with all of its branches still intact, would come off with one horizontal cut across the trunk—a sight he had never seen.

Bucky had already axed deep angled cuts into the right side of the trunk, just below where the branches started upward in a green, upside-down "V." Conrad quickly caught up with him.

"Where's that sonofabitch gonna fall?" asked Conrad.

Little Boy heard the question and shouted for them to move back. "It's going to land right where you're standing." This sent Conrad scrambling up the slope, struggling over the hacked mulberry and pine, to find a spot between two large firs. Albert quickly followed. Neither sat down, so they could move if necessary. The valley grew quiet as the pounding of the pile driver at the other side of the ravine stopped. The only sound was the breeze that continued to tilt the naked spar gently from right to left.

"Are they watching, too?" asked Conrad.

"I figure they can see with binoculars," answered Albert.

For several minutes, they stood silently. Bucky's back was arched, humping the saw back and forth, spewing chips of bark that dropped quickly out of sight into the ravine below them.

"You ever see anybody fall off one of those things?" asked Albert.

Conrad shook his head. "Saw a guy break his neck once when the top of the tree came off in the wrong direction and split the trunk down the middle. Pulled him into the tree 'cause his topping belt was too tight."

Was it Conrad's tone, or perhaps the hint of pleasure that flickered across his face when he said it, that made Albert see Nariff Olben again—standing bent-over, straining to push a railroad tie under the Shay? Now he felt terrible fear for Bucky. He could feel Bucky being tossed from the tree, into the ravine, or being splattered against the rough wood, broken like a rag doll by the power of the mighty fir, striking back with all the violence it could muster as this puny human tried to wrest it from its 800-year-old birthplace.

"Here it goes," shouted Conrad.

Albert looked up to see the green tip—its branches and point now quivering—begin to tilt slowly outward, first hinting that it might fall directly over Bucky, who now hugged the trunk several feet below. But then it shifted, with a gust of wind, and broke cleanly from the tree, pitching out into the open air, suspended for a moment by a heavy gust, then dropping earthward, hitting the cleared space with a thud that shook the ground, and then catapulted outward, over the ledge and into the ravine.

"Jesus," shouted Albert. He turned to Conrad, but Conrad only pointed upward, where the towering, naked, and now headless fir whipped in a violent circle at the top—a rubbery, liquid motion, with Bucky clinging to the trunk, his arms wrapped around it as far as they would go, the thick belt snug around his back and the back of the trunk.

For several minutes the tree swung in a wide circle. Albert didn't take his eyes from Bucky, wondering each time whether this was the swing that would toss him off. But Bucky hung on, as the tree slowed.

For several minutes after it finally stopped, Bucky didn't move. He held firm, perhaps trying to recover from the awful spinning.

"I'll bet he pukes," said Conrad. "I've seen some of 'em come off there and not be able to walk for two days."

But eventually Bucky loosened the belt. He leaned back against it. He seemed to drink in the cool breeze, and for a moment, even take in the long view down the ravine and to the west, but then inched his way slowly upward.

"What's he doing?" asked Albert.

"Shit if I know," said Conrad. "He must be so fucking loony from that ride that he can't remember which direction is down." Albert wondered if it might be true. He held his breath as Bucky slowly climbed up onto the flat top of the tree—which Albert guessed was perhaps a couple feet wide—first to sit on it, and then, finally, to actually stand up.

Bucky now stood directly on top of the spar, standing with his hands on his hips, 200 feet above them. With a smooth motion, he unbuckled his belt, opened his zipper, and began to piss into the ravine, pointing directly at the trestle on the other side. With three sharp blasts, the steam whistle—with Petey Hulst at the controls—saluted him, which Bucky acknowledged with a wave and a long stream of urine.

"I'll be goddamned," said Conrad, with a respectful smile.

The Swedes finally arrived. They started falling the firs in the area near the spar and the ravine's edge—where the rail line would connect-up, once the trestle was finally complete. The trestle now reached almost halfway across the ravine—a heavy pile driver and steam engine sitting at its front edge.

Bucky and Little Boy finished rigging the spar tree, with its elaborate network of cables, pulleys, and support rigging. Heavy guide wires ran from its peak to iron spikes buried deep in the ground. To allow the choking bell to speed back and forth between the spar tree and the spot where the fallers had dropped individual firs, haul-back lines ran from the upper rigging to pulleys attached to tall stumps scattered in a wide circle around the spar tree.

With the arrival of a group of buckers, led by a thin, muscular man named Edwards, the remote camp now became home to more than thirty men. Though the work flowed smoothly, the tensions in the group surfaced the first night the buckers showed up. The question was whether to post sentries around the camp.

"What the fuck for?" asked Bucky Rudman.

"Just in case they try to attack us," said Edwards, with anger in his voice that anyone should question him.

"Who is *they*?"

"Whoever killed the animals and filed the spike ain't finished yet," answered Edwards.

"And they're going to chase us over here?" asked Bucky. "Leaving aside the fact that we've been working on this coast of that goddamn ravine for near two weeks and we haven't been attacked once...leaving all that aside. You are saying that they got it in for us so bad that they are gonna—number one, climb down that there trail on the opposite side of this ravine; number two, hike across a mile of hard terrain; number three, ford an icy mountain stream that freezes your nuts off; number four, climb this goddamn goat trail on this side, and then—what, shoot us?"

The coolness had returned to the breeze, which now nipped at the large fire that Conrad and the Swedes had built for cooking dinner. Two of the Swedes, Johansson and a tall, thick-necked blond named Bergen, had volunteered to cook. They had already skinned and chopped several squirrels that had been hit by falling limbs, tossing them into a black kettle with potatoes and carrots.

Bucky warmed to the scene. "In fact, this here is the perfect setting. A bunch of sceered loggers, perched atop a cliff. Sitting round a big roaring fire. Just them and eighty million acres of woods—filled full of cougars and lynx and bobcat and coyotes and—hell, who knows— maybe even a grizzly or two come down this far."

"You take these men for fools, Rudman," said Edwards softly.

The tone of voice was calm, self-assured. Edwards held Bucky firmly in his gaze. "By making fun of them, you don't remove the legitimate concerns of these men. We have got what is clearly one case of sabotage, and another case that sounds pretty much like there may be a traitor in our midst. This company needs to take that seriously, and that includes sentries."

Bucky now smiled broadly. "Well, I'll be damned, Edwards. I thought I detected just a bit of union-talk in that."

Edwards nodded, but didn't smile.

"Which one? No. Let me guess." Bucky peered closely at the man, whose age Albert guessed was no more than twenty-five. Yet something about him made him seem older. "Just by the cut of the hair, the angle of the jaw, you look like an AFL man."

Edwards finally showed a slight grin. Even when Bucky was playing the asshole, he was hard to resist. "Card-carrying member, just like most of the rest of the buckers on this crew."

Johansson belched as he tossed more logs on the fire. The fingers of night chill had reached inward from the black woods. "I just got no use for you people with your unions," he said, through a rolling Swedish accent. Albert found the "J's" that were pronounced like "Y's" made the speech sound slightly comical.

"Wait one minute on that, Johansson. There's still a matter on the floor that hasn't been settled." Bucky's voice picked up speed, and Albert couldn't tell if he was about to go on the attack or start playing to the crowd. Bucky chose the latter. "Our Mr. Edwards, the AFL man here"—Bucky swept an arm in Edwards' direction— "says we ought to set up some sentries around the camp tonight. This Mr. Edwards seems like a pretty reasonable fellow, so let's see a show of hands of how many men are willing to volunteer to stand watch tonight... Wait, first I wanna say that none of my men are interested."

Johansson spoke up immediately. "Same is true with my crew. Swedes sleep. Don't do sentry work."

Bucky was now standing, thumbs underneath a set of wide black suspenders, broad smile—master of ceremonies in front of the fire. He swung left and right to make sure that everyone knew he was checking each man to find out if he had volunteered.

When the hands of only two buckers rose, Edwards let out an audible sigh and smiled. "Okay, Bucky. You win. No sentries."

"See, you union men are smarter than people say," said Bucky, with an over-eager tone of friendliness. "Only two out of the whole bunch of you AFL buckers didn't have enough sense to choose sleep over sentry duty."

Edwards started to protest when Johansson cut him off.

"What good are your unions, anyway?" Johansson's voice showed none of the good humor of Bucky's performance or Edwards' response. "You kill and destroy—you and your unions do. You stop men from working. Why? What right do you have to do this? I understood in my life early that in America a man was free. No one could stop him from working, from getting ahead. Yet I get here, and this is what I see?"

Several of the men who had been other otherwise occupied, now turned to the conversation.

Johansson persisted. "What do you people got against Skybillings? These are good men. Bud Cole is an honest man. Why do you want to be doing this damage?"

Edwards' initial surprise at the change in the tone of the conversation faded as he listened to Johansson.

"We didn't do any of this damage, Johansson," said Edwards crisply. "Get that straight. Our people don't resort to these kinds of shenanigans. If we have a beef with an outfit, we'll strike it."

Bucky Rudman laughed, now sitting on a log facing the fire. "So you are denying that the unions are doing all of this to Skybillings?"

"That's right," said a man with dark hair and furrowed skin the color of sandpaper. Albert thought his name was Herrera, but he wasn't sure. He was one of Edwards' crew. "AFL don't do this to logging companies. What Skybillings is facing is the damn bastards from the CIO. These are the tricks they learned from the Wobblies, from the Communists—derailing trains and blowing bridges. It's got all the markings."

"You gents are more refined—is that it?" Bucky seemed proud of the question.

"That's right. Voting, marching, striking—but we don't do none of this other shit."

"Some say that just makes you all pussies." The voice was that of Little Boy Whittaker. Even Bucky seemed shocked that Little Boy spoke. Little Boy leaned forward toward the fire—his upper arms seemed ready to split the sleeves of his denim shirt.

Little Boy's voice was low. "Clare Ristall says that's why the AFL don't belong in the woods. Anybody who isn't willing to kill is worth shit representing loggers."

Neither Edwards nor Herrera answered, and Bucky was silent. Several men shot quick looks at one another.

Most of the men around the fire said little while they ate. Then most either peeled away to wash their dishes in a small waterfall not far from the camp or wrapped themselves in their bedrolls for sleep. But Albert remained with the group, as did Conrad, Little Boy, and Bucky.

"Let me ask you a question," said Bucky finally, looking at Edwards and Herrera. "Assuming that you don't do this sort of thing, what would you do next—if you did do this sort of thing?"

Edwards seemed suddenly uncomfortable. "You mean what would I do to stop Skybillings? To close it?" He paused for several seconds, thinking about the question. "But if I tell you what I would do—and then, if it happens—everyone will think we did it. Why should I take that chance?"

"No, you got my public promise," said Bucky. "Just what we might call an intellectual exercise—that's all. And I figure you wouldn't be dumb enough to do what you predicted, assuming you was behind it."

"Unless, we knew you'd think that, so we'd be sure to do exactly what we predicted." This time it was Edwards' turn to smile.

Bucky didn't answer.

"I'd put dynamite on that trestle out there in the valley," said Edwards finally. "But I'd also figure that everybody in Skybillings expected that, so I'd work up to it. Not now. Maybe when it's about to connect to this side. Or just when the first train heads over it."

Bucky nodded, listening, watching the flames. Johansson and Bergen were listening closely to Edwards, as were several of the buckers.

Herrera now picked up the theme, as he leaned toward the flames. "I would do just what they're doing so far. Kill the animals. Then maybe somebody turns up missing."

Johansson interrupted. "Let me understand you, sir. You would be killing one of the men? This is what you are saying?"

Herrera seemed uncertain now. He looked at Edwards, who was expressionless. "The point is to scare the hell out of the place. Get them all wound-up on themselves, everybody pointing at everybody else. Suddenly, somebody turns up with a knife in his back."

Albert felt several men shift slightly. Even Bucky's forehead furled, but Little Boy's face was unmoved. The flames were settling lower into the ground. The cold air encircled the men with a chill that Albert hadn't felt in what seemed like weeks.

For several minutes, no one spoke. Edwards and Herrera had fallen silent. Albert studied their faces—young, intelligent, even handsome. How could they become so dedicated to a union, he wondered? Then he turned to the three Swedes still listening: They must have gone through just as many battles and hard times in the woods, but they wanted none of it—the unions, the strikes, even the grumbling.

"You a reader, Rudman?" asked Edwards after several minutes. His voice now seemed slightly out of place, discordant against the harmony of the gentle breeze and sparks and cracks of the remaining fire.

"True Detective and the Book of Revelations," said Bucky with a smile. "They got a lot in common."

"Indeed," said Edwards with a smile. "Ever read any poetry?"

"Poetry?" Bucky looked stunned, then scrunched his forehead in a look of worry. "Edwards, I try my very best to avoid poetry. I feel it weakens my male capabilities."

Everyone laughed, including Edwards. His face seemed even more handsome when covered with a smile. Albert decided that Edwards was a good man, though he couldn't understand him or how he—like Clare Ristall—came to his way of thinking.

"Your male capabilities notwithstanding, let me quote a poem by an old Englishman."

"Jesus. You memorize poems?"

"One or two."

"Don't women find that a little questionable in a man?"

"Most women love to hear poems from a man," said Edwards with a broad smile. "And believe it or not, Bucky, some men don't court women just with their dicks."

Bucky shrugged.

The faces of the circle turned to Edwards, who cleared his voice, seeming slightly embarrassed, and spoke the words softly:

*In a thing as mighty as an oak,*
*A wind that could so quickly fell a bloke,*
*Stands not a single hope,*
> *even along the jarring edge of winter.*
*For in that tree*
*That stands stout and stable like you and me*
*Is the bond that withstands the angry and cold night that draws*
> *nearer.*
*Worry not! You sailor, warrior, fighter of night's soulless dread,*
*The oak still stands,*
*Its singular and lonely leafs holding hard and tight above the frozen*
> *land.*
*The morning will wake fresh, and perhaps warm,*
*As will you,*
> *mighty and powerful yet, if indeed terribly worn.*

Edwards smiled when he finished, as if the truth of the poem rung out loud and clear.

"That's the damnedest thing I ever heard. I got no idea what that is all about," said Bucky.

"Renewal, rebirth—all built upon the struggles of those in the past," said Edwards, with a warm smile. "The winter comes, the leaves die, they disappear, even though a few hang on. But come the spring, the mighty oak renews, regardless of the snows of winter, the death of December. That's us, Rudman. That's the unions. We don't quit, no matter how hard things are; no matter how bad the weather gets. No matter how much others might want to kill us. We persevere and come back, just like the mighty oak and its beaten, but unbowed, leaves."

The two Swedes said something to one another that Albert couldn't understand, but otherwise the group was silent. Until Little Boy's voice—quiet, high-pitched, but still firm—surprised all of them.

"It doesn't mean that at all," said Little Boy, his face pockmarked by the yellow glow of the fire. "The poet is honoring the last man, the last one who hangs on through the death of winter, regardless of every-thing." He paused, as he let out a sigh. "It don't say nothing about unions and groups."

# Chapter 22

The woods awakens only when the moon rises full above it. In the shadows, in the coal-black recesses, the animals of the night emerge, moving across the paths of men, searching their prey, re-establishing their territory, smelling ancient smells, abiding by distant callings.

As Albert lay on his bedroll, well outside the main circle of men, most of whom clustered near the fire, he sensed the changes in the woods around him—a creature, of sorts, in and of itself, that lay only a few feet from him, and that yet enveloped him, enveloped all of them. Soon after Little Boy expressed his interpretation of the poem, most of the listeners drifted off to find their bedrolls. Albert had found a flat spot, near one of the stumps that held a guide-wire for the new spar. Thick with drying fir boughs, the location seemed ideal to sooth his sore back, and get him well beyond the circle of men.

As soon as he rolled the blankets around him, he fell instantly asleep, lost in a dream about exams on novels he could not understand and had not read. Just at the point that he was walking into the room to take the test, he realized that the teacher was his mother, but she had aged terribly. In fact, he studied her more closely, to find that it was not his mother, but his grandmother, with stern expression, anger brimming at his lack of preparation. He tried to explain, but the words would not come out, just gibberish that everyone laughed at as he tried to speak.

He awoke with a start, awakened by his own mumbling as he was trying to speak to the figure in the dream. Though the air was cold— his breath came in puffs—he swept off the blankets to cool himself. For several minutes, he fought with the vestiges of the dream as he tried to go back to sleep. But little by little, he woke up, finally crawling back into the blankets to huddle into a ball against the cold night.

Several feet away, he could hear the loud breathing of Johansson. Edwards was just beyond, snoring loudly—which surprised Albert. He had assigned snoring as a liability of old age or a behavior characteristic of stupid people, not something that afflicted the young or the handsome. Occasionally a spark cracked from the fire, which was now only embers. The circle of fire and conversation that had glowed so brightly only a few hours before was now still.

As he lay there, fully awake, staring upward, he sensed that other sounds had taken their place. He stared up at the spire of trees that rose overhead, straight and silent, reaching their black boughs inward toward one another to frame the brilliant white of the moonlight. With wafts of breeze, the trees creaked loudly, like a squeaky screen-door hinge—perhaps protests, decided Albert, that things so mighty and so solid could be forced to bend, even so slightly, in front of the force of something so light and unseen as a night breeze.

If that's the case, what the fuck must they think in the face of stinking Swedes with springboards and razor-sharp, double-tooth saws? Even Albert had found something uncomfortably violent in watching it all. As he and Conrad continued to help Bucky and Little Boy rig the spar tree, he watched them: Mountainous biceps and chests; they stripped down to bare skin early in the morning, standing on springboards cut into notches in the trees perhaps ten and even twenty feet above the forest floor, so they could bring the monster down more easily, without fighting the buckling knots and sticky pitch at its base. Throughout the day they worked, never stopping for lunch. Instead, eating sandwiches with one hand while pulling their end of the saw with the other.

But there were also images that stood out in his mind—Bergen, the assistant, and Johansson, continuing to saw despite a front of rain that had swept through. Stripped to their waists, the steam rose from their shoulders as the sharp curls of red, oily wood sprung outward from the ends of their saws, like spools of confetti in New York ticker-tape parades.

The other image was worse, somehow. Albert had longed to actually watch a massive fir fall to its death. The idea of a creature so massive, so strong, finally giving in to a logger's saw had drawn him even as a child. What would something so big sound like when it fell? How would the ground rumble?

But when he actually had watched it—the day before, as the fallers finally got themselves organized and began clearing the landing for the trestle—he felt only a blankness within him. Because the fir was so big, and so close to where they were working on the spar, Albert, Conrad, Bucky, and Little Boy had stopped to watch the final moments.

In this case, Johansson and another man, who Albert found surprisingly unpleasant-looking for a Swede, had sawed the giant for nearly eight hours. Still standing on their springboard, they kept the saw digging furiously, faster and faster, even as the fir began tilting slightly. But the men stayed on the board, which now rocked from the movement of the tree, driving their saw deeper and deeper, refusing to slow, refusing to pause, unwilling to accept the finality. Until finally, with the crown of the fir beginning to rustle those of its neighbors overhead, both men dove off the board, sprinting down a slight incline and dropping behind a stump for protection.

The sound that followed lay somewhere between a raging wind that grew steadily stronger, and ripping fabric. The tree tilted on its base, lost its footing, swept suddenly upward, as the sound roared to a mighty crash, and then silence—the sound of wind and tiny pieces of branch and bough settling to earth delicately, almost in silence.

But it was not this scene that Albert saw in his mind, as he wrapped the blankets tightly around him to protect what little heat he had from the prying cold. It was the scene later, as the Swedes emerged from their hiding places—proud, tall, standing ramrod straight. As they did, Albert noticed clearly, on Johansson and the other, thick bulges below their belts, straining hard at their work pants. For some hours, he didn't think much of it, until it hit him late in the day—they'd had erections. Loggers who sawed down Douglas firs got hard when the giants fell.

Something in this struck Albert as coarse beyond belief. Not that he cared particularly about the tree. It was there to be cut down. But why would a man get aroused in doing so? There was a personal aspect to the act that seemed rotten to the core.

At this point, he decided that sleep was gone for the night. So he rolled onto his side and tried to see down into the ravine, but by now the moon had disappeared beyond a lens of clouds. Even blacker than usual, he thought. Not even an outline of the trestle, though the spar tree stood straight down the hill from him.

In just a few hours they'll start in again. He flexed his back muscles, feeling the pain still there from the pulleys that he arranged on the cable so Little Boy could haul them upward. They'll start, I'll start with 'em, and my ass will be on the ground because I haven't slept, because I've worried about erections on a bunch of dirty Swedes.

For several minutes, he willed himself to not think of anything. To let his mind go blank, to drift with the wind, to fall inside the dark recesses that were all around him. But the drifting, instead, took him elsewhere. Arriving, without explanation, at Little Boy, and the comment he made about the poem. Albert didn't have any clue as to what it meant, either the poem or the two interpretations. But he did know that the men fell silent after Little Boy spoke, though he didn't know if it was due to respect or agreement, or if they thought he was such an unusual person that they wouldn't bother even to respond.

Little Boy. The comment about a union being worthless if it wasn't willing to kill for the cause was frightening. But did he mean it? The men exchanged nervous glances, as if to ask, "Is he the one?" Albert rolled this idea around in his head for a moment. Could Little Boy be the one sabotaging the camp? But why? He was close to Bucky Rudman, but he was hardly a revolutionary.

The talk in the crew had Little Boy as one of the radical Reds. Out of Victoria. Something about the central committee and a strike on the docks at Vancouver that led to a riot. Myles Norgren told Albert he'd never heard of Little Boy ever being active in the movement. Yet this kind of talk, together with the fact that Little Boy did act a little odd, was enough for most of the crew to begin whispering.

From the beginning, Albert thought it was a joke. That the guy who didn't talk and kept to himself could be the culprit. He especially found it odd because, in another sense, being a union man meant you were just part of the mainstream. The buckers—behind Edwards and Herrera—were AFL. Union men. Sound, reliable. Clare Ristall, he was CIO, but still viewed by most in the crew and the valley as a good fellow.

Then why was it that a person like Little Boy, who held to himself, listened to symphonies on the radio, was singled out for his political views?

He rolled over in the blankets again, now to give his back some relief from the hard earth. The pine boughs had long since squashed into nothingness. Yet as he turned, the earth felt even harder against his belly and his legs.

What would his mother think of these conclusions—these conclusions after only a few months on his own—he wondered, as he tried to get comfortable in this new position. Would she be pleased that he was beginning to see—no, to feel—the harshness of the logging life? Or would she be angered by his growing disgust for unions, and for the men, like Clare Ristall, who promoted them?

But those thoughts vanished when he heard a stirring in the bushes. He turned, but the clouds covered the moon. The sound of an owl in the distance, the rustling of perhaps a mouse or mole in the thatch not far from his feet. But this sound was different—twigs broke, like the sound of feet stepping quietly across a noisy floor.

For several minutes he listened. But now the only sound was an owl, followed by a coyote cry from the edge of the ravine. Albert tilted his body around to get a look at the rest of the circle. Johansson was a bundle of blankets that heaved upward in steady breaths. Edwards the same. Farther in the distance, Albert could make out a line of other forms, all asleep.

He listened again. There, once more. A crisp split of a twig. Who would be walking around the group?

Albert could feel his heart beating faster as the thoughts rushed through him. Hadn't Edwards said that the next thing he'd do would be to kill someone? Albert checked again. Edwards was still asleep—or at least seemed to be. But where was Herrera? Albert didn't know where he had lain down for the night, but he decided to prop himself up on an elbow, to see if he was on the other side of Edwards.

Albert moved so slightly that his muscles ached. Upward, slowly, inch upon inch, he finally could see over the top of Johansson, but he still couldn't tell who was on the other side.

Probably just someone taking a piss, he decided. After all, they had all drunk gallons of coffee.

Finally, as he felt a thickness grow in his chest, his legs begin to burn, his breathing catch in his chest, he tossed the blankets back rapidly, jumped to his feet, and strode directly toward the sound. He didn't think, didn't look, just walked, stepping on twigs and rocks, until he got far enough away from the group. He swept his shorts down and started pissing—a long low stream, with white steam arching upward as it fell.

As he did, he felt his heart slow down. The water made a welcome sound, a sound he knew and understood, and his bladder finally felt relieved. It wasn't a goddamn man, thought Albert. It was some sort of critter. As he pulled his shorts up and turned to walk back to his bed, however, his eyes fell directly on two gray eyes peering back at him from the moonlight.

Deep from inside the boughs of a massive pine, perched on the bottom branch, stood a mountain lion, a cougar. The moon, now peeking from behind the clouds, illuminated the front paws and head of the cat, muscular in the moonlight, mouth open, breath escaping in white puffs. The cat stared at Albert, cold, alert, as if measuring him.

Albert froze, locked in the animal's stare. Should he shout? Run? Or remain motionless? He didn't know. But the cat didn't move. So he didn't either.

For several moments, they looked at each other. The cat, studying his form, even shifting from one foot to the other, which sent a shiver through Albert, but he remained motionless.

Are you what's behind all of this, Albert wondered as he studied the animal. He could now see the powerful muscles just above the front legs, the sweep of the shoulder—was it gray, perhaps brown?—upward to the ridgeline of the back. Was it you who killed Zoe's animals? The thought flashed through his mind as he studied the red tongue and the whiskers. Were you the shape I saw at the bottom of the rock slide? Albert tried to recall the image from that night—a man, perhaps, but it might've been an animal like this one. Are you behind all this—all this rage and anger, this fear of spirits and ghosts, these attacks on Skybillings?

For a moment, as he studied the wild beast, Albert even had the fleeting thought that maybe the spike hadn't been filed at all—that all of this, the anger, the hostility, the finger-pointing—was the coincidence of bad interpretation, an apparition in the moonlight, and a silent, unseeable mountain lion. And he, Albert, was in the middle of all the confusion and misinterpretation.

But as his focus returned to the animal, he realized that the cat was gone. At first he thought it was just that the moon had hidden the shadow once more. But he studied the tree carefully, and the form was no longer there.

For several minutes, Albert didn't move. He searched the brush, the pines behind it, even the edges of the ravine. He wanted one more glimpse. One more chance, for a second or two, to take the full measure of this animal. To get some inkling of what secrets it held and, in some odd way, capture a hint of the answers he sought.


## Chapter 23

Meredith Cunningham didn't dress like a publisher of a newspaper. She was partial to large-print dresses, which on a large frame, made her look mammoth. The impression was reinforced by tiny, round glasses tilted down on her nose, a patch of brilliant red lipstick, and gray hair, cut short. And a small carnation, pink today, that she clipped just to the left of a string of white pearls.

But while her looks may have been unorthodox, her outlook on the world was not—at least not for a newspaper publisher. The voice of the Everett Chronicle was clear: Business was the backbone. Commerce the lifeline. And workers fit in around the edges.

Not that Meredith Cunningham was anti-labor. She pointed out some of the unfair practices of shipping companies on the West Coast long before Harry Bridges—leading a group of longshoremen in San Francisco—took the maritime workers out on strike in '34. But militancy, work stoppages, slowdowns, and strikes—especially aggressive, violent maneuvers that Bridges liked to use in trying to establish the legitimacy of his union—Meredith Cunningham would not tolerate. No workers could ever hope to pick themselves up with those tactics. But more important, the Northwest economy could never truly recover from the Depression. So both on the editorial page and in person, she roared against the growing power of unions.

Besides, she'd had enough of the union battles that had wracked Everett for years—and made it clear in her editorials. Dead sick of sawmill battles, is how she put it in one. Men are supposed to work, not strike. You don't buy groceries if you are standing on a picket line. And on, without waver.

This was what Clare Ristall now faced, sitting on the other side of her oak desk cluttered with newspapers and stacks of dog-eared, typewritten pages. Her managing editor, a mousy man named Herbert Earle—who Lonnie Harrison kept calling "Earle Herbert"—sat on a chair beside the desk. But Meredith was the questioner, Meredith the decision-maker.

Clare had tried to avoid the meeting. But Lonnie Harrison pointed out that he, not Clare, was chairman of the Democratic Campaign Committee, and he decided that newspaper editorial endorsements may be what turned the election. "All this goddamn talk about strikes ain't doing nothing to improve your chances," said Harrison to Clare when he called to let him know that he'd set up the appointment with Meredith Cunningham. "But you get that windbag publisher to say you're okay, and the good folks up the Seakomish Valley will do the same. You need this editorial, Clare."

The comment had rankled Clare. When Harrison had first raised the prospect of Clare's running, Harrison had gone out of his way to say that Clare's union organizing was a mark in his favor. It guaranteed name recognition. It was why the campaign committee even started paying attention to him. But now, somehow, Harrison acted as if all of that had become a liability.

Clare argued with him. "If you've got a problem with the union, Lonnie, you can always find somebody else to run," said Clare. This brought a hardy laugh from Harrison. Even on the long-distance line, Clare could tell it had caught him by surprise.

"Nothing like that," said Harrison. "Nothing like that. You're our man, Clare. Just that this race is closer than we expected. You gotta get those endorsements. So meet me there next Friday at ten sharp."

Clare knew what was going through Harrison's mind. The race was tightening, alright. He could feel it himself, and the newspapers were full of the talk. Loggers on the street or at Talbert's seemed less interested in shaking his hand. Lydia reported more criticism when she handed out leaflets door-to-door. The Republicans continued to raise talk about how the CIO was going to strike and close down the woods, and it was being heard.

So Clare accepted the fact that he had to struggle for each advantage he could find. But it didn't make looking across the desk at Meredith Cunningham—at ten on a Friday morning—any easier. And listening to Lonnie Harrison prattle on with her about friends they had in common made Clare momentarily consider doing what he suggested earlier to Harrison: pulling out of the race entirely.

But he put the thoughts out of his mind. Winning the seat in the legislature was important for the union. He would be the first CIO man in the House. From there, he could call attention to the bastards in the AFL—and the spineless contracts they agreed to with the logging companies. For that matter—though he wasn't sure—he would probably be the first logger in the House. Not a bad feat in itself.

So as Meredith shot the breeze with Harrison, Clare focused on finding a way through the granite of Meredith Cunningham. If she thinks she owns Everett, that's fine. I'll give it to her. If she thinks she's the kingmaker, then let her play the role. If its commerce that's her manna, then I'll find a way to provide it.

Clare didn't have to wait long. "I've got your Republican opponent coming in an hour, Mr. Ristall, so I'll cut to the chase," said Meredith. Her voice was surprisingly soft. If Clare wasn't looking at 200 pounds of flowered print and short gray hair, he might've thought he was speaking to a sixteen year old. "In twenty-five words or less, why should the Chronicle endorse you?"

Clare had thought through his response for an entire week. He knew that the standard campaign lines would fail with Meredith Cunningham, so he decided to try to catch her off guard. "You should endorse me because I'm the only one who can put the labor strife in the Seakomish Valley behind us," said Clare.

The answer had the exact effect Clare intended. As if to say, "You?"—Meredith's head tilted backward quickly, jolting the flesh under her chin. "I'm all ears, Mr. Ristall."

Clare looked at Lonnie Harrison, whose face looked ashen and lost. Clare suspected that, given half a chance, Harrison might have been willing just then to take him up on his offer to pull out of the race.

"There are two main reasons for the labor trouble right now," said Clare. "One is that the strike two years ago didn't settle anything. It only made things worse. The employers weren't willing to sign a standard agreement with the workers, so every employer, every sawmill and logging camp, has a different agreement. Workers don't have any real protection. It's the luck of the draw. Second, the AFL's largely to blame for that. They put the loggers in the gutter. Forgot 'em. Made them pay big dues, but didn't give them a vote. And didn't get anything solid for them from the last strike."

Meredith Cunningham said something to Herbert Earle, who scampered out of the office. Clare noticed that when she spoke, narrow creases fanned out around her mouth. When she turned back to Clare, her mouth now seemed square, exposing a perfect set of very white teeth. "Internecine warfare isn't my interest, Mr. Ristall. And I'm still waiting to hear how you're better than your opponent in putting the labor strife, as you put it, behind us."

"It's all tied together," said Clare quickly, leaning forward, both hands on the corner of her desk. "As long as the AFL is in charge, we'll never have a standard contract. We'll never have standard conditions. We'll never get the wages we need. So the men will always be angry, mistreated, with no real protections—*and* they'll be underpaid." Clare glanced at Herbert Earle as he came back into the room and dropped a thick folder of papers onto Meredith's desk. "The CIO will change that. We'll ensure a standard contract. We'll ensure standard conditions. We'll make sure that every logger and every sawmill worker can count on a decent wage."

She looked up at him now, over the top of her round glasses, as if waiting for him to finish.

Clare added, "Yes, in the short term, we may need to strike. But if we do, it only means that over the long term, the men will settle down if they get a fair, standard agreement."

Meredith dug a stubby index finger through the rolled papers that Earle had given her, licking her finger carefully each time after she had flipped several pages. Clare felt the room grow still. A fan just above her desk, on a bookcase, had stopped. Lonnie Harrison seemed to be studying his shoes.

After several minutes of silence, Meredith looked up. "You pay much attention to shipping, Mr. Ristall?" She leaned forward, with a rosy lipstick smile.

This time, it was Clare who was caught off guard. "You mean, shipping lines? Boats?"

"I mean, yes, boats, water, you know, that sort of thing...." She stopped for a second and pointed to Puget Sound, which spread out beneath her window.

"Not a lot. But I'm not running for a longshoreman's position." Clare said this with a friendly smile.

"No shit. I actually had that figured out. My point is simply that you probably know all about Harry Bridges, the slimy gent who runs the Longshoreman's Union down in San Francisco." She now poked one of the stubby fingers toward Lonnie Harrison. "Lonnie, you're a friend of Harry Bridges, aren't you?"

Lonnie cleared his throat. "Harry Bridges? Ummm, yes. I mean, no. Just met him once or twice. Can't say that I actually know him..."

Meredith turned away from Lonnie before he finished. "Mr. Ristall, I heard the same arguments from Harry Bridges when he started bitching about how the AFL was ignoring the Longshoreman's Union. How it wasn't looking out for the workers. How the ship owners were getting to do anything they wanted." She paused now as she leaned back in her chair, pulled out one of the lower drawers and plopped her foot on it. "Harry Bridges sat right in that chair in 1934 and explained how he was the one who had to step in and deliver what the stodgy old AFL never could—better wages, the union shop, and god-knows-what-else. And that he—not the old line AFL boys—could get an agreement that would be fair to all parties and that everyone could live in peace and prosperity."

She ended the sentence with a cold smile, then lifted from her desk the thick roll of papers that Earle had brought in. "But you read this, Mr. Ristall, and you find that Harry Bridges was full of shit—Grade A, Number-One shit. Because you know as well as I do what happened after Mr. Harry Bridges spoke those words. We got the biggest strike the West Coast ever saw. Profits of shipping companies, warehouses, and lumber mills dropped like a rock. Freight is moving slower than ever, and costs are up. And the Port of Everett hasn't had such a bad year since 1929."

Now she sat upright quickly in her chair. "And then that bastard Bridges decides he needs *another* strike. So they strike again last year. And we'll probably see one this year, too."

Meredith Cunningham's eyes danced. She'd found a topic close to her heart. And she wouldn't be satisfied with giving Clare just a lecture, she insisted on an economics course—about the fundamental failure of unions, of collective bargaining, the closed shop. Lonnie Harrison never looked up. He coughed violently once when she launched into an attack on the "Communist influence" in the unions, especially the CIO.

Clare listened attentively, nodding occasionally, leaning slightly forward in the hard chair, trying to show that he was willing to give her view a fair shake. Despite Meredith Cunningham's blustery exterior, Clare knew she was a thinking person. So while she lectured, he also struggled to find the angle that might sidetrack her. If he needed her endorsement, he was going to do everything he could to get it.

"You ever been in a logging camp, Miss Cunningham?" asked Clare. The question broke into a sentence on how Harry Bridges was a Communist who should be shipped back to Australia, where he came from.

"Me? Yes. I've visited the Ashford & Southern logging operations several times," she said quickly. Her flower print seemed to wave in the wind as she resettled herself in the squeaky chair.

"I don't mean Ashford & Southern. I mean some of the other operators in the woods, Miss Cunningham," said Clare. "The gyppo loggers, the little guys, the runts—these are the companies, if you want to call them that, that employ a good many men out there."

Her eyes looked bored. "State your point, Mr. Ristall."

"It's just that one hell of a lot of loggers still work in conditions that you would find totally unacceptable..."

"C'mon" she snapped. "That's malarkey. That's why all you loggers decided to strike in '35. You do remember that, don't you?"

"The '35 strike guaranteed one thing: That if you work for the big companies, you've got a few protections." Clare's voice seemed strained. "But that's my point. Those protections aren't uniform. They're all over the map. The same with the pay. It's all over the map, too—because the AFL leaders decided to cozy up to the employers and they virtually got nothing. But even more important is that— without a uniform contract—those big companies are going to start backtracking. Most of them already are."

Meredith Cunningham groaned. "So you're going to squeeze the shit out of the good companies because of something they might do? You're going to spread violence through the woods to make a political point?" Before Clare could answer, however, she suddenly stood up. "Frankly, Mr. Ristall, I find your arguments lifeless. I think what's going on is the same thing we've seen with that bastard Harry Bridges and his longshoremen."

She walked to the door and opened it. "I think this little union is your bully pulpit. Your moment in the sun, as it were. Bridges became a household name in every port on this coast because he manhandled the dockworkers into believing they've got some terrible threat lurking out there. In my book, you're up to the same game."

"Game?"

"That's what I said—game: Building your own little empire. Making the companies dance to your tune." Her smile turned hard. "Add a nice little post in the State Legislature and, who knows? Old Lonnie Harrison might decide to stop screwing the girls in Olympia and spend his energy on getting you elected to Congress."

Clare smiled politely. "And what can I do to convince you that is not the case?"

Meredith Cunningham shot back an answer almost before Clare had the sentence out. "Renounce a strike in the woods, and we've got something to talk about."

❊　❊　❊

Lonnie Harrison insisted on stopping at the first bar they found after they left the Chronicle. He ordered a scotch, drained it, then ordered another. "That settles it," said Harrison with a rasp. "You've got to call a press conference on Monday and say, 'No strike.'"

Clare drank two gulps of beer and stared at Harrison. "The hell I am. You think all that stuff I said to her was all just a bunch of bullshit?"

"No, no," Harrison shook his head. "I didn't say that. I know your heart's in this union stuff, for Christ sake, but you don't stand a chance of getting her editorial support—or the vote of anybody who reads her—if you go forward with this strike crap."

"I didn't say there was going to be a strike."

Harrison's face fell in folds around his eyes, making him look like an aging hound. Only his skin was paler. "Save that crap for somebody else, Clare. Not me. I know where you're going." Harrison now smiled broadly, though the edges of his mouth sagged. "Look, from my own personal point of view, I think you're right on all this strike stuff. But I think you can do a hell of a lot more for these people if you're in the State Legislature than you can with all this rabble-rousing up in the woods."

Clare slapped his bottle onto the table, sending a stream of suds flowing out of the neck. "Is that what this is to you, Lonnie? Is that what all the old codgers in Olympia think about this?"

Harrison cast an embarrassed look toward the other tables, smiling quickly as the roomful of eyes turned their direction. "Relax, will ya? You're wound-up like a clock, Clare." Harrison took out a folded sheet of paper from inside his jacket. "Look, it ain't just a know-it-all, windbag newspaper publisher that we gotta think about, okay? I've got a memo here from the guy who runs our canvassing— all the door-to-door shit. And he's saying that people are getting scared with all this strike talk. They're afraid, Clare. Jesus, they just got their jobs back—they don't want to lose them again."

Clare leaned close to Harrison. "That's the goddamn point, Lonnie. They *are* going to lose their jobs if they don't get a union that has some balls." Clare settled back into his seat. "Meredith Cunningham moans about the Longshoreman's Union and those strikes. But if those strikes never happened, you know what? All those guys working down there on the docks, right now, below her goddamn window, right here in Everett—those guys would be working longer days, they would be getting less money for every hour they work, and there wouldn't be any union hall to help them if they do lose their jobs."

Harrison waved for the bartender, a young woman, to send another scotch over. "You are one boring son of a bitch, Clare," said Harrison in exasperation. When she arrived, Clare noticed the sharp points at the tip of each breast, barely concealed by a thin sweater. She smiled at both men as she put down the drink.

Harrison nodded toward her as he tilted the glass back and finished half in one swallow.

"Right there is another reason you should want to come to Olympia," said Harrison, as his eyes finished watching her return to the bar. "You still get to screw women like that even when you're as old as me." Harrison broke out in deep laughter that sputtered into a hacking cough.

When it was finally over, he leaned close to Clare again. "There's one more thing," said Harrison. Clare expected more talk about the waitress. "Our guy who runs the canvassing"—he now nodded toward the sheet of paper—"well, he's been hearing other talk, too."

"Other talk?"

Harrison nodded, wiping a crooked finger across the rim of his glass and then licking the finger. "Yeah. Talk about how some of the business people aren't real happy with you."

Clare laughed. "This is news?"

Harrison smiled. "Just news that they, well, feel so strongly about it."

"Lonnie, just say it."

The old man hesitated. Clare suspected that Harrison actually felt fondly toward him, even if he didn't approve of his approach. "Our guy says that, from what he is hearing, you should watch your step, you know what I mean?" He glanced quickly around the bar, now half full. "He says there is some ugly talk. About the AFL boys and the company goons working together to trim your sails."

Clare hadn't heard such talk directly. But he'd certainly heard about it. Sammons has raised it only a few days before. "Watch yourself, Clare," Sammons had said. "I know these guys. These are guys who will kill you if they think it will help 'em."

Clare considered Harrison's warning and expected him to press harder. But that was all he said. He made small talk on the way to the train station, where Clare dropped him. But when he was pulling out his bag, he turned a warm, tired smile to Clare.

"Let me ask you this way," said Harrison. "What would it take to get you to call off this strike?"

"For Christ sake, Lonnie," said Clare, moving the heavy bag onto the platform.

"No, I'm serious. You want a call from the governor—is that it? Some special committee assignment or something when you get elected? We can arrange it, Clare. You could hold hearings or something—is that what you'd like? Hold hearings on all these bastards you hate in the AFL. We'd get you tons of publicity. Even the New York Times and TIME magazine are writing about this chaos between the unions. I know one of the reporters. You'd be a national sensation."

"Lonnie, this has nothing to do with political posturing. How many times do I have to say that? This really, truly, absolutely, cross-my-heart-and-hope-to-die has to do with protecting men who are in the woods. I was one of them. I saw this shit. I know the AFL is a pack of ass-kissing do-nothings, and they need, at the very least, a swift kick in the butt."

Harrison was silent.

"Look, Lonnie," continued Clare, "I am going to build this union—if it takes everything I have. That includes winning a seat in the Washington State Legislature. But if I need to call a strike, I am going to do it—legislature or not."

Harrison studied him. The old man's eyes swam in a gauzy liquid. As the train tooted its arrival into Everett, Harrison finally bent over and picked up the suitcase. "I want you to understand," he said, as he hoisted the bag into his grip, "that I have never trusted anyone in my life whose price I didn't know."

※   ※   ※

Lydia balanced the two bags of groceries on one knee and rummaged through her purse for the key to Clare's front door. She was angry. She should've had it out and ready, but she was late. She didn't like the idea that anyone would know that she had a key to the house. But she glanced quickly across the street as the door opened. No curtains moved.

She dropped her purse and hurried to the kitchen, pulling vegetables and stew meat out of the bag. She checked the clock—three hours. Clare said he'd be home by six, Carl and Marilyn Raglin would arrive at seven-thirty, and the Stewarts at eight. Clare hadn't asked her to prepare dinner. He had decided that he would put off the meeting with Lonnie Harrison and the Everett Chronicle, because the dinner with two important union officials and their wives—Carl Raglin of the Sailors' Union and Billy Stewart of the Longshoremen—was more important. That way, he'd be home and could do it himself.

"I can do it," volunteered Lydia. "I can cut the teachers planning meeting short."

Clare refused. "School's only a week away and you've put too much of your time into the campaign already."

But Lydia insisted. She'd heard Clare's end of the conversation with Lonnie Harrison on the phone two days earlier. She sensed the point, though Clare avoided the detail.

So Lydia had gone by Walther's on her way home, bought enough stew meat to make Claudia Walther peer closely at her. She had then dropped her daughter and Clare's daughter at the church for the weekend youth retreat on Sylvina Lake, ten miles north of Seakomish. "Are you sure you wouldn't rather stay home and visit with your father's guests?" asked Lydia of Shelley Ristall.

"My father's guests are always boring," she said, lugging a bag out of the car. "All they do is argue about politics. Besides,"—a twinkly smile suddenly filled the gaps between the freckles—"it will let the two of you be alone." This sent both girls into fits of laughter. A stern look from Lydia quickly settled them down. She gave both a peck on the cheek and hurried to Clare's house.

Lydia was aware that the relationship was becoming more serious—and public. The girls were the first to pick it up—partly because they were such close friends to start with. The other teachers could see it, though few said much. People at church knew it, leading to many knowing smiles from the ladies on Sundays. Which meant that Lydia often did not go. But increasingly, Lydia didn't mind. She was not a public person. And there was something in the feeling of being part of a couple—and the world recognizing it—that pleased her.

There was something else too. She discovered it while campaigning for Clare. Even talking to total strangers about a candidate makes you feel closer to him, she thought, but especially if you've been seeing him for six months, or was it a year? Lydia rapidly tossed the chopped vegetables into the pot, careful to layer them around the edges of the meat. It would be a year—a year in November that Clare had first asked her out.

She checked the clock—another hour before Clare returned. She put in the stew, and started setting the table. She noticed that her hands looked raw and the skin broken, from all the hands she'd shaken at the depots and grocery stores down the Seakomish Valley during the past several months. She selected green cloth napkins to accompany the china, as well as wine glasses with green crystal stems. When she was done, she surveyed the scene. A perfectly set table—more like something from one of the mansions on Queen Anne Hill in Seattle, not Seakomish.

But Clare had insisted that she put out the best china. "These guys love money," he assured her. "They all want it. And it's something they can understand—it doesn't matter how much they rail against the companies. Besides, it'll convince them I'm no Communist."

The comment had troubled Lydia more than she let on. There had been more talk lately. She'd picked it up when she and another teacher knocked on doors to campaign for Clare. There was more of it in the local papers. Communists were behind the militant unions. The Longshoremen were swimming with Reds. The CIO was backed by Moscow.

A cloud of steam rose as she lifted the lid, sending a hint of beef throughout the kitchen. She took out lettuce and radishes and peeled the skin from onions; then sliced apples for cobbler.

Communists in the CIO. The words sounded too sinister, too ugly. Life in the woods was one thing. You came to accept its harshness. But talk of Communists, that was something that didn't feel right in Seakomish, or anywhere down the valley, for that matter.

She willed the thoughts out of her mind. If she was going to entertain tonight, she needed to feel entertaining. She checked the stew, turned down the burner, then went to the bathroom to put on her lipstick.

✻    ✻    ✻

For four hours, the wine flowed. Halfway through dinner, Clare got two more bottles from the basement, always showing them first to Billy Stewart, who sniffed the cork and rolled a sip around in his mouth before letting Clare fill the rest of the glasses.

By midnight, the ladies had turned their attention to the art collection, which Lydia now knew almost as well as Clare. The men retired to the living room, wine glasses in hand. Clare brought a tray of cigars, which all three promptly lit.

"Impressive," said Stewart, a man whose jowls seemed twenty years premature.

"A Bordeaux," said Clare.

"I don't mean the wine," replied Stewart, blowing a long stream of smoke toward the ceiling. "Union men are supposed to be poor, remember?"

Clare laughed, sitting slowly into a straight chair opposite Stewart. Raglin bit off the tip of his cigar and lit it. But he remained silent, as he had most of the evening.

"We can join the ladies on a tour of the paintings," said Clare lightly. "My favorite is an early drawing by Whistler, just around the corner in the hallway."

But Carl Raglin cut in. "Clare, why don't we move to the point of all this?"

Clare seemed puzzled initially, but then smiled when he met Raglin's look. "Always direct, Carl. I like that." Raglin didn't answer. "The reason I wanted to meet was twofold. I thought it was a good chance for all of us to meet face-to-face. To get to know one another."

Raglin rubbed the gray beard that made a long face seem too long. Lines creased the forehead.

"The second reason is that I need your help," continued Clare. He looked at both men, sizing up their likely reaction before he spoke the words. "I'm asking for help from both of your unions when the CIO men in the Seakomish Valley go out on strike. I want to close down the port of Everett."

Stewart dropped his cigar onto the carpet, grabbing it before the ashes fell off. Raglin continued to stare at Clare without expression.

"We are going to shut down all AFL operations in the Seakomish Valley," continued Clare. "Just for a few days. Maybe a week. I'm asking you to refuse to load or ship any logs from AFL camps."

Clare knew the request was colossal. He hardly knew either man. The CIO in the Seakomish Valley was hardly a union—in the eyes of most. And the Sailors' and Longshoremen's Unions had been pulled into the labor battles down the coast ever since '34.

"Jesus H. Christ," said Raglin, in a near shout. "What has got into your head?"

"We're not talking a month-long strike. Just a day or two," said Clare quickly.

Raglin sneered. "Do you have any idea how much money that is in lost wages just for members of the Sailors in Everett?"

"Some idea, yes."

"You're goddamn right—a lot. When did Harold Pritchett give the okay for this? C'mon, he's the head of the CIO lumber workers in the entire Northwest, after all."

"He didn't." Clare looked at both men quickly. "I'm doing this on my own."

Clare knew that as soon as he asked for help from other unions, this question would arise. Had this strike been cleared by the CIO central office? The answer was no—officially—though Clare had met with Pritchett several weeks before and outlined his plans. Clare recalled Pritchett's big smile when Clare had finished.

"You know that you are out of your mind, don't you?" Pritchett's smile was still there.

Clare rushed in with his answer. "But this is vital to loggers in the Seakomish..."

Pritchett held up two large hands. "Wait a minute, Clare. Let me finish. There is no way that you are ever going to win up there with a half-assed wildcat strike like that. You have to understand that before you start. And there is no way that the Central Committee can endorse you. Not right now, anyway. We're doing everything we can to avoid looking like rabble-rousers—officially, at least."

Pritchett paused, then pulled a checkbook out of his desk. "But I would like nothing better than to have wildcat strikes pop up all over the Northwest—you know, create a little additional friction for the AFL; give 'em something to think about. And I am happy to write a check for the cause."

Clare smiled, but declined. "No need, Mr. Pritchett. The financing is taken care of." He thought back to the odd look on Pritchett's face when he said he didn't need the money.

Clare was about to turn back to Raglin's question when Billy Stewart broke it.

"So let me get this straight," said Stewart, leaning forward in the chair. "You want the Longshoremen and the Sailors' Union to stop hauling in Everett only?"

"That's the main port that handles logs from the Seakomish Valley," said Clare.

Stewart evaluated this. His eyes locked on Clare without moving. Finally: "Clare, that's a very tall request. You know damn well that the last port strike ended only a few months ago. And now this? We're already up to our asses in alligators, and we don't need more."

Clare launched into all the reasons why it could be done. It wouldn't be long, only long enough for the timber companies in the Seakomish Valley to recognize that the CIO had some real clout. They could even just delay—slow down a little. There wouldn't be any violence. No pickets.

But Carl Raglin interrupted before Clare could finish. "I'll tell you this, Clare. The Sailors' Union never much liked all this radical stuff that the Longshoremen like. We approach union work like it was a business." Raglin shifted in his chair. "This just smells of penny-ante tactics. Either you do a strike or you don't. You don't just shut down here and there."

Stewart now jumped in. "How the hell you ever gonna get elected to the legislature if you're running a strike?"

"First, the people of this valley want a union with backbone," said Clare. "Second, if they don't elect me, it doesn't matter. Getting the CIO organized is all that counts. At the very least, my running for the legislature will get more people to pay attention to us."

Clare could hear the women returning. He knew that he couldn't get final promises from either man, but that wasn't his goal. "I have only this request," said Clare. "Just think about it. Don't decide right now."

As the women finally returned the living room, Raglin looked like he was about to speak again, but he finally shook his head and relit his cigar.

❀   ❀   ❀

It was always at this point that Lydia felt the guilt sweep over her. The picture of her husband that still sat on her bedroom bureau kept coming back to her. But with each motion of Clare's warm hands along her back, the sensation overwhelmed the memories.

She felt Clare's hands sink lower, onto her buttocks, moving gently, softly, dipping deep into the warm crevasses. Within minutes, she knew that she would be pleading him to press harder and deeper. But for now, Clare kneaded and rubbed, ever deeper, followed quickly by the wetness of his tongue.

Within seconds, she turned and swept him into her, holding him firm as she felt the thrusts begin and break over her. Deeper and louder, she felt the wave shudder throughout her. Until finally, they lay softly in one another's arms, listening to the midnight rain.

Lydia looked forward to the long conversations that followed their lovemaking. Part of it, she knew, was to keep her mind away from the guilt, from the thoughts of what her daughter would say, or Albert, if they found out. But part of it also was that she felt a closeness at these times that she missed so much.

Clare lit a cigarette as he lay tangled in her legs. "What did you think of Carl Raglin?"

Lydia rolled over and propped up on a pillow. All that was visible was Clare's outline. "Shouldn't you be reading me sonnets instead of asking me about Carl Raglin?"

"Sorry," said Clare with a sigh.

Lydia gave him a soft hug, laughing. "I was just kidding." She rolled back against the pillow and considered his question. "I thought he was very civilized, but a little standoffish, I guess. What about you?"

Clare blew out a breath of smoke into the darkness. "Typical Sailors' Union representative, I guess."

"Typical?"

"Yeah. Parochial. Conservative."

"I take it he said he wouldn't support the strike?"

Clare got up and walked to the window. He pulled open the curtain and looked at the rain. Lydia could now make out the puffs of smoke against the streetlight. Though Clare was not a large man, he was muscular. His arms and chest seemed coated in a thick band of muscle, his stomach rippled. From running from too many widow-makers when he was a kid, he told Lydia. Now, as she watched him, she was struck by how powerful Clare looked—something that few others understood about him.

"Did I tell you that Lonnie Harrison told me I've got to drop the strike if I want to get elected?"

"No you didn't."

Clare turned to face her. "He said that I should announce Monday that there's not going to be a strike."

Lydia laughed. "And you told him to go to hell?"

Clare shrugged. "Mostly. But I knew he had a point." Clare frowned as he sat on the bed. He drew aggressively on the cigarette. "Sometimes I wonder who I'm kidding, though."

She waited. This was Clare after midnight. At sea in the forces that he'd set in motion on his own. But now questioning any—even all— of them.

His voice was small. "What kind of arrogance does it take to run for the State Legislature while you're about to organize the biggest strike this valley has ever seen? And then, to beat it all, telling the publisher of the Everett Chronicle—eyeball-to-eyeball—that you aren't?"

"Who said it's arrogance? What about compassion or concern? You deserve credit for trying to do both, because both would help all of these men, and their families."

Clare laughed. "Did I tell you that I ran into one of Bud Cole's men last week—Lightning Stevens?"

"You're full of news," said Lydia as she reached for his package of cigarettes. She rarely smoked. But news of Bud Cole was enough to bring out a craving for a cigarette.

Clare shrugged. "Bumped into him at Walther's store. He said that it looks like they've had more sabotage up there."

Lydia exhaled a cloud of smoke, but didn't say anything.

"He said the cook's cats had been mauled, probably by a human. They used some kind of tool to scoop the heads out."

"My God," whispered Lydia. "What kind of a person would do that?" She paused, then added. "Albert hasn't said a word about it."

"Maybe he hasn't because Bud and the crew have all decided that I'm the one who did it," said Clare with a laugh.

"You're serious?"

"Quite."

Lydia now strode to the window. "That is absolutely ridiculous. Why would they think that?"

"It's easy," said Clare, now laying back on the bed again. "They think I'm behind everything—the train wreck, the spike, now the animals. They figure we want to stop Skybillings. It's the CIO. We want to destroy everything, you know. So, I'm guilty."

Lydia now sucked hard on the cigarette, her mind sorting through the problem. "This is stupid. This is so bald-faced stupid that no one, in their right mind, could believe this." She paused now, exhaling smoke. "First of all, why would you bother with them? They are too small. No one gives a damn what Skybillings does."

"That's exactly what I said to Lightning," said Clare, his voice relaxing slightly. "You know, Lightning Stevens is a decent fellow. I've known him for years. So I said, 'Lightning, look. I got much bigger fish to fry than Skybillings. There is no way that the CIO is gonna bother with Bud Cole and his outfit.' Besides, I told him that we don't work that way. If the CIO has a problem with an outfit, we'll lay down a picket line. We don't go around killing people—or cats, for that matter."

Clare snickered. "Of course, I didn't tell him the other reason why Skybillings' got nothing to worry about...."

He paused, but Lydia looked out the window, without responding.

"What with Albert working there, Bud Cole has an ironclad guarantee."

Lydia turned now to study Clare's face. She'd often thought about the contradiction she was stepping into, falling in love with a man whose political activities could indirectly—no, actually, very directly—endanger her son. But she had finally resolved the issue. She had done what she could to keep Albert out of the woods. She'd used every argument she could think of. She had to be willing to let him make his own choices and to live with the results. Yet Clare's statement added a new complexity. Lydia had never expected him to purposely avoid shutting down Skybillings just because of Albert.

"Clare, you don't have to do that." She walked to the bed and sat down, reaching for his hand. "Albert knows the choice he's making."

"Well, frankly, I doubt that's true." Clare closed his eyes, as Lydia rubbed his shoulder and arm.

They didn't speak for several minutes. Lydia leaned back against the headboard, thinking about Albert. He also hadn't ever said anything to her about the fact that the spike was filed, causing the accident. She'd heard it from one of the teachers.

Clare ran his hand along her stomach, down her leg. Then back up again, ending with trying to tickle her below her armpits. Lydia let out a shriek.

"Clare Ristall, you are nothing but trouble," she said, as she kissed him gently on the forehead. He laid back, warming in the comfort of her body. For several minutes, more silence.

Then Lydia spoke softly. "Has Bud Cole ever talked to you about any of this, Clare?"

For a moment, she thought he had gone back to sleep. But then his voice came softly.

"Never." Clare rolled over and leaned onto an elbow, looking into her eyes. "And he never will."

She shook her head, confused.

"He never, ever will talk to me about any of this because he is incredibly jealous of me, and he cannot stand to face it."

"Jealous of you, how?"

Clare let out a sharp laugh. "Is that a serious question?"

"Very serious. Why wouldn't he want to talk to you?"

Clare now reached out and pulled her toward him, letting a hand rest under a breast. "You and I both know that Bud Cole would give his eye teeth to be where I am right now—and where I was about a half hour ago."

Lydia slapped him gently. "Bud Cole is hardly jealous of you, Clare."

"He is, too," said Clare. "He has been in love with you for years. He just doesn't have the guts to say it, or the brain to do anything about it."

Lydia lay her head on Clare's chest as he stroked her hair. He continued to laugh about Bud. But Lydia heard little of it.


## Chapter 24

The mountains lay in summer splendor.

Though ice clung to the tops of the peaks and the glaciers remained immobile even in the hottest sun, the granite below became whirls of blue and gray. Every day, the sunshine bore down on the snowfields. Every day, the fields gave up more and more to the heat, filling streams with an icy torrent that rushed across the floors of ravines with a whooshing sound that pretended to be the wind. In between, the woods held a royal greenness, dappled by hues that ranged from the yellow green of skunk cabbage to the deep green of rhododendron. In the warmth of summer, the greenness took on a bolder, stronger shade, unfettered by the grayness of winter or the watery air of springtime. With the warmth, the woods came into its own—brilliant, sparkling, powerful.

But Skybillings was changing this, albeit only slightly in such a universe of forest, but changing it nonetheless in the acreage on the sloping shoulders of Three Sisters Ridge. From the tips of the peaks, Skybillings must have looked more like it was painting the mountains than logging them. As it moved up the first ridge, then reached onto the other, the green ground—once matted thick with firs—turned deep brown, splotches on the face of the woods that hinted slightly of red at midday, black at dusk.

And across the mighty chest of Three Sisters now stood the beginnings of an unlikely railroad trestle—a creature with spindly legs, lashed tightly at its knees and ankles with heavy crossbeams, and support posts zigzagging their way up and down. Its feet buried deep in granite. Every day the creature reached further across the ravine, almost laughable in its unlikely course, but insistent, refusing to give in to the heavy pull of gravity or the evening winds that slipped off of Three Sisters.

Bud slowed the speeder as the panorama of the trestle against the gray-brown rock face opened into view. He brought the speeder to a stop, as he always did when he was alone at this spot, the landing, just before the track turned inward and began the steady descent downward, toward camp.

From the first day he'd laid eyes on this land, Bud had realized how unlikely it was that anybody could ever get a trestle to the rich fir on the other side of the deep ravine. Given its depth and the steep drop-off near the bottom of the Three Sister's face, the gorge would force the trestle flat up against the rock face; then the trestle would have to twist-in slightly three quarters of the way across. Even Ashford & Southern had given up. When Bud bought the land, he had consoled himself with the knowledge that he wouldn't have to try—a belief quickly dashed by Witstrop's demand in exchange for more money.

Now the trestle was no longer a dream. It was certainly well over 500,000 board feet of poles, bents, caps, braces, stringers, and—on its top—railroad ties and, in places, track. It even had a name, dubbed "Bachelder's Folly" by Valentine when Harry first announced the plan for the work, but then adopted by Bachelder himself. And it had a personality of its own. It shook with each slam of the pile driver. It popped and creaked in the heat and cold. In the rain or morning frost, its slippery footing became a ticket to death on the rocks a hundred feet below.

But at midday, with the summer sun tilted now just above Three Sisters, it opened the ridgelines to the west and offered a perspective that few, if any, men had ever seen. As the lunch whistle blew, the crew working on top, or those securing braces underneath, settled at the farthest point—near the last set of bents—to get the best views. From that vantage, it was a panorama of ridgelines for perhaps fifty miles to the north and west.

Bud heard himself laugh as he turned and gave the speeder gas. Even the loudmouths, he thought—St. Bride, Valentine, Conrad

Bruel, and Appleseth. He had even seen them on top, eating their sandwiches, staring off into the distance, taking in what was simply a breathtaking view. Even the gruffest had to stop, at least for a moment.

Bud used the speeder to move quickly back and forth to Seakomish on the Skybillings rail line. The speeder was nothing more than four small railroad wheels welded to a metal platform, with a gas engine and a throttle. Bud had rigged-up two seats in the front, and an open space for hauling gear in back.

Bud let out the throttle slowly, rounded the curve, then opened it completely, shooting the speeder down the incline, the cool wind in his face. He grabbed his coat from under the seat and pulled it on. Hurrying to Seakomish to meet some kind of photographer seemed absolutely crazy, but—once again—Bachelder had talked him into it.

The letter was polite and seemed legitimate. "I am a private photographer specializing in logging photography. I am led to under-stand that your company has undertaken a trestle-building operation that is somewhat unusual, and I would like to record it." The letter was signed Julius Olmeier, from Anacortes, Washington.

"This is all I need," said Bud when Fergie dropped the letter on his desk after mail call. "Why the hell would a photographer want to come up here? Can you imagine the hell we'd have to put up with? Half the damn crew would claim he was part of the conspiracy."

Bachelder had read the letter and taken a completely different view. "Why not? May be just what they need."

Bud had laughed, thinking it was a joke. But the more he consid-ered it, the more it seemed to make sense. Bachelder's argument was that this was just what the crew needed to divert their attention away from all the other troubles Skybillings was facing.

Bud slowed the speeder as he approached the gorge part of Roosevelt Creek Valley—a narrow canyon of raging water with only a little room along one ledge for the railroad track that wound its way down to Seakomish. Dennis Elspeth sat along the track, smoking a cigarette, watching Bud approach.

"I'll be needing to see your passport and birth certificate, sir," said Dennis, with a thick formal air.

"Go to hell," said Bud as he pulled to a halt. He got out and shook hands with Elspeth, who sat again on the rock beside the track.

"How's it going, Dennis?"

Dennis was one of the riggers from the early days of Skybillings. Thick, stocky, his chest and neck bulged with muscles. "This job ain't half bad," he said with a smile, "as long as you don't have to shoot anybody, and especially as long as that "anybody" ain't one of your own men." Dennis nodded to the stream with his shotgun, as Maynard Olsen climbed out of the bushes next to Roosevelt Creek.

"I had you in my scope just for practice," said Maynard to Bud over the roar of the water.

Bud broke out into a gut laugh. "God it's good to see a couple of friends for a change." He sat on the side of the speeder and took out his tobacco pouch.

Dennis now turned serious as he and Maynard joined Bud on the speeder and began rolling their own cigarettes. "We've been watching for a week now and we ain't seen nothing, except for Fergie bringing the logs in and out. Not a soul."

Maynard seconded Dennis' point. "We've been keeping our eye on the other side of the stream, too, but nothing. And been watching up above." He paused now as Bud took in the geography. Nobody could get through here without walking on the track, or in the water, thought Bud—and this was the only human way into the Skybillings show. You'd have to be a mountain goat to get in any other way.

For several minutes, Bud filled them in on news from the camp, about Zoe's rules about getting rid of the stench, the animals whose heads had been torn off, and the crew's readiness to stage a hunt for cougar. He finished by telling them how much of the trestle had been completed.

"It don't make no sense," said Maynard, with his thick lisp forcing Bud to listen more carefully. Several chipmunks now scampered within reach of the men.

"What don't make no sense?" asked Bud, sensing that Dennis and Maynard had spent most of their time on sentry duty feeding the animals.

"It don't make no sense to put a trestle in there, Bud. That's too damn close to Three Sisters. Start blasting in that rock, you never know what may come down on your head."

Bud knew all this. Inside and out. Every detail of what might happen when the blasting started—from the shale slide at the base of Three Sisters that might move suddenly and wipe out the section of trestle already standing, to the boulders that could be loosened and slam onto the trestle—and the crew—from above. He talked it over with Harry, regularly, and repeatedly. He rethought it. Reconsidered the decision. But always came back to Harry's point: "Do you want to log that ridge or don't you?"

This inevitably led into a moral dilemma, which Harry excused once again out of hand. "To hell with 'em," was Harry's response to Bud's worry that men, maybe lots of men, might be harmed. "These are men who sign up for hard labor. They take chances. If they don't like it, they can quit. Did anybody ask you your opinion when they shipped you to France?"

Maynard now bent down and tossed the chipmunks a few pieces of bread, drawing several squawking jays onto the alder trees sprouting out of the rocky surface between the tracks and the rushing stream.

Bud smiled in response to Maynard's point. "It's true Maynard, it's a risk, but that's the only way this show is gonna keep going." He paused to watch two chipmunks scuffle with a jay for a piece of bread. "So it's not even a decision."

As he said it, he knew it sounded more certain than he felt.

The men smoked in silence, feeling the sun on their faces, watching the animals. When he was done with his cigarette, Bud explained that they would be relieved soon by Bucky Rudman and Little Boy.

This brought a laugh from Dennis. "Bucky sitting here with a shotgun and nothing else to do. If you want a definition of what it means to be trigger happy, that's it."

Bud shrugged and started the speeder. It let out a rattling, gassy rumble that echoed in the gorge. "It's either sentry duty or go down and blast rock under the trestle," shouted Bud with a smile.

Dennis pointed to the ground at his feet, as if to say he'd rather choose sentry duty. Maynard had already disappeared back to his point next to the water. As he gave the speeder gas, Bud wondered what had gone so wrong that a logging company now had to post sentries—with shotguns.

❖ ❖ ❖

Julius Olmeier looked like Charlie Chaplin.

At least that was Bud's first impression when he saw him standing on the platform at the Seakomish Train Depot. Even after Olmeier spoke, with a slight English or Danish twist in his voice, Bud still couldn't get the notion out of his head. And in a deep-base voice to boot. But Bud decided it was the small stature mostly—thin frame, narrow face, delicate hands. And the little tuft of dark whiskers, tucked just under the bottom lip.

Bud had loaded two large trunks of equipment into the back of the speeder, and set-off up the mountain. Olmeier settled into the seat next to him, a long coat wrapped around him. He slipped a thick corduroy hat over his head, which he held tight as they raced along Roosevelt Creek.

"Nice of you to make this trip for me, Mr. Cole," shouted Olmeier against the wind. "I think you will be pleased with the results."

Bud smiled, though he wasn't sure how a bunch of pictures of his crew would make him very happy. "You know much about woods work, Mr. Olmeier?" asked Bud, easing slightly on the engine to make talking a little easier.

Olmeier smiled and nodded, his hand still on the corduroy cap. "Sure do. It's my living—woods photography, I mean. I do some studio work in Anacortes, but mostly I visit the logging shows."

Bud found that he liked the young fellow. Partly due to his looks. As Olmeier spoke, even his mannerisms reminded Bud of the fun of Chaplin's movies. But he also liked the young fellow's sincerity. He couldn't have been more than twenty-two or twenty-three, but he had a spark that Bud admired. "You got a family, Mr. Olmeier?"

"A small son and a daughter—I hope—on the way." He laughed, somewhat embarrassed.

"Do you mind my asking how a young father makes a living by taking pictures of a bunch of dirty loggers?" asked Bud.

Olmeier laughed. "That's a question my wife asks sometimes, too." He shrugged and was silent while Bud negotiated the narrow gorge, waving at Dennis Elspeth as they passed. Dennis waved his shotgun and smiled.

"That man was carrying a shotgun," said Olmeier.

"I know. I put him there." Bud turned to Olmeier. "You were telling me about earning a living from making pictures of loggers."

"Oh, yes. My wife occasionally expresses concerns along those lines, but it's better than one might expect. I visit the camps to take the pictures. Then I visit them again, a few months later—if it's alright with the management, of course—and offer the photos for sale to the men. You can actually make a respectable living at it."

Bud considered this as they rode in silence for several miles. The incline had increased, so the speeder worked harder, making conversation more difficult. Bud noticed that Olmeier seemed lost in the scenery around them. For a long time, he focused entirely on Roosevelt Creek running next to them. He asked Bud several questions about it—where it started, what it was like in springtime—then turned his attention to the rising peaks on either side.

"Do you mind my asking why you chose this area to log in?" asked Olmeier, straining to be heard over the speeder and the wind.

Bud looked at him, trying to determine the origin of the question. Normally, that was a question he would have tossed away with a curt response or simply ignored altogether. But now, it was the kind of question that made him at least pause. Was there something more to it?

But from Olmeier, the question seemed innocent, and Bud found that he actually enjoyed telling the story—about looking for land, not finding any down low, having to come to the high ground, getting a good price from Ashford & Southern, and then deciding to put in the trestle to reach the best stand of all.

Olmeier seemed to think about this, though he didn't answer. He was once again lost in the scenery, twisting in his seat occasionally to watch the peaks pass overhead. Bud noticed that his coat was badly worn. The elbows were patched. Someone had re-stitched the lining along the bottom, several times, with different colors of thread. Bud saw that one of the belt loops was missing entirely, forcing Olmeier to cinch the belt tightly.

"Wasn't there something about burial grounds up here? About Seakomish graves?"

Bud slowed the speeder to navigate the turn onto the steep section of track running up to the mountain. As he did, the gas fumes caught up with them, mingled suddenly with the scent of dead fish. Bud sniffed the air, wondering who had been fishing in Roosevelt Creek and left dead fish along the stream, but he turned his attention back to Olmeier.

"It's true," said Bud. "We're right there. Right in the middle of the grounds."

"That worry you at all?"

Bud laughed. "Not in the least. Why?"

Olmeier shrugged. "Personally, I tend toward the side of being a bit superstitious. Don't like to admit it. But it's true."

Bud gave the speeder throttle, scaring a flock of mourning doves off the edge of the track. "I 'spect you've heard about the troubles up here, then."

Olmeier nodded, absently scratching his goatee as he watched the birds fly, but he didn't say anything.

Bud smiled at him. "But you decided to come up here anyway."

"I did."

"Mind if I ask why?"

Olmeier now offered a big full smile. "Because this is the biggest damn trestle of its kind—far as I know—and no photographer worth his salt would miss it for the world."

"Ghosts or not?"

"Ghosts or not."

❋    ❋    ❋

As they continued to climb, Olmeier reported on his recent visits to other camps, starting up in British Columbia, then working down through the valleys of Washington. This was a good time for making pictures of the logging crews, he reported. More of them were operating than any time since the '20s. More men with money to buy pictures. More bulls-of-the-woods—camp bosses—willing to let him visit.

"But damn dangerous now, isn't it?" asked Bud as they neared the top of the climb.

Olmeier rubbed his goatee again, turning a frown toward Bud. "My last job was bought mostly by the sheriff's department down in Longview."

"I don't understand."

"It seems that the last place I photographed broke into a nasty battle the day after I left." Bud groaned, but Olmeier cut him off. "You needn't worry. Had nothing to do with me. Some hooligans showed up the next day, tried to close the place down, and the bull decided they ought to fight." Olmeier took a deep breath. "Ten sent to the hospital, one dead."

"So why did the sheriff want your pictures?"

"They decided that it was an inside job. Some of the guys on the crew were in cahoots with the hooligans. They wanted to take a look to see if any of the faces matched the descriptions of troublemakers that were doing the same last month down in Auburn."

Bud let off the throttle, bringing the speeder to a halt. The staccato call of a woodpecker rocketed overhead.

"In Auburn, too?"

Olmeier's eyebrows arched. "Oh, you didn't hear? Several men were killed at Sawyer Brothers in Auburn last month. Same thing. Some kind of sabotage on the inside. Three, in fact, including some businessman who was there for some reason. Name was Patterson, or Pinkerton, or something like that."

Bud let out the clutch and they surged forward, sending Olmeier's head back against the seat.

❀   ❀   ❀

When they reached the top of the mountain, the high-pitched screech of the steam whistle echoed off the face of Three Sisters. Bud quickly pulled the speeder to a side platform.

"The Shay will be through in no time with a load of logs," said Bud, as he turned off the engine. "We might's well cool our heels for a half hour or so. Besides, there's a good view of the trestle from over here."

Olmeier jumped out of his seat and ran across the track to where it almost butted against the rocky edge of the ravine. He shielded his eyes from the sun as he studied the outlines of the trestle against Three Sisters Ridge.

Olmeier whistled softly, but was otherwise silent.

"Whaddya think?"

Olmeier turned quickly, as if he'd forgotten that Bud was there. "I think that this is one very large trestle."

Bud walked to the edge, trying to make out the trestle in the growing shadow that engulfed it. He could see Bachelder on the front end of it, standing like a captain on a ship that seemed to be racing headlong into a mountain wall. Underneath, men scrambled along the gridwork braces. Several crawled across the solid rock at the base.

"Once the final section is finished, we can start hauling out all that timber over there," said Bud, pointing to the cold deck piles on the distant side of the canyon. "We've been logging that for a month, but can't get it out without the trestle."

Olmeier seemed to be photographing the setting with his mind. He studied carefully the distant ridge, now increasingly brown where the Swedes had dropped perhaps a hundred firs. Then he turned to the trestle, studying its cross-hatched support beams below. Then he took in the emptiness just above them—the 10,000-foot hard, granite backdrop of Three Sisters.

❀   ❀   ❀

The hour was late. The sun had long since disappeared behind Three Sisters, and the cool of the late afternoon had set in. Harry Bachelder was in a terrible mood.

"Goddamn it," snorted Harry, as Bud and Olmeier made their way out to the end of the trestle. Bachelder's face was dirty. Grease covered his arms.

"What's wrong?" asked Bud.

"Management," said Harry in a half-shout. "That's what's wrong. Management. Personnel. Unions. America has gone to hell, do you know that?" His face froze momentarily, as if to give the question the weight it deserved. "I cannot understand how a herd of such under-educated fools that you have hired for this logging operation can be so goddamn bull-headed and so goddamn lily-livered at the same time."

Bud smiled politely, nodding in the direction of Olmeier, who seemed to not hear any of it. He stared off into the blue-gray haze, which illuminated several white ridges running toward the north.

"Harry, I want to introduce you to Julius Olmeier," said Bud. "He's the photographer."

Harry swept his attention to the young man, who smiled and held out his hand. Harry grabbed it and shook it, even though he left deep black smudges.

"You're the photographer, eh?" Harry's face brightened slightly. He swept his hair back, leaving black smudges now on his forehead. "When do you plan on making pictures of this trestle?"

"I've been trying to read the light. Perhaps in the forenoon tomorrow, if that's okay?" Olmeier still looked away as he spoke.

"Sure, sure," said Harry, the scowl now gone completely. "That's fine…"

Bud cleared his throat and spit over the side.

Harry added quickly, "…assuming it's okay with Mr. Cole."

Bud nodded to Harry. "That's fine by me."

"That's perfect," said Harry quickly—with a broad smile now across his face. "I figure we'll tell the crew and everything will take care of itself."

Bud studied Bachelder for a moment. "Harry, why do you seem so pleased by all of this?"

"Maybe I just have got the crew figured out wrong," said Harry, now with a thin smile. "Maybe they aren't stupid at all. Maybe you hired a crew that is too goddamn smart, Bud. You see, nobody wants to go down and drill holes for the dynamite in the granite down there. Too risky, they say." He nodded downward, to the crisscross beams that formed the framework of the trestle and the flat ledge of granite directly below. Harry now reached for a rag that lay under several hammers and started wiping his hands. "I figure that when they find out that the best logging photographer in the country is going to make a photo of them down there on that rock, I'll have to beat away the volunteers."

Olmeier laughed nervously. "They don't want to go down where?" He searched below, trying to find the spot Harry referred to.

Harry raised an eyebrow slightly as he took several steps forward and stopped at the very end of the trestle. He leaned gingerly onto a wooden railing that was nailed across the front edge. "See that rock face down there?"

Olmeier leaned over, peering at the rock ledge that was more than fifty feet below them. The ledge jutted straight out from the face of Three Sisters, sloping slightly toward the ravine. Most of the surface was flat, broken only by a few cracks and fissures. A gust of wind abruptly shook the entire structure, causing Olmeier to grab the railing.

"She's a little temperamental," said Bachelder, with a slight hint of apology in his voice. "This time of evening the wind comes off the rock face up above. Once we get her connected to that piece coming over from the other edge of the ravine, well, you won't feel the gusts like that anywhere. It'll be gentler."

Olmeier studied the long ladder that ran downward from where they were standing, down through the middle of the trestle. "That's how we get down to the rock you're talking about?"

"Yup. Our guys go down that to lash the braces down below here." Harry pointed to the wood beams that held the bent's posts together. "And that's how we're going to get down to that ledge where we are going to set the dynamite, so we can blast holes in the granite, so we can set more of these babies into them." Harry now kicked the top of one of the posts that formed the ribbing of the massive wood frame.

Olmeier studied the scene for a long time, looking upward, then toward the facing ridge, then the ridge behind him. He asked what time the crew started work and when they finished. Several men appeared from underneath, making their way to the top of the ladder. Once at the top, they began the walk back to the crummy.

Olmeier's face seemed darker. "I'll make you a deal, gentlemen," he said quickly. The wind caught his hair, ruffling it into his face as he spoke. "I will be happy to climb down your ladder, with my camera and tripod, and photograph your men as they get ready to set the dynamite."

Harry smiled and held out his hand. "You got yourself a deal, Mister," he said quickly.

Bud pushed down Harry's outstretched hand. "Not so fast, Harry. Remember, I do still own this joint. Plus, I think there is a 'but' in Mr. Olmeier's deal."

"Yes there is," said Olmeier, now wiping a strand of hair that got caught in his mouth. "The 'but' is simply this: I'll go down that ladder, if you'll agree to do one thing for me." He turned and paced several yards away, then turned around.

"This trestle is able to carry a train out this far, isn't it?" asked Olmeier of Harry.

"Yes, as a matter of fact," said Harry quickly.

"What?" Bud's tone conveyed the question on his face.

"I would like a photograph of the locomotive on it, along with a few of your men," said Olmeier quickly.

"That's a deal."

Bud exploded. "Goddamn it, Harry. I'm tired of reminding you who runs this company. And just what the hell are the two of you talking about exactly? This is crazy. This goddamn trestle isn't done. How hard is that to see? How can you get a train...?"

"Nothing to it," shot Harry. "I was planning to run the Shay out here—at least part of the way—just to test the thing a little. There's no danger. It'll hold. I just want to see where the stresses are, before we link up the final section."

The steam whistle shattered the silence, announcing that the crummy was heading down the mountain. Anybody not on board would have to walk back to camp. "We'll take the speeder," said Bud, as Harry paused slightly after the whistle blew.

Bud studied both men. "Are you sure you want to climb down there, Mr. Olmeier?" asked Bud. "One slip and you are dead.

Those kids of yours..."

"I am confident of my ability to navigate a ladder, Mr. Cole."

Bud shook his head and frowned, then studied both of them. He turned to take in the trestle itself, then turned back to Harry. "Is this another of those cockamamie schemes you are famous for?"

"No. It's not. It is very customary to test the strong part of a trestle with the equipment you're going to run across it. If it's a question of risk, I'll be happy to pull it out here on my own—Fergie can start it. I'll stop it."

Bud drew in a deep breath. Both hands still stood on his hips.

"Jesus." He shook his head slowly. "This is against everything I know, but I guess I'll agree. But here is my condition, gentlemen." He turned directly to Olmeier, after looking about to make sure that all the workers were out of earshot. "You said you took pictures of that crew down in Auburn."

Olmeier nodded.

"I want you to tell me if you see any of those same faces in Skybillings that you saw down there."

Olmeier smiled quickly. "I'd be happy to, except for one thing. I have a terrible memory for faces. They all blend together. But as soon as I have your pictures developed, I'll compare the faces to the negatives from Auburn. If anyone is in common, I'll send you a telegram immediately."

Bud studied Olmeier, whose face seemed older in the deepening dusk. The thought that he was making a terrible mistake crossed Bud's mind—as did the thought that he was making a series of them and that he would pay a dear price—but he pushed it off. "Alright, it's a three-way deal—but no one talks about it."

❊   ❊   ❊

The next morning brought brilliant sunshine that Olmeier deemed perfect for shooting.

As soon as the crew found out about the photographs, Bachelder had more volunteers than he needed. Within a half hour of arriving at the trestle, he'd selected his men. Less than an hour later, Olmeier had already positioned, actually posed, them along the rock surface below—hammers, picks, and dynamite carefully placed for maximum photographic effect.

Olmeier steadied himself on the ledge, his tripod on a flat piece of rock just in front of him. He stumbled slightly, sending shale skittering across a narrow gutter of rock and then dropping in free fall several hundred feet to the firs below.

Olmeier nodded and smiled, but otherwise ignored it. A hawk swept upward suddenly, out of the canyon, veering away just as it neared Olmeier's head. But that was the only movement, save a steady breeze from the ravine below.

Everyone stayed in the exact position in which Olmeier had placed them. Bud steadied himself on one knee, resting his right arm on the other. Conrad Bruel did the same to Bud's right; then Little Boy Whitaker next, his foot touching a crate of dynamite. Just slightly above and behind them on the ledge stood Valentine, Edwards, and St. Bride—all with arms folded. The line was finished by Bachelder, whom Olmeier had posed with his right side to the camera, his body facing St. Bride, his head turned slightly, his hands slipped casually into his pants pockets.

Olmeier snapped several times, then moved the camera, rear-ranged their positions, and snapped several more—this time climbing onto a rock outcropping, just to their right.

"Jesus, Julius, you're gonna get killed," said Bud. But Olmeier didn't respond, setting the camera gingerly upon the ledge, then finding footholds to haul himself up. Behind him was open air.

Once on the ledge, he redirected the shot. This time, all of the men sat across the face of the rock, arranged in a semi-circle around the box of dynamite. The sun climbing higher over the ridge behind him lit the faces in the bright white that Olmeier sought, against the massive poles of the trestle that dug into the ledge just behind them.

"What's a man get out of all this?" asked Valentine—a complaint, not a question.

"Shhh," snapped Olmeier, clicking furiously as a band of clouds arrived, then opened the scene fully to brilliant sunshine. After perhaps ten minutes of snapping pictures—with the men remaining motionless, or trying—Olmeier clapped his hands and shouted, "That's it. Now you can blast away."


## Chapter 25

Clare Ristall maneuvered the rowboat through a shallow channel, trying to avoid the sandbars that appeared at low tide. In the distance, two young men stood barefoot in the sand. Both held narrow garden spades, which—like their forearms—were covered with wet sand. Clare had hired them to dig clams for the dinner the next night. They waved when they noticed him.

Low tide in the San Juan Islands—even on Samish Island, which wasn't technically an island because it was connected to the mainland by a short dike—exposed long swatches of dark sand, separated by occasional streams of seawater flowing toward the deeper channels. Some people hated the view and the smell—they called them "gunk-holes." Clare liked low tide because you could observe the sea at work. He even liked the pungent mix of warm seaweed, exposed barnacles, and sharp saltiness that filled the air. But he especially liked the easy access to oysters and clams that low tide provided. He decided that they were the perfect food for a group of hungry loggers.

Clare pulled the oars hard to bring himself into the deeper water. Here he could let the tide pull him further into the broad channel that ran between Samish Island and Lummi Island. Because ships used the route to reach Bellingham from Everett or the Strait of Juan de Fuca, he always kept a close watch. But on a Friday afternoon in mid-summer, there was little traffic.

He pulled in the oars and tossed the small anchor overboard, to hold him in the middle of the channel. It was the best place to get the full sweep of what he loved about living in this part of Washington— the Cascades, still snow-tipped in summer, running the entire length of the horizon to the east; the deep blue channel, edged by the dark sands of low tide on Samish; and, to the west, the rise of Lummi Island, which was more of a mountain than an island, rising like a humpback whale out of the water, and now bathed in green-black as the afternoon sun continued to flee west.

As a result, brilliant afternoon light illuminated the log lodge, which he had rented for the weekend of meetings, that stood back slightly from the shore on Samish. He often came here to think, usually by himself. He rented it from a banker he had gotten to know in Seattle soon after the War. The banker was a Hoover Republican, but they'd struck up a friendship anyway.

Clare knew the building had been there for years, but didn't know how long. He assumed that it was built in the mid-1800s to house a crew of loggers who were likely cutting the old Douglas firs that, at that time, grew right up to the shore. They'd drop them over the cliffs into Puget Sound, then move them with tug boats that pulled large log booms—floating corrals of logs held together by cables—to mills in Bellingham or Everett. A three-story fireplace of granite boulders stood in the middle of the massive room, with four log posts providing the building's structural support in the distant corners. Bedrooms lay just off of the great room, on two levels, and an old iron stove that was as wide as three regular stoves anchored the far wall.

The declining afternoon sun was now leaving the lower parts of the house in deep shadows, though the ridge of tin on the roof still gave off a slight glint of reflection. Clare studied the large structure. How many loggers had lived there over the years, he wondered. Had to be hundreds, since logging right along Puget Sound had been active until the turn of the century. But how many logging companies would have provided this kind of facility for loggers? Probably none. This would have been where the company owners lived. The company big shots. They probably invited the bankers from Everett or Seattle to come here for fishing holidays.

As he picked up an oar and slipped it through the oarlock to begin the journey back, a thought crossed his mind: He was about to organize a strike against companies that may have been founded in this very building.

❖    ❖    ❖

Clare greeted each man as he stepped off the bus. Sammons had given him a list of the names, but he didn't need it. He recognized all of them.

Harold Rauck of Northwest Logging. Claude Harper of Ashford & Southern. Milt Rumshin of Cascade County Logging. Olie Ness and Sherman Baxter of Stardale Logging. In all, twenty-five. Clare knew most of them from visits to the logging camps, starting way back in '35 when he led them in the Seakomish Valley Local of the AFL.

Now he was welcoming them to Samish Island for a day of fishing in Puget Sound, followed by a salmon, clam, and oyster feed that night. Then plenty of beer, wine, and scotch around the stone fireplace afterward. The goal of it all was to make sure that these men would, once again, be the spine of a strike that would close all logging in the Seakomish Valley. Only this time on behalf of the CIO.

"Okay fellas, toss your bags into any room, then follow me out to the water," he said to the group, which was accompanied by Sammons and Fitzgerald. "We've got plenty of rods and reels—and a ton of rowboats—for everyone."

The group of men stopped for a moment as they entered the building, taking in the massive room and the stone fireplace at its center. Several wandered around, touching the rough-hewn log supports in each corner, others sat down in the deep chairs in a circle near the fireplace.

"Hell of a place you got here, Clare," said Willy Hanson, a thick-chested man with a hint of a Scandinavian accent. "This here your summer home?"

Clare met the teasing tone with, "Nah. Too tiny for my tastes. Needs a little more elbow room."

He quickly clapped his hands. "C'mon. Times a-wastin'. I want those fishing boats in the water so we got something to eat tonight."

It took them only two hours, even with a breeze that made the boats drift into the middle of the deep channel. Fifteen salmon, three steelhead, ten cutthroat trout. Clare, Sammons, and Fitzgerald gutted and cleaned the entire haul in minutes and got them, along with the oysters and clams, ready for the fire. Clare also brought along several bushels of red, beefsteak tomatoes and fresh-picked corn that he'd gotten at a farm just outside of Mt. Vernon.

The dinner was ready in minutes, and the men scattered out along the beach and seawall, just in front of the lodge, to eat. As with the night before, the sun brought warm red light as it moved slowly toward the great hump of Lummi Island. Clare made sure that all the men had enough food, bringing around fresh platters of salmon as they ate. He also had Sammons making sure all of them got two beers, if they wanted them—but no more, at least until everyone was done eating and settled in front of the fireplace inside.

Clare worried that too much beer would make serious discussion impossible, but that too little could make it too threatening. A couple of beers, a full stomach, away from the wife and kids, sitting in front of the fire with your fellow loggers—Clare decided that was just right.

❊   ❊   ❊

"You guys want some more to eat?" Clare's voice broke over the loud conversation around the room. A chorus of "no's" responded. Most of the men had already settled around the fireplace, many on picnic table benches carried from the beach, others enveloped in the soft leather chairs, and the rest spread across the wood floor.

Clare stood to the side of the fireplace, his hands in his pockets. "Let me get right at it, fellas. I asked all of you to come here today so that I could explain to you personally what I believe we need to get done in the next couple of months. Honestly, I don't know if that means a strike—it might. And if it does, I want to make sure you are all in agreement and that you feel that you've had a chance to have your say. The only way to succeed is if we are all together."

The faces were friendly, many nodded. Sammons and Fitzgerald sat together at the end of one of the picnic benches. Sammons with folded arms; Fitzgerald looking out the window.

Clare got out the facts first. That he had met with each of the companies in the Seakomish Valley since March. That he had laid out the CIO demands—a ten-cent an hour pay increase; a standard contract that would be used by all companies; and recognition of the CIO as the sole bargaining agent for loggers in the valley. He said he had given all of the companies a deadline of August 1, and that several had already agreed. But most had not.

Clare paused to take in the room. All eyes were on him.

"I still hope that the rest of the companies in the valley will agree to these terms. There's still time for that—but not much. If they don't, this is what I think we need to do. First, we strike all companies that haven't agreed. Second, we put up picket lines around each of them— and we don't let anybody go to work there, whether it is guys who have stayed with the AFL, or it is scabs that the companies bring in."

Clare paced in front of the fire, his head bent down. No one spoke, though he wasn't sure if it meant they disagreed with him, or if it was just because they knew he was about to start in again.

"Let me raise two points that I suspect are on your minds." He now stopped pacing and faced them. "You fellows supported me by striking in '35. I told you, 'Follow me, and we will fix this.' Well, you did. And we didn't fix a damn thing. That was because of the dismal failure by the AFL. I believed in that strike with my whole heart—and I still do. What I don't believe in anymore is the leadership of the AFL."

Several men raised their hands, but Clare held up his hand. "Just one more point, fellas, and I will stop. The second concern I know that all of you have is that it sounds damn near crazy to ask men to give up their salaries by going on strike in light of how tough things still are. I know that is a big request. But I believe that the employers in this valley will always underpay you and undervalue you unless we show them that we will all stick together."

For perhaps a minute, nobody spoke. The men seemed to be weighing the last pieces of Clare's arguments, or perhaps beginning to formulate their own.

"And I want all of you to know that I personally will provide each man who goes out on strike with strike pay. I can't say how much that will be right now; that'll depend upon how many fellas go out. But I will guarantee that it is enough money to feed your family."

The first one to speak was Sherm Baxter—a barrel-chested man whose full brown beard seemed to hide most of his face. Clare had known Sherm Baxter from before the War, when they both worked for Ashford & Southern.

"I supported the AFL strike and I support this one. There ain't no way that we're gonna get our rights from these companies if we don't show them that we have got the balls to take action." Baxter now stood up from one of the leather chairs. "I don't know what the rest of you think, but this is the time to make our mark. I support Clare a hundred percent."

This brought several "I agree's" and nodding heads. One of men who had spoken now stood, introduced himself as Dave Nelkins of Big River Logging, a rail-thin man with hollow cheeks.

"Clare, I am totally in support of what you are doing here. But I do have a question."

Clare nodded. "This is the time to ask 'em."

"When we go out on strike, what does that mean exactly? I wasn't around here in '35." He paused and looked around at the men, as if slightly embarrassed. "Personally, I would prefer we try to find some agreement with the owners before it comes to that. I have two little ones to feed."

Nelkins sat down and nodded to Clare, who smiled but did not respond. Clare sat on the hearth and waited for others to speak. Several men looked at each other, then a man with a shiny bald head, about fifty, stood up.

"I'm Wally Becker, and I am the CIO representative at Falls Timber Company. I am supporting this strike, whole and complete."

Another man stood up saying that he worked for Deek Brown & Sons. "I have been a long-time member of the AFL, but I cannot stand what they did in the '35 strike. They sold us down the river. But let me say this: I just don't want to see any bloodshed. I don't think that serves our purpose. So what do you see us doing, Clare, as far as picketing goes? Will there be violence?"

Clare jumped to his feet because he saw that Sammons was about to answer the question.

"We will set up picket lines to keep all AFL workers out and to stop any outsiders that the companies may bring in," said Clare.

The man stood again. "But what does that mean? Do we just push people back who want to walk through?"

"Well, hopefully it won't come to that," said Clare. "Most often, like in '35, you just talk down the guys who are wanting to go through the line. You know—enough guys on our side, standing around, telling the scab or the AFL-er that he doesn't want to take on this fight."

Bernie Walker, a man with a stiff crew cut and olive complexion, raised his hand on the side of the room. Clare knew he was a strong CIO supporter, but he also knew he had a bunch of children. "You know, Clare, how I feel about the AFL and how I agree that they have left us to fend on our own." He took several steps toward the middle of the room as he spoke. "But it is very hard for me, Clare, to walk away from a paying job. My wife and I have just gotten back on our feet. We have the food we need. But I would be looking at the real possibility of losing our house."

Walker paused briefly to look around the room. Several heads nodded. Others studied the floor. "So my question here, Clare, really boils down to this: Are you absolutely sure a strike is necessary? Is there some other way?"

Clare studied the ground, his arms crossed, as he considered Walker's question. But before he could speak, Sammons jumped to his feet.

"What in the hell is wrong with you guys? We have talked long enough to these companies—"

Clare spoke over him. "Sammons, please sit down."

But Sammons continued. "We need to get in there and close 'em down, finally, and we will have the muscle to do that."

"Sit down, Sammons!" Clare barked the words, which finally brought the desired result. Clare drew in a deep breath. He continued to look at Sammons, ready to stop him again, but Sammons just shook his head, got up, and walked out.

When he was gone, Clare turned back to Bernie Walker. "Your question is the key one—and it deserves a fair answer and, if you like, a lot more discussion. In my mind, the answer is yes, we need to strike—assuming that a lot more logging shows in the valley refuse to sign the agreement. We have negotiated in good faith. We have given them plenty of time. We have made it clear that we want the CIO—not the AFL—to represent loggers."

Bernie smiled, but shook his head. "But why not live with what we've got for a while longer? That's my vote. Christ, Clare. Things are still too much in upheaval—and who knows what tomorrow will bring? And as for striking, well, goddamn, the whole world is on strike. And a lot of those strikes just lead to more strikes. Look at the strikes at the mills up and down Puget Sound. And the dockwork- ers—hell, half the time the port of Seattle is closed. And that just leads to even more trouble."

Bernie paused now and turned to the men near him. "C'mon, I heard some of you guys saying the same thing. Come on, tell him."

Clare didn't speak. He waited for others to stand. No one did, but two men sitting next to Bernie said they agreed with him. "There's no sense in striking," said one, a burly man whose name Clare momen- tarily could not recall. "We need to give it more time."

Clare stood and waited. No one else spoke. He again looked at as many faces as he could—trying to make eye contact as he swept the room. Many looked weary. Many sported sunburns from the day of fishing—made all the brighter by the warmth in the room. He noticed that Sammons now stood in the kitchen, arms folded, leaning against the long dining table.

"Okay," said Clare with a smile. "Anybody else want to weigh in?" Several heads shook no. He waited another moment, but still no one spoke.

"Okay. So let me speak to each one of these issues. First, as for waiting longer, my answer is no. Time is not our friend. We do not have the luxury of letting this draw out because the longer it does, the less likely we will win. Second, a lot of you don't see much of an opportunity right now. After all, things are just getting back on track, and you are finally feeling a little more secure in your jobs. Here is what I say to all of that: This is the opportunity of a lifetime. This is a time when every part of the world is pulling against every other part, whether it's the state of business, or it's the battles among the unions, or it's the politics in this country."

Clare now paced along the side of the room. "This chaos we have seen in the past few years is our big chance, don't you see? Because of all of these deep doubts we see around us and that we all feel, and because the business world is still trying to find its footing, we find ourselves in a time when the new order of the world is being created— it is being written right now, as we speak. What happened before doesn't much matter. But what we do now can change everything."

Clare stopped and faced the men. "And if anybody is about to lose their house over this, I want you to come and show me your paper- work, and I will make sure that the payments are made until you are back on the job."

❊    ❊    ❊

Seventeen to eight.

The vote was better than Clare expected. He knew it would never be unanimous. That was too much to hope for, especially after so many men expressed doubts. But in the middle of it all, he feared that maybe he couldn't even keep the majority.

So seventeen to eight was just fine. He knew that he had enough to call the strike if the hold-out companies refused to sign. And he knew they would never sign. If they had any inclination to do so, they would have done it already.

## Chapter 26

Lydia had looked forward to Whitey Storm's wedding. He'd been her student several years before. But he'd often come by the house after Fred's death to help with the chores. Lydia knew that his mother, who also taught at the high school, made him do it, but she was struck by how willing he seemed to be. Albert, who was much younger than Whitey, had also liked helping Whitey with mowing the lawn, even though his help wasn't much more that watching Whitey do the work.

She found it hard to believe that was so long ago—and now Whitey was getting married. She was glad Clare suggested that they go together. She wouldn't have gone by herself.

For Lydia, the cool summer evening brought back such memories: Methodist Church. Maids of honor in soft yellow. Men with corsages pinned to lapels. And the air, heavy with the scent of carnations.

So long ago, she thought as she walked with Clare into the back of the church. She swore she could feel the alter at the front pulling her toward it. If they just kept walking, it might become real all over again—a young woman not that long off the train from Iowa, wondering why and how she got here; a handsome, dark-haired young man with a smile of brilliant white, dimples at the edges, with a tiny point in the middle of the chin. To Lydia, Fred Weissler was the perfect man—a thick chest, muscled arms, with soft skin that she loved to touch.

"Where do you want to sit?" asked Clare in a whisper.

"Whitey's side, I think."

Clare mumbled something to the usher who directed them to the right side of the church, as the organ played gently in the background. The thoughts about Fred Weissler and the night—was it almost twenty years already?—gave way to the sea of faces that nodded and smiled as they made their way to the front of the church. Earl Talbert, Deek Brown, an old man she didn't know but who almost tore off Clare's hand as they walked past; the Mayor, the Valentines, Lightning Stevens and Alma, Myles Norgren, and Bud Cole. Bud nodded slightly as she and Clare passed, but she pretended not to see. She didn't notice whether Clare responded.

The usher showed them to a pew just behind Whitey Storm's mother and father. Part of her was angry with Clare for even asking which side of the church she preferred, because he had obviously arranged for this seat long before. Yet part of her liked it. As they sat down in the nearly full church, she felt the eyes of the congregation upon them—approving, smiling. Despite the union anxiety growing in the valley, most people who lived and worked there liked Clare Ristall, and she sensed the feeling sweeping over her as well.

Across the aisle sat her daughter Liz with Clare's daughter, Shelley. Both girls waved as they sat down, and Clare suddenly rushed across the aisle to give both girls a peck, which brought a comment from two rows back and polite laughter as Clare re-took his seat next to Lydia. When she turned to see who made the comment, she also noticed halfway back a group of Skybillings loggers—Petey Hulst, Bucky Rudman, and another several she couldn't name—all sitting on one pew. At the end, sitting next to the aisle, Albert.

When he noticed her, he smiled slightly and nodded. She returned the nod, then righted herself as the organ music rose.

Lydia willed her mind back to the girl, Whitey's bride, who was now standing at the church door. She forced herself to think of the girl's soft lace that cascaded down her shoulders and sat lightly atop the simple white dress. Otherwise, she would have started crying. She was not a woman who was easily moved to tears. Didn't even have to try very hard to avoid it, unlike many women. But now the tears were there—welling up from so many different times, so many different lives. Tears from her own wedding and their happy years. Tears from the funeral, in this very church. And tears from the son who sat only a few rows behind her, but lived in a world so different than the one she wanted for him.

As the congregation rose and the bride began walking slowly down the aisle—preceded by two bridesmaids—Lydia looked at her face: soft, radiant, beautiful like all nineteen-year-old girls, she thought. Stepping from a world of innocence into another world of inno- cence—at least for a little while. A world of houses and children, of learning to live with a partner for the first time ever, of sharing confidences and new adventures and physical intimacy. An avalanche of exhilaration.

As the bride reached the front of the church, and the congregation seated itself once again—in a rustling sound that reminded Lydia of a burst of wind—she wondered: When did that feeling change? Clare suddenly put his arm around her and hugged her shoulder. She smiled and briefly came back to the service. But the past pulled at her harder. It was the day that Bud Cole knocked on the door—a moment that would be forever locked in her memory.

She'd been washing dishes. She and Fred were going to go to a school play that night. *Coming up Roses*, in fact. She'd helped direct it because the drama teacher had been in a car accident three weeks before. Albert and Liz were running about her feet. Albert had just tipped the cookie jar, breaking it into pieces across the kitchen floor. So when she got to the front door, she was angry.

For an instant, she thought that was why Bud Cole just stared at her without speaking. His face was set hard. No smile. His eyes seemed glassy, tired. She wiped her face with the towel still in her hand and apologized for looking so angry. It was that Albert had just broken the cookie jar—and she was in a hurry because of the play tonight.

Then she realized that Bud's expression hadn't changed. And she realized that he wasn't in the woods, even though it wasn't quitting time. And she realized why he was there.

A soloist now sung. Mildred Peabody from the Catholic Church. Lydia listened to the voice and felt herself aloft, suddenly, with the airy notes—the sense of freedom, of love. No sense of danger in those words. No warnings of death. Of surprise in the middle of a Friday afternoon when you have to get the kids to a babysitter because *Coming up Roses* will start at seven o'clock.

Bud told her the news straight out. A limb came loose. Fred didn't see it. They couldn't get him to the doctor fast enough. Lydia, I tried. I carried him out myself, Lydia. Will you, please, ever forgive me? But Lydia couldn't hear the words, or the plea, or the pain. She swam in her own deep sea—of last words spoken, of last words she wished she had spoken. Did he suffer? No. Did he know it was coming? No, he was looking down. Then the sea grew deeper in an instant—the children, how to tell them, how would they do without a father, how could she raise them by herself? That was the thought that took her under, she decided—she was by herself. Alone. Again. So quickly.

As she watched Whitey kiss the bride and the congregation broke into applause, she tried to remember when Bud actually left that afternoon. But she couldn't find it. Only the words he spoke. Then he was gone somehow. Disappeared, at least from her memory. Mrs. Carlson was there. And Emma Jean Talbert. And Barrett Fletcher was there giving her a pill. She remembered him saying she should cry. She really should cry. But she didn't. And didn't for days, maybe weeks. Then, all at once, for what seemed like months, all she did was cry—away from the children, out of sight of the other teachers. Locking herself in the toilet stall, flushing repeatedly. Or running into the woods behind the woodshop. Or just burying her face in the pillow and gulping for air through the awful wet fabric.

The strains of Mendelssohn brought her back to the church, just as Clare stepped into the aisle and crooked his arm for her.

"Lydia, you're just gorgeous," said Meredith Pritchard, the fire chief's wife, as she passed. Lydia smiled.

"It's true, Mother," whispered Liz, who walked just behind them with Shelley Ristall.

❄    ❄    ❄

Albert smiled at his mother as she passed.

Perhaps it was the light. Or the soft blue, which she rarely wore.

Or even something about walking with her arm linked inside that of a man. Albert wasn't sure, but his mother did look different tonight. Even before Bucky Rudman leaned over and made a comment about her, Albert noticed—was this the first time, he wondered—that his mother was an attractive woman. Not like the girls she taught. Not like his sister, who, even at sixteen, walked with a sway and carried her breasts proudly. No, his mother had a kind of beauty that you noticed in family pictures from years past—women of simple style, but with beauty that spoke from slim lines, delicate mouths, serious, yet soft, eyes.

Albert stood as the ushers guided each row of the congregation out of the church: Deek Brown's men; the foreman—what's his name—from Ashford & Southern; the Talberts; the Pritchards; he nodded at Elmer Fastund and his wife; the Clarks; the Evans, Harry and June. But even as the parade of faces passed, Albert struggled with another thought: That what he saw in his mother's face had its origins in the arm she now held tight as Clare Ristall escorted her out of the church. Albert had never seen his mother express interest in any man but his father. She had her books, her students, the school activities, and her roses. He'd hardly considered that his mother might want companionship with the opposite sex.

But as she passed, as she nodded, as Bucky jabbed him in the ribs, Albert finally saw a woman in his mother—a thought that, in itself, wasn't troubling. But what did trouble him was the notion that somehow Clare Ristall was responsible for this unexpected change.

As Albert emerged from the church, soft streaks of pink light striped the blue sky overhead. A group near the bottom of the steps stopped suddenly on the last one, stranding Albert and the rest of the Skybillings men at the top of the steps. At the center was Clare Ristall—smiling, shaking hands with Earl Talbert—while Mrs. Talbert hugged Lydia. A cluster of others moved in, also laughing.

"You're going to win the race," shouted Elmer Fastund, to which Clare shook his head and shrugged.

Albert had only learned about Clare's race for the state legislature when he got home the night before. His mother mentioned it in passing as she put dinner on the table. "It looks like he has a decent chance," she said, smiling. Albert tried to sound positive. He asked questions. What was her role in the campaign? But he found the whole notion preposterous.

What he wanted to ask was how a union agent—CIO for that matter, planning a strike in the Seakomish Valley, and undoubtedly with a hand in the labor turmoil that was spreading through the state—could muster enough local support to mount a run for the state legislature. Much less look like he was going to win. Damn people in the Seakomish Valley were dumber than he thought.

"Does the CIO-business get in the way?" he asked as Liz swept into the dining room and plopped into a chair.

"In the way of what?" asked Liz.

Albert sighed. "If you want to participate in the conversation, why don't you get down here on time?"

"Just remember who the visitor in this house is, okay?" She smiled sweetly as she scooped potatoes onto her plate.

"Enough," said Lydia softly. "The question is whether Clare's CIO work creates a controversy for his also running for the seat in the state legislature."

Albert nodded, as he scooped from the bowl of potatoes and passed them to Lydia.

"I suppose to some extent, it does. On the other hand, it also helps. A lot of local people down the valley feel that the unions need to stiffen against the companies and the AFL can't do it."

"Even if it means they'll lose their jobs in a strike?"

"If it means they will have better working conditions in the future, I suppose the answer is yes."

"What's so terrible about the companies?" Albert's tone was friendly, but also pointed.

Lydia studied him as she took a platter of chicken from Liz and placed it in the middle of the table. "I take it you think they have nothing that could be improved—working conditions-wise, hours, safety, dangers."

"I didn't say that."

"I thought you did. Sorry, I misinterpreted." She smiled at Albert.

"No, I only asked what was so wrong with the companies. I recognize that they can always be improved. But I wonder if they are so terrible that it makes sense to close down the woods or—worse yet—to start breaking heads. The woods are dangerous. No union will ever change that."

The rest of the dinner was spent in near silence. Liz prattled about how exciting Whitey Storm's wedding would be, and the color of the bridesmaids' gowns. But neither Lydia nor Albert responded.

As Albert looked down from the church steps, he wondered if he was responsible for all the misunderstanding. Since he'd come down from the woods the afternoon before, he hadn't said much to his mother other than the discussion at the dinner table. He found a way to excuse himself to his room, then read himself to sleep. By the time he was ready for the wedding, Clare had already picked her up.

"Just because he's going out with your mom doesn't mean he's a bad guy," said Bucky Rudman, as the crowd finally opened and they were able to make their way down the steps.

Albert looked at him and received a broad smile and a slap on the back. Albert laughed softly because he didn't think his thoughts were that obvious. "Don't get me wrong, I hate most of the union guys," said Bucky softly as they passed behind Clare and Lydia. "But as far as union guys go, he's not a bad one."

Albert nodded, as the crowd thinned and the Skybillings crew gathered in a knot at the edge of the sidewalk—Conrad Bruel, Bucky, Lightning Stevens and his wife, Myles Norgren, and Bud Cole. Petey Hulst smiled broadly, wearing a gray tweed suit, vest, watch chain, and spats.

"Jesus, Petey, you're a handsome devil," said Bucky.

"Had to tell those bridesmaids to keep their hands to themselves," chortled Petey, his wiry black hair sticking out at points above his ears.

Lightning Stevens and his wife were in a close conversation with Jake Dobinns, the town druggist, while Bud stood to the side with Deek Brown, a tall, thin man with a bald head.

"Hello, Albert," said Bud, surprising Albert with a hand thrust outward. Albert shook it, surprised that the hand was softer than he expected. "Hi. How are you?"

"Just fine," said Bud. "Deek, I'd like to introduce you to one of the new men on our crew. Albert Weissler."

Brown shook Albert's hand, squeezing it so hard that the fingers hurt. "Nice to meet you, son. Any relation to the English teacher there?"

"She's my mother."

Deek Brown now stepped back half a step and looked out the bottom half of his glasses, directly at Albert. "Well my goodness, now I see the connection," he said with a friendly smile.

Albert felt himself blushing and searched for words. "They usually say I look more like my Dad."

"As a matter of fact, that was the connection I was making," said Deek. "Your dad was a fine man, Albert. He worked for me many a year ago, along with this here whipper-snapper." He jammed a thumb into Bud's chest, just above his shirt pocket. Now it was Bud's time to turn red, which Albert had never seen before.

"Don't let this fellow kid you, Albert," said Deek, clearly enjoying Bud's embarrassment. "I tried to get him and your dad to actually do some work, and they'd be wanting to do nothin' but talk and laugh and carry on. I'd sneak up behind 'em and you know what they were planning? To make their own company and compete with me. Right under my nose, Albert. Can you get over it?"

Brown's easy, friendly style made Albert smile. He wasn't a handsome man—long nose, long face. Deek looked like a bundle of stretched skin that, nevertheless, still sagged under the chin. But despite vertical wrinkles that lined both sides of his face, there was something young and exuberant about him. Albert couldn't tell if the kidding was his true personality, or if it was just the side he turned to the world at church gatherings, but Albert liked it. Deek Brown gave you the impression he was related to you.

The bride and groom suddenly swept past and raced to the top of the steps, where the bride prepared to toss her bouquet to a handful of young girls at the bottom. Albert noticed that his sister and Shelley Ristall were among them. He heard Conrad Bruel say to Bucky, "That's the one I screwed," but before he could turn to find out which of the girls he meant, he heard Deek Brown's voice between the shrieks of the girls.

"Gonna stay in the woods, son?" Albert thought Brown was asking the question of Bud Cole, but Bud just smiled when Albert turned.

"Me?"

"Yes."

"Well, I haven't given it a lot of thought," stumbled Albert. The girls continued to shriek and a handful of rice fell on them. "I was thinking maybe newspapers. Reporting. University of Washington has a good journalism school." Though the words came out of his mouth, they surprised Albert. He knew the thoughts were there—they had been since early in high school, he had even written to the university for information. But he had never spoken of them, least of all to men he hardly knew.

"I want to write books," he continued. "Novels." The words shocked him, but they continued to roll out. "Like Hemingway. I figure I could start with a reporting job."

"There's a war coming," replied Deek. "That's where reporting careers get made. Course, it's a good way to get your head shot off." After a pause he added, "It's a fine profession. Your mother must be very proud, seeing as how she's an English teacher and all."

Albert suddenly felt embarrassed. "Yes. I'm sure she is."

❊   ❊   ❊

The girls surged forward as a group, but the bouquet fell to the ground. Several lunged for it, but in the shuffle, it got tossed back into the air. It sailed upward, over the bride and groom, and fell directly onto Clare Ristall's outstretched hand.

A delighted roar of laughter emerged from the crowd. "There's the church, Clare, might as well do it now," shouted Earl Talbert. Lydia turned brilliant red, but a wide smile crossed her face.

"But I don't know whether it means a win in November or a win in other circles, Earl," laughed Clare, squeezing Lydia around the waist. Once again laughter from the crowd, combined with clouds of rice as the bride and groom raced out of the church and into the back of a Ford.

"He's such an asshole," whispered Deek Brown to Bud, nodding toward Clare Ristall. Albert had fallen into conversation with Gary Walther and his parents, but he picked up pieces nonetheless.

"Don't say it too loudly or they'll lynch you," said Bud softly.

"What's she see in him anyway?"

"Money, for one."

Deek considered this, then studied Bud for a moment. "You ever give any thought about her?"

Bud colored. "How do you mean?" He paused and looked directly at Deek. "You mean—me?"

"Jesus, Bud, it's not the last thought that might occur to a man. Lydia is a fine-looking woman. All that stumbling and stammering tells me you have given it some thought." Deek smiled broadly.

Bud suddenly didn't like the conversation, especially in this crowd. Albert was just a few steps away, and the crowd continued to mill around them. He searched for a quick route out. "Lydia was like a partner. Like Fred. It never seemed right, under the circumstances. Besides..."

"Besides what?"

"Jesus, Deek, another time, okay?"

Deek laughed, turning his gaze back to Clare, who stood with

Lydia in a group including the Talberts, the mayor, and several Skybillings men.

"Goddamn woods is ready to erupt," said Deek quietly. "There's talk of a big strike that'll throw half this valley out of work. But they treat him like some kind of hero. And they're ready to put him in the legislature."

"I figure he's got a hand in my troubles too," said Bud.

"You mean the sabotage?"

"Who else? That's what he wants to do—shut everything down."

Deek Brown seemed to think about this as the Ford spun its tires and roared onto Main Street headed for the reception at the Masonic Hall. It was followed by a convoy with horns blaring and lights flashing. White shoe polish across the side of the Ford read, "Seakomish today. Hot Springs tonight."

"You got that wrong, Bud," said Deek as the noise disappeared. "Clare's too smart for that. That's the stuff that scares too many people. He wants 'em to believe that the sacrifice is worth it—that they'll gain long term. Filing spikes and letting Shays fall onto loggers don't make people comfortable."

This was a view that Bud was still not willing to accept, though he had heard it from many people.

"You ain't alone in this, you know," said Deek. "Train wreck killed several men down near Auburn last month. It was a little show. Not one of the big companies—course, the big shows are getting pounded, too. Strikes, wildcat and otherwise—Hoquiam, Aberdeen, down the Willamette Valley. But the wreck in Auburn—a small operation like yours. I heard that one of the men killed was some business guy from Seattle."

"If you ask me, Clare Ristall is at the bottom of what's going on with me," said Bud. "I can't prove it. But I can feel it."

Deek Brown laughed. "You been thinking too much, Bud. A logger thinks too much and his head explodes."

Bud was ready to argue, but Deek slapped him on the shoulder. "C'mon, young man. Let's get some cake."

❖   ❖   ❖

The room was a whirl of sound and color. Albert had never been in the Masonic Hall in Seakomish. It had always been the big brown building on the corner, near the Methodist church. Busy on Sundays and several nights through the week, the hall had been a prominent landmark of his childhood, but never a stop within it.

Albert sat with Gary Walther, his best friend in high school, along the wall facing the line of tables mounded with cookies and peanuts, with a punchbowl at one end and a flat wedding cake at the other. Several bridesmaids formed a half circle at the end of the table, with the bride and groom in the middle, and both sets of parents after that. The room thundered with conversation and laughter.

"What did Conrad say outside the church about the girls?" asked Albert, speaking loudly so Gary could hear.

This started Gary laughing. "About which one he had fucked?"

"Hold it down."

"You asked the question, I didn't."

Albert just shook his head. "Which one?"

"You really want to know?"

"Yeah."

"You're sure."

"Goddamn it, Gary."

"Your sister." Gary broke into a roar, watching Albert's face the whole time.

Albert didn't speak, but studied Gary to determine if this was actually a joke. When he decided it wasn't, he slumped against the chair. "That goddamn little shit."

"What's wrong? She's old enough."

An accordion started at the far end of the hall, muffling the noisy conversation for a moment, but then sending it even louder, to accommodate the interference. Albert continued to groan. Did his mother know about any of this? He spotted her in the distance, shaking hands with the group of parents. Clare had his arm around her.

"C'mon Albert," said Gary, slapping him on his knee. "Get modern. It's 1937. Girls do that stuff today."

"Shit, Gary, she's sixteen. She's not twenty-one—or even nineteen." He spotted Liz with Shelley Ristall, standing in a circle with several men from Deek Brown's crew. He noticed that Liz's skirt was several inches shorter than Shelley's, and she swayed as she spoke to the men. What would his mother say if he pointed out to her that while she was fighting to keep her son out of the woods, her little daughter was screwing a man who was at least twenty-one, and probably a lot older than that—and an odd son of a bitch to boot? For that matter, he could be a murderer—at least he said once that he thought about it.

The conversation suddenly came back into Albert's head. They were up on the mountain. Conrad was angry with St. Bride. "Have you ever thought about killing a man, Albert?" That was the question. Albert couldn't understand it at the time, and he sure as hell couldn't understand it now. But could Conrad have been the one who filed the spike? St. Bride had been riding on the Shay the day of the accident. Could Conrad have been trying to kill St. Bride and make it look like an accident?

Albert studied Conrad, who had suddenly appeared behind Liz. He noticed that Conrad stood directly behind her, leaning hard into her from the back. From his angle he could see them meet, and press firmly against one another—although to those in their circle of conversation, it must have looked simply like they were pushed together by the crowded room. Albert cursed, as the other piece of that conversation with Conrad came back. Something about poking the fresh meat in Seakomish. How they wanted a hard logger. Goddamn if he ever thought it might have been his sixteen-year-old sister getting poked.

"Come-on, Albert, let's kiss the bride," said Gary, getting up suddenly. "You're boring when you get depressed."

But Albert only shook his head.

Gary leaned down. "Stop worrying about who she is fucking and start thinking about who you ought to be fucking, okay?"

"Get stuffed, Gary," snorted Albert, too loudly, since several faces near him turned. He pretended to cough and walked to the other side of the room. Well away from his sister, and where he couldn't see his mother.

Did Gary put his finger on it? Maybe he was just jealous of his sister. He'd never laid a hand on a girl's breast. Never put his hand between a woman's legs. The closest he'd ever gotten was a couple of pecks from Susan somebody—Wallington or Wallingham—after the junior prom.

Jenny Caldwell, Gary's girlfriend, suddenly swept into the room—in a chiffon, lacy dress, blond hair, blue eyes that were so deep they seemed to have no centers. "Albert, sweetie, how are you?" She gave him a hug. "God I'm late. Where's Gary?"

"Over there, trying to kiss the bride," said Albert.

"What a goddamn asshole. I'm away for two hours, and he's kissing other women." That was the surprising thing about Jenny. Beautiful, popular, sweet as apple pie—but who could curse like a logger. She never let it show, however, unless she knew you well. "I had to go to Everett today for one of those shitty secretarial training interviews. Sorry I missed the wedding. Was it beautiful and splendorous and romantic and all that shit?"

Albert also liked her cynicism. "All of the above."

"You know something?" Jenny now leaned close to Albert's ear, giving off a scent of cinnamon and peaches. He wanted to lick her. "What's her name—Whitey's bride—she's fucked everybody this side of Stardale in the last week."

"What?" Albert shook his head, about to tell Jenny he didn't want to hear.

"It's true. She decided that she didn't want to break her marriage vows so she's had a different guy almost every night the last week—just to fill her appetite for a while. Don't it sound delicious? Bucky Rudman—isn't that his name?—from Skybillings had her last night."

Albert leaned back in his chair. He felt like a rag. He hated the wedding. He wanted to take the train back into the woods.

Jenny continued brightly, her voice still low. "Rumor has it, he does some kind of thing where he asks the girl whether she's ever ridden the top of a spar tree before...."

Gary Walther appeared, bent over and gave Jenny a long kiss, and started babbling about how beautiful she looked, which gave Albert the opening to slip out the side door. Several knots of men stood outside in the cool evening air, tossing chords of laughter and clouds of smoke upward.

Lightning Stevens, Myles Norgren, and Bucky Rudman leaned against the side of a wood-paneled station wagon. Clare Ristall spoke to them quietly. Everyone smiled, though Albert saw Bud Cole eyeing the group from another circle, several yards away. This contained Deek Brown, Earl Talbert, and several men from Deek's crew who Albert didn't recognize. Petey Hulst had just come out of the hall, wiping perspiration from his forehead.

"I haven't danced with a twenty-year-old in roughly fifty years, Albert," said Petey, sitting on the steps. To Albert, his breath sounded like the air being forced into a pipe organ.

"They can keep a guy going alright," said Albert, trying to sound bright.

"Didn't honestly remember that those creatures were that soft."

"Yeah."

"Reminds me of the first time I ever kissed a girl, Albert," said Petey with a broad smile. His eyes crinkled at the edges. "Couldn't get over how goddang soft that skin was."

Albert decided that he had been cursed. Even Petey Hulst was talking about sex, to say nothing of his sister—and for that matter, possibly even his own mother—both of whom were also likely practicing it. With that thought, he gave out a groan.

"You okay, Albert?" asked Petey, a voice of concern. "Too much cake?"

"No, sorry Petey. Just too much going on in my mind."

"Young fella like you? Shouldn't have that much on his mind. Just good times. Having fun. Girls."

Albert nodded and smiled. He settled on the porch step beside Petey. The stars overhead were brilliant.

"Can you name 'em?" asked Petey when he noticed Albert looking up.

"No. You?"

Petey pointed a brown, crooked finger at the eastern sky. "That's Sirius, there above the peak. Brightest star in the sky. Off to the right is a star named Alpha Centauri." Now he whirled a finger to the west. "In about an hour, if you look right there—near the tip of the little dipper—you can see Venus. An hour later, Mercury."

The music inside the room had now begun to increase, and the floor thumped with people dancing.

"How'd you learn about the stars?"

"Dunno. Too old to remember. Part of a man's education I guess. Probably came about the time as I learned about the spirits." Petey paused, studying the skies. His face looked like the face of a magician, to Albert. A face of points and leathery-brown skin.

"Did you really conjure up Bucky Rudman's great uncle?"

The question seemed to catch Petey by surprise. He turned back to the sky while he thought. "Yup. About a year ago, I reckon. Red kilts. Pipes—no, no pipes, just kilts. Bucky talked to him about why he left the old country."

Albert looked at Petey as he spoke—almost a gnarled man, thought Albert. A man who could die soon, who some people assumed could go any minute. Albert figured that people had been thinking that for the better part of fifty years.

Albert turned to Petey. "Do the spirits really just show up?"

"The spirits? Most times they do." Petey took out a tin of chewing tobacco, offering some to Albert, who shook his head, then dipped a finger through the black goo and slipped it into his cheek. "Not always, but most."

Albert had wanted to ask Petey about this, but always felt reluctant. For a long time, he thought the men were joking when they talked about Petey and the tarot circle. Albert understood tarot cards. But the circle troubled him—no, fascinated him. Especially after the death of Nariff Olben and the other men. The prospect that Petey could somehow contact the dead seemed at once laughable and tantalizing. The suddenness of Nariff's death continued to trouble him. At one moment he was alive and telling stories. The next he was gone. In fact, during sleepless nights or mind-dulling rides on the crummy, Albert had often tried to break down the end of Nariff's life into seconds, then parts of seconds—so finely, in fact, that he decided that there was a point at which Nariff was technically dead, but the air that surrounded him still held the living oxygen that had been in his body a second or two before.

For Albert, this introduced the notion of a kind of plane of death: On one side was the living, breathing human, with a personality and a conscience and awareness; on the other, merely a body, of chemicals and water and bacteria—with no soul, no life. But in an instant, perhaps just at that split second of death, the human existed, in a sense, across both of those planes. Would that mean that, sometimes, under some unusual circumstances, that the human, or perhaps its essence or its soul, could break the plane, perhaps, and come back?

These were not ideas that Albert discussed with anyone. Yet these were ideas that had also received inspiration, if even only indirectly, from Petey Hulst's circle. That loggers could engage with the spirits— or claim they did—suggested to Albert that maybe his ideas had more to them than he thought.

"How do you decide which spirits to contact?" asked Albert after a long silence. He could hear somebody giving a toast to the bride and groom inside the lodge.

"Sometimes I decide," answered Petey. A lone coyote wailed painfully in the distance. "Other times, people ask."

Petey studied Albert. "You got somebody you'd like me to call up, Albert?"

Albert shrugged. He looked at Petey, then off into the darkness. The coyote wailed again, now joined by another. "As a matter of fact, I do."

Petey's voice was soft. "I bet I know who it is," he said. "Nariff Olben, right?"

Albert smiled, but shook his head. "No, my father."

## Chapter 27

While Whitey Storm's wedding seemed to draw half the loggers in the valley, the county fair in Stardale seemed to draw them all.

By noon, the fair grounds were filled with several hundred people—children racing from the merry-go-round to the Ferris wheel; ladies touring the sewing and canning exhibits from the 4-H, men smoking and jawboning, or joining in the competition—log rolling, topping, axe throwing, even tug-of-war. The games always started during the day; the political debates and horse races filled the afternoon, clearing the way for the county dance on Saturday night.

Jenny Caldwell pulled her father's Ford in front of Albert's house at 10:00 a.m. sharp, with Gary Walther in the seat beside her. "How do you get your old man to let you drive this thing?" asked Albert, as he crawled in the back seat.

"I'm very persuasive," said Jenny, flashing him a quick smile, as she jammed the car into first gear and roared toward Main Street.

"Only child," said Gary, with his arm around the back of her seat, even though he had to stretch to reach it that far. "The old man gives her anything she wants."

"Don't be an asshole, Gary," said Jenny sweetly.

Albert always enjoyed the drive down the valley to Stardale, but never when Jenny drove. It wasn't just that she was a fast driver. It was that she usually had four or five things on her mind at the same time. This morning, it was Albert's sister.

"Gary says you didn't know about Liz." She cast him a wicked smile and winked. Albert barely noticed, as he watched the car wander into the other lane.

"Watch the goddamn road, Jen," shouted Gary.

"Sorry." She turned back to the road, now glancing at Albert in the rearview mirror. "You really didn't know about her and Conrad Bruel going at it?"

"No. How the hell was I supposed to know? I work in the woods these days, if you haven't noticed. Not around here enough to hear every rumor."

Gary turned around suddenly. "Jenny claims that they were humping in your mother's house."

Albert groaned. He decided that, despite Whitey's wedding and the county fair, he would've been better off staying up at the Skybillings camp for the weekend.

"It's none of my business. So I don't give a damn," was all Albert got out.

For several miles they drove in silence through the canyon just west of Seakomish. Albert willed Jenny to watch the road, which—to his surprise—she mostly did. This allowed Albert to relax a little and, though he hated to admit it, enjoy looking at her from this angle. Her nose tipped up slightly, sliding gently into a small mouth, and a smile with dimple bookends. As she drove, she slung a shock of honey-blond hair out of her face, occasionally exposing a slim neck to his view.

"Do you think Conrad had anything to do with the Skybillings train accident?" asked Jenny suddenly. Her eyes were on him from the mirror again.

"Jenny, why are you so damned interested in this guy? He's a fool. How should I know if he had anything to do with it?"

"But he could've, don't you think?"

"Anybody could've. Any of them. Or anybody on the outside."

"But wouldn't you find it interesting if he did? I mean, that the person who was screwing your own sister was the same person who got all of those men killed?"

Albert guessed that this was a planned ambush. Jenny the gossip, the one who always knew the details, smelled something delicious and had to go after it.

Though Albert didn't want to discuss the accident or who might be responsible, his anger over Conrad screwing his sister—and his sister doing it under his mother's nose—propelled him into the topic anyway. "Even if Conrad wanted to do it, he isn't smart enough to pull it off."

Jenny tried to hold back a laugh. "I just thought of something."

Albert refused to meet her eyes in the mirror.

"Is Conrad Bruel a member of one of the unions?" She threw him a cute smile.

"What's that got to do with anything, Jenny?" Albert could feel the anger in his voice.

"Jenny...," said Gary in a low, cautioning tone.

"Well, if Conrad is a member of the CIO—and of course, Clare Ristall is the head of the CIO around here—then it's possible that your house has had two of the CIO organizers sleeping under one roof."

"Shut-up Jenny," said Gary quickly.

The words stung Albert. Was this just Jenny Caldwell's active imagination? Her effort to get a rise from him? Or was this like the news about Liz? Did the whole valley know that not only his sister was sleeping with Conrad, but that his mother was sleeping with Clare? Jesus. The woods were far better than the valley. At least the trees that threaten to kill you in the woods bear no malice.

Jenny studied him for several miles, but Albert pretended not to notice. "I was just kidding," she said finally, as they pulled into fair grounds.

"Forget it," said Albert abruptly.

"I really was just kidding," she added softly, as she backed the car into a parking space. She looked straight at Albert. "I just wanted to see how you'd react. Your mother would never do anything like that." She jammed her foot on the brake and put the shift into neutral. "If she did, she'd know that kids like me would spread it all over."

She smiled once more in the mirror as she turned off the engine.

❈     ❈     ❈

"One more heat."

Bucky Rudman's shirt displayed deep blue stains under each arm. His tin hat lay at his feet, the center of a circle of equipment—ropes, two axes, and clamp-on claws for his boots. Little Boy Whittaker looked strangely dapper next to him—relaxed, not sweating, despite the noon sunshine.

Most of the Skybillings crew was gathered around Bucky—some reclining on the sawdust, others eating hotdogs and drinking beer. This was the "topping" competition, one of the biggest attractions at the fair. Toppers from throughout the valley joined in the competition to see who was the fastest at climbing a spar tree, axing off the top ten feet, and scrambling back down. Two spar trees were rigged close to one another, held tight to the ground by a network of crisscrossing cables. They stood a hundred or more feet tall at the start of the competition, but shrunk quickly. Albert guessed they were now down to no more than fifty feet.

"Give him hell, Rudman," shouted Myles Norgren. "The least you can do is make the outfit proud."

"Samuelson's one of the best toppers in the state," said Bucky quickly. This surprised Albert, who had settled in with Myles and Lightning Stevens on a bench. Bucky rarely missed a chance to brag—which gave Albert the clear sense that, for perhaps the first time that Albert had ever witnessed, Bucky was actually doubting himself. Albert had heard of Rolf Samuelson. He worked for Ashford & Southern and had won the topping competition for several years. He beat Bucky by two seconds the year before.

Petey Hulst stood up and patted Bucky on the shoulder, offering him a can of snoose. "Gets the blood flowing." Bucky stuffed a plug in his mouth.

The referee blew a whistle. "One minute, gentlemen. Last heat. First to Rolf. Second to Bucky. Third to the best man of the two."

Bucky pulled on the belt that held the rope and axe. Little Boy handed him his tin hat. "Goddamn hat. Just slows you down."

"Regulations," said Little Boy. Bucky snorted.

Rolf Samuelson and Bucky lined up along a chalk line drawn on a piece of cement. The crowd pressed in, the music on the bandstand in the distance now revved up with accordion and piano. Albert noticed several couples doing a jig on the stage with the performers.

"On your mark. Get set." The referee paused slightly: "Go!" Bucky was the first to the tree, wrapping his belt around it, clicking the belt back into the hook, then digging upward with his clamp-ons. But Rolf Samuelson was taller. Within ten steps up the tree, Rolf had overtaken Bucky as both men sent chunks of wood flying from where the clamp-ons dug in. As the crowd grew, the roar grew as well. Chanting and shouts of encouragement, mixing with the thumping on the bandstand. St. Bride was taking bets around the crowd. Albert noted that he was giving odds to Rolf Samuelson.

Within seconds, wedge-shaped pieces of wood showered the crowd as the men slammed their axes into the two-foot-thick wood. Most looked down, to avoid the sawdust, but a few cupped their eyes and continued to shout. Myles Norgren was nearly hoarse. "Come on, Rudman, kick his ass! C'mon Bucky."

Though Samuelson was taller than Bucky, his height worked at a disadvantage as they hacked at the top of the spar. Bucky's thick stubby arms drove the axe faster and deeper, until finally, the top of the spar moved slightly, then dropped straight down with one more whack of the axe. Like a fireman down a pole, Bucky sped down the spar tree with the belt hardly gripping, until he rushed across the finish line, just as Samuelson topped his tree.

The crowd roared for Bucky, who took in deep gulps of air. His face swam in glistening sweat, eyes bulging, chest heaving, but a rich smile on his face.

"We're fifty bucks richer, LB," said Bucky through his gasps to Little Boy, who tossed him a clean towel. "Know what fifty bucks will get us in Everett?" His face now slipped into a nasty leer, even as the crowd continued to clap. Rolf Samuelson finally loped down the spar and put his arm around Bucky. "I guess big ain't always best," he said to Bucky.

"That ain't what they'll say up in Everett tonight, Rolf," replied Bucky with a laugh. Samuelson shook his head and slapped Bucky on the back.

"Congratulations, you old oversexed-fart," said Rolf. "But you better keep some of those winnings for some shots from Doc Fletcher."

Conrad Bruel ran into the group from near the bandstand. "Goddamn it, I need some help over here. Skybillings is gonna get killed in the tug-of-war unless I get some help."

Albert studied Conrad's face once again. He was ugly. Square faced. Square jawed, with slightly buck teeth. On the other hand, he decided it wasn't any surprise that this is what Liz would like. Big, smart-mouthed, without a brain to his name.

Several Skybillings men deserted Bucky's victory celebration and made their way to the grandstand. Even though Albert decided he would try to find Gary and Jenny again, Myles slapped him on the shoulder. "C'mon young man. You gotta understand that one of the best parts of logging is kicking the shit out of the other logging shows at the county fair," he said with a laugh. "Besides, this way we know who we have to look out for when the wildcat strikes start."

Albert laughed awkwardly and followed the crowd, leaving Bucky still breathing hard. Even Little Boy headed for the grandstand.

Several Skybillings men let out a cheer when they saw the rest of the crew coming. Several of the Swedes, Edwards and Herrera, Appleseth, Valentine, all seemed pathetically small, standing across a blue line drawn on the cement from a line of burly men from Ashford & Southern. Lightning Stevens ran to grab the end of the rope. Myles grabbed a piece in front of him. Then Conrad, Little Boy, and even Bucky finally showed up, along with Rolf Samuelson.

Albert suddenly felt a waft of summer breeze that mixed the strangely sweet smell of peanuts and cotton candy with perspiration and tar from the parking lot at the edge of the grounds. Several women from the 4-H poured coffee from urns set up on tables near the edge of the grandstand.

"Ladies and gentlemen, you are now going to see how the best men in the forest are going to crush the women and children from Skybillings," shouted one of the Ashford men. His tone was light and friendly, so it brought only good-natured catcalls and whistles from the Skybillings crew.

"We whipped you on the spar tree and we'll be happy to do it again," shouted Bucky Rudman, who held the position next to the blue line. Behind him stood Little Boy, then Conrad, St. Bride, Appleseth, Herrera, Valentine, Edwards, Norgren, and finally, Lightning Stevens. Albert didn't know the names of the other side, though Rolf Samuelson took the head position directly across from Bucky. He spit on his hands as he grabbed the rope.

A county commissioner wearing a red vest stepped up and raised the rope. "You know the rules, boys. Anybody touches the line in any way, loses." He cleared phlegm from his throat, mumbling a dull "excuse me," to the grandstand. "You can reach across all you want, just don't let your foot go across."

"Christ, we know the goddamn rules of tug-of-war, Dale," shouted a man from the grandstand. Dale turned with a scowl, but couldn't find the voice.

"This is the first heat. The second goes this afternoon. And the winner will be crowned tomorrow—with $150 going to the crew who wins."

"Goddamn, let'em pull, Dale." Again the same voice, but Dale didn't turn this time. He simply blew the whistle, surprising both sides.

For a moment, the rope stood limp while both sides looked at each other. Suddenly, somebody from Skybillings tugged, almost pulling Rolf Samuelson across the line. In an instant, both sides were tipped outward from the center line, straining and grunting, while the crowd shouted encouragement. For several seconds, it looked like Ashford & Southern was finished. Rolf's feet grew closer and closer to the line, but when Bucky Rudman reached for a tighter grip, somebody on the other side pulled, reversing the advantage—this time almost tipping Bucky into the line.

The men from the Skybillings side started shouting. "Goddamn boys," growled Conrad, as if to himself, then letting out a huge grunt.

This seemed to tilt the contest for a split second, but was immediately overcome by a unified pull by the entire Ashford & Southern team that drew Skybillings quickly forward as the entire line collapsed toward Ashford & Southern. Bucky fell across the blue line with his belly, Little Boy on top of him, all the way down the line. The crowd cheered and Dale blew his whistle.

"Ashford wins the first round. They'll take on the winner of the round this afternoon," he shouted to the grandstand.

The crowd groaned, wanting more. "That was too fast," shouted one of the old men from the front row. "Give it to 'em again."

"Ashford won," shouted Dale. "That's it. Contest is over."

"We don't give a goddamn who won," shouted the old man back. "We just want to see another pull." This brought clapping from the crowd.

"Ain't no more companies ready to pull," shouted Dale back. His hand was shaking as he raised the whistle to his mouth and blew it sharply, as if to punctuate his point.

"How about AFL versus CIO," asked Edwards loudly when the two crews finally were back on their feet.

"What?" Dale hadn't heard the suggestion amid the confusion.

"If the crowd wants more, how about an unofficial contest between AFL and CIO," repeated Edwards. The crowd applauded loudly.

Dale shrugged. "I don't give a damn." Another cheer. "They can if they want."

Most of the rest of the men on both sides started nodding. "Alright," said Dale. He resumed his position in the middle of the rope, not trying to hide his exasperation. "AFL men from Skybillings and Ashford & Southern over here, CIO from both companies over there."

Albert now watched an odd spectacle—men being forced to shift allegiances, instantly and publicly. From company to political cause, with no time for hesitation. Even with the turmoil in the Skybillings crew, few had indicated their allegiances, except for Herrera and Edwards' men. Most of the rest ignored the debate over which union truly represented the loggers. But here—on a piece of cement in front of a hundred people—both companies had to choose.

Edwards and Herrera, as well as Appleseth and Valentine, immediately took up the AFL side, along with several of the men from Ashford & Southern. St. Bride, Myles Norgren, Conrad Bruel, and several Swedes stepped to the CIO side, along with most of the

Ashford & Southern crew. Albert noticed that several of the men on both sides exchanged surprised looks with one another; several just stood in the middle, still sizing up which side to join. Pull with your friends or pull with those who think like you? And how many of them hadn't thought one wit about it prior to that second, Albert wondered.

"Goddamn, we don't have all day," snorted Dale. He was now looking at his watch. "If you want to go through with this, then take your positions. Or let's say the hell with it."

The last few men settled in—Lightning Stevens stepped to the AFL side, directly facing Myles Norgren. Bucky did the same, but Little Boy took a piece of the CIO rope.

"Time to choose, Albert," shouted Bucky.

Albert felt the eyes of the crowd land on him.

Albert searched for words as he turned to Bucky, whose face suddenly looked surprisingly stern. Gone was the laughter of the defeat to Ashford & Southern a moment earlier. Dale blew the whistle. "Get in here kid, on the double. I don't got all day."

Albert studied both sides. Evenly matched, mixed of Skybillings and Ashford & Southern, some burly, some thin, all standing perfectly still, with a thick round rope threading through each of their hands. With a sudden burst, Albert sprung onto the cement and walked directly to the middle of the circle, turned to the grandstand and looked at the crowd, then took one step to the left—onto the AFL side. A chorus of cheers and boos arose, with Bucky Rudman patting him on the back.

"Take the inside slot, Albert," said Bucky, giving him the piece of rope just inside the blue line. Directly across the line now was Little Boy Whitaker, who cast Albert a slight smile.

"On three," shouted Dale. "One, two..." He blew the whistle sharply and stepped away. In an instant, the advantage went to the AFL. Albert felt the rope surge backward, almost tossing him onto his back. He dug his feet into the cement, straining against the thick strands that smelled like hot, wet hay. As he pulled, trying to hold his position, he heard the breathing and grunting behind him—steady ahhs and uhhs, split by gasps and roars as the rope teetered left and right, drawing Albert close to the line, then Little Boy, then back again.

Unlike the first match, Dale bent low along the blue line, watching closely every time Little Boy's or Albert's feet came close. But despite repeated close calls in both directions, the two sides held firm. Was it five minutes? Ten? Albert's wrists knotted, then his forearms and biceps, as the grunting behind him grew louder and the grimaces on the faces across the line grew uglier. Little Boy's face was all wrinkles and curls, framed by muscles that arched up from his shoulders and bulges on the top of his arms. Behind him, Myles Norgren's beard dropped beads of water.

It was the sight of Conrad that somehow gave Albert renewed strength. No longer could he feel the wrench-tight muscles in his arm; all he could feel was the rage he felt the night before when Gary first mentioned Liz. With a hard jerk, Albert heaved his body full force against the rope, pulling Little Boy and the others toward him rapidly. But before they came across, Albert heard a loud *thumpf* as the rope snapped directly above the blue line and both sides collapsed backwards, followed by the sounds of crashing tables and screaming women.

Despite the awful aching, Albert got back to his knees to see what the cause was, only to see that—when the rope broke—the end of the AFL side had crashed into the stand with cookies and coffee. The ground was covered with black goo and scattered glass. Rolf Samuelson was helping Edwards and Valentine to their feet.

"I declare it a draw," shouted Dale at the blue line. He spat onto the ground and walked away.

❀　❀　❀

Albert had just begun to get up when the sweet smell of violets swept over him with a wet kiss on his cheek.

"You were wonderful!" shouted Jenny. She hugged him, then ran to the end of the line and did the same to Gary. Albert hadn't even noticed Gary join in, but now he was wiping coffee from his pants.

"How about me?" asked Bucky Rudman, as Jenny locked her arm inside Gary's.

Jenny blushed. "Sorry."

Albert wondered if that wasn't the first time he'd seen Jenny Caldwell blush. Maybe she decided that Gary would take it wrong, but he didn't seem to notice. Instead, he suggested that they find some food. The rest of the two crews mingled loudly, punctuated by laughter and slaps on the back. Albert heard Bucky razzing Little Boy for joining the "wrong side." Myles asked Lightning Stevens if he was a Republican, too.

"You mean just because I pulled on the AFL side?"

"Something like that."

Albert couldn't hear the answer because he was pulled along by Jenny Caldwell, who now linked her arms inside both Gary's and Albert's. The three of them wandered across the middle of the parade grounds, occasionally running into people, then laughing, and doing it again a few steps later. They found room at the end of a picnic table near a corn and hot dog stand, where they sat for the next two hours.

For most of the time, Albert just listened as Jenny talked. Rumors about girlfriends. Gossip about teachers. Stories from schools down the valley. Comments whispered quietly as friends and classmates and parents wandered past. The gym teacher walked past with his wife and small daughter, nodding hello.

"How are you, Mr. Leopold?" asked Gary.

"Fine Gary, how's life in the woods?" Leopold shook hands with all of them.

"You want an honest answer?"

"Why not?"

"I'd rather do anything than work up there." Gary leaned closer to Leopold. "You know how many pigs work in the woods?"

"How 'bout you Albert?"

Albert had never liked Leopold. He was arrogant, in Albert's view. Too ready to criticize. "It's great. Fine."

"Hard job."

Albert nodded. "Yup. But we'll come through."

"You boys take care." Leopold picked up his daughter and wandered away.

As soon as he was out of earshot, Jenny said, "You know he shacked up with Lisa Mueller last week don't you?"

"Leopold?" asked Gary and Albert in unison. They both turned and watched him walk away.

"His wife was visiting her mother in Seattle," said Jenny smartly. "Snuck Lisa in through the back door."

Albert considered this as Gary continued to press Jenny for more details. How did she know? Was she sure?

"I don't know, Jen..." said Gary.

"You don't believe me?

"I don't know."

"All men want it, you know." She took in Albert with her look.

"They like the fresh stuff. Unsullied." She flashed a knowing smile.

That was pure Jenny, thought Albert. Wrapped up neatly in just a few sentences. Direct, blunt. Street smart, despite her cotton-candy looks. Albert felt hopelessly inexperienced around her. Gary was so lost that he didn't even know it.

For the next hour they said little, drinking their sodas and watching the world parade by. Most of the Skybillings crew, several of Deek Brown's crew that Albert recognized, faces from the other high schools in the valley, teachers, neighbors, and local politicians. As two o'clock approached, however, a large crowd swung through the middle of the parade grounds, centering around the state governor, who had arrived to give a speech. Next to him was Clare Ristall, who clung firmly to Lydia as they smiled and chatted with a group of well-wishers.

As they swept through, Albert turned the other way, though there were so many people that he doubted his mother would see him.

"You going to the debate this afternoon, Albert?" asked Gary, studying the crowd blankly. The debate between Clare and his opponent was scheduled to follow the governor's speech.

"Haven't decided," Albert lied. If there was one thing he fully intended to do, it was to hear Clare Ristall. Albert hoped the Republican would demolish him.

"You heard about Shelley, haven't you?" Jenny's voice was low, well short of the other tables.

"You mean Clare's daughter?" asked Albert.

"How many Shelley's do you know?"

Albert knew who she meant and wanted to hear whatever Jenny knew. But this was Jenny's profession. If you want the gossip too much, she gains even greater control. Better to relax. Pretend only passing interest. So Albert watched the crowd file toward the grandstands.

Gary finally asked the question. "What'd you hear?"

She smiled brightly, but spoke to Albert. "Shelley hates her dad. Has for years. Says the worst stuff behind his back. But she's careful. Only says it to the people she trusts."

This was in the range of what Albert had hoped for when Jenny raised the subject. Dirt on Clare Ristall was always useful. "Why?" asked Albert.

"Why what?"

"Why does she hate him?"

Jenny shrugged and sipped her soda. "Never heard that much. Just that it has something to do with the mother. Something about when she died. Ever since then, they haven't talked. They just say enough to get along." Jenny paused. "I would've thought you'd have heard of all of that."

Albert shrugged. "Why should I know about what Shelley Ristall thinks?"

The cute smile again. "Oh, maybe because Shelley is one of your sister's friends. And, oh, maybe because your mother just walked within ten feet of us with Clare Ristall's arm around her."

Albert got up. He didn't know what time the debate started, but he didn't need Jenny nosing in his family any more than she already had. "Am I really that interesting, Jenny?"

"What do you mean?"

"I figure that it must be that my family is more interesting than any in the valley since you spend so much time thinking about it. First Liz. Then my mother. Then both again."

Jenny's voice was friendly. "You know he's rich, don't you?"

"Clare?"

"Rich as in paintings and antiques. Shelley can get anything she wants."

This wasn't exactly news to Albert. He'd heard for some time about the apparent oddity of a union man with money—much less in the middle of the Depression. But since he had never discussed Clare with his mother—who presumably knew about Clare's financial status—he never heard exactly.

Jenny sensed that she'd again caught Albert's attention. "He goes to Seattle every now and then and buys paintings. Really funny stuff. Ugly. Shelley's shown it to me. And he's got a bunch of furniture that isn't like yours or mine. It's got all kinds of curly-cues. Shelley says that he gets it from an antique dealer in Vancouver. Bet you didn't know that, did you?"

She was right. He didn't know it. Gary rescued him from having to answer. "Is that why Shelley hates him?" asked Gary.

"Why would she hate him because he's rich?" snapped Jenny. "That's a stupid question. Would you hate your old man if he gave you all the money you wanted?"

"I guess not."

Jenny paused, as if working out a complex calculation. "Why do any of us hate our fathers? It's because they're always telling you that you don't know anything and that you've got it easy."

She looked at Albert, who simply looked back. The talk about Clare, about fathers, coming from the mouth of Jenny Caldwell, made his head hurt. How many times had Albert thought about Jenny, especially up in the woods? Yet in that beauty lay something that he wasn't sure he understood.

She flashed him a smile, but then turned away quickly.

❊    ❊    ❊

Albert enjoyed the refuge of the top row in the grandstand. He could avoid the crowd, avoid the comments he was bound to hear.

He slipped in just at the end of the governor's speech. Though he didn't hear much of it, what little he heard reminded Albert of why so many people didn't like him. He was boring and spoke in a monotone.

After he was done speaking, and the Stardale Mayor introduced the debate—saying it was really just "a couple of more speeches"—he introduced Clare, who bounded to the platform, which was draped in red-white-and-blue bunting.

"Since the best political speech is one that's already over, I'll be brief," said Clare to a wave of laughter. "We aren't electing a US Senator or Member of the US Congress in November. We're electing a representative to the State Legislature. We want somebody who knows us, who knows this valley. Who will go to Olympia and get on with the day-to-day business that affects us."

Clare had the cadence, thought Albert. The words fell just right. A few one direction, followed by a nod of the head. The next sentence the other direction, again a nod, and a quick smile. Albert had to admit that there was a natural flow here—and, to his surprise, it didn't seem dishonest. As Clare spoke, he even found himself laughing along with the rest of the crowd at Clare's quick wit.

"Union boys aren't supposed to know much," said Clare with a big grin. The audience laughed. "But we do know about fair wages. We don't have 'em yet, up here in the woods. We know about safe working conditions. But we don't have them either, up here in the woods. We know about fair representation, but we don't have that up here either." This brought a loud round of applause, but a few "boos" as well, mostly from Deek Brown's crew.

Clare deftly nodded toward the "boos" and smiled. "It's differences that make horse races, boys—Mark Twain said that. And I know we got some differences. I'm CIO—that's my job. I don't make any bones about that. But in November, try to lay aside the internal disagreements we have. One day, we'll all be brothers in the same movement—I'm going to do all I can to make that happen. Bring peace to labor. Peace to the woods. Let the workers finally get their fair share from the bosses."

This brought a solid round of applause. "In the meantime, if you vote for me, I'll use the power of the state legislature to see to it that you get better wages and better working conditions. I can bring some pressure. Once that's done, we can work all the rest of it out later."

With this, Clare thanked the crowd, waved, then sat down. A loud round of applause followed him down the steps to his seat, where he bent down and kissed Lydia before sitting down beside her.

This is why I'm in the back row, thought Albert. He watched his mother closely for signs that she might have kissed him reluctantly, but he couldn't find any. The fact was, she seemed to lean into it.

Clare's opponent, Rudolph Tollafson, walked to the podium—a round, wide man, with cuffs that seemed to drag on the ground. He wore a white shirt, but no tie. His face was brown. His jaw square and sharp, much like his head. To Albert, he looked like two people—everything square above the shoulders, everything puffy below, all jammed together at the neck.

"I'm all for short speeches," said Tollafson. "But Clare Ristall gives such short speeches that he forgets to tell you some important things." This brought a polite laugh from the audience. "Like he forgot to tell you that his boys are set to close down the woods here in the next few weeks. I wonder what that'll do for your wages? How many groceries can you buy if you work for a logging show that the CIO has struck?"

This brought a round of applause. A man sitting on the row below Albert leaned toward another and said, "He's got a point there."

"Clare will tell you that he's all for the working man, but he's spending all his time looking for ways to get the logging companies in this valley to stop working. I got no beef with men wanting better union representation. If it's AFL they want—fine. If it's CIO—fine. But don't stop the work, for God's sake."

Albert detected a slight shift in the crowd. Several near him leaned forward. Others whispered to one another and nodded. Albert tried to make out his mother and Clare in the front row to get some idea of how Clare was reacting, but the afternoon sun blinded him. Rudolph Tollafson was a shadow against it.

For several minutes, he outlined his proposals. Increase the wages, but don't have the government set them. Cut taxes for working people. Make the legislature pay more attention to safety in the woods—issues that largely echoed Clare's, but with somewhat rounder edges.

"I'm gonna keep my speech short, too," he said, scratching his jaw. "But before I sit down, let me say that this election ain't between Republicans and Democrats. It's between common sense and foolishness. I, for one, think that the way to straighten things out is to go to Olympia and work for those things Clare talked about, and forget all this foolishness about striking. People have had enough turmoil. Let 'em get down to business."

The crowd broke into applause, punctuated by a few cheers. Several of the men below Albert stamped their feet, making the grandstand shake. But before it subsided, Clare had bounded again to the podium—each candidate was given five minutes for a rebuttal.

"Rudy is pretty convincing," he began. "No, he is totally convincing." He paused, to take in the audience as they digested this surprising admission. Albert wondered which way the strategy was going. "I'd be tempted to vote for him." Again, a pause, Albert noticed a few smiles flicker around him, wise to Clare's angle.

"Just one problem." Another pause. "Rudy forgets that his Daddy wouldn't have been able to buy the property he grew up on if the Wobblies hadn't struck for a fair wage back before the War. Rudy forgets that he, himself, wouldn't have been able to meet the payments on the farm—like a lot of us—if we hadn't struck as an industry a year or so ago. Now, we gotta take the next step. We have got to get the kind of union that truly represents the working man—not some bosses off in Chicago or Florida. We need a union that negotiates for all of us—doesn't let us fend for ourselves."

Clare's pace picked up slightly. Albert thought he seemed buoyed by the looks on the faces. "I'll grant you that strikes can hurt. I know that laying around the house or walking the picket line don't buy groceries. But I'll tell you this"—now Clare was jabbing the air—"if we want the boys and girls in this crowd to be able to get fair wages when they grow up, and if we want to get fair wages now to pay the way for their growing up, then we gotta have the courage and the fortitude to make the hard choices."

A warm breeze carried the sound of a merry-go-round from across the fairgrounds, along with wafts of buttered popcorn. But most in the crowd didn't notice. All eyes were on Clare Ristall.

"I'm willing to risk what I have in this world, to make the working life better in this valley," his voice rising, "but easy answers and easy solutions ain't gonna do it. We've got to make the hard decisions that are going to actually do some good. Giving in to the company bosses may be easy, but it ain't right."

The crowd applauded loudly. Several men shouted, while others rumbled their feet on the grandstand. Albert decided that if rumbling counted in elections, Clare was a sure bet.

❊    ❊    ❊

"Where you going, Jenny?" asked Albert.

"Down to the river. Why not?"

They had just dropped off Gary. Now they were pulling down Main, away from the direction of Albert's house. "Great night for a swim, don't you think? Full moon."

"Jesus Christ, Jenny. Are you nuts?"

"What's wrong with a moonlight swim?"

"Swimming's got nothing to do with it. Gary will kill us if he finds out we went swimming without him."

Jenny jammed the car into second to navigate the steep incline off Main Street, onto the river road. "Gary trusts me, and he trusts you. He'd never think anything of it. Besides, he had too many hotdogs. He felt like garbage."

The thought of going swimming with Jenny Caldwell—all alone, on a moonlit night—was something close to a dream. But the circumstances were wrong. She laughed suddenly, dribbles of giggling. "I just figured it out, Albert. You're afraid of me."

"Afraid of you?"

"Yeah." This time the laugh was louder. "You're afraid that I might try something and you won't know what to do."

Albert told her to keep her eyes on the road. The river raced along the side of the road. The houses of town were now well behind them. The sharp black outline of a steep rise on the right.

Jenny suddenly swerved to the left, down a narrow gravel lane. Albert had the sense that she floored the gas, but the car jolted and bumped so bad that he couldn't be sure. For several seconds, the headlights jumped wildly—like yellow searchlights strafing the night forest.

"What in God's name are you doing?" asked Albert as she swerved to miss a deer, then spun the car sideways into an open gravel parking lot next to the river.

Jenny stepped out of the car, pulled the keys, then walked quickly around the other side. Albert watched her race behind a bush, out of sight; then reappear a minute or so later. This time she stood next to his door.

"God did I have to pee," said Jenny. Albert groaned, but before he could speak, she swung the car door open and slipped onto his lap. "Sorry to be so direct about all of this, but I figured I'd have to wait years if this was up to you. Push the seat back."

Albert's nose was filled with the scent of violets and tickled by the wispy strands of blond hair. He felt a sharp hardness in his pants, directly beneath her thighs. "I suppose you think I don't know what to do," Albert heard himself say with a laugh. But it sounded brittle and wiltingly accurate. He wished he'd been silent.

"I figure you know what to do, but have never done it." With one hand, Jenny pushed the seat latch and the seat slid back, giving her enough room to wiggle forward. She slipped down, kneeling between his legs. "You ever had a blow job, Albert?"

"Jesus, Jenny. What are you...?"

"A blow job." She now settled her hands directly on his pants, one over his zipper. "Do you even know what a blow job is?"

But the pounding in Albert's chest drowned the words. As he tried to answer, he felt the moist lips engulf him and pull hard, then softly, then ease away and brush him lightly. Was it five seconds? Less? Albert's hands grasped Jenny's blond head, pulling her into him tightly, until he felt her full weight finally upon him and her lips nuzzle his face.

Albert's hands slid underneath the sweater, then lower, into the warmth between her legs. Within seconds, he straddled her, tearing at her blouse, as the Ford rocked. But Jenny suddenly slipped away and resettled in the driver's seat.

"Sorry," she said sweetly, adjusting her sweater. "I only do blow jobs on the first date. Besides, Gary would be pissed if I let you screw me."

Albert lay spread-eagled on the passenger side of the car—his pants bunched around his ankles, his shirt tilted upward at the belly, a cold puddle underneath him. Jenny tossed him a hanky. "This'll probably take care of that," she said, as she started the engine and jammed the car in reverse. "My dad would go nuts if we stained the seat."

"You know what?" asked Jenny quickly, as the car roared back onto the river road.

"I hate to even ask."

"I think I want to try Conrad Bruel next."


## Chapter 28

The Seakomish train depot, where the Skybillings crew met the crummy on Monday mornings to start the long ride up the mountain, stood alongside the highway that ran through the valley. At four in the morning, even summer mornings, the cut through the mountains carried a sharp wind, fluttering the jackets and occasionally nipping a cap off a head.

As he stood there, Albert felt the blackness of the morning in his soul. Still no light, not even a hint. He stamped his feet and blew into his cupped fingers. Several knots of men spoke quietly, but most stood on the platform alone, huddled tightly against the cold. He turned his back into a particularly bitter gust, finding himself facing Bucky Rudman. "You need more meat on the bones," said Bucky good-naturedly. But Albert turned away, preferring to study the tracks.

The crummy finally appeared in the distance, slowly pulling next to the depot platform. The crew lumbered into the seats, huddling with coats and blankets for the hour-long, open-air ride up the mountain. It had a metal roof, but no windows.

"Let's go boys," shouted Ferguson, the engineer. "Great Northern freight comes through here in five minutes on Mondays." This brought a surge of men into the crummy, just as Ferguson let out some throttle and the crummy began to move. This sent Bucky tumbling into Little Boy, who stumbled and then fell across St. Bride.

St. Bride cursed and pushed Little Boy, who righted himself just as he slammed a forearm into St. Bride's chest. Several others jumped into the melee, some trying to pull Little Boy and St. Bride apart;

others joining sides. Albert sidestepped the knot of bodies that were spread across the benches and floor until Ferguson let out more throttle and he, too, fell on top.

He landed on this stomach, but quickly rolled against one of the benches. Arms and legs seemed to smother him, taking away his breath. He pulled on one of the benches, feeling a hand above him that pulled him up. But before he got to the bench, a wall of cold water swept across him, sucking the breath from his chest with an icy bitterness.

The melee stopped immediately, as the crummy continued to pick up speed. Albert could hear a locomotive whistle somewhere behind them.

"Goddamn it—all of you!" shouted Bud Cole, standing on the front bench with an empty bucket in his hands.

Albert dragged himself onto a bench, as the others did the same. He saw that St. Bride had a gash across his eye, and Bucky's eye was already puffy. But Little Boy looked unharmed, as did the others who had joined in.

"I'll fire all of your fucking asses if this continues," shouted Bud, raising his voice to cover the wind and the gaining whistle of the Great Northern diesel not far behind. "I hope every one of you freezes your dick off on the ride up the mountain." Bud put the empty fire bucket back onto the floor of the crummy.

That was all he said. He sat down in his seat again, and bound his coat around him. The others did the same as Fergie pulled the crummy onto a side rail, which took them to the Skybillings line that ran up the mountain. It was less than a minute later when the pounding Great Northern train rumbled past them on the main line.

Albert tried to wring some of the water from his pants and huddle against the side of the crummy, out of the wind as much as possible, to keep his legs from freezing.

Despite the intense cold and the wind along Roosevelt Creek, his face felt hot. Had Bud Cole thought that he had something to do with it? Jesus, he'd just lost his footing. Surely, Bud wouldn't think he'd get mixed up in a pushing match.

Albert spit over the side and cursed. He looked around to see how the others were reacting, but most had already gone to sleep. It appeared that none of them had gotten as wet as he had. He cursed as he huddled his arms to his chest.

He knew, already, that sleep would not come on the ride up the mountain—sleep he'd counted on when he tossed and turned throughout the night. He comforted himself at the time with the notion that he'd get an hour on the way up. I'll be fine by the time I get on top. Now this. To say nothing of the fact that the boss thought he was part of the trouble.

Maybe Clare was right. Albert shuddered at the thought and cursed out loud. He checked to see if anybody noticed, but no one had heard.

This thought settled in his mind for several miles. It was in his mind as he noticed the fingers of light beginning to silhouette the tips of the peaks overhead. It was in his mind as he actually lifted his face into the hot exhaust plume from the crummy, to gain a little more warmth. Foolish. Only fumes and dirt, so he looked back down again.

Albert laughed suddenly. On the walk from his house to the depot, he decided that the day couldn't possibly be worse than supper the night before. Worse than the conversation with Clare, followed by the conversation with his mother. But here he was, soaked, reprimanded, accused yet innocent, cold as hell, and wide awake.

He lifted his foot onto the bench in front of him as the growing light exposed a small puddle of water below. Edwards, Myles Norgren, and Conrad Bruel all shifted slightly at the new pressure, but nobody opened their eyes.

Which conversation had made him angrier? He couldn't decide now. At the time, each one seemed worse. But now—who was to tell? And maybe he reacted to both of them wrong—especially in light of how poorly the day had just started.

At first, the conversation with Clare angered him more. Clare had come over for Sunday dinner, along with several of Albert's mother's friends—mostly other teachers from the high school. Albert had enjoyed the dinner. The conversation drifted through gossip about several former teachers. Then banter about politics and literature. The afternoon started with a debate over Huey Long and if he could've beaten Roosevelt and ended with general agreement that the Depression would remain as one of the most defining moments of US history—though Terrence Stubbs, the principal, argued that Teddy Roosevelt's legacy would endure much longer.

Albert listened intently. Tried to jump in wherever possible. But generally found the group too vocal and opinionated—his mother among them, as well as Clare, of course. As much as Albert hated to admit it, Clare once again handled himself remarkably well—much like the performance at the debate. Slowly, Albert found himself liking Clare more. The know-it-all-edge that Albert had expected, and knew was there, wasn't apparent.

Albert also witnessed, up close for the first time, the relationship that was growing between his mother and Clare. He tried not to watch them, because he thought they might catch him, but he listened. To the "dear's" and "thank-you's." To the genuine warmth that appeared to be there. His mother's hand would occasionally rest on Clare's shoulder as she placed a dish on the table. Clare seemed to listen with interest when she spoke.

Though he didn't want to admit it, they did seem like a couple. The others treated them that way. Making plans for the next weekend with both of them, together, not just separately.

Despite his doubts, Albert had enjoyed the meal. But as the guests drifted into the backyard after dinner, Albert found himself seated on a bench next to Clare in the far corner. Two couples that had been chatting with them suddenly decided to go inside, leaving them alone.

"How's the woods?" asked Clare, as he got up.

"Fine, just fine." Albert began to move toward the house, but Clare stood next to the bench, making it hard for Albert to politely step past.

"You thinking on making it a career?"

Albert shrugged. "Haven't thought of it much, really." He pondered just how far politeness forced him to go.

"Hell of a dangerous place—the woods."

Albert sorted through the variety of smart responses he could make to such an observation, but he decided to remain, at least temporarily, in the realm of civility. "That's true," was all he could muster. Again he moved toward the door, but Clare seemed planted.

"I might be able to line up something for you in Olympia if I get elected." Clare smiled suddenly. "Of course—that's a big if."

Politeness again. "Oh, you'll get elected with no problem." Albert even offered a quick smile.

"I don't know. New Deal's going broke. Stock market's still shaky. Governor's angry with all the Democrats. People are still nervous."

Albert didn't answer. He didn't understand where any of this was going. So he remained where he stood, studying Clare's relaxed posture. One of his feet was on the bench—he chewed absently on a piece of clover he had picked from the lawn. "I could maybe get you to help out on one of the committees, or something. Your mom says you like to write." Albert noted that the uncertainty about his prospects in the election were now suddenly gone.

"I'm happy with what I've got."

Clare turned to him and studied him. "You're a hell of a talented young guy, Albert. I'd hate to see it wasted."

"Wasted? How?"

"In the woods."

Albert couldn't choke back the anger rising in him. "Working in the woods is wasting your life? You represent loggers, don't you? How can you call their lives wasted?"

"I didn't say their lives were wasted. I said that you would waste yours if you spend it—or lose it—in the woods."

Albert suddenly felt firmer ground around him. He at least sensed now where Clare was going. "My father didn't waste his life, Clare."

"No, but he lost it, didn't he?"

Even Albert could tell that Clare wished he had the sentence back. "I didn't mean that Albert," he said quickly. "I didn't mean any disrespect."

Albert nodded, but didn't know what to say. Clare was silent. He took several steps down to the small stream that wandered through the back yard. "Beautiful garden your mother has."

"What are you trying to say to me, Clare?"

Clare tossed a small piece of bark into the stream, watching it float past his feet, then out of sight. "I guess what I'm saying is that I think a young fellow with your potential should realize it. Seize it. He shouldn't go into a line of work that kills as many as it lets get away. Hell, you could get into the University of Washington. Maybe get a teaching degree or something. Or get a job with one of the offices in downtown Seattle—insurance or something."

Clare paused now, looking for words. "Besides, it's going to get rough up there." He stopped.

"You mean because there'll be a strike."

"There may be—you don't know."

"C'mon Clare, if you think I'm so smart, don't insult me."

Clare laughed softly, but with no humor in his voice. "Albert, it's not my business to tell people my business. You know my occupation. You know what I think we've gotta do. Will that mean a strike? Probably, sometime, maybe, maybe not—but no guarantee either way. All I'm saying is that any strike, almost by definition, means violence. You add that to what working in the woods is like in the first place, and it doesn't make sense for a young guy who could do a hell of a lot more with his life."

Albert's response was fast and certain. "So you don't want my blood on your hands, is that it?"

Clare laughed nervously. "Albert..."

"No, let me finish. I think I understand. You are going to call a strike. That is going to lead to a few busted heads along the picket lines—maybe including Skybillings. And that may mean that my head is among them."

Albert now paused for breath. "And that would be pretty damn embarrassing for you—at least as far as my mother is concerned—wouldn't it? Her baby boy with a head bashed in because of a little necessary union violence. But the problem isn't that the unions called a strike. The problem isn't that the union grunt pounded the baby boy with a tire iron. The problem is that the baby boy had the audacity and guts to be there in the first place. Isn't that what you're telling me, Clare?"

Albert's breath came hard. He felt his heart in his throat, but Clare wouldn't get angry, which made Albert even angrier.

"No, that's not it at all Albert," said Clare calmly. "You asked about the chance of a strike. That's got nothing to do with you—hell, Skybillings will be able to go on for years, probably, before any unions get around to bothering with them. The big companies are what count up here. You know that. Ashford & Southern, Deek Brown, and all those guys. All I was saying was that—based on my own years of working in those woods and my own experiences up there—I want to try to prevail on you to make a better choice for your own life than the woods. Get out of the woods now. That's my advice. The faster the better."

"You're not my father, Clare," snapped Albert. "So let me make the decisions I want to make."

As Albert looked up into the growing fingers of daylight over the ridge, he smiled at that last comment. It was one thing to watch Clare grow closer and closer to his mother. It bothered him, yes. Something in it felt uncomfortable. But he also knew it was childish. His mother was an adult, a woman, who no doubt longed for companionship. So in that sense, Albert was growing more accustomed to it. Yet perhaps Albert had finally fallen upon the central issue. Clare was not only trying to be his mother's husband, or so it seemed; he was trying to become her son's father, or so it felt. And that was a blasphemy that neither politeness nor reserve in Albert's soul could ever tolerate.

❅ ❅ ❅

The water on Albert's legs had begun to dry—or at least warm. He no longer felt the iciness in his legs. The crummy was now pulling through the portion of the climb that sliced through a narrow canyon. He looked straight down, to see Roosevelt Creek racing underneath a small bridge, its surface white with froth, chopped only by large boulders of granite. The water moved so fast that its sound even drowned out the laboring crummy.

But instead of the water, he saw his mother's face—flushed, full of emotion, from the night before. A face he'd looked at a million times, but last night, a face he had never seen before. In his eighteen years, arguments with his mother were never loud, never direct. They always moved deftly in parallel realms, or they swept along in politeness and even silence. But this was different.

The guests had long departed. Albert was packing his bag with clean clothes for the trip back to the camp the next morning. His mother had appeared silently at his door.

"Do you have a minute?" Her voice was friendly, but still formal.

"Sure." Albert had packed his entire supply of underwear, since he had decided that he wouldn't come home the next weekend.

"Did you have a good chat with Clare tonight?"

He looked up quickly, to see if she was chiding him. But the look on her face was still friendly, indicating clearly that Clare hadn't told her about it. "Yeah. Fine. We had a good talk."

"That's good." She paused. She seemed to be uncertain about the direction of the conversation. She helped him fold his underwear. But then she walked to the window.

"Has this window been sticking?"

He looked up. "No. Should it?"

"I just wanted to make sure you were comfortable—what with the warm days."

"It's fine, Mother."

He watched her as she walked around the room, peering at the high school photos and the pictures of FDR. "We haven't had much time to talk this weekend."

Albert continued to pack. He hated this. She was an intelligent woman. Sometimes he thought she was brilliant—literature, the arts, all that. She was comfortable in public. She could think fast on her feet. His mother was unlike any of the women—in fact, even the men—in Seakomish. He always was disappointed that because she was his mother, he couldn't have her as an English teacher in high school. He and Liz got Old Man Brady instead.

But this was a field in which Albert knew his mother was entirely unequipped—that is, in speaking openly, directly. He knew her failure so well because he knew he suffered it as well.

"I need to speak with you, Albert." She sat finally at the chair behind his desk. She placed her hands on the desk, folding them neatly.

"That's what we're doing."

"No, I mean I need to tell you something."

Albert tried to concentrate on his underwear.

Her voice started, then faltered. She cleared her throat and began again. "Clare has asked me to marry him."

As the scene replayed once again in Albert's mind, he kicked the bench directly below Myles Norgren, shattering his sleep. "Goddamn it Albert, what's wrong with you?"

"Sorry, Myles," said Albert quietly. "I just fell asleep. Jerked or something."

Norgren shook his head, then settled against the back of the bench, closing his eyes again. "Just jerk the other way next time, will ya?" he said with his eyes closed.

"Sure."

Albert's reaction the night before had not been so visible, at least outwardly. He felt heat in his throat. Water in his eyes. So he continued to work diligently on his underwear.

"Did you hear me?"

"I heard you."

"What do you think?"

Albert felt lost. First a battle with Clare Ristall. Now this. What could he say? What possible answer could he give his mother that was truthful, but that wouldn't hurt her? "I think that...." He broke off.

She sat silently, waiting. He finished the underwear, then pulled his pants out of the laundry basket, throwing himself just as aggressively into this new task. She did not speak.

"Mother, what does it matter what I think?" asked Albert finally.

"Because you're my son. Because you've got brains."

"Have you asked Liz's opinion?"

"She's still a kid, Albert. I intend to tell her. But I haven't done so yet. I wanted to talk to you first. To solicit your thinking."

Albert considered this. He wasn't sure she really wanted his opinion. She wanted his approval. "Do you love him?" Albert felt the words almost stick in his mouth, but they came out. How could this be a conversation he was actually having with his own mother?

"Yes, I do, as a matter of fact." She paused, as he glanced up at her. She seemed to be sizing up his willingness to discuss the subject. "I'll be honest—I didn't for a long while. I kind of thought he was, well, kind of arrogant. But I've gotten to know him. He's as warm and caring and loving as any man I've ever known."

Albert looked at her inadvertently when she spoke the last line, but he quickly turned back to his task.

"This is a hard subject for me, Albert."

He nodded.

"But I need to talk about it."

"Fine."

"I know that mothers and sons usually don't—" Her voice dribbled away. "What I mean is that mothers don't usually confess their feelings about men to their children. It isn't done. Emily Post would be mortified." She now got up from the desk and began pacing. Her voice rose, gathering the force she usually reserved for books or politics. "But I think that, well, you're an adult. So your opinion is important to me. But beyond that, you remember your father. You remember the life we had. The love. And your blessing, I suppose you could call it, is important to me."

Albert recalled this scene vividly as he studied the swirling waters of Roosevelt Creek, still racing along next to the crummy. The stream bent sharply, sending spray upward, while whirlpools lashed a granite boulder at midstream. Just like me, he thought. Swirling with uncertainty. What to say? Tell her what she wants to hear? Or tell her what I think? He felt swept along by a current of unfamiliar emotions, yet saddled by doubts about just where his responsibility lay.

He had stalled for time. Asking her what her plans were. When she might get married. Where they would live. Whether Liz would get along with Shelley Ristall. How the town might react. But finally, he started running out of questions, and she didn't leave. She waited, her hands now on his desk again.

Albert took a deep breath. "When I asked you about going to work for Skybillings, you were honest with me."

She nodded and smiled slightly.

"You made it very clear that you thought it was wrong. That I had made the wrong choice." He paused, looking at her to gauge her reaction. "I didn't agree. But you were honest. Is that what you want from me?"

She didn't respond. She simply looked at him.

"Assuming that is true, then I'll tell you my opinion. I think you shouldn't marry him." He now rushed through the words without pause and without looking at her. "I think Clare Ristall is arrogant and self-centered. He's all things to all people. He has money. Everybody loves him. He is popular—at least until his damn strike starts." Albert paused to take in his mother, whose eyes did not move. "The only thing missing is that he doesn't have a wife."

Her eyebrows arched and her eyes took on an intensity he'd never seen before. "You really think that? You think that this is all part of some decoration he feels is necessary for his public persona?" Her voice was rising.

Albert shrugged.

Lydia started laughing. "Albert, tell me this is your idea of a joke."

"You wanted to know what I thought."

"You think that I'm a *prop*?" Her voice wavered. She wiped both hands through her hair. "That's how much credit you give me?" Now she walked in front of his desk, then back again. "You think I'm not bright enough to spot it if Clare was just trying to *hire me* as his wife? My God, Albert, how did you grow so cynical?"

"Why were you so cynical about whether I should go to work for Skybillings?"

She laughed slightly now—laughter he had never heard from her. "Is that what this is about? Is this time to get even, Albert? This has nothing to do with Skybillings."

"It does."

"How? What does this have to do with where you work or what you do?" She stopped abruptly and held him in a hard gaze. "If you haven't noticed, Albert, this—for a change—is about me. Not you, not your career, not your job. Me, Albert. Your mother. Lydia Weissler. Do you understand that?"

Albert felt clawing in his throat. He hadn't expected such a confrontation. "My opinion"—he felt his voice quiver, so he took a breath and started over—"My opinion was that working in the woods was right for me. I asked for your permission and you said no—working in the woods is dangerous, it's reckless, it's got no future, it's a dead end."

"It is all of those things. Would you like me to list more?"

He grinned flatly, waiting for her to finish. "But that's not the point," shaking his head as he spoke. "It may be all of those things and more, like you say. But the point is that you wouldn't hear my side of the story because you had all the answers, Mother. You told me you saw it clearer because my sight was clouded—I was too close, too set, too convinced, you said. I couldn't see the facts, you said. I was about to make the same mistake that Daddy did." He saw a flicker of a response at that. Perhaps a slight softening. "All I am saying is that, just like that may have been true of me then, it is certainly true of you now."

She was silent. She hadn't moved from the desk. Albert heard the door downstairs open and close. He briefly wondered where Liz had been, but his mother still held him firmly in a frozen gaze.

"You were chasing after your father, Albert. You were chasing after a dream that never should have been in the first place. I simply was trying to save you from the same fate. I was trying to save your life."

Albert's voice was soft, but distant. "And what dream are you chasing after, Mother? What dream is clouding your vision?"

This question stuck with him throughout the night, throughout the hours of sleeplessness, of staring out the window, throughout the ride up the valley—because her expression looked so pained after he said it. Part of him wanted to grab it back, but there it remained—cold, judgmental, but so much how he felt that he did not make a move to alter it, or its effect. Nor did her response soften the effect.

She studied him for what felt like hours, then drew a deep breath, and smiled gently. "Perhaps we are too much alike, Albert. Maybe that's the problem," she said, and then walked from the room.

Albert felt the crummy lurch and turn, opening the entire crew to brilliant sunshine for the first time on the trip up the valley. Albert turned away from the blazing light, as the others cursed the interruption of their slumber.

## Chapter 29

Bud decided at the fair what he needed to do. He needed to be a logger again. To feel the saw in his hands, to fight the ache that came from hours at the end of an axe.

He caught John Valentine as he was stepping off the crummy.

"I'm going to be working on your crew for the coming week," said Bud, after several of the men had already gotten off.

Valentine stepped to the side to let the rest of the crew pass. "Why in the world would you want to do that?" asked Valentine. "Have you gotten bored with management?"

"You might say that."

Valentine studied him for a moment. "You know, you started this ride this morning by tossing a bucket of water on your crew in the freezing cold, and you're ending it by telling me that you want to saw logs for the next week. You sure everything's okay, Bud?"

Bud had known Valentine longer than anyone on the crew, except Lightning Stevens. He didn't see eye-to-eye with Valentine on virtually anything—politics, religion—and he hated his arrogance. But their long history had built a trust between them.

Bud thought about the question, but didn't answer. He was back at the fair—twenty-four hours earlier. Against his better judgment, he had listened to Clare Ristall's speech. And while he listened, he could not fathom what was happening, not just to him, but to common sense. He had, yet again, studied his own men at the fair—as they chose sides for the AFL versus CIO tug-of-war; as they wandered around the fairgrounds; even as they sat in the pews ahead of him at Whitey's wedding. Each time, he tried to see something in them that would tell him what he needed to know.

But it was when he listened to Clare's speech, he realized that he needed to stop thinking about all the nonsense for a little while and go back to what he did best.

"You're serious, aren't you?" asked Valentine when Bud didn't respond.

"I wouldn't be saying it if I wasn't."

They started walking toward the trestle. "Bud, I've got plenty of people to do the job, you know. And I would remind you that bucking logs is heavy work." Valentine's voice was low, to keep others from hearing.

Bud stopped suddenly. "If you ever again imply in anything you say that I have gotten soft, I will fire your ass in a split second."

Valentine studied him, without answering. Then he smiled. "Okay. I will be sure to remember that."

❊    ❊    ❊

Bud knew how foolish he had been once he laid his eyes on the terrain. The slope this far up on Three Sisters was so steep it was nearly impossible to maintain your footing, creating a constant strain on ankles and knees. Even worse, the fallen firs—many nearly twenty feet at their base and many pushing 200 feet in length—lay at haphazard angles to one another. Some had fallen directly next to where they had stood, others had fallen sideways—thus on top of, and now crisscrossing, others—and many, once freed from their earthly bonds, had toppled down the steep hill full speed and lay jumbled atop one another at a small rock outcropping.

For the first day, the head bucker, named Svenson, didn't seem to know what to do with Bud. Here was the owner of Skybillings, who suddenly appeared, along with Valentine, with the announcement that he would be part of the crew for the next week.

"Work him hard, Sven," said Valentine as he turned and headed back down the slope.

"So now, Mr. Cole, what do you want to do?" asked Svenson—a tall, barrel-chested man whose English was much better than Bud remembered. "Since you are the big boss, you can choose. Okay?"

Bud shook his head. "Nope. You're the boss for the next few days, Svenson. Tell me what you need done, and I'll do it. I am here to work."

So Svenson assigned him to the bucking crew that worked the jumble of logs above the rock outcropping down the slope. He worked with three other men, all Swedes who spoke English, but who switched to Swedish when Bud joined them.

Bud had grown up in logging by working largely as a chokerman—whose job began after the buckers were already done. He'd also done his share of felling trees, but he'd never done much work as a bucker—which, within an hour of starting, he decided was the worst job in the woods.

The pain set in immediately. First, just from holding himself on the steep hillside; then, getting enough traction to drive the saw hard enough to actually cut the wood. The next was the awful pain in his arms—the Swedes were used to the work, so they didn't seem to tire.

At one end of a ten-foot-long two-man saw, though, Bud felt his arms and back tighten, then hurt intensely, but he kept working.

The job was relatively simple. Each man took an end of the long saw. They measured each fir into sections, anywhere from thirty to forty feet long. They notched the bark with their axes, to get the saw started, then—taking up their positions on either side—began what was usually several long hours of sawing before the log groaned then broke in two. Near the wide, bottom end of the large firs, it could take a whole day, given the extraordinary width of the wood and the sticky pitch that gummed the saw.

Perhaps it was the pain. But Bud's mind could go far away, which it often did. Back to the fair, to Clare's speech, to Whitey's wedding; sometimes further back, to why he suggested buying a sawmill, to why he thought there was any chance he could save Nariff with the Shay on top of him; and as far back as the Great War, and the awful cold and mud and stench in the trenches, and then, the days that he and Fred spent in Paris at the end of it. Dry, alive finally, and drinking. He tried to remember the bar where they'd gotten so drunk they couldn't walk. Paulina's was the only name he could come up with—though he was sure that it wasn't right.

But Bud's mind also could stay right where it was—on the unforgiving slope, under a burning hot sun—his thoughts buried deep in the saw rut, in the smell of the pitch, the taste of the wood chunks that flew through the air, in the cut that grew deeper and wider as the saw rode back and forth between the men stationed at either end. Sometimes even, the thoughts took him so deep into the hot wooden rut that he would be startled by Svenson's voice at the other end of the saw— sharply, in English, shouting to him.

"Hey, Bud Cole! Hey! Slow down, dammit!"

Bud would look up from the wood, to see Svenson's flaring nose and his brilliant red face streaming sweat. "Holy Jesus, but you are wearing me down. You are pushing the saw too hard, sir. I cannot keep up."

❀   ❀   ❀

He knew these things from the hard bucking.

He knew that he shouldn't have let his wife Kathryn go. He laughed because he realized that he hadn't thought about her for probably ten years. But still—it was a stupid decision to let her walk out…. Yes, she was heady, and full of herself, but potentially, very possibly even, loving. Did she love him at the time? No. But he knew that she could have—and that she was much more likely to love him than he was to love her.

He also knew that he shouldn't have restarted Skybillings after the crash. It was stupid. It was stupid because Fred was dead, and he needed Fred's calm head to make the company run. It must have been the crazy alcohol that was still coursing through his veins, he decided, that made him take up this hopeless cause of Skybillings once again.

He also knew that he shouldn't have abandoned Lydia after Fred's death, even though she had turned cold, verging on rude. He should have tried again. Should have asked her to meet again, somewhere, and to speak openly and honestly about how she felt. He could have reasoned with her. He could have assured her that the future was bright—and that there was reason to forgive.

And he decided that he should have never come back to the US after the War. Should have stayed in Paris, learned the language, and found a job somewhere. He had a high school education. He could have found a wife and would have had four children already who were half grown—no full grown. They would be twenty or so—but he stopped the thought when he found himself thinking that they would be about Albert's age.

He came to all of these conclusions not just while he was bucking the logs—as the ruminations and notions and far-away thoughts swirled about him—but at night, as he lay on his bed, feeling the stiff arms twitch, the legs tighten to the point of pain that woke him. He would get up at night and walk to help ease the stiffness. Then he would get back into bed, sleep a couple of more hours, and do it all over again.

But often the sleep still wouldn't return—and when this happened, he would take his sleeping bag and his flashlight, and walk into the woods, just above the camp. He climbed to an opening in the trees— the only flat ground in the steep rise—that gave him a clear view of the lake, as well as the camp below. Here he would roll out his sleeping bag, crawl in, huddle himself together into a ball to force out the cold, and fall into a deep sleep.

His week of bucking was almost over, and he was grateful. The sleep got worse as the week progressed, as the stiffness and pain became more extreme. He cursed it—the pain, the lack of sleep—and he especially cursed the fact that he had to even face such problems at all. After all, there was a time when Bud Cole could work for days, and not feel it. He had proven this and shown this. He and Fred had chased around Seattle and Vancouver until all hours—and they'd been ready when the morning bell rang. But now, it wasn't that way.

So he was here, on this damned hill, sitting on top of his sleeping bag, smoking a cigarette. Was it two in the morning? Four? He didn't know. The lake reflected the halo of the half-moon as it neared the peaks behind the lake. That would make it closer to two, he decided.

When the cigarette was done, he crawled back into the bag. He folded his shirt into a square first, then laid it on one of his work boots, which he used as a pillow. It held his head just right, and kept it warm despite the damp night air.

The lake gently lapping, the slight breeze and the creaking firs—these sounds relaxed him. The warmth crept into his legs and arms, but he was occasionally startled by his head twitching. This would wake him slightly, but he knew it was the sign of coming sleep.

At this stage—drifting along the edge of sleep, but not quite there—his thoughts floated away from the work and the questions. Laying on the forest floor, at the feet of the giant firs, he felt like just another part of the forest; no different than the ferns or the fallen logs from decades past, tucked in and among the granite boulders and tall rhododendron bushes.

As he drifted, he could see now from way above himself, hovering hundreds—maybe thousands?—of feet overhead. Everything to the north was dark green and quiet, even the snowcaps of the highest peaks lay shrouded in nighttime shadow. And below him—just the roofs of the camp and cabins and the tool sheds.

And Fred was there with him now. He was alive once more. Bud could see him. Isn't it funny, thought Bud—that I would think that he was dead when he is actually standing right here? Then it all became confused, and he was riding down the mountain with Fred's body in his arms.

He felt uncertain and afraid suddenly—just as the earth rumbled violently with a brilliant white explosion that tossed him into a thicket of thorns at the back of the landing. He couldn't see. His eyes were clogged with dirt and leaves. For several seconds, he lay there, feeling his legs, touching his chest and stomach for blood. Until his senses brought him back.

Albert could see his mother's face across the valley. Was it a picture? A billboard? But it moved. She moved. The lines in her face seemed deeper from this distance, from where he stood. But when he tried to get closer, the valley stretched wide, and she lifted farther away. Her voice, already faint, grew fainter. Then it erupted in a rumbling, shaking explosion that tossed him hard against the wall.

Albert sorted through the array of colors swimming in front of his face, as voices filled the bunkhouse. Little Boy kicked his bed, drawing him fully awake and then out the door, with shoelaces dragging. He could feel the red glow as he rounded the corner of the building, and as he did, another explosion ripped through one of the tool sheds.

The camp was a sea of red and black. Fire from the tool shed leapt in peaks, then drew in air, then leapt again. The mess hall was shrouded in thick smoke, and the firs just above the tool shed sizzled, lacing the smoke with a wet, oily scent. Bud Cole, wearing boots but no pants, had already formed a bucket brigade, starting on the dock and running past the mess hall. Buckets of water sloshed from man to man until they reached the mess hall, which stood directly in the path of the advancing flames.

"Over here, in between Norgren and Conrad," shouted Bud, whose face was streaked with black. Albert jumped into the line, and began handing buckets forward.

"What happened?" Albert shouted to Conrad above the roar.

"Dynamite." Conrad's voice carried the sneer that was on his face. "Somebody loaded dynamite in the tool shed and decided to light it."

Albert felt cold. The heat made his face burn, but it was overpowered by the cold water and the sharp breeze. He looked at the rest of the men in the line—all tired, many still startled from the sudden awakening.

Valentine, Edwards, Lightning Stevens, and Bucky Rudman dug furiously with shovels on the side of the tool shed facing the bunk-houses and the woods. "Wider!" shouted Bud. "We gotta get it wider! Otherwise we're gonna lose 'em."

"We can't go any wider without burning our asses," answered Bucky in a shout. Bud grabbed his shovel and jumped to the front of the line. A line of buckers fell in with axes and shovels.

For almost an hour, the battle remained much the same. But the buckets of water, together with the disappearing sources of fuel, began to have their effect.

By the time the first gray of dawn appeared, the fire was finally finished, leaving the crew knotted in groups—half-dressed, covered in sweat and soot, some sitting, others standing limp with axes and shovels, staring at the scorched blackness that was once the tool shed. In the middle of the black circle were deep holes where the two charges of dynamite had erupted.

"I saw him." It was St. Bride's voice. He was standing on the porch of the mess hall. The voice was gruff but still piercing. The crew turned to where St. Bride was pointing. "I saw him go in there with dynamite."

Bud had just doused himself with a bucket of water—his bare legs now dripping, as he bent down to finally tie his shoelaces.

St. Bride's pitch rose. "He had it in that black case he was carrying this morning down in Seakomish. I saw him put them in."

Now the voice of Little Boy Whittaker broke across the camp—a high, mournful, yet angry voice. "You're a liar, St. Bride. You never saw nothing." Albert had never really heard the voice this loudly before. It sounded like an animal.

Bud Cole stepped onto the porch. "What are you saying, St. Bride?"

"I'm saying that I saw him carrying that dynamite."

Bud turned to look at Little Boy, who now curled up slightly, turning away from the crowd. The men started rumbling as they considered these charges. Appleseth and Valentine talked to several of those around them in louder voices. Albert could make out the word "sabotage."

"St. Bride, let me sort out who did what here," said Bud as the morning light began to finally illuminate the camp and the gray smoke that hung above it.

"He's a fucking saboteur, that little prick. He's here to kill us all 'cause he's a Red that's set on destroying men who work for a living." St. Bride's face was black with whiskers and mud—a wild smile at the center.

But the smile was replaced with a howl as he lurched backward, smashing hard into the log wall. His left arm was instantly red with blood; just behind it, a wooden hatchet now stuck halfway into one of the logs. Across the camp, Little Boy was still hunched over—having thrown the hatchet with all of his might.

Someone shouted, "He's lost his fingers!" But St. Bride's voice rose again. He held out his hand, two fingers missing, pointing the man-gled hand at Little Boy. "You're just afraid to admit it, you fucking Red. I guarantee by my two dead fingers that you're the traitor that's behind this tool shed, behind them animals. I saw you, and you know I did. And you got Nariff Olben's blood on your hands." He continued to hold out the hand, blood oozing. "He's the traitor, boys. He's the one deserves a noose."

Little Boy stood alone, not far from one of the bunkhouses, his face black with soot. Though one moment he stood perfectly still—a wisp of breeze ruffled his black hair—the next he had crossed the twenty yards to the mess hall and landed full-force on St. Bride, who collapsed onto the porch floor.

This drew the crew into a thick circle next to the porch, with shouts of encouragement for both sides. Bucky Rudman dove into the melee, as Bud Cole and Valentine lunged to pull him off.

Albert felt his stomach surge at the back of his throat. Not from the blood. Or even the fighting. But from the looks on the faces. Animal looks—eyes wide, nostrils flaring, saliva and dirt dribbling from mouths as the men clawed at one another. Clare's warning suddenly flashed through Albert's mind. Could it get worse than this?

Bucky finally pulled Little Boy away from St. Bride, with a choke hold around the throat, exposing every vein in Little Boy's neck. His shirt and face were covered with blood. Valentine and Bud Cole held St. Bride, while Zoe applied a tourniquet to the fingers and pressed hard with a rag that grew quickly redder.

"Alright, alright," shouted Bud. His legs were streaked with blood.

Some of the men continued to shout support for one side or the other. "Alright goddamn it!" shouted Bud again. This brought silence, save for the angry cries of blue jays perched on the roof overhead and the heavy breathing of both men.

"This ain't no kangaroo court, you got that?" Bud's voice shook.

"If he's guilty, he's guilty," shouted Appleseth in return. This brought a chorus of "yeah's", and a surge in the crowd toward Little Boy. But before they reached him, Bucky Rudman spun Little Boy around, shoving him against the wall directly behind him, and turned to face the surge himself.

"You touch a hair on his head, and I'll pull your windpipe out of your throat, Appleseth," said Bucky calmly, but loudly enough for the rest to hear. This stopped the crowd. "This boy didn't do nothing. I can personally vouch for it. He didn't set no dynamite. He didn't kill Nariff, either."

"But St. Bride saw him." Appleseth's voice rose, followed by a deep gurgling shout from St. Bride. "He's your traitor, boys. He's your traitor!"

Bud Cole now stepped between Appleseth and Bucky, pushing each back with one hand. "That's enough. Everybody..."

But Appleseth slapped his hand away. "Get out of the way, Cole. If you don't have the backbone, we've got it."

Bud turned to him angrily, but did not speak.

"You heard me," continued Appleseth. "This crew is fed up with letting panty-waists like this..."

But Appleseth never got the full sentence out. With a swift upward motion, Bud slammed his fist into Appleseth's jaw, spinning him off the ground, then doing it again when he came down. Appleseth finally landed in a heap on the ground.

Albert expected that would be the end of things, since Appleseth's face already spouted blood, his eyes shut. But Bud reached down and picked him up by his suspenders, slamming his right fist into Appleseth's belly, forcing broken teeth out of the tall man's mouth. As Appleseth slumped forward from the blows, he fell across Bud, who tossed him to the ground. When he landed, Bud took one step back, then, as if kicking a football, he recovered the step and slammed his right foot full speed into Appleseth's back.

Bud looked at the crew, his body heaving as he gasped air. His voice was full of phlegm and billows of heavy breathing. "Any the rest of you want to argue about this? Huh?  Any the rest of you wanna file a goddamn complaint about how I'm handling this?" He suddenly slammed his foot again into Appleseth, this time the back of his legs. "Huh?"

Albert saw several of the men exchange glances after the last blow. Myles Norgren looked at Lightning Stevens, who took a step closer to Bud.

"You want to tell me how to run this show? You want to tell me who is guilty?" Bud's voice grew as he spoke. He searched the faces, turning to take in the whole semi-circle. His back was arched and full. "Appleseth here thought I didn't have backbone," he shouted. "Any of the rest of you boys agree?" He paused now, wiping a bleeding hand across his face, as Appleseth lay motionless at his feet. "Any of you want to tell me how to run the show? Huh? Speak up, goddamn you!"

A sudden gust sent the smoke from the smoldering tool shed across the camp, leaving most coughing, which seemed to distract Bud. As they struggled with the smoke, he laughed—a deep, angry laugh—then picked up one of the buckets of water and sloshed it onto Appleseth, who suddenly stirred.

"We start work in two hours," said Bud softly as he started walking toward his bunkhouse. "Two hours. I want every one of you mother-fuckers to be there."

# Book Three: Fall 1937

**Chapter 30**

"There ain't a goddamn thing I can do, Bud," said Charlie Deets, turning in the swivel chair behind a gray metal desk. "I am one sheriff. I got one deputy. And I got rumors up my ass about the CIO getting ready to shut down this valley."

Charlie Deets might be sheriff, but to many people of Seakomish, he was known as Fats. Something that newcomers always found surprising, since Deets was rail-thin. He'd gotten the nickname thirty years earlier, when he was well over 300 pounds.

Bud had always liked Deets. Not because he thought he was exceptionally hard working. But because he was honest. You may not like what Charlie Deets had to say, but you'd hear it straight.

"Look, Charlie," said Bud. "I'm not asking you to figure this thing out, okay? All I want is for you or your deputy—either one of you—to visit the camp one more time. Ask a few questions."

Deets got up from his chair and closed a window against a sudden rain squall. He smiled while Bud talked, making his cheeks sag with the excess flesh that used to be filled. "What you're saying is that you want us to scare a few folks, right?"

"Something like that."

Deets started laughing, as he reached into a chest pocket and withdrew a can of chewing tobacco.

"What's so funny?"

"Just that I never took you for being so god-darn naive, Bud." He sucked a black gob off of a bony finger.

"Naive? How?"

"First of all, it didn't do a lot of good the last time I came up there. Second, it's a little hard to believe that my coming up there again and questioning your crew all over again is going to scare away your traitor—if that's what you're even dealing with." Every time Deets leaned back, the chair gave out a low, slow squeak. "And in my mind, that is one hell of a big if."

Bud slumped into one of the hard wooden chairs facing Deets' desk. He let out a long breath. "Well, Charlie, if you got a theory, I'd be more than happy to listen."

"I don't got any theory. Hell, if I had theories I'd be working for J. Edgar Hoover." Deets stretched his long frame around the side of the desk and spit downward, into a small brass spittoon. He wiped his mouth with a dark shirt sleeve. "But if you're asking me to give odds. Well, hell, I'll be happy to give you some odds."

Bud waited. This was how Charlie Deets approached everything. He talked to you straight, but always from angles or, if he had a beer or two in him, from circles.

"In my book, it's maybe a hundred-to-one that it's somebody on the inside. Don't see enough evidence from what you told me. Maybe fifty-to-one it's the union boys—Clare Ristall and those assholes. But if they're gonna go after anybody, it's gonna be Ashford & Southern or Deek Brown or Zollock—not you, but I figure you already know that." Deets now stood, dipped another plug and coated his lip. A fan in the corner clicked every second or two. Bud wondered how Deets kept from going crazy.

"In the even-money category, I'll suggest two things." Deets now leaned forward, jabbing a thin middle finger suddenly into the top of the desk. "I figure that it's either somebody who wants to get you or one of your crew. You know, a personal thing. A grudge. Hatred. Somebody fucked somebody's wife. That kinda thing. You been keeping your peter in your pants, Bud?"

"Goddamn it, Charlie."

"Okay, okay. Or"—now he sat again, the chair squeaking—"if it ain't that, then you mighta stumbled into one of them crazy Wobblies that's still holed-up there in the woods from thirty years ago."

Bud snorted and waited for Deets to laugh, but the long man simply stared back at him. His eyes sagged away at either side, causing ridges that cut into his cheeks. "You aren't serious," said Bud.

"Serious about which one?"

"Are you talking about that goddamn Olaf Carn story? The crazy old Wobbly who's living in a cave and haunting logging companies?"

Deets now leaned forward. "Look Bud. Let's assume for the sake of argument that it ain't an inside job, okay?"

"Jesus, Charlie."

"Will you shut up and listen for a second? If it ain't somebody on your crew, then somebody came in from outside. That meant he had to get past your sentries, so he had to know that section of track and woods like the back of his hand. And he had to spend a lot of time sneaking around your camp—setting that dynamite in your tool shed and killing those pet cats earlier."

Charlie let out a long sigh, as if his point was clear. But then added, "So, that points to somebody who is very experienced in those woods. Maybe somebody who's lived in them. It also points to somebody who knows all the ins-and-outs of that rail line coming up Roosevelt Creek—like somebody who worked on it when it first was built. That was Ashford & Southern, wasn't it?"

"Yeah, they put it in just before the war."

"Okay, mighta been somebody who worked for them, or with them. How many of your men worked for A&S?"

Bud shook his head. "Don't have a clue."

Charlie looked unhappy at Bud's response. "Olaf Carn fits both descriptions—whether you like it or not. He was with A&S when they built that line." Deets' brows now shot up as he leaned abruptly forward in the chair. "Plus, come to think of it, he'd know how to file a spike. Wasn't that what caused the Shay accident?"

Bud shook his head. "It's all wrong, Charlie. You're all wrong. That story about the goddamn Carn or whatever his name is ain't a hell of a lot more reliable than the stories about the Indians."

Deets smiled and raised his eyebrows, but Bud interrupted. "Now Goddamn it, Charlie. I don't want to hear that Indian ghost shit either."

Deets put up both hands, as if to stop Bud from advancing. "I didn't say a thing about Injun ghosts, okay?"

"Do you know an old codger named Petey Hulst?" asked Bud.

Deets started laughing. His shoulders heaved back, as he shook his head. He also showed a set of long, yellowed teeth. "Goddamn yes. You mean Petey Hulst is working for you?"

"He's the whistlepunk. Damn good at it too. It's just that he gets these guys thinking about all that Indian crap and the stories about Olaf Carn. And it damn near scares the shit out of them."

Deets slapped his hand on the arm of his chair. "God, I remember when he worked for A&S, years ago. He conjured up some ghosts or something—or said he did. And I hadda go up there and calm the hell outta the whole camp." The laughter died slowly in him. "I think they had Jesus Christ himself walking around up there. Half the men were ready to shoot the other half."

Deets leaned forward again, with a painful squeak. "Say, he worked for A&S, didn't he?"

"So?"

"So."

"For Chrissake, Charlie…"

Deets shrugged. "I 'spose it's a little far-fetched to think that that old fart would be involved, but I was just trying to help."

Bud lit a cigarette. "We had this photographer up to camp this week," said Bud. "Olmeier. Julius Olmeier."

Deets nodded. "I've heard of him. Travels all over the state."

"Right. He said something about trouble in Auburn. You heard anything about it?"

"Heard anything? Christ, yes. Some business guy, friends of the governor or something. Got his head opened on a show down near Auburn. As a matter of fact, it was kinda like your situation, now that I think about it. A train went over a cliff a couple months ago because somebody filed a spike. This business guy went up to look into it or something. Or he worked for some company from New York that was gonna buy in."

"What did the cops say?"

Deets laughed. "What do you think? Said they were too busy with all the other shit going on. Couldn't look into it."

"You get the impression that Bonnie and Clyde could rob half of the banks in this state and none of the law enforcement officials would have time for it 'cause of all the goddamn labor trouble?" Bud smiled but didn't mean it.

Deets nodded slowly. "'Perfect day for a little robbery, said Bonnie to Clyde. The AFL and the CIO have everybody tied up in knots. Let's rob the rest of 'em silly.' That's what's going on here, Bud. You got that part right for sure."

"Exactly," said Bud as he stood up. "By the way, Olmeier said he thought the guy's name was Patterson. Does that sound right?"

"Which guy?"

"The one that got killed in Auburn. Pinkerton or Patterson. He wasn't sure."

Deets shook his head. "Neither one. Bulletin that came my way said Petrisen. I remember exactly. That was the name of the little crossroads where I was born down in Carolina. I remember thinking that when I read it."

Bud nodded and closed the door.

"It's Olaf Carn," shouted Deets through the closed door. "Living in one of them caves. Just mark my word."

Bud laughed and got into his car.

❀    ❀    ❀

Bud had dreaded the next stop for weeks. Perhaps that's why he delayed it for as long as possible. He stopped at the house to eat lunch, then to Walther's to order groceries for the camp, then to the post office. As he dumped the mail onto the passenger seat and got ready to start the car, he noticed the two letters on top—one from Julius Olmeier, the other from Panama Northwest Shipping Company in Seattle.

He ripped open the Olmeier letter and unfolded a neat, typewritten note:

*Dear Mr. Cole,*
*I am afraid that I must disappoint you. I cannot compare photos*
*of the men in your company with those I took at the operation in*
*Auburn because it appears that someone exposed every role of*
*film that I took when I visited Skybillings. I am not certain*
*whether this happened after I returned to my studio or during the*
*last evening of my stay in your camp. At any rate, I want to*
*apologize to you, and to say that I hope I have the opportunity in*
*the future to complete this work.*
*Thank You for Your Hospitality,*
*Julius Olmeier*

Bud leaned back in the seat, as the rain started once more. The sky was dim gray. A perfect setting for this kind of news, thought Bud. He tossed the letter back onto the pile and picked up the one from Panama Northwest.

Who the hell would've exposed that film? He sliced the end of the envelope with his finger. Does that prove that somebody inside the crew is involved? Or is it coincidence? Maybe it happened after Olmeier got home. Bud slammed his hand into the steering wheel and cursed, as he drew the Panama Northwest letter out of the envelope.

*Dear Mr. Cole:*
*Kindly contact me as soon as possible to arrange a time for a*

*meeting. New developments require us to speak at the earliest*
*possible convenience.*
*Sincerely,*
*Bertram Witstrop, President*
*Panama Northwest Shipping Company.*

Bud gritted his teeth. He let his eyes focus on several women walking past, hurrying against the darkening sky. Then on a truck with old tires loaded on the back, that crawled slowly down Main Street. Then on the rippling flag just above him, on top of the post office. There were times during the worst of the Depression he walked right along this street, right through this kind of weather—with these kind of people around him, the streets full of trucks like the one with the tires—and he would have given anything he had to get a chance to restart a logging company, to get back on his feet, to restart what he and Fred thought could work, even thrive.

But now, sitting here, sitting in the same spot like so often before, everything in him wanted to turn the car out of Seakomish and drive away as far as possible. To Seattle and then Portland and then to California and say to hell with all this. Work in the woods down there. Hell, even the fields. He could pick lettuce, haul grapes. He could hire onto a steamer out of San Francisco.

He slammed the steering wheel again, so violently this time that a man and woman walking into the post office stopped to look. He sat silently, hoping they wouldn't see him. When they went in, he started the car and backed out. But rather than turning up Main and heading toward Seattle, he drove two blocks to the union office and parked in front. Clare Ristall's car was already there.

Bud drew in a deep breath and smiled to himself. He put both the Olmeier and Witstrop letters into his pocket and got out of the car. He felt a chill in the air too, leading to another curse. How far behind this was the snow, he wondered as he climbed the stairs. He knocked, then walked into the office.

Clare was on the phone, his shirtsleeves rolled up. Though he turned and nodded to Bud as he entered, two women Bud didn't recognize worked at a table across the front of the office.

"Can I help you?" asked the older woman.

"I'm Bud Cole. I have a meeting with Clare this afternoon." She looked back at Clare, who nodded for Bud to have a seat. She pointed at a chair in the corner and Bud settled in, watching the women fold leaflets into envelopes. They quickly settled into a conversation about a campaign meeting in Everett the next night—some kind of political convention, or gathering, though Bud couldn't make it out exactly.

Clare's voice fell away, so Bud couldn't make out the conversation. Though, once again, he thought he detected something about a convention and he heard Everett mentioned several times. But his mind went back to the two letters in his pocket. He didn't have any sense what either one really meant, but he feared that neither was good news.

"Bud Cole," said Clare suddenly, grabbing a coat from the hangar. Bud hadn't noticed him hang up the phone.

"How are you, Clare?" Bud thought his hand would be crushed by the handshake.

"Great, except for the fact that I have to give a speech tomorrow night at the civic center up in Everett and I haven't put down the first word on paper." He smiled broadly, a warm smile. Bud re-considered the approach he planned. Maybe just make some excuse, maybe some comment about the campaign, and get the hell out. But Clare had already turned and was speaking to the two women.

"Ladies, Mr. Cole and I are going to get a cup of coffee at the diner. Will you tell any callers that I'll be back in an hour or so?" Both nodded and smiled, as Clare led the way down the stairs. "Hope you didn't mind," he said, turning to Bud. "Didn't know what you had on your mind, but I figured we probably didn't want campaign ladies listening."

They stopped awkwardly at the sidewalk. "Choose your poison Bud—either a walk or a cup of joe?"

Bud chose a walk, so Clare started up the hill toward the high school. "It'll keep the blood flowing on a day like this, what do you say?" said Clare lightheartedly.

"Sure," said Bud, now buttoning his jacket. "Yeah. Sure will."

"Hope you don't mind my being too direct, but I was a little surprised by your note." Clare smiled. He came only to Bud's shoulder, but something about his easy style didn't make him seem like a smaller man to Bud. "Seeing as how you boys are AFL and all."

Bud didn't take time to reconsider his approach. He'd thought it through repeatedly, so he launched it. "I've been having a hell of a lot of trouble up there, Clare." Bud paused to glance at Clare, who nodded but didn't say anything. They had crossed First Street and were approaching the playing field on the east side of the school. The sidewalk led uphill from there.

"That's what I've been hearing," said Clare. "Of course, I was terribly saddened to hear about the three men in that Shay crash. God, that was awful." Clare glanced at Bud quickly. "I am very sorry."

Bud nodded and walked in silence for several steps. The Seakomish River appeared on the far side of the field. Bud noticed that wind was catching the foam that boiled up as the river passed over the rocks near the park. "I don't know if you heard, but we had an explosion in the tool shed about three weeks ago. Somebody set it off with a couple sticks of dynamite."

Clare stopped. "Dynamite?"

Bud nodded.

"Jesus Christ." Clare shoved his hands in his pockets. "You talked to Charlie Deets about it?"

Bud shrugged, feeling the anger in his chest. "Course I have."

Clare stopped now. "And what'd he say?"

"He said that there's nothing he can do since we're just small fry. Says he's too busy dealing with all the labor troubles."

Clare now stared directly at Bud, without expression. Bud noticed that Clare had something of a baby face—a look of city schooling and easy life, though he knew he'd worked most of his life in the very woods that Bud had. "So why are you telling me this, Bud?" asked Clare. His voice was matter-of-fact, not unfriendly, but the attempt at light banter was gone. He seemed to be searching for words, as if it wasn't entirely clear why Bud was even discussing the subject with him. "What do you want me to do—somehow to stop the CIO, to let the AFL own the woods, just so Charlie can look into your problems? Is that it?"

Bud studied Clare. He had thought about this conversation many times. And he knew just how he had to approach it. Watch Clare's face, watch how he reacts, listen carefully to his answers, and try to surprise him.

Bud smiled and laughed softly, as a school bus roared past them. "No, no, that's not it at all, Clare. I'm realistic. I know there ain't nothing that will stop you boys from trying to organize your union and get your share."

Clare nodded his head and smiled slightly. "Glad to hear it."

"No, what I had in mind was something much more direct." Bud stuck his hands in his pockets and turned to face the river. The breeze caught the foam, then tossed it lightly on the blue-green waves, where it disappeared instantly. The trees running upward on the other side seemed more black than green.

"And that is?"

"And that is that I figure you boys are behind all these troubles I've been having and I'm here to tell you that I've had enough." Bud turned to face Clare, but the face gave no hints. It was hard, set, flickered with hair that blew across the forehead. "I figure that from day one, you CIO boys have had your hand in all of this. The spike that got filed. The animals that happened to lose their heads. The explosion and dynamite."

Bud paused, giving Clare a chance to respond. But Clare remained silent.

"So I just wanted to say this to you," continued Bud. "I may not have much in this world. God knows, before you boys are done, I might not even have a fucking logging company. But I want you to know, Clare, that I got a memory. I got one hell of a mean spirit. And I will person-ally repay you—with my own two hands, if necessary—for what you are doing to my crew and my company."

Bud was suddenly thankful for the wind. The gusts cooled the sweat he felt on his chest. Besides, it covered the tremor in his voice.

For several seconds, Clare remained motionless, his eyes locked on Bud. Still no movement, no expression, no change in how he stood. He seemed lost in the words Bud had just spoken, as if measuring them. After several seconds, a small smile flickered across his lips and his eyebrows dipped. Still he didn't speak, as another bus roared past. This time the bus driver waved, so both men waved back. Bud didn't recognize the face.

When Bud turned back to Clare, he had a full smile across his face. "Jesus, Bud, there for a minute, I actually thought you were serious," said Clare with a hearty laugh. The smile was deep, revealing dimples on either cheek.

Bud was instantly furious. "Goddamn you!" he shouted against the wind. "I am serious. You think this is some kind of fucking joke? I got three men dead because of you goddamn CIO assholes and you coulda killed fifty more with that dynamite. And you think I'm joking?"

Clare took a deep breath and seemed to tilt into the breeze. It caught his jacket and made him look suddenly like a sail, with his hands in his pants pockets and his elbows cast outward. The sense was of a schoolboy playing in the breeze. But now he turned to Bud, his face hard. "Well, I was hoping you were kidding Cole, because that is one of the biggest goddamn pieces of horse shit I have ever heard in my life. Any man who even claims to own half a brain would have the good sense to admit it was a joke and go on his way."

Bud listened, not surprised by the response. In fact, he fully expected it. But he was surprised by its forcefulness—and a little pleased.

"So you think that the CIO is behind all your trouble up there, do you?" continued Clare. "Funny how no other company in these parts has had your trouble. Funny how we're so dead set against you, Skybillings—a pimple on the ass of the logging industry, I might add—that we'd be willing to kill some of your crew, but we haven't bothered with killing anybody at companies three times your size, at, oh let's see, at Deek Brown, or Ashford & Southern, or Zollock. At companies that count." Clare paused briefly, then added: "This is a strike we are planning, you dumb son of a bitch—not some kind of murder spree."

Instantly, Bud felt like hitting him, but he held himself back. He tried to draw the cool air into his lungs.

"Spare me the insults, Clare," said Bud, his voice surprising him with its strength. "I don't happen to care what you think of me. And I sure as hell don't expect you to admit any of it." He paused now, and pointed a finger at Clare's chest. "But even if you destroy Skybillings, I want you to know that I will personally come after you. I will personally, with these hands."

Clare was now laughing, shaking his head. He turned away, then turned back suddenly. His face flashed with anger. "Jesus, I have gone the extra mile for you, Cole. I have put my prestige, my very leadership of this union on the line for your penny-ante little operation."

Bud shook his head.

"No, no, I'm serious. Hear me out. Do you know how many times my people have wanted to come after you? Huh?"

"That's bullshit, Clare..."

"It isn't bullshit. It isn't bullshit." Clare's voice was now a shotgun, spewing out words in flashes that slammed into Bud. "They have wanted to go after you. I've said no. I've said you're too small. I've said you're too far up. I've said that you're a decent guy—that you treat your workers well. I've told them that let's at least go after the big boys and then—only later, only if need be—we'll talk about Skybillings."

Bud felt the heat in his chest again, so he turned to the wind, but it had died.

"Do you know how they look at me when I say that, Cole? Huh?" Clare's eyes bulged, his voice hoarse. "You won't answer, but you know, goddamn it. They think I'm weak. They think I'm easy. They think I'm in bed with the goddamn companies—that's what they think."

Bud wanted to leave. He hated the whole confrontation now. But Clare continued, his voice more and more strained. "And then you come up here and tell me that I'm behind your troubles." Clare now lunged for Bud, grabbing him by the front of his coat, but Bud stepped back, sweeping Clare's arms away.

But he couldn't stop the assault of words. In fact, it seemed to gather more strength. "You tell me that I'd set dynamite, that I'd blow up a Shay, that I'd try to kill people up there—when Lydia's son is working up there? Jesus, what kind of animal would I have to be?"

Bud was shaking his head, though he wasn't sure what to say, but Clare still didn't stop. He was laughing now. Laughing furiously, with a hard smile. "That's it. That's it!" he shouted.

"Goddamn it, Clare, let's just drop all this..."

"No, I won't drop it, Cole. You don't like this, do you? You don't like being exposed this way as a raving lunatic?" Clare now was quiet, laughing as if to himself. "But what's really going on here is Lydia, isn't it? That's what's got you so up in arms. That's where all this shit you've been spewing out comes from."

Bud turned now and started walking back toward the car.

"That's it, isn't it Cole?" Clare was now right behind him, still laughing. "You've always hoped that Lydia would turn to you, haven't you? Ever since Fred died, you've wanted that, haven't you?"

The rage was growing in Bud as he walked, so he hurried more. But Clare persisted. "But she never wanted you, did she? She was never interested. So what do you do? You come around attacking me. You hate me, Cole, because Lydia Weissler loves me."

Bud turned and faced Clare directly. "That's nothing but horseshit Clare, and you know it."

"I do? I do?" The laughter was replaced by a broad, wicked smile. "I know that for the past ten years you've been waiting and hoping and wanting, but what have you got? Not a goddamn thing, that's what. You haven't had the guts to even try. So what do you do now? First, you ask her only son to go to work for you—even though his old man died on your watch." Clare now leaned close and winked at him, conspiratorially. "Not bad, Cole. The wife stiff's you, so you get at her through the kid."

Bud wanted to swing at him, but he held his breath.

"Now you come after me." Clare paused. "But I got one question for you, tough guy. After you kill me, Cole, who's it going to be next? Maybe Lydia ought to be next. What do you think? Why not just do her in?"

Clare stopped now, his chest heaving. Despite the wind, Bud could see perspiration across his forehead and above his lips. He seemed depleted suddenly. The violent barrage of words seemed to have left him empty. "You're one sick man, Bud. I feel sorry for you," said Clare quietly, as he turned and began walking back toward his office.

※　　※　　※

Bud leaned onto the rocks and vomited into the swirling black water. He cupped a hand of cold water across his face, just as another wave hit him. He lay on the rocks, his stomach a knot of muscle and pain. The perspiration that he felt up his chest and across his face remained, despite the cold water and the growing wind.

He knew the river. He knew its bends and its rapids. He could swim in even the swiftest of its currents. So this is where he knew he had to come when he had left Clare. The sky was already the dingy dark of early night. The wind had started up again. But he knew he couldn't go home. Not to his bed. Not to the memories that Clare's barrage had awakened.

As he lay still, the cold spray washing across him, the bubbling roar of the Seakomish filled every pore of his body. As it did, he saw the picture of Fred Weissler, that day, as Fergie pulled into Seakomish. He saw his hands. The dried cold blood, as he got in his car and drove to tell Lydia.

Bud's stomach now seemed more settled. At least the uncontrolled spasms were gone, so he sat on the rocks. He realized that his body was soaked. For a moment, he wondered if it was raining, but he couldn't tell. It didn't matter, not this close to the river.

Even in his pain, he didn't care what Clare Ristall thought of him. He knew that despite his initial kind words, that Clare hated him—had for years. And Bud always suspected it had something to do with Lydia. Clare was right—many people around town assumed that Bud and Lydia would end up together. Earl Talbert was the only one with balls enough to actually say it to his face. And Bud didn't dislike the notion. Lydia had been a friend, almost as close as Fred when Skybillings first started. Even with the terrible loss they'd both suffered through Fred's death, Bud felt that there might be hope someday.

But that was dashed so quickly. Lydia had sealed him off—away, distant. The pain had been unbearable for many months. But he put it somewhere into a corner, where he wouldn't think about it.

Now Bud stood and stripped off his shirt and peeled off his soaked pants. He tossed his shoes several feet back from the water and dove into a deep pool. The inky icy-cold blackness swept over him, as the violent roar suddenly disappeared. Now just the gentle sound of bubbles, the lightness of buoyancy, of floating, of feeling the jets of current wrapping and curling around his body. He'd gotten used to swimming in the icy waters many years before, so the cold didn't bother him. Within seconds, it felt like his natural home. It felt like this was where his life was, where his life should go.

He lay back in the deep pool, out of the torrent at midstream that would have swept him away. His mind was lost momentarily in the wonderful freedom of the water. Yet even it could not keep the thoughts away. Was it so obvious that even Clare could see how much he longed for Lydia? He thought he'd hidden it away so many years before. But now even Clare Ristall could see it.

Bud swept his arms forward, bringing his body into a roll—adding even more buoyancy. He pulled back once more, laying out, his body fully extended. As he did, he felt a shiver run through him, not from the cold of the water, but from the awful comment by Clare—you couldn't get Lydia, so you took her boy instead. Bud struggled to stifle the feeling of nausea he suddenly felt again, even in the water. He brought himself to the surface, and felt himself shout, though he couldn't hear his voice in the roar.

Was that what he had done? Clare was a political whore. But was he right about Albert? Was he right that what Bud Cole had buried deep down in his soul was an anger at being rejected—and doubly, at being blamed for his partner's death—that was working its way out by trying to harm the boy?

Bud felt suddenly angry. That was bullshit. Clare knew it was bullshit. He brought it up just to raise doubts. But why truly had he, Bud, invited Albert to join Skybillings? Bud didn't know, and hadn't really thought about it. Just that at that particular moment, on that day when he sat there with Albert and the church crowd, it just seemed right.

Bud came to the surface and drew in deep breaths. He tried to put all of the confrontation out of his head. But then the rest of it hit him. Nothing in the confrontation yielded one piece of evidence that gave Bud any clearer sense of what was going on.

He went through all of this chaos with Clare and still had no clue who was going after Skybillings. Was the CIO involved? Bud still had no idea. But he had to admit that Clare's arguments had seemed plausible. The emotion he thought he saw in the face seemed genuine. And he had to admit, something in the voice, even in the mocking laughter, seemed to well up from true pain.

Bud was suddenly aware of a flash of light striking him. He spun in the water, but then several beams of blinding yellow light hit him full force. He tried to dip and resurface twenty or thirty feet downstream, but the lights found him again, just as he heard voices and made out two shapes running toward him.

"You outa your goddamn mind?" was all Bud could make out as he finally gave up and swam toward the shapes. He recognized the tall, thin body of Charlie Deets. His deputy was carrying two more flashlights just behind.

Bud pulled himself onto the rocks and stood up, just as the two of them reached him. "What in the fuck has got into your mind, Bud Cole?" shouted Deets. In the indirect light cast off by the flashlight, Bud could detect the anger.

"Decided to take a dip."

Deets pointed the flashlight directly into his face, sending a sharp pain through Bud's eyes. He turned away, and realized that he was standing only in a pair of shorts.

"Me and Foster come down the River Road and saw your car," shouted Deets, above the roar of the river. "We thought you'd been conked over the head or something."

Bud shook his head. "Sorry. Just had some thinking to do."

Deets now leaned close to Bud, so close that Bud could make out the yellow teeth—and a hint of alcohol. "I figure you got yourself some thinking alright," said Deets gruffly. "Clare Ristall stopped by this afternoon to tell me you threatened to kill him."

Bud laughed sharply, wiping water from his face, and for the first time, he felt the terrible chill from the wind. But Deets' flashlight didn't leave Bud's face. He seemed interested in studying how Bud took the news.

"Clare says I oughta arrest you. You know that?" Deets face was still close.

"That's the damndest thing I ever heard, Charlie. He's trying to blow up my show and you're gonna arrest me?"

The sheriff studied him for a moment, then dropped the flashlight beam. "Get home, Bud. I oughta toss both your asses into the clink, but I'm not sure it's worth the bother."

## Chapter 31

As he lay in bed, Albert heard a rattling sound just outside the bunkhouse. At first, he thought it was a raccoon, but then he heard muffled voices and a sound of tin metal. He listened for several more minutes, but then the sound stopped. No one else in the bunkhouse stirred.

Albert crept out of his bunk and looked out the window. In the moonlight, he could see several forms walking quickly into one of the equipment sheds, the one that held most of the tools. Someone had propped the door open. He could see flashlights swaying in the direction of the platform near the crummy.

"What the hell is all the racket?" asked Lightning Stevens sleepily. Albert turned to see him climb out of his bunk.

"Take a look," said Albert.

Lightning looked out the window. "I'll be damned. Little Boy, Bucky, wake up! Somebody's stealing us blind."

Within seconds, everyone in the bunkhouse was up and Lightning was running out the door. He caught St. Bride coming out of the shed with two toolboxes.

"What the hell are you doing?" shouted Lightning.

"We're quitting this half-assed outfit before the whole goddamn place blows."

Norgren now stood next to Lightning, as the rest of the crew poured from the bunkhouses. "Quitting, hell. You're robbing us blind," said Myles. He stepped forward to take the toolboxes, but several of the Swedes blocked his path.

"We're leaving this half-assed outfit and we're taking our share of the belongings," shouted St. Bride. Then he turned to the group of men forming behind him. "If you boys stay here, you're dead.

Somebody's got it in for this two-bit outfit and not a one of them's got the balls to do anything about it. What's Bud Cole done for you?"

St. Bride's voice grew. "I'm asking you boys this: You wanna die like those cats did? Huh? With their heads scooped out?"

St. Bride now started laughing, as Parsons, one of the buckers, picked up the argument. "It don't matter how many sentries this scum operation posts, they ain't gonna stop the ones who are wanting to kill us. And for my money, it ain't nothing but a Communist traitor right in the ranks. But Bud Cole don't got the guts to do anything about him."

Albert studied the growing mass of men, now milling around outside the mess hall. The flashlights lit the ground in front of them, but the faces remained shrouded in darkness. Valentine, Petey Hulst, Edwards and his AFL men, along with half the Swedes, gathered behind Lightning Stevens, while the others gathered in a thick group behind St. Bride.

Zoe stood on the porch, watching the gathering. Then she disappeared into the mess hall.

Lightning spoke loudly, to the whole crowd. "You men want to go, that's fine. I think you're imagining ghosts, but...."

Several shouted for him to be quiet, that he was just one of the scabs, but he shouted louder in response. "I don't give a damn if any of you—all of you—go. But you aren't taking those tools. We got a job to do up here, and we can't do it if we don't got tools."

St. Bride spit on the ground. "You and I both know that if we walk out of here, Bud Cole ain't gonna pay us. So we're gonna get what's owed us."

"You take any of those tools, and you'll do it with a hell of a lot less fingers than you got now," said Lightning.

St. Bride turned to the men assembled behind him. "You boys worried about that?"

"Hell no!" was the nearly uniform response, and most of the men began to turn and walk away.

But Lightning Stevens launched himself directly into St. Bride's chest, knocking him to the ground. Bucky, Little Boy, Conrad Bruel, and others followed. Whether he was swept forward by the men around him or simply launched himself like the others, Albert caught Parsons' jaw with a forearm that sent both of them tumbling. He tried to punch Parsons with both fists once they hit the ground, but Albert felt a whoosh over his head, then what felt like a hammer on his back.

As Albert struggled to roll away, a gunshot echoed overhead, which brought the melee to an immediate stop.

Zoe stood on the porch, slowly moving the shotgun downward so that it was leveled at the group. The men—half on the ground, the others fighting on their feet—froze.

"Those of you who want to go...just get the hell out of here," said Zoe quietly. "Mr. Ferguson, get the crummy ready and take anyone who wants to go down to Seakomish. Immediately. Don't even go back to your bunkhouses." St. Bride said Zoe's name, but she spoke over him. "Hold your words, Mr. St. Bride. The time for discussion has long since passed." She paused, as she took in the whole group. "And no one touches any of the tools."

Silence. No one moved.

"You heard her," Lightning Stevens said softly.

"Let's go, boys," said St. Bride finally. Though a few hesitated for a moment, all of them finally turned and started walking toward the crummy, with Ferguson running to catch up.

❄ ❄ ❄

Albert wondered how Skybillings could keep going with only half the crew. As he figured it, most of the buckers were gone—as were the men Bud Cole would need to load the logs once the trestle was finished. And many men who'd worked the entire time on the trestle left, though Bachelder made one last plea to get them to stay.

All of which meant that Bud Cole shifted virtually all of the crew to new jobs when he returned. Lightning Stevens and Norgren took over the section crew, in charge of laying the tracks across the top of the trestle. Valentine ran the crew that secured the cross braces to the timbers underneath. Bachelder took over the few remaining Swedes who, together with Bucky and Little Boy, wrestled to complete the final three-log bent that would finally complete the trestle.

Bents were "the legs" of the trestle—the massive support structures of logs and crossbeams that were set into the granite ledge. Each was constructed of four or five ramrod straight, full-height firs, lashed tightly together at the top with lumber crossbeams. The firs fanned out widely at the bottom, making the bent resemble a rough-hewn, upside-down V. Three more sets of crossbeams held the lower section together. Across the top, heavy wooden beams connected the bents to one another horizontally.

Most of the bents were built in place, from the bottom up. But some required special attention, such as additional reinforcement, which was the case of the final one. Bachelder had directed that it be assembled on the far side of the ravine, to make it easier to lash the especially long timbers together—which, in turn, required that it be lifted into place on the skyline.

But when it was ready to be lifted, a cold snap hit. An icy wind roared off the face of Three Sisters Ridge, making the trestle itself shudder.

Every time the bent was snaked across the gorge on the skyline, it shuddered, making the winches whine as they attempted to hold the massive post-and-beam structure taut. Each time, Bachelder directed the bent to be taken back, to wait one more day. But more than a week passed—the section crew finished the track to the end of the completed portion of the trestle; the crossbeams were all made secure. Virtually the entire operation now awaited completion of the last section, but the wind sharpened, followed by snow squalls.

"I told Orville, I told Wilbur, it just ain't natural," crowed Bucky Rudman as they watched the trestle cover with a light dusting of snow. The men huddled in several makeshift shelters of two-by-fours and canvas, waiting for the squalls to pass. Bachelder insisted that both the pile driver and the steam engine keep running. So they continued to chug, waiting, like the men on the edges, for a break in the weather.

Lightning Stevens huddled next to a blazing fire, warming his hands. The light snow had stopped, but the wind continued. Albert perched on a log next to the fire.

"Can you figure that guy out?" Albert nodded toward Bucky Rudman who, rather than warming himself in front of the next fire, was now taking bets down the line on whether Skybillings would ever get the trestle up and the logs out.

Lightning laughed. "That's Bucky Rudman. Never one to worry about the situation, no matter how bad." He looked back to Albert, who shook his head. "Hey Bucky, what're the odds?" shouted Lightning toward Bucky.

"Up to five-to-one against," shouted Bucky back. "Care to bring down the odds?"

Lightning laughed and shook his head. He looked back toward Albert. "Gotta keep your sense of humor, Albert."

"I just hate the goddamn cold." Albert stood up and stamped his feet. As the snow began to fall again, the ugly brown emptiness facing him across the gorge begin turning a soft white. The broken stumps, the torn ground rising upward from the clearing, were soon obliterated by a gauzy white.

"How long you think we can stay up here before the heavy snow hits?" asked Albert.

"This time of year, heavy snow may only be a matter of hours." Lightning stood up and walked to the edge of the ravine, peering up at Three Sisters Ridge. "She's socked in up above." He came back to the fire, buttoning his jacket tighter and pulling on a pair of work gloves. "But it ain't cold enough to come down. I figure we've got two, maybe three weeks."

Albert considered this. Three weeks didn't sound like enough to move all the logs, especially since the center of the trestle was still waiting to be finished. "What happens if the heavy snow hits before we're out?"

Lightning chuckled. "I told you when you first came to work here, that a good logger doesn't think too much. Scares the hell out of him." Lightning stopped there, as Petey Hulst joined the group. He pulled out a tin of tobacco and dug in hungrily.

"Bud's fit to be tied," said Petey in his high-pitched whine, hunching toward the fire, away from the weather. "I told him—my leg says that there's a heavy snow on the way the next two days, so he better get ready."

"Your leg?" asked Albert.

"Mm-hmm. Ever since the Frisco quake. I broke it clear through, just below the knee. Ever since, I can tell the weather on her. Cold weather coming it hurts right into my crotch."

"What's Bud gonna do?" This time it was Myles Norgren.

"After he's done cursin' and shittin', he's gonna send us all back to the camp. Wait her out down there."

Albert took this in, recognizing that he still didn't have an answer to his question about a heavy snow that might block the route down to Seakomish. He'd heard stories about blizzards that could come up suddenly, followed by ice this high up. He'd read in school about how, in the 1800s, trappers who got caught up here never came out. But he didn't say anything. He contented himself with the fire, and the small warmth it created in his fingers, and with studying the trestle, now solid white in the snow.

In its whiteness, it didn't seem to defy gravity quite as much. It gave the impression of solid ice—or perhaps a white flower trellis in a garden. As he studied it, he heard the pile driver's engine cut off and the door of the cab slam. In the white distance, Bud jumped onto the trestle and started walking back to the side—a fleck of gray floating in a sea of white.

## Chapter 32

For two days, the men were locked in camp. The first night, two feet of wet snow fell, followed by dropping temperatures. Zoe found extra blankets, and the crew moved from the bunkhouses, which didn't have stoves, into the mess hall. After supper, they shoved the tables to the sides of the room, spread their mattresses on the floor, and brought in another half cord of wood to keep the room heated throughout the night.

Bud Cole, however, insisted upon sleeping in his own bunk, despite Zoe's protests. "You are going to freeze out there, Mr. Cole," she insisted, as the rest of the crew settled into card games.

"I've got paperwork to tend to," said Bud. "Besides, I got a stove, remember?"

"That stove isn't going to keep you alive, Mr. Cole. This cold will freeze you right through those walls."

Bud didn't answer. He took one of the extra blankets and left without saying anything else.

Bucky Rudman was the first to comment. "Poor son of a bitch. You survive dynamite and train wrecks, and it's a freak snow that closes you down."

"To hell with him and his business," snapped Conrad. "What about us? Damn stupid we're up here, this time of year. Men die of freezing cold like this every year."

Bucky slapped him on the back. "That'll make Hell all the better, when we get there boy. You just gotta have a little faith."

But Conrad's mood and the danger from heavy snow didn't sour the crew. Zoe brought out Saturday-night beer for everyone, along with large tins of cookies. Delbert McKenna found country music from a radio station in Montana, which brought several crew members to song. In the corner near the door, as usual, Valentine's circle gathered for Bible study, while Petey Hulst moved his tarot cards into the kitchen. Several men gathered around a large round table that Zoe used for packing lunches, as Petey prepared.

Albert decided to join in, since the only other option was regular cards, and he didn't have any money. Petey started with Delbert McKenna, who shifted nervously in his seat. "I ain't sure this is Christian exactly," said Delbert.

"Jesus Christ his-self read tarot," said Petey, who began laying out the cards.

Delbert squinched his eyebrows at this news, but decided not to argue with it. Next to him, Conrad Bruel rolled his eyes in Albert's direction, as Petey shuffled the cards. Myles appeared from the mess hall and pulled up a chair. Two of the Swedes also appeared—though Albert didn't know their names. Petey became perfectly still as he studied the deck. The sound of laughter filtered in from the mess hall, but the kitchen was silent, save for the loud, nasal breathing of Delbert McKenna.

Petey put one card down. It was a picture of the devil. Delbert's thick cheeks quivered. The next card was a woman in a wedding dress—this brought a smile—followed by the fool and, finally, the hanged man. Delbert waited while Petey seemed lost in thought.

"How old are you, Delbert?" asked Petey finally.

Delbert's face turned ashen. "Why?"

"Just answer the question."

"I'm fifty-five or fifty-six, depending." He waited for Petey's response, but didn't get any. "Jesus Christ, Petey, tell me what they say. Am I gonna die?"

Petey shook his hand. "No, they say that you'll finally lose your virginity before you're sixty."

Delbert's relief at learning he wouldn't die was quickly replaced by embarrassment. "How did you know...?" But Delbert stopped short, casting several sheepish looks around the circle.

Next came Myles, who Petey predicted would fall into a sizeable amount of money. "What the hell is a Communist gonna do with money?" asked Norgren, but Petey said the cards said nothing more. One of the Swedes, the biggest one, was next.

Petey said the Swede would marry soon. That his first-born would become a doctor, but would die violently before he had a son of his own. The Swede, named Gunnar, laughed nervously, then said something in his native tongue, to which Petey said, "Sorry. I just tell you what the cards are saying."

As Petey moved down the line to Bucky Rudman, who had just joined the group, Albert realized he was next. Part of him felt like Delbert—that there was something slightly anti-Christian in this. The other part of him wasn't sure he wanted to know any of this—least-wise not in front of this group.

But Bucky's future gave Albert more time to think. Petey studied the cards closely, for perhaps five minutes. No one spoke. Only the sound of the wind that now blasted the kitchen window with snow. Finally, after much deliberation, Petey announced that Bucky should quit his job.

"Quit?"

"That's what I said," said Petey.

"What business—topping trees?"

"Yup. The cards say topping."

Bucky's faced turned somber. "Why should I leave?"

Petey shrugged. "Dunno. I just see here that you have to leave—either on your own or otherwise."

"But goddamn it, Petey, I love what I'm doing. Taking off the top of those goddamn beasts is the best feeling a man could have."

"I see you hanging from the top of a fir," said Petey slowly. "Hanging, but not moving. You're tangled in some lines." Petey paused now, looking directly at Bucky. "I see a group of men running toward you, but then stopping suddenly. And then not hurrying."

When Bucky remained silent, choosing to watch the snow against the window, Albert could feel the eyes of the group turn to him.

Petey studied the cards closely. He smiled occasionally but his face remained largely empty—folds of skin cascading inward, down a narrow neck. He stroked his handlebar mustache while he studied. Albert noticed that Petey's fingers were narrow and delicate, like those of a musician.

Occasionally, laughter or coughs drifted from the mess hall, but it was clear that most of the crew had gone to bed. The potbelly stove even fell quiet, though the kitchen felt warm—and tight. The snow continued to claw at the kitchen windows, as Albert waited for Petey to speak. Occasional glances fell his way from the others, but most looked down, waiting.

"I have looked through the cards," said Petey quietly. Albert felt himself clutch the edges of his chair tightly. "But the cards are silent."

Several men began to speak, and Delbert whistled. "Quiet," snapped Petey. Albert jumped at the voice, but tried to pretend that he had to cough. "The cards do not speak to me. But, in itself, that does not carry any meaning. Only that we are not to be shown answers through this medium."

Albert let out a deep breath and leaned back in the chair. He noticed Myles Norgren smile.

"So I suggest we choose another medium," said Petey, standing up and pulling several candles from the drawer. He put three in a triangle in the middle of the table and lit them. When he blew out the match, he said, "It is my habit that when the cards remain silent, to open myself to the spirits. To listen intently. To understand if there is special meaning."

Delbert let out a gasp, while Myles snorted, instantly infuriating Petey. "Goddamn it, I won't stand for such blasphemy," he said sharply. "If you don't want to participate, then leave—now." No one got up. Myles nodded, but didn't speak.

Petey sat down in his seat once more. "Please place both hands on the table, palms down." Each of the men did so. "Now place your right palm on the hand to your right." The Swedes and Bucky hesitated, but finally they, too, settled their hands on the hands next to them. "Thank you," said Petey softly.

Albert concluded this was a terrible idea. He wanted to slide back and walk out. But he was too embarrassed to do so. So he tried to imagine what the woods would look like tomorrow in the deep snow.

Petey's voice began again. "Please turn your minds to the wind that is above us." He paused briefly, as if to let each man identify the sound, which was now coming in gusts. "Please concentrate only on the wind."

From what Albert could tell, the rest of the crew had gone to bed. He heard no other sound from the next room. Bucky Rudman's palm felt rough on the back of Albert's left hand, and—for a moment—Albert worried that his own palm was sweating so fiercely that it would slide off of the back of Myles Norgren's hand. But Petey's voice broke into these thoughts. "I can feel that not all of you are concentratin'." He cleared his throat roughly. "You can only hear the wind. Your mind is in the center of the wind. It draws you, it fills you, it carries your soul aloft, it bores into the center of your existence."

Suddenly the wind rose loudly, buffeting the mess hall with a blast that made the seam lines between the logs begin to groan. Delbert let out a shout, but again Petey spoke in his high-pitched wheeze. "We enter the other world with humility. We enter the other world as seekers, as seekers of truth." Now he stopped, as the wind whistled overhead. Albert felt a sudden chill, almost a sense that the wind had entered a small crack in a window. Though Petey's voice continued, it fell into more of a rhythm—less of words, and more of sounds. The warmth in Albert's hands crept up his arms, as the cool wind now seemed to rush through the mess hall, racing to look into every crevice, every corner, scurrying along the log walls, between the men, into the recesses that had previously been hidden from it. It raced, then eddied—as if stopping to take note, to observe a placement out of order—then to race onward.

Was this the wind of the mountains? Was this the wind of the winter storm? Its fierceness was masked by a gentleness, its inquisitiveness was matched by a strange, laughing anger, its arrogance was the humility of the oceans and the sunny desert and the frozen tundra.

The high-pitched, rhythmic voice spoke through the wind. "We are your servants, who, in humility, ask you to show us answers of your choosing." The wind rose once more, followed by the sing-song voice. "Who visits us tonight?"

But Albert now felt drawn by the force of the wind. He felt like he was racing along with it—a molecule, at its center, without form or substance, only fluid movement that swept him faster and faster. And in the distance, he could make out a figure—was it just a few feet ahead or was it miles? It moved slowly, but its form was unlike any form he'd ever seen. It stood tall, like a grown man, but odd projections came out from either side—rounded on the right, dangling on the left. Was it a man? Some sort of creature? Albert turned into the wind, and felt drawn down into the middle of it.

Again the rhythmic voice: "If you have a message for us...." But the form did not move, or speak. Albert tried to look harder, but the cold seemed suddenly to envelop him as the form started to turn. As Albert felt himself drawn onward by the wind, the form turned— slowly, slowly—until it faced him. And Albert could see that it was not one form, but two—a man, a tall dark-haired man, carrying another form, a much smaller man, who looked like he might have been injured. The tall man stooped low under the weight.

Again the rhythmic voice: "But we cannot see your face. Come closer." Yet as Albert felt himself racing ever faster toward the figure, he suddenly could make both faces out in an instant: The tall man's face was that of Bud Cole, the man he carried was Albert.

The scream that Albert let out brought half the crew out of their chairs. Bucky Rudman was shaking his shoulders, but the screaming wouldn't stop, until someone must have closed the window, and the frightfully cold wind stopped.

## Chapter 33

"Anybody home?" asked Harry as he knocked on the door of Bud's bunkhouse and then poked his head in.

Bud's feet were on his desk, his eyes set on the slice of wet snow building on the windowpane.

"Zoe sent me," said Harry. "She claims you're gonna freeze your pecker off out here." Harry dropped another blanket onto the one already folded neatly on Bud's bunk. "Actually, she left out the pecker part. I added that."

Bud shrugged and tossed the book he'd been reading onto the desk. He slipped his glasses off his large face and rubbed his eyes. "I'm not about to freeze with a half cord of wood just outside and a box of matches under my bed."

"What's a little snow, right?" said Harry, sitting down on the bed. "It'll be gone in a day or so." He picked up the book Bud had been reading. "What the hell is this—*American Labor, 1910-1925*? This is certainly the book I would've picked for a snowy evening by the fire. Bet there's some good sex in it."

Bud laughed. "Got it down at the Seakomish Library the other day. When I went down to talk with Clare Ristall." Bud then went on to tell the story of the confrontation with Clare, his claims about trying to protect Skybillings, and Bud's dip in the river.

"I'll be damned," said Harry. "You went swimming at night?"

"Hell yes. Used to do it all the time when I was a kid."

Harry laughed. As he flipped through the book, the letters from Olmeier and Witstrop fluttered to the ground. "If you want a good laugh, read both of those," said Bud. After Bud had opened them in his car, he had jammed them into the book and hadn't looked at them since.

Harry took out wire rim glasses and slipped them onto his face.

When he was done, he let out a sigh. "Who the hell would've destroyed Olmeier's film?"

"A damn good question," said Bud. "Add it to all the other riddles around this place." Bud paused as Harry studied the other letter, from Witstrop. "Logging never used to be this complicated, Harry."

"What's this on the back?" asked Harry, holding Olmeier's letter further away to make out the handwriting.

"What?"

Bachelder held it up near the kerosene lantern. A neat, handwritten P.S. was scrawled across the back of the page. He read aloud, "P.S. If it's of any interest, the name of the man who died in Auburn was Petrisen—not Patterson like I said. Not sure this is of interest, but it's the only thing I could offer in lieu of photos." Harry gave Bud a quizzical look. "What's that mean?"

"I didn't even see that the first time I read it," said Bud, rubbing his eyes. "Guess I was too mad. I think he's referring to some fellow who got killed down in Auburn. On a logging show. He was telling me about him on the ride up from Seakomish."

Bachelder continued to frown.

"What's wrong?" asked Bud.

"Petrisen."

"Yeah. The sheriff mentioned the same name—when he was telling me that I could go to hell. Like I said, some guy who was standing in the wrong..."

"Petrisen." Harry cut off Bud. "Wasn't that the name of the guy who was in Witstrop's office that morning we went in to ask for the loan?"

At the time, Bud had still been rattled from the close call he and Harry had in the union riot in Everett. They both reeked of gasoline. And he knew there was virtually no hope for more money—so he hadn't paid much attention. But he did recall a man walking out as they walked in.

"Kind of a weasely-looking guy," said Bud vaguely. "Tall, thin."

"Right. Had a fist full of papers. Witstrop sent him away as soon as we walked in. I could swear his name was Petrisen."

Bud slapped the desk. "I'll be damned. You're right. When we walked out, I remember the secretary saying the name."

Both men looked at each other, then sat in silence.

"Tell me again what the photographer said about him," said Harry. So Bud recounted the report he'd heard from Olmeier: That this

Petrisen had been killed while doing business with a small logging company down in Auburn, that he had worked for some kind of a company from New York, or somewhere—Olmeier wasn't positive.

"I heard basically the same story from the sheriff." Bud stopped. The conversation with Charlie Deets was coming back now. "Deets said that this logging show—this one in Auburn where Petrisen got killed—went through the same thing we did. Sabotage. Somebody had weakened a bunch of the spikes and a train went over the edge."

Bud hadn't thought much of the sheriff's comment at the time. Sabotage wasn't all that unusual any more, and the battle with Clare Ristall, followed by the snow, had wiped the thought from his mind. Now he began piecing it together again—taking Bachelder through it step-by-step.

"Let me write this down to keep it straight," said Bud, pulling a pencil and tablet from the drawer. "A logging company in Auburn—a small company, like ours—gets sabotaged, just like us." He scribbled on the pad, then started again. "Somebody dicks around with the spikes— just like they did with us. And somebody gets killed"—he stopped to write—"just like with us. And," Bud emphasized the word, "the guy who gets killed happens to work for the same guy who funds Skybillings— Bertram Witstrop of the Panama Northwest Shipping Company." Bud paused, studying the sheet, letting the facts settle in his mind.

"And a photographer who took pictures in Auburn and who took pictures here suddenly finds that his film has been destroyed," added Bachelder.

Bud stepped to the window and looked out at the snow. The lights in the mess hall were all off, but a faint glow fell upon the deep snow from the kitchen window. Somebody was still awake. That seemed funny, thought Bud, since he guessed it was after midnight. For a moment, his mind fell back to the practical problem before them. The snow was clearly more than a foot deep—he could see it built up high along the railings on the front porch. Very soon, it wouldn't be a question of whether the trestle would ever get done before winter. It would be a question of whether he was waiting too long to get the men to lower ground. Several feet of snow could fall at this elevation within a few hours—dramatically increasing the chances that they could be stuck there for weeks.

But Bachelder's voice brought him back. "So why does Witstrop want to see you?"

Bud turned back, leaning against the log wall. "Could be anything. Why aren't the logs rolling? We've run out of money. Got to speed up repayment on the loan." Bud sat on the bed. "It ain't good news, whatever he has in mind."

Harry stood up and walked to the desk, bending low over the tablet where Bud had written all of the events involving Petrisen. He sat down, studying them closely, then began writing. When he was done, he handed the tablet to Bud. "I've listed everything that's happened to Skybillings—spike, animals heads torn off, tool shed, and dynamite—although I probably should've added all the talk about traitors and half the camp leaving."

"And what does this tell us?"

Harry pulled his pipe from his pocket and filled it. He shook his head without speaking.

"It isn't possible, is it, that Witstrop's behind this somehow?" Bud's voice rose at the end.

"Doesn't make sense. You don't hand over big money to a company and then sabotage the guys you gave it to."

"But he's gotta have something to do with it."

"Can't even be sure of that. His man could've been down there doing the same thing with that company that they were doing with us—giving them money. He might've just happened to be standing in the wrong place at the wrong time. A widow-maker or the loose end of a cable."

"I understand that," said Bud quickly. "That's probably what happened. What I can't figure out, though, is that this company is the spitting image of ours—it's small, out of the way, nobody ever heard of it, number one. But number two, the spikes are filed." He paused. "Harry, I been in the woods for damn near twenty years, and I have never seen that before. Especially with two companies so much alike."

"Could be just all the union crap going on."

"But such small fry?"

Harry shrugged. "Possible."

"Possible, but not likely."

"Sounds like Clare Ristall convinced you," said Harry flatly.

Bud didn't like the tone, partly because he didn't like the sound of the statement. He was so convinced that Clare was behind all of the trouble that he was willing to confront him directly, even to raise it with the sheriff. Now he was going the exact opposite direction—suspecting the very man whose money had gotten him this far.

Bud let out a long sigh as he looked out at the snow again. The wind was now kicking up swirls of white that clouded the glow from the kitchen. He'd never been this high up in such weather. He'd always gone out of his way to make sure Skybillings was closed well before anything like this hit. But here they were—in a logging camp, twenty miles up, locked in a blinding snowstorm. Bud wondered how whoever had it in for Skybillings was even able to enlist the help of God in the effort.

## Chapter 34

But God surprises. By morning, the bitterly cold wind turned into a Chinook wind—warm and moist. The snow had drifted high against the bunkhouses and sealed the wide porch of the mess hall. But the sudden warm breeze began melting the pack instantly.

For most of the day, the crew dug its way out of the camp, then fastened heavy metal snow blades to the front of the crummy. As Fergie plowed forward, the men jumped off every quarter mile or so to shovel the accumulated snow to the side. This got them to the trestle in two days of work.

"Jesus, she's still standing," shouted Bucky Rudman as the crummy edged over the top of the rise.

"What the hell did you expect?" asked Bud Cole.

Bucky shrugged. "Sorry. Just wondered if Bachelder here could build a bridge that wouldn't fall down in the snow."

Bachelder jumped off the crummy as it neared the trestle. "Don't doubt me, Rudman. The only thing you need to figure out is whether or not you've got enough smarts to set that bent into place without wrecking the whole operation."

Bachelder led the way onto the trestle, now clean of snow and drying in the warm air. Albert could smell the warm wood of the railroad ties. Even the iron tracks gave off a welcoming, rusty scent.

Albert had rarely seen so much water rushing beneath him, even when he stood on the bridges over the Seakomish. As the water roared across the rock, it slammed against the trestle posts, sending a gentle vibration through the structure. Albert wondered if Bucky Rudman's question about the trestle might carry more truth than jest.

Where once stood nothing—save for open air and the summer updrafts that lifted the flight of hawks—now stood two tall, wooden, man-made sentries, each set deep in granite, each trailed by two ribbons of steel that wound their way back to the green edges of the ravine. Each waited silently for the final piece that would link them to be set into place. After all, these were sentries not of opposing forces, ready to battle for supremacy on the vast ocean of green forest and gray rock; they were, instead, children of the same father reaching out to grasp one another, to hold one another tight, to stand arm-in-arm against whatever threats the world around them might pose.

"Alright men," shouted Bachelder. "This is what we've got ahead of us today. Bucky's going to bring that bent across again, but this warm wind ain't a hell of a lot lighter than the cold wind a few days ago. So I want to try something different." He explained that each man would position himself at various locations along the crossbeams under both portions of the trestle. This way, they could help steady the new bent when Bucky brought it into position. He picked ten men to cross over to the other portion of the trestle—via two narrow planks that ran between the two ends; the rest were sent below the portion they were already standing on.

As Harry spoke, Bucky stepped gingerly onto the planks that spanned the open air between the unfinished ends of the trestle. Was it fifty feet across? Maybe more. He looked down the whole time, as if studying the firs standing far below him. Watching Bucky walk across the planks in midair—without railings, and nothing but rock and ravine below—gave Albert a queasy chill. Bud Cole followed, as did several other members of the crew.

When they were all finally across, Bucky fired-up the engine to drive the skyline.

"The crossbeams are all dry this morning, so nobody's in danger of slipping," said Bachelder, speaking to the men on both parts of the trestle. This led many to look down to where the rushing water disappeared into clouds of white as it shot off the rock ledge and into open air.

Myles Norgren shook his head. "Jesus, Harry, you want us to crawl down next to that?"

Bachelder seemed surprised. "Next to what?"

"That!" said Norgren, pointing down at the roaring water. Bachelder looked down, as if noticing it for the first time.

"You can swim, can't you?" asked Bachelder.

"Jesus." But Norgren didn't argue more.

Bachelder resumed his explanation of the plan. "We've got ropes tied up and down the new bent. In this breeze, they'll be dangling and flopping all over the place. When Bucky brings it close, try to grab one of them or whatever you can and try to stabilize it against the wind." As if by design, a sharp gust took his cap, but he grabbed it before it blew over the side. "Any questions?"

Albert noted that Bachelder skipped the part about how the men could be crushed if the bent swung hard into the trestle. Several glances suggested to Albert that some of the men wished they had walked out with St. Bride and the others.

"One more thing." Bachelder cupped his hands around his mouth so everyone could hear him over the wind gusts. "I want all of you to tie ropes around your waists and then cinch them to the post or crossbeam next to you. This SOB is gonna shake like hell if that bent hits—and Norgren here suggests to me that some of you would prefer not to go swimming."

Albert breathed a sigh of relief when Bachelder directed him to a crossbeam under the main part of the trestle. While he dreaded crawling around underneath any part of the thing, he hated even more the prospect of having to walk across the gorge on the two planks.

"C'mon Weissler, down the hatch," shouted Bachelder as the steam engine gave a full-throttle roar. Albert hurried down the ladder. He pulled off his gloves to attach the loop around the closest post, then knotted the rope to his belt.

The two crossbeams below him were manned by Conrad and Myles. Just above him sat Little Boy and Lightning Stevens, and above them three Swedes. Fifty feet away, on the other portion of the trestle, ten more men were similarly settled.

"Hi-ho!" shouted Bachelder. "Let's kick it in the ass, Bucky!"

Slowly, the bent lifted off the ground on the far side of the ravine, shedding brush and slabs of mud and snow as it rose, then inched its way out into the open air. The skyline squealed against the massive load as the bent moved slowly toward them.

At first, it drifted lazily in the breeze, but then took on a slow pendulum sway. Albert looked down to double-check the rope holding him, just as the bent slammed against the other portion of the trestle. The sound was more of a rifle shot than of wood hitting wood. Several of the men on the crossbeams lost their grip, but none fell.

"Hi-ho-hi-ho!" shouted Bachelder, followed by four quick blasts on the whistle by Petey, which told Bucky to immediately reverse the movement of the skyline. As he did, the bent pulled the skyline low, causing more high-pitched screeching. The change in direction, together with a sudden *whoosh* of the warm wind, pushed the bent outward over the ravine. "Hold On!" shouted Bachelder, just before the mass of wood roared back into the trestle—this time the portion Albert was on—with a thunderous crash that nearly knocked several men off. Albert slammed into the crossbeam with his chest.

Again the bent swung out, but now Little Boy jumped to his feet, untied the rope that had secured him to the trestle, and stepped carefully along a crossbeam to its tip—extending far over the rock ledge. He sat down, wrapped his legs around the beam like a rodeo rider, and tied a lasso knot into the rope.

"Jesus Christ!" shouted Bachelder from above. "This isn't some goddamn rodeo, Little Boy!"

Even though the bent was moving away, Little Boy swung his lasso around several times then rifled it toward one of the crossbeams. It looped around the end for several seconds, but then slipped off as the bent moved further away.

Albert drew a deep breath and untied the rope that held him to the center post. He repositioned himself on the cross beam just below Little Boy—closer to where the bent would next strike the trestle— and he quickly tied a lasso loop into his rope as well. As he settled, he squeezed his legs tight against the hard wood, just like Little Boy.

For several minutes, all was still—save for the rapid-fire cursing from Bachelder about how both of them had lost their minds. The warm breeze tossed the bent awkwardly above the ravine, coming closer as if it were going to smash once more, but then drawing it away. But when the breeze switched again, and the bent finally roared once more toward the trestle, two lassos launched immediately— snaring the protruding crossbeams.

The resulting thud of wood against trestle loosened Albert's leg-hold, but he and Little Boy instantly looped the rope ends around the nearest fir posts. The ropes seemed ready to snap, but the wind gave up the battle, and the bent held tight—settling gently against the trestle.

Petey gave a series of short toots on the whistle, which brought out a roar from the crew. Albert let out a deep breath, as Lightening clapped Little Boy on his shoulder. "Little Boy, goddamn it—where did you learn that trick?"

"Just a little something you pick up bronc roping in Calgary," said Little Boy, with a hint of a smile.

Lightening turned to Albert with a wink. "Didn't know you had it in you, young man."

"I probably didn't," smiled Albert.

By the end of the day, the towering bent had been set perfectly into place and concrete poured into the rock to hold it.

Bud Cole was jubilant. Even as the men worked to lash the new bent into place, he seemed to skip from one to the other, slapping them on the shoulders and shaking their hands. He even shook Albert's hand, though Albert had feared a tongue-lashing for taking such a chance. For several minutes, Bud stood directly in the middle of the new section, hands on his hips, peering upward at the rock face of Three Sisters Ridge that jutted directly upward.

Bachelder finally put a stop to the celebrating. "We'll never get this sucker finished, Bud, if you don't let the men do their work," he said, joining Bud in the middle of the new section.

"There isn't a goddamn soul down in Seakomish that would've given me thousand-to-one odds of putting this trestle alongside Three Sisters Ridge," said Bud, looking up at the peaks again. "But here it stands, by God. Here it stands, Harry."

❖   ❖   ❖

Bachelder had to smile as he watched Bud, whose tanned face crinkled with joy. He hadn't shaved since returning from his visit with the sheriff. He'd barely eaten since the snow set in.

But the Bud he looked at now—taking in a finished trestle and the death-defying hubris it took to make it stand—was much different from the Bud he'd looked in on several times during the heavy snow.

As Fergie, the engineer, waddled across the trestle, Bud grabbed his hand and shouted, "Fergie, look at this. Day after tomorrow you'll be driving across this baby and we're gonna be rolling logs into Seakomish." Bud stomped both feet a couple of times, as if to demonstrate to Ferguson that the trestle was real, that it was actually connected, that it wouldn't crumble under the extra pressure of a grown man who suddenly felt like a boy again.


## Chapter 35

Fergie's face looked pinched and sweaty. He drew in long gulps of air before he was able to blurt-out the news he'd just learned in Seakomish: "They've struck the entire valley. Everything's shut."

Bud's face went blank.

"What are you talking about, Fergie?" asked Bachelder.

"I was down to Seakomish—me and Zoe and Delbert—to re-stock the groceries." He drew heavily to get enough air. "We heard it first thing when we stepped out at the depot. Clare Ristall and the CIO boys have closed down all of the big logging operations in the valley. Closed down tight." A large group of men had begun to gather at the end of the trestle.

"Where? How many shows?" asked Norgren.

Fergie shook his head. "Can't say. Just heard that it was everybody."

Lightning Stevens whistled, while conversation raced among the men. Edwards cursed loudly, saying that the CIO was nothing but a bunch of Communists. Conrad Bruel suddenly spoke, "I bet they're on their way for us now."

Bud seemed to consider this point, but turned back to Fergie. "Any violence?"

"I heard somebody say that there's some broken heads up at Zollock & Sons. Two or three in the hospital, but that's it so far." Fergie turned to the rest of the men facing him. "And I heard that Ashford & Southern was closed down solid." This brought an audible gasp from the men.

"Jesus," said Lightning. "If somebody that big shuts down, these CIO bastards are stronger than I thought. Conrad may be right. They could be coming up here."

Bud shook his head. "No, no, no. I took on Clare Ristall directly the other day, and he swears nobody will come after Skybillings. At least not now." He looked around the group, whose size now had grown to virtually the entire crew.

"But what it all means for us—I can't tell you," added Bud. He stopped quickly, as if surprised that he spoke so directly. He turned and looked at the approach to the trestle, behind where the Shay now sat. No one was there. Not yet.

"How many of us?" he said suddenly, to no one in particular. The men started counting among themselves.

"Forty-five," came a shout from the back. Bachelder quickly added ten more who were still down at the bottom of the trestle.

"Okay, fifty-five men," said Bud, wiping his hand across his whiskers. "I want six men on this trestle, twenty-four hours a day, starting now—one at either end and one in the middle, both on top and half-way down, sitting in the crossbeams. I want two more to go down the line toward Seakomish and double up with Dennis Elspeth and what's his name who's helping him."

Bud caught a look on Lightning Steven's face that seemed to question the decision. "Problem with that, Lightning?" asked Bud.

Lightning seemed caught off guard by the question. "No, not at all. Just wanted to ask—should we arm the sentries?"

"I'm going down to Seakomish on the speeder when we leave here and I'll send back whatever I can round up," said Bud. As Bud spoke the words, Albert noticed that Bud looked at him for a moment, but quickly turned to Bachelder and began making a list of who would be on the first watch.


## Chapter 36

The worries among the men couldn't dampen the excitement the next morning. The talk at breakfast was louder, with more laughter, since this was the day that the Shay would cross the trestle for the first time.

Albert drew in the cold air as the crew all stood on the trestle, turning occasionally to see whether the Shay had rounded the bend from the valley. But the air was still. Fergie must still be climbing the mountain, thought Albert.

Albert felt the cold settle harder in his stomach. He looked down, studying the rushing water that flickered well below the openings in the railroad ties. The mist from the water cascading down the face of Three Sisters drifted sideways, chilling the air even more.

"Never thought I'd live to see anything like this," said Bucky Rudman.

Lightning Stevens stopped behind him. "I used to walk down there in that ravine, looking up at Three Sisters. I never figured anyone would ever stand up here." Several others slowed down to take in the view, now opened to the west. A line of blue-green ridges disappeared into the distance.

Albert turned to look, but his eye fell on the Shay that now chugged into the opening on the edge of the ravine. Several others spotted it too and began trotting the rest of the distance across the trestle.

"I'll be danged if I'm standing on this thing when that beast starts rolling across," shouted Bucky.

"What's wrong, Rudman?" shouted Harry Bachelder. "Don't you have any confidence in Bachelder's Folly?"

"God didn't ever intend anything this spindly to be carrying a railroad train, Mr. Harry. That's all I got to say. It's a violation of the rules of God and man."

Bachelder flipped him the finger as he strode across the trestle toward the approaching Shay. Albert had to admit that the trestle seemed totally implausible—it had from the very start. But now that it was finished, it seemed even less likely—plunked, like it was, on the hip of a rock ledge, below a granite face that stood perhaps 10,000 feet high. To Albert, the trestle didn't seem as much an act of engineering, as an act of desperation, clinging like it did to the rock. Or perhaps an act of hope, or faith—that something in that rock would hold it erect, that the thousands of tons of pounding iron and steam and lumber crawling across it would not force it to give in to gravity or, for that matter, common sense. But in the end, probably, it was all just an act of charity that the mountain itself agreed to extend to the realm of men.

Fergie had brought the Shay, along with the three flatcars that trailed it, into the clearing at the side of the gorge. Harry stood beside it, pointing and motioning to Fergie, who seemed to be studying the length of the structure. As Albert watched them, the gray timbers of the trestle gained new color with the ascent of the sun. Its shoulders glistened in rainbow hues as the mist drifted overhead, the base now brilliant green with shards of red—the occasional vine maple already showing slight autumn colors.

"What the hell are those two discussing?" asked Bucky.

"Probably trying to decide which part of the locie's gonna hit the rocks first," said Conrad Bruel. This brought a chorus of boos.

"Ain't gonna collapse," said Lightning Stevens. "Not the way Harry built it."

The Shay now stood at the edge of the ravine, its nose just reaching onto the trestle. Perhaps twenty feet in front of it, with his back to the men watching him, stood Bachelder. Even from this distance, the men could tell that he was studying the front of the engine closely.

Slowly, Fergie brought the steam up, the boilers sending clouds of white into the crisp air. With Bachelder stepping backward carefully, motioning with his hands to Fergie, the Shay began to move gently away from the edge of the canyon. First the front wheels, then the cab, finally the entire engine and all three cars edged their way onto the narrow track.

The Shay floated. In one glimpse, Albert could take in the icy peaks of Three Sisters overhead, the water raging across the rock ledge below, and the long, gray trestle standing between the two—now topped with a smoking locomotive and three rail cars. Foot by foot, Bachelder backed his way across the trestle. He seemed to be judging how the trestle was taking the weight, though Albert wondered why he was being so careful. If it was going to collapse, Bachelder couldn't do anything about it. He and Fergie were finished.

As the train drew nearer, Albert could make out the faces of Fergie and Bachelder, who occasionally turned toward them. To his surprise, neither looked troubled. Both faces were intent, but relaxed. Just below the cab of the Shay, hanging on a rising upcurrent, was one of the hawks from summer. It rose up suddenly to eye level with Fergie, before dropping downward again and then disappearing into the ravine.

The men on the edge of the ravine watched in silence. As soon as the Shay had left the other side, all chatter stopped, though Albert heard a soft, "I'll be goddamned," from time to time.

But now, as the Shay drew nearer, the chugging of the boilers was enough to scare the grouse and robins from the thatch still left after the logging. Albert watched Bachelder step carefully backwards, peering downward, then signaling, until he finally stepped on the track that was planted firmly on the ledge. When he did, Fergie gave the Shay enough power to reach the top of the knoll where the men stood. Then he set the break and jumped down.

Slowly, the men started to applaud. Albert thought Valentine started it. But it might've even been Bucky Rudman. One by one, the whole group joined in. At first, Bachelder ignored it. But then he realized it was intended for him, and he finally stopped, and nodded slowly. The long, leathery skin sagging on each cheek seemed to open, as the head bent slightly. When he removed his hat and nodded, Albert noticed that his forehead was brilliant white.

❁   ❁   ❁

"Hi-ho, let's kick it in the ass, boys!" shouted Valentine suddenly.

The pounding of both steam engines rumbled through the ravine, as the men began to scatter among the cold deck piles that littered the hillsides. Lightning and Norgren headed directly up the hill, Valentine to the right. Albert peered up the hill, where Bachelder stood.

"This is it," he smiled, much as he did the night before, just after supper. Harry had suggested they take a walk along the lake.

"Bud wanted me to ask you to do him a big favor," said Bachelder. He seemed hesitant to Albert. As if he didn't agree with Bud. "We'd like you to work as riggingslinger on one of the choking crews tomorrow."

Albert stopped. "Me? Why me?"

"The answer is that we don't have enough men with experience to run the crews and we need to count on the men we trust—even if they don't have experience." Bachelder's tone was matter of fact. Nothing complimentary. Nothing particularly encouraging.

Riggingslingers were hated. He'd hated St. Bride more than he could say. Now he guessed it was his turn. But there was something in the request that he actually liked. Bud Cole had confidence in him. Even Bachelder must've had some. And Valentine too.

Perhaps this was why he hadn't argued. He'd agreed, even readily. But then the doubts hit him. He knew he'd get Conrad. He'd get maybe a Swede or two. What would he do if they disagreed with him? Or argued? He hardly knew how to choke, much less be a riggingslinger. He lay awake half the night, wondering.

The sun was now up fully, the air full of screeching from the steam engines and Petey Hulst's whistle. Albert surveyed the pile where Bachelder stood. It was forty feet high, most of it leaning against the spar tree. One of the Swedes, who everyone just called "Swede," ran the donkey. "Vee ready my boy?" he shouted. A smile showed not a single tooth in his mouth.

Albert nodded, and looked around, to find Conrad and Adam Jost staring back at him. Conrad's face was a smirk. Albert had seen the look of defiance many times. But rather than challenging it, Albert jumped onto the deck and scrambled to the top, signaling the Swede to bring the boom upward.

"Let's go, Swede," shouted Albert. "Boom over here." Instantly, the steam engine revved and the mighty boom swung.

Even over the straining donkey, Albert heard Bachelder's voice. "Goddamn it, Conrad! Get your ass onto that pile." Albert noticed a moment of hesitation, but Conrad suddenly turned and jumped on the pile.

Even in the first few logs, Albert was surprised. His worry over the uncertainties of the men was replaced by the complexity of the job. He felt like he'd been given a puzzle. Which log to move first. Which would jostle the next. Which would take the entire pile down the side of the mountain. As Albert pointed, and the men choked each log, then as he scrambled onto the next ones, he felt the worries subside.

It was a job of geometry, he decided. Whereas St. Bride's choice of logs had seemed haphazard, even purposely dangerous, he realized that one could use a little sense of angles, relationships, and a little common sense, and take the pile down quickly and safely. He even detected a sense of that growing in the men. None of them said anything, other than grunting and shouting signals to one another. But he felt Conrad's mood begin to shift. Adam looped the cable around the logs a little faster.

By lunchtime, the deck was half gone and the Shay ready to move out. The last log was especially hard to buckle, because of its size. When Albert saw that the choker wouldn't hold underneath—and Conrad hesitated to crawl under the load—Albert scrambled down the pile and slipped underneath. Once again, he felt the Shay rumble as Fergie let out the brakes. But he quickly snapped the cable, closed the bell, and slipped out from underneath the rail cars.

With a swift arm motion and a staccato, "Hi-ho," Albert signaled to Fergie and the wheels began to turn. Slowly, down a slight incline, then onto the trestle itself. As Albert watched, he had a sense of a freighter leaving the dock, of hundreds of tons of dead weight floating in the air. Once again, the hawks sailed along beside the cab, screaming at Fergie.

Albert felt his back suddenly collapse forward, taking the air out of him. It was Bucky Rudman, slapping him over the shoulder. "Congratulations, Albert," said Bucky with a raspy laugh. "You ain't no virgin anymore."

The crew roared with laughter. As he shrugged, he turned to see that Bud Cole was standing just above them, looking down. He hadn't seen Bud return. He hadn't seen him cross the trestle. For a moment, Albert wondered why Bud had the small smile on his face.

## Chapter 37

For three weeks, the strike stopped most of the timber movement from the Seakomish Valley. The largest companies were the first to be hit. Ashford & Southern closed immediately, followed by others. As the strike spread, Seakomish took on the look it had only recently lost during the height of the Depression: working men milling about on Main Street, lines at the WPA office and the local church food give-aways. But now it was punctuated by fistfights between AFL stalwarts and CIO believers. Charlie Deets hired extra deputies from Everett. Earl Talbert closed his bar by eight in the evening to avoid fights.

The only logging companies that continued to operate were the smallest firms, including Skybillings. Bud watched the community begin to sag under the pressure of the strike, often wondering why Skybillings was being spared. But while he took advantage of his good fortune, he never concluded that they were out of danger. He posted the extra sentries, bought second-hand rifles at a hunting-goods store in Everett, and shipped them back to Seakomish on one of the Shays.

What he was going to say to Witstrop confounded him: Why not just ignore the request for a meeting? Skybillings was moving enough timber now that he had the cash to cover his repayments. That couldn't be too upsetting to Witstrop, could it? But Bud knew that wouldn't do. There was unfinished business here.

When the secretary showed him into Witstrop's office, he looked around briefly, thinking Witstrop hadn't arrived yet. But then the black leather chair behind the desk slowly began to swivel. Bud was surprised by what he saw. Witstrop looked older. Was it the mustache—perhaps longer, untrimmed? Perhaps the color in his face?

Witstrop didn't get up or offer to shake Bud's hand. He only motioned at one of the straight-back chairs in front of the desk.

"You need to move more logs, faster," he said abruptly.

Bud half expected him to laugh, but the face was frozen. "We're already moving more timber than anyone else," said Bud.

"It's not enough. I need more. What do you need to get it out?"

Bud stared at Witstrop. "Need? You mean men?"

"Men. Money. Equipment. I don't give a damn. I just want more timber out of there as soon as possible. Is the trestle done?"

Bud nodded, still trying to sort out what lay behind the sudden demands. "You may not have noticed that there is a strike up in Seakomish right now. And we're the only one of any size operating." Bud looked directly into Witstrop's eyes. They were gray and gave a surprisingly young look to a chubby face. But they were unblinking, locked on Bud. "Hell, we're getting all the timber out of there that you demanded and more."

Witstrop slapped the desk and jumped to his feet. "Listen, Cole. I don't need any explanation of history. I know damn well what we discussed. What I'm talking about is what I need now. And either you move more timber or I'm going to call that note." He paced quickly in front of the tall windows overlooking the water.

Bud decided to meet force with force. "How the hell do you expect me to move more timber?" asked Bud at the same decibel. "Can't you see the light outside that window? It's black as night on the mountain by 6:00 p.m. these days and first light doesn't come until seven the next morning. I'm already operating dawn to dusk."

"What about the size of your crew?" asked Witstrop. "Can we bring in more men? Find more locomotives? Do both? I'm not the expert, Cole. You are. Figure something out." Witstrop stared at him.

Bud shook his head. How many months had he struggled to get the trestle built—even though it was virtually impossible? How many battles had he fought with his crew to log such terrain? As he looked at the sun, setting behind the Olympics, an image of the trestle, standing tall against Three Sisters, was firm in his mind. And yet now that it was built, now that Skybillings was somehow, miraculously, avoiding the strike that had shut the valley, Witstrop was demanding more—much more than he'd ever indicated before.

Bud leaned back in the chair, his eyes still on the mountains. "What happened to Petrisen?"

"Who?"

"Petrisen. Your helper. He was here when we met with you last time."

Witstrop looked puzzled, much as he had the morning that Harry said he could build the trestle. For a moment, Bud thought he seemed trapped. "Petrisen? Moved on. Went to work for a firm in San Francisco."

Bud laughed. "Petrisen was killed on a logging show in Auburn."

Witstrop rung for the secretary, then ordered two cups of coffee when she opened the door. "Where did you learn that?" he asked when she closed it.

"What does it matter?"

Witstrop drew in a breath, then let it out slowly. "He was killed doing some business for Panama Northwest. How is that of any interest to you?"

The secretary came in and placed a cup of coffee in front of each man, then hurried out. Bud took a sip, opening a small notebook. "My understanding is that Petrisen was killed on a visit to a small logging show in Auburn. Like you say—doing business for Panama Northwest. I also understand that this operation was a small company—much like ours. And that this company had been fighting sabotage for several months, including filed spikes on their rail lines—just like ours."

Witstrop tapped a finger absently on the side of his coffee cup. He held Bud in a careful gaze for several seconds, then smiled. "Alright Cole. My hat's off to you. Good detective work." He paused again. "I'll give you the answers you want, if"—another pause—"if you can move the timber I want."

Bud nodded.

"And none of this should ever be repeated," said Witstrop.

Bud nodded again.

"Petrisen was doing business with that particular logging company in Auburn. He was out there because they were having the very trouble you've been having—sabotage. Several filed spikes, like you said. Train wreck, similar circumstances. Petrisen died when a cable cut loose from a spool and wrapped him around the neck."

Bud tried to keep the picture out of his mind as Witstrop continued. "Basically took his head off. When the foreman took a look at the spool, it was clear that the cable had been filed in several spots."

Witstrop seemed to be weighing his words as he rang for more coffee. He waited until the secretary left before he began again. "Damndest thing was that she was having an affair with him," said Witstrop, nodding toward the door. "Had been for years. I didn't have a clue."

"Why would they want to kill him?"

Witstrop shrugged. "I don't know the answer to your question entirely."

Bud gave a sarcastic laugh. "When the hell are you going to level with me? My men are..."

"Relax, Cole. I'll tell you all you need," said Witstrop sharply. He drew in a deep breath. "First off, it isn't the unions. That's all a smokescreen. What with all the chaos in the woods, it's a perfect time to carry out any crime. Even if the authorities have time to look into it, they're going to conclude it was just unions bashing unions."

Witstrop paused, sipping the coffee and wiping his fingers across the bottom of his mustache. "Let's just say that this is the perfect time for companies to have at each other tooth and nail."

"What's that supposed to mean?"

"It's supposed to mean just what I said," said Witstrop quickly. "That the battle in Auburn involves who is going to control the woods."

"You mean, not the AFL or CIO, but some company instead?"

"That's it. The real question is about which company will own the biggest operations so they can squeeze out the rest."

Bud tried to sort out what Witstrop was saying. That the battles between the unions weren't behind his troubles—that Clare Ristall was right? That Skybillings was a pawn in the middle of a battle between Panama Northwest and God knows who? He considered this—then remembered the extra money that Witstrop had pushed on him months earlier with the message to hurry up his operations.

"I will be damned," said Bud, his voice low. "You mean that I've been a pawn in this thing all along?"

Witstrop shrugged. "I suppose you could call it that."

"You are one nasty son of a bitch, Witstrop. I've got men up there ready to tear each other apart, thinking that there are traitors in the camp, looking to lynch anything that moves in the dark. And you mean to tell me that this is nothing more than somebody who's out to get you?"

"You may well have traitors, Cole, regardless of what's behind this. There's plenty of ugliness to go around."

"And if I've got this right: They want to shut me down because I'm getting money from you, and somebody wants to stop you from controlling the woods."

Witstrop nodded, then added, "And I want to stop them."

Bud shook his head. "You speak as if this is some kind of business deal—as if lives didn't depend on it; as if Petrisen hadn't died over it, or three of my men; as if my whole operation isn't struck by fear." Bud stopped to gauge Witstrop's reaction, but there was none. "And you've got the balls to ask for more timber? To have us risk our lives even more, for your goddamn game to grab control over the woods?"

Witstrop chuckled softly. "So now you're a moralist."

"I'm no moralist. I just think that you have damn few morals to put me and my men in this position with no warning."

"Don't blame me, Cole," snapped Witstrop. "You never asked about any details. You didn't care why the money came to you or where it came from. You just wanted the money. You just wanted to prove you had the little company that could. You were willing to do anything to put all that failure of the past behind you. So spare me your moral outrage, Mr. Cole. You're in this up to your neck, just as much as I am—the only difference is in the details."

Bud felt exhausted. He'd risked lives, including his own, by stepping into the middle of a battle he hadn't understood, or didn't bother to even wonder about. And Witstrop was right. Skybillings was, in its simplest terms, a test of whether Bud Cole still had the presence and mettle to build his company again. When he had walked into Witstrop's office, he had felt that he had done it, finally. Now he wondered. Perhaps he had only succeeded in playing a fool, blinded by his own ambition.

Bud noticed that the sky outside was completely black. No silhouette on the horizon. The night-lights from ships in the Seattle Harbor winked at him. For several minutes, neither man spoke. Witstrop looked down at the movements under the lights in the shantytown along the waterfront.

He nodded down toward them, as Bud stood up. "The poor bastards that live down there, Cole, didn't end up there because the system was moral. They got that way because the system was immoral—corrupt, riddled with errors and shortcomings, and run by swindlers and crooks, by deceivers and charlatans who wrap themselves in lofty promises and, even worse, unarguable goals."

He turned to face Bud. "But the goals and the promises were either mirages of lies and privateering, or simply the pipe dreams of the well-intended. Whatever the case, those poor shits down there got that way because they fell into a system run by humans, who make countless errors, Cole—some intentional, some not. We can't correct that system through high-minded morals, but through doing what has to be done." Witstrop paused. "And trying to do it in the way that seems right, despite the bumps."

Witstrop paused again. "I'll make you a deal. I'll let you off on everything you owe me up to this point, if you can move the kind of timber I said I needed."

Bud looked down at the men walking among the shanties and let out a long sigh.

❊   ❊   ❊

Bud decided not to think about it. If Witstrop was going to give him more money, he was going to take it. To hell with morals. To hell with the dangers. Maybe Witstrop was right—he cared only about himself. But something in the blackness of the night, in the danger he now realized he was in, made him blot out the doubts.

For three hours he drove north. Not stopping until he reached Bellingham.

On the water, he thought. Near Canada. A damn good place to find what he needed—men who didn't ask questions, drifters, out-of-work sailors, unemployed loggers from the northern Rockies. And all with thick, hard backs. Plus, he knew he could find equipment—perhaps an extra Shay—that had been cut loose from the logging shows on Vancouver Island. But most importantly, it was hours away from the Seakomish Valley. No one would know him, or ask what he was doing.

Within two days, he had assembled two groups of twenty-five men each. Some may have been union men, but they kept it to themselves when Bud announced that he was willing to pay twenty-five cents an hour more than anyone else.

A scraggly, old riggingslinger challenged him on a street corner near the AFL office. "If you're hiring strikebusters, mister, I ain't gonna be one."

"Nobody's striking my show," said Bud loudly, so a group near him could overhear. "But if you're afraid of doing business along the edges of a strike, I don't want you anyway."

Bud turned to leave, but the old riggingslinger called him back. "Jethro Callup's the name—they call me Jess." He thrust a rough hand toward Bud, who seized it. When the fellow smiled, Bud saw that he was missing several teeth, but somehow it didn't disrupt what was basically a handsome, if heavily lined, face. "Come on over, boys," shouted Callup to the group nearby. "This is our new boss man."

Bud put Callup in charge of keeping the men organized. They had to ride in flat cars behind two Shays that would make their way to

Seakomish and the Skybillings camp. The Shays would travel separately, on different days, and both at night. Callup and several of the
men arranged tarps along the edges of the flat cars, so that when the
Shays approached Seakomish, the men would lie on their stomachs,
the tarps draped over them.

"Nothing but cable and equipment under there, right Mr. Cole?"
shouted Callup with a wink to Bud as they arranged the first flat car
headed toward Seakomish. Bud smiled, and urged the men to hurry.

One of the youngest of the group shouted down from the flatcar to
Bud. "What happens if they stop us? What're we supposed to do?"

"You got two choices," said Bud, opening the trunk of his car. "You
can either run like hell, or you can flash one of these." He held up
several shotguns from a long brown box.

The young man jumped from the car, took the guns, and climbed
back aboard the flatcar.

"But I'll be riding right alongside you," added Bud quickly. "And
they don't get used until I say so."


## Chapter 38

The wind roared through Bud's hair, bringing with it an alertness that
he wished he could escape. In the alertness lay the doubts; in the
doubts lay failure.

He could feel the breathing of the man sitting next to him in the flat
car—rhythmic, heavy, dried sweat mingled with muscatel. When Bud
climbed onto the car in Mt. Vernon, he noticed in the dim light that
the man looked Spanish, perhaps Filipino. A sailor, no doubt. Can't
know much about logging, Bud decided. But strong arms, willing to
work hard for good money—that's what Bud needed.

A flatcar full of men like him, thought Bud, as the rhythmic pounding of the track below him numbed his legs. Except for Callup, he
didn't know one of their names. Yet he had armed them—bought the
guns, sent them into the middle of a valley torn by a strike.

One of the men suddenly stood up and grabbed one of the car's side
posts, which jostled wildly. He unzipped his pants and leaned outward.
For a moment, Bud thought he would fall, but he held firm, then slipped
back under the tarp. A few murmurs, followed by the sooty wail of the
Shay locomotive as it crossed the main road at Stardale.

The picture that kept coming back was Witstrop. The mustache, and the thumb and index finger wiping outward on both sides to whisk away any driblets of coffee. And the matter-of-factness of it all—Skybillings was a pawn and he wasn't the least bit troubled to say so. But something in the honesty of it all, the unapologetic self-interest, had somehow simplified things for Bud. Had it finally awakened the emotion in him, he wondered? Was it that, when all was said and done, he was no different than anyone else—presented with a little money, Bud Cole would operate in his self-interest?

And he certainly did, thought Bud. He'd taken Witstrop's offer in a second. Offer me more money and I'm on your side, thought Bud. And only now—deep in the night, with the twenty-five men around him and the course set—did the doubts return. Riding into the middle of a strike with shotguns. Knowing you were a pawn in a bigger match and not walking away. Testing the will of God by working too late into the season and risking death from the heavy snows that, even now, Bud could smell in the cold night air.

He tried to close out the doubts with planning. Step-by-step and this would work. Get the Shay through Seakomish. Then up the valley and onto the mountain. Then work like hell for as long as the weather would hold.

Bud felt the Shay lurch suddenly and begin to slow down. It felt too soon to be entering Seakomish. Though the night was black, he sensed they were several miles still below the town. Maybe near the flat, where the tracks paralleled the river. Several of the men stirred.

"We there?" asked one voice from across the car.

"No," said Bud quickly.

"Then how come we're stopping?" asked another.

"Everybody be quiet. No sounds." Bud heard a quiver in his voice. He listened carefully as the Shay finally rolled to a stop. He thought he heard voices near the cab, but couldn't be sure over the sound of the idling locomotive. He got onto his knees to peer through a hole in the tarp.

Two men stood alongside the track, talking to Fergie, who perched on the side of the Shay. "Who you hauling for?" asked one.

"Skybillings." Fergie's voice sounded firm. Businesslike.

"Skybillings, eh?" The next voice was thick and ugly. Bud thought he recognized Billy Sammons, one of Clare Ristall's henchmen. "You work for Bud Cole?"

"He's the owner. Yup."

Bud adjusted himself slightly so he could see more clearly through the slit in the canvas. He could see Sammons standing next to Fergie, with Seamus Fitzgerald—whom he recalled often seeing going in or out of Clare's office in Seakomish—just behind.

Sammons peered closely at the Shay, as if purchasing a car. He studied the steam lines closely, then stepped into the cab, with Fergie watching every move. "I reckon maybe we oughta take her over, don't you think, Seamus?"

Bud could see that the two men carried rifles. Fergie must've stopped because they had waved the rifles.

"How much you think we could get for a Shay, Seamus?" asked Sammons with a low laugh. "$10,000? We could pay a lot of striking loggers for a long time with ten grand. It'd be the end of the AFL in this valley right there."

Bud slipped back to the bed of the flatcar. "Let's pick 'em off," said a voice from the far corner. "I can get a shot off easy from here." Some of the men began shuffling toward the far side of the car. Bud didn't know if they were getting ready to run or to attack Sammons and Fitzgerald.

"No," whispered Bud as loud as he could without being heard over the idling Shay. "We use these guns only if attacked, goddamn it. Just don't move. They'll let us through."

"But they'll kill us if they find us," said a frightened voice near him.

"We can rush 'em," offered another.

But the discussion stopped suddenly as a loud metallic bang rumbled through the body of the flatcar. Bud didn't know where it came from, but it brought instant silence—heavy breathing, bodies shifting on the hard iron to ease numb legs, but silence.

All three voices were now directly beside the flatcar. "Pull over onto that siding over there, old man." It was Fitzgerald. "I declare officially that the CIO workers of the Seakomish Valley now own this locomotive and these cars."

"Now just a minute," shouted Fergie, only a few feet away from the car. "There ain't nobody striking Skybillings. So me and this here Shay is going on through to Seakomish."

Fitzgerald laughed loudly. "These two barrels say you aren't going through to anywhere, old man."

Bud heard coughing and what sounded like someone spitting.

"There, you motherfucker!" shouted Fergie, who'd obviously spit in the face of one of them. Fitzgerald cursed loudly, while Sammons roared with laughter.

"I'll be goddamn if you don't look awful," snorted Sammons. "You been had by an old railroad engineer."

Fergie cursed and started running for the front of the train. Bud decided it was time to step in. He tapped shoulders around him and began rising to his knees. He knew that if the men who were now crouching next to him lunged outward, Sammons and the Fitzgerald would be overwhelmed. "On three," he whispered. "One...two..."

But just as he began to move, he heard a car horn and the sound of tires screeching to a stop. A door slammed; then an angry voice in the distance.

"Goddamn it, Sammons, what's going on here?" Bud finally placed the voice: Clare Ristall. Had he seen the stopped train from the highway? Clare was now running toward them on the gravel track bed.

"What are you doing here, Clare?" asked Sammons loudly.

"I might ask you the same question, Sammons." Clare was angry. He sounded the same way he did that day by the school, thought Bud.

"We stopped this here Shay. We're ready to take it over," said Fitzgerald.

"On the goddamn main line to Everett? Are you out of your mind?"

"Where else are we gonna stop it?" Sammons voice was rising.

"Freights from Spokane go through here at all hours. You know that. You want to get this goddamn Shay run over and all of you killed, and the fucking track torn up for the next six months?" Bud smiled to himself. Clare Ristall may be an arrogant son of a bitch, but he at least had a brain. "Why didn't you move them to that siding up ahead?"

"We were just doing that, Clare," said Sammons. "Hold your horses, will you? No freight is due through here in the next two hours."

"Since when did you become an expert on the Great Northern schedule, Sammons?" The pitch in Clare's voice grew. Bud sensed something else in it too, but he couldn't put his finger on it. Something maybe in the intensity. Was there an element of fear? Perhaps, but he conveyed none of it to Sammons. He seemed aggressive and uncompromising.

While the two argued, Bud furiously tried to sort through what to do. The strikers had two rifles, while his crew had several shotguns. Should they shoot it out? Or should they try to escape along the river?

"Alright, pull over on that siding, old man," shouted Sammons to Fergie.

"What logging operation owns the Shay?" asked Clare. The anger seemed to have dissipated somewhat.

"Skybillings," said Sammons, so softly that Bud could barely hear.

Bud thought he heard scuffling, a loud thud, and somebody obviously fell to the ground. Then grunts. Bud decided not to chance looking out. He assumed that one of the thugs had overwhelmed Clare. But Clare's voice was crisp and loud.

"There, you dumb son of a bitch," shouted Clare. "That's what I think of your plan."

Had Clare hit one of them? Bud listened, but now only heard the sound of the wind that had suddenly picked up. Sammons and Fitzgerald were silent. Only Fergie's voice rang out. "I been trying to tell these bastards that very fact, Mr. Ristall," shouted Fergie from the cab. "I told 'em—ain't nobody striking Skybillings. I told 'em. Skybillings got no complaints with the CIO."

Bud let out a sigh, but suddenly realized that several of the men were getting ready to rush Clare and the others. "We'll hit them with the tarp and you begin firing," said Jess Callup in a loud whisper.

"No," whispered Bud quickly. "Nobody moves, or I'll shoot you myself." This settled the men, as the locie continued to power up.

But the sound of Clare's voice was too loud to be smothered. "I told you we are not striking Skybillings, Sammons."

"We ought to, Clare. This is bullshit."

"I said no. I'm running this goddamn strike, not you. And I said no. We don't waste our time on this shit."

"They're bringing in new Shays, Clare," said Fitzgerald. "They're building up their company while we spend our time on the others."

"Seamus, use your goddamn brain. It doesn't matter how many logs Skybillings moves in the meantime. They're nothing. It's the big boys we want—Ashford & Southern, Deek Brown, and Zollock & Sons—not these guys. Not now. Later maybe. But not now."

Fitzgerald was angry. "We're giving away a Shay and all this equipment for nothing."

"And what are you going to do with a Shay? Planning to go out and do a little logging yourself? Maybe a little weekend fun?"

"We could sell it."

Clare laughed loudly as he shouted to Fergie to start moving. "Since when were you put in charge of fundraising, Seamus?"

Fitzgerald was silent.

"Exactly," said Clare. "I'm the deep pocket—remember that. Your job is to organize some picket lines, make sure your men are ready with ax handles, that they get their hands a little dirty when they need to. You stick to striking, okay? And I'll stick to running the strike."

Bud felt the car lurch suddenly, then stop, then lurch again and begin rolling. The voices slowly faded. Bud eased back onto the flatcar floor. He could feel the water running down his arms. He hadn't realized that he was soaked. Several of the men clapped. The Filipino sailor let out several long sighs.

"Is this why you're paying us an extra quarter an hour?" asked Callup, when Bud finally settled back.

"No," said Bud, with a small smile. "As a matter of fact, it isn't."


## Chapter 39

After the strike began, working men often gathered in small groups along Main Street in Seakomish to pass the time and learn the latest strike news.

Of special interest was Clare Ristall's office. The small groups of loggers who gathered in the Seakomish Cafe for coffee in the mornings or sat on the benches in front of the post office in the afternoons kept a close watch on the comings and goings. The visits by the local ministers—no doubt as part of the food bank effort—captured only passing interest. As did the visits by union stewards from each of the logging shows.

But a visit by anyone driving a new car drew special attention. It had to be the owners—logging company owners, come to negotiate—no doubt.

The cluster of men about to walk into the Seakomish Cafe at the end of the strike's third week appeared to have frozen in their steps when several tall men—and one short one—in black suits strode from Clare's. Down the steps, onto the sidewalk they swept—officials from the state capital, perhaps? Did Clare get the governor to step in? Or was it an owner?

Within minutes, Clare emerged and appeared to be in a hurry—opening the door of his pickup, firing the engine and backing out absently, without noticing the group of men. But as he began to pull away, he spotted them in the rear-view mirror and jammed on the brakes.

"Howdy, boys," shouted Clare gamely as he jumped back out of the pickup. "How's it going?"

"It ain't," said a tall man with a mustache. "It ain't since three weeks ago Monday." Four other men, dressed the same, stood beside him.

"How long do ya think it'll go, Clare?" asked another. No one asked about the men in the new cars.

"Hard to say. Depends on the owners—on whether they'll agree to close out the AFL. We gotta go till they do."

The faces nodded, but said no more. Clare looked at each man in the group—several he knew had families. "You boys getting along alright? The Methodists and the Baptists have food supplies. I made arrangements for special food-pay for any man out of work. You can get it at the bank. I talked to Halvorson the manager myself this morning."

Again, the group nodded. "So we win when they all say no to the AFL? Not just one or two companies. Is that it, Clare?"

"That's the way we decided, yup," said Clare. "That's how the vote came out."

A young man, perhaps twenty, suddenly spoke. "What's so damn wrong with the AFL, anyway? I was enjoying my work. I was making more than I made before. Now I'm making nothing." He spat loudly onto the ground.

Another joined in. "I'm a CIO man, Clare. But frankly, I never had too much trouble with the AFL myself." He quickly smiled and nodded toward Clare. "That's not saying, Clare, that I'm backing out on ya. I'm with the strike. Cause those bastards are practically in bed with the owners, the way I see it."

Clare smiled. He cast glances at each of the men. Proud men, he thought. Each of them. Willing to work hard and willing to take a chance on a new union. But only able to last so long. Only able to understand a cause as long as it didn't begin harming their children.

Clare leaned back on the fender of his old Ford and crossed his arms. "You know who that was who just left my office?" He drew in a breath of the warm autumn air.

Several shook their heads.

"Do you know who Tuttle B. Ashford is?" asked Clare.

"I'll be goddamned," said the tallest of the group. Clare wasn't sure if his name was Thompson or Thomas, but knew he worked for Ashford & Southern. "That there was Tuttle Ashford?"

Clare nodded, with the warm smile still on his face, as the man continued. "I worked for that company for twenty years and I never saw him—only heard stories about him. The little fart in the middle was Ashford, wasn't it?"

"You met with him?" asked one of the others who had sat down on the bench. Several other loggers had joined the group in the meantime, now numbering more than a dozen.

"Yup. And it looks like Tuttle Ashford himself has agreed to recognize the CIO—and only the CIO."

The group of men cheered, slapping Clare on the back. "But that's not official," said Clare quickly. "The best way to destroy this is for word to get out. Mr. Ashford has to talk with his board, which will take a day or so."

"Jesus, that could be the end of the strike," said the young man who had previously complained. "We could all go back within a day or so."

Clare raised both hands. "Again, let's be cautious here boys. Even if he agrees, there is no certainty that the other companies will. But it's a damn good sign." The men erupted in a noisy chatter about which company might be the next to close out the AFL. Zollock & Sons? Deek Brown? But Clare refused to be drawn into the speculation. Too many dangers. Too much chance of everything going off track, he warned.

As the volume of the conversation continued to grow, Clare climbed back into the pickup and swung toward Highway 4.

❀   ❀   ❀

Not telling the gathering of men that he also was on his way to see Deek Brown, Clare decided, was the right decision. No sense driving rumors even harder. But as he got off the crummy that took him up to Brown's camp, he allowed himself a moment of satisfaction. Maybe the strike was about to be over. Maybe Deek Brown was going to give him the same message as Tuttle Ashford. Perhaps that's why Deek had sent for him.

But the moment faded quickly. A line of men, CIO men, stretched across the gentle incline that led up to a group of bunkhouses. Most of the men stood idly, hands in pockets, a few with arms folded, each perhaps fifteen feet from the other. Shovels, axes, hammers, and an assortment of other equipment—all that could be grabbed quickly—lay near them. Immediately opposite them, about twenty feet further up the slope, stood fifteen or twenty of Deek's men. Each wore logger gear, and each carried a rifle.

"Been this way since the strike started," said Sammons gruffly, as he stepped off the crummy behind Clare. "Lookin' at each other. Nobody movin." Sammons chuckled loudly, a self-satisfied growl. "But then again, Deek ain't moved any timber since we closed him down, neither."

"And he ain't gonna for a long time," said Seamus Fitzgerald.

Several of the CIO men recognized Clare and greeted him by name. So he stopped, careful to ask each how he was doing. He worked his way along the line, as the Brown crew watched. He noted that they held their rifles ready. The last CIO man in the line slapped Clare heartily on the back, which seemed to startle the rifles in the opposing line.

"Sorry, fellas, nothing to worry about," Clare shouted good naturedly to the AFL men. "Just a little exuberance among the workers of the world." This brought laughter from the strikers, but angry stares from the Brown crew. Clare was about to make his way toward them, when he recognized Deek Brown standing on the porch of the building in the distance. He motioned for Clare to come through, and the line of men opened silently. It closed quickly before Sammons or Fitzgerald passed, but Clare waved for them to stay with the CIO strikers.

Deek Brown looked drawn. His face had the look of too little sleep. "Any problem getting here?" asked Brown flatly when Clare had finally reached the porch.

"None. Not at all." Clare tried to sound friendly, but not overly so. Lydia had warned him not to ooze, despite his natural tendencies—especially with opponents.

Brown opened a thick door and held it while Clare passed into what appeared to be an office—a room that was long and narrow and probably was once used as a mess hall. At the far end, stood a wide desk—perhaps a teacher's desk, but scuffed and marked as if someone had been working it hard with a jackknife. The room echoed loudly as they walked its length. The hollowness reminded Clare that there was no other furniture. Not even a hard-back chair.

Brown reached the desk, sat down slowly in a swivel chair that creaked when his full weight dropped into it. He gave no indication as to where Clare should sit, or stand. So he simply stood to the side, waiting for Brown to speak. For several minutes, however, he was silent, scribbling quickly on a small note pad. He ripped off the page and handed it to Clare, who read it quickly.

When he looked up, Brown was smiling. "That's the final offer—take it or leave it." The smile confused Clare. Where did it come from? Did Brown think he would accept? Or was there something else in it, a kind of respect? Despite the hatred Brown felt, had he seen enough of Clare's operation to finally come to respect it?

"You know this won't do, Deek," said Clare softly. His voice did not argue. Nor did it criticize. He worked hard to simply keep it factual. "It's just not enough to offer to boost pay. That's grand in itself. I personally thank you for it. But that's not only what is at stake here."

Brown suddenly filled the room. "I am so fucking sick of this holier-than-thou union shit, Ristall, that I'd blow a hole right through you if I thought I could get away with it. You've shut down this whole Seakomish Valley because you want to be the only one to bargain for loggers. I got one question for you: Who gives a goddamn about who is the bargainer if those men of yours get ten cents more an hour and a week's paid vacation a year?"

Clare had to admit that Brown had put his finger on the key question—the question that had underlain all the union tensions in the state for the past several years. And the question that was foremost in Clare's mind. If the owners started making real concessions, how long would his members agree to hold out in an effort to squash the AFL—Clare's ultimate prize? Would they overlook the fact that the AFL ignored their plight in the '35 strike and cut a deal with the owners who tossed the workers' demands to the wind?

Before Clare answered, the door at the end of the hall groaned and a man of perhaps fifty walked in. Clare thought he recognized him, but couldn't place him. "Thought you might want to say hello to Jimmie Stearns," said Brown as the man strode across the long room.

Clare laughed. "Deek, I've got to hand it to you. You don't leave one stone unturned."

As the man approached the desk, Clare reached his hand out, but Stearns ignored it. Despite this, Clare's buoyant mood was undeterred. "Imagine old Deek Brown bringing in the AFL's chief organizer in the State of Washington." Clare swept a hand across his forehead, as if brushing perspiration. "Whew. That's what I call power."

Stearns glared at Clare. Clare thought he seemed uncomfortable—as if he'd expected the battle to be one of sheer muscle, not one mined with jest and sarcasm. "I'm here to tell you, Ristall, that the AFL has accepted this offer from Mr. Brown."

Clare studied both men. He actually liked Deek Brown. Found him to be an honorable logger, who treated his men fairly. It troubled Clare that they had to strike good logging shows as well as bad. He even found Deek's tactic with Stearns and the AFL impressive. Most logging bosses in the Northwest woods wouldn't have tried so blatantly to drive the two unions at each other.

"Let me get this straight, Mr. Stearns," said Clare as he began to pace. He pushed his hands into the pockets of his pants. "The AFL doesn't bother to complain about the pay or the vacation time at all. Then the AFL opposes our decision to strike—raising all kinds of hell about how what we're doing is going to hurt the workers in the long run. Then you magnanimously agree to accept this here offer—which you would have never received without us or our strike—and now you expect everyone to go back to work. That it?"

"I don't care what kind of smart ass English you want to use to describe it, Ristall. What my union is doing is just what I said—we're taking Deek's offer. And we are going to announce on Monday morning, on Main Street of Seakomish, that the AFL has done just that, and that we have signed a five-year agreement. Then we're going to tell any man who wants to—and we ain't gonna ask his union affiliation, either— that he can go back immediately—all he has to do is show up on the job two hours later. That's it."

Clare smiled, and clasped his hands gently together in front of him. "Let me tell you what I think. I think that you, Mr. Stearns, can tell Mr. Brown here all you want about how your men are going to come in here and take his offer and run his operation. And come tomorrow morning, I will tell you that your men will be nowhere to be seen and my picket line will still be in place."

Deek Brown cleared his throat loudly, then stepped to the window, opened it and spat violently. He slammed the window closed before addressing Clare. "I'm tired of the debate, Ristall. If you don't take the offer, this operation will be running tomorrow—that's a guarantee. We'll do it with any kind of AFL-er, scab, roughneck, or hooligan we can find—but your strike is finished."

Clare nodded and placed the piece of notepad that Brown had

given him on the top of the desk. "Well, then, I guess our business is finished, Deek. I appreciate your inviting me and at least attempting an offer." He turned to Stearns and nodded. "Mr. Stearns," he said as he began walking to the door. His steps echoed loudly in the empty hall.

But before he opened the door, he turned to face both men. "You know, I might have failed to mention one thing, Deek. Sorry." Clare's voice sounded apologetic. Still soft. Still even. "Did I mention to you that I met with Tuttle Ashford today?"

Brown's face hardened, but he didn't answer.

"Yes, I think I did forget." Clare now drew Stearns into his gaze. "Mr. Stearns, Tuttle Ashford owns Ashford & Southern..."

"I know who Tuttle Ashford is," snapped Stearns.

Clare nodded, but now turned back to Deek Brown. "And Mr. Ashford has agreed to recognize the CIO and to accept our demands of full representation. And, by the way, he has agreed to offer those same conditions you scribbled out on that notepad."

The enormity of the news struck Brown with a force that even Clare had not expected. Brown's lips sunk deep at either end.

"He's lying," said Stearns quickly. "Ashford would never accept that."

"Let time be the judge," said Clare with a smile as he closed the door.

## Chapter 40

The trip down the mountain on the crummy was boisterous. Clare retold the story several times, and each time Sammons and the Fitzgerald burst into laughter when he described the look on Deek Brown's face.

"I gotta hand it to ya," shouted Sammons over the roar of the wind. "I think the CIO just got control of this valley." Suddenly he clasped Clare on the shoulder, sending a sharp pain through Clare's back. "I didn't think a city slicker like you ever had it in ya. I really didn't." For the first time ever, Clare thought the emotion was genuine.

The afternoon sun hung low over the ridgeline to the west. Clare had always enjoyed the Jaster Creek Valley, even when he had worked it with Cascade Timber before the War. Something about this stretch of the track, with the valley beginning to open. The sun would glitter brilliantly over the tips of the ridge, casting deep shadows below.

"What comes next, Clare?" It was Fitzgerald, who sat across from Clare. "What are you gonna do after you win this strike?" He smiled with a wink. "Maybe chase the AFL out of the whole state? Run for governor, eh?"

Clare put his feet onto the bench and adjusted himself against the hard seat. "It's way too early to decide we won," shouted Clare over the wind. The crummy tooted and slowed as it rounded a wide bend. "We still don't know what Ashford's gonna do. He may still tell us to go to hell—in which case, that little bluff I pulled a minute ago is going to come crashing down on us."

Fitzgerald waved his hand. "Nope. You're just too superstitious to say what you think. I'll predict Ashford & Southern will go with the CIO. And it's gonna turn out just like you said." He fumbled for a pack of cigarettes and handed one to Clare.

As Fitzgerald spoke, Clare noticed light flickering down the track. It caught his eye because the track bent tight against the mountains, which lay in afternoon shade. The light seemed to move from left to right, then back again. Sammons and Fitzgerald also turned, as the crummy began to slow.

"What the hell?" Sammons voice had lost its giddiness. He grabbed his satchel and unzipped it. Fitzgerald had already climbed to the front of the crummy, peering around the side to get a better look. Clare stood next to him, then began surveying the surrounding country. Either side of the track was flat for a few feet, though thickly wooded. Then both sides shot upward sharply toward the ridges on either side. To the right, a small stream roared alongside the track.

Sammons leaned over the left side of the crummy. "Who do you reckon it is?" he shouted. By now, the flickering light had become four or five lanterns, all moving back and forth, being swung slowly by a group of men holding shotguns and what looked like baseball bats. Perhaps a dozen black railroad ties lay across the tracks directly ahead.

"I never knew the AFL had it in 'em," answered the Irishmen.

"Can we fight 'em?" shouted Sammons, but Clare's voice overpowered both of them.

"Over the side, boys," shouted Clare. "It's the only way out."

Without waiting for an answer, Clare lunged outward from the step of the crummy—pushing himself as far as possible. In an instant he felt the terrible jolt, then began rolling downward. The taste of dirt mixed with the grass and straw in his mouth. When he finally stopped, he lay silently, listening. He thought he heard the crummy brakes or the whistle, or perhaps screams. But he could identify voices, well in the distance. Angry shouts. Then, suddenly, two more thumps and groans. Fitzgerald landed almost on top of him. Sammons just a few feet down.

"You alright?" whispered Clare, as Fitzgerald began groaning. Sammons was now on his feet nearby.

"What the hell we gonna do? They got us pinned down," whispered Sammons.

"You alright, Seamus?" asked Clare again, as he picked up Fitzgerald and stood him on his feet.

"Yeah. Just all beat up."

Though the voices grew closer, the lanterns weren't yet visible. "We got to go straight up this ridge," said Clare, as both men tried to steady themselves. He pointed to the heavy wooded rise directly in front of them.

Sammons cursed. "You out of your mind, Ristall? We'll never get out that way. That ridge is too high."

But Clare didn't wait. In an instant, he was into the woods and climbing upward, hanging onto the scrub as he climbed. The shuffling and groaning told him Fitzgerald was just behind, and Sammons just behind him. For the next two hours, Clare led the way up. Occasionally he spotted the lanterns below them, but getting closer, and could hear the shouts of the men. For the first hour, it was clear that they were close behind, but then the voices had dwindled. Even the flickers from their lanterns had disappeared.

Clare sat on the edge of a rock, while Sammons and Fitzgerald rested. "I'll be goddamned," said Sammons in a whisper. "How the hell do you know where we are?"

"Keep it down, Sammons," whispered Clare.

"Jesus, no sane man would follow us up this far," snorted Sammons. "What them AFL pukes can't do to us, the shit-ass bears will. We're lost out here, ain't we?"

Clare didn't answer. He listened to the rustling of the wind in the firs overhead, the crackling of twigs in the distance. Several times, he peered intently into the blackness.

"You two ready?" he asked quietly after several minutes.

"Ready for what?" asked Sammons.

"We gotta keep moving. My sense is they're close behind us."

"For Chrissake, Clare, no AFL man can follow us up this far," said

Sammons loudly. Suddenly, two gunshots crashed against the tree overhead, scattering the men onto the ground. Several more rang out, then silence.

Without speaking, Clare pounded each man on the shoulder and began moving upward again, staying close to the ground as he moved. Fitzgerald and Sammons followed. Clare knew that whoever was shooting was close by, but they were shooting at sounds, not at anything they could see. So he tossed rocks and twigs in all directions, usually drawing shots away from them.

As they moved slowly upward, the terrain became increasingly difficult—steeper, fewer twigs and rocks, sharper drops. For perhaps a half hour they climbed, but the fatigue and darkness finally began taking its toll. They fell often, tried to grab hold, then slipped back.

"We're caught," whispered Sammons in a loud wheeze when he stumbled, but couldn't regain another foothold. "We can't go up anymore."

Without hesitating, Clare slapped Sammons across the side of the head. This brought a surprised grunt, but silence. "Just stay as close to me as possible," whispered Clare matter-of-factly. "Don't lose sight of me."

For several minutes, the men worked their way along a face of solid rock. Fitzgerald tried to get a foothold to climb over it, but Clare directed them to move sideways, just below it. Several more shots rang out.

"There's more than one of 'em," said Fitzgerald quietly. Clare could see several lanterns just below. Within a minute or so, he knew they would close in.

"Hold my hand," said Clare, jutting his hand into Sammons's belly. "What?"

"Just hold my hand, and grab Fitzgerald."

Clare felt a thick hand grasp his as he continued to step gently along the rock ridgeline. He probed the rock face with his other hand—often reaching far ahead of him—as he moved. The swinging lanterns were now accompanied by voices in the dark.

Clare felt the rock turn inward suddenly. The opening. He reached several feet beyond it and, as he expected, felt the rock rise again just as sharply. "Hang on tight and step carefully." This was the narrow fissure in the ridge that Clare was looking for—barely wide enough for a mountain goat and littered with sharp, uneven rocks, but passable.

Within seconds, the three men stepped into the narrow opening in the ridge. Sammons stumbled twice but the other two picked him up. The sharp rocks scraped on either side—much closer than Clare had recalled. He knew that Sammons would likely find it hard to breathe, which he knew would also make him panic. So he whispered to both men to hold their breath. He could feel the warmth on his left hand—perspiration or blood, he couldn't tell—from where he felt the sharp rocks to guide him.

Within little more than a minute, they passed through the top of the ridgeline, totally lost to their pursuers. Once they emerged, the outcropping of rocks suddenly fell away. As it did, the terrain underfoot began to run downward gently, and Clare insisted that they keep moving downward as quickly as possible. The sounds of heavy breathing filled the air. Every few moments, Clare stopped the procession to listen for the pursuers. But on this side of the ridgeline, he heard only the wind and the sound of their own breath.

"If we keep moving downward," said Clare in a soft voice, "we'll hit a small stream. We follow it, and we'll be into Seakomish within six or eight hours."

Sammons sat loudly onto a log, his breath still coming in gulps. Clare could see now in the moonlight that his face was streaked with blood and sweat. Sammons studied Clare for several minutes without speaking.

"I had you figured all wrong, Ristall," said Sammons finally.

Clare didn't speak.

"I had you figured for one of them pencil pushers." Sammons' dirty voice brimmed with respect. He looked up the ridge again toward the notch that had saved their lives. "How the hell did you know that was up there?"

Clare smiled. "I've worked in these woods a hell of a lot longer than you ever guessed, Sammons." The night wind blew gently as the three men stood once more and began picking their way down the mountain.


## Chapter 41

The new men brought a surprising spark to the Skybillings crew. Bucky Rudman had a new audience for his jokes. John Valentine had a new flock of potential converts. Petey Hulst had a new circle for tarot. Zoe had a new class to educate in table manners.

But the most noticeable change was in the surge in timber moving from the far ridge across the trestle and down the valley. From dawn until near darkness, the crew worked the mountain. The only hint that a strike had shut down most of the other operations in the Seakomish Valley was the extra sentries that Bud had posted along the trestle and on either ridgeline. Every member of the crew did sentry duty every third day, with the sharpest eyes assigned to patrolling the trestle at night.

Bud had scattered the new men among the existing crews, seemingly at random. Several of the younger men joined Valentine's crew, but—for reasons Albert couldn't fathom—several of the most experienced were assigned to him.

Albert asked Bud if it wouldn't be better to let Jess Callup, who'd been a riggingslinger on Vancouver Island for twenty years, to take over his job.

"Why?" asked Bud, as they grabbed lunch buckets from Zoe.

"Because he's more experienced. He knows this job."

"How do you think he learned?"

To Albert, this reasoning sounded dreadfully like conversations with his mother. But he also decided that letting on that he was ready to step aside for Callup was not something he wanted others to hear. So he simply accepted Bud's decision.

Despite Albert's doubts, things worked smoothly. In fact, he actually enjoyed working with Jess Callup. Something in Callup reminded Albert of Nariff Olben. Was it the way he walked? His slight limp was the picture of Nariff. Maybe it was the jokes and all the stories about his worldly travels. Or perhaps it was the practical advice he offered—never pushy, but seasoned by decades in the woods.

Albert sought Callup's views from time to time, though Albert found that he had developed a comfortable rhythm of his own. He carefully studied the cold deck piles, one by one, as they prepared to load them. He walked around them, then crawled over the top and studied them from there—unlike Valentine and the other rigging-slingers, even unlike Bud Cole himself, who all headed for the top of a deck and started there.

The end of the first week after the new men had joined the crew, Callup started telling stories—some dirty, most making fun of himself, and lots on how any job is better than working in the woods.

"Albert, did I ever tell you about a feller name Red Sullivan?" asked Callup, as the crew waited to hear Albert's directions.

"Never did," said Albert with a ready smile, knowing that this was the opening of a story. The other three men in Albert's crew exchanged glances with Albert, who only smiled.

"Red Sullivan was an ornery little bastard," said Callup as he sat on a log at the base of the cold deck. "I worked with him up along the Strait of Georgia—felling fir right over the cliff and into the water." Callup slapped his hands together to signify a falling timber hitting the water, then followed with a whooshing sound as the tree went under.

Albert studied Callup's face as he spoke. Weathered lines that cut deep troughs into his cheeks. If there was any problem with Jess Callup, Albert decided, it was that he was too ready to talk—another reminder of Nariff.

"Goddamn it down there! Let's get moving!" The voice was that of Bud Cole, shouting from further up the slope. He was standing with his hands on both hips, staring at Albert.

Instantly, Albert jumped to his feet and scurried up the pile. Within seconds, he had given the orders on which logs to pick first and soon after, the skyline swung downward and the choking bells landed with a crash. The Carlson brothers—twins who were assigned to Albert—quickly loaded the first log, while Callup and a man named Harrison, one of Albert's least favorite members of the new crew, struggled with theirs. Albert scrambled down the pile to help with the hang-up, but before he got close, Callup gave the hand signal and the log swung upward violently—narrowly missing Albert.

"Sorry, young feller," said Callup to Albert. "I knew you was worried about Mr. Cole there, so I thought I'd speed things up for you a little."

Albert's face felt hot. He hadn't come that close to a rifle-shot log—and death—since the first week he worked for St. Bride. As he wiped away the mud and shards of bark, he knew the heat he felt was more than just the close call. Giving the high sign to hoist a log was not the job of a choker—even one with twenty years' experience. It was the job of the riggingslinger, even one with only two-weeks experience.

Callup slapped him on the shoulder. "Sorry, Albert. I didn't mean to get in your way. Was just trying to help, what with Mr. Cole pushing you so hard."

Albert told him to forget about it. But the incident stayed with him the rest of the day. The tone in Bud Cole's voice was sharper than he'd ever heard it before. He couldn't blame Callup, in some ways.

For several days, Albert was careful to keep the crew moving, even trying to keep Delbert McKenna organized. Bud had added Delbert to the crew for odd jobs that came up. Usually one of the choker men would have to run down the slope to get an axe or shovel, but Delbert now had that job. And Albert had the job of trying to make sure Delbert got the job done.

"You got two of the oldest coots on the crew under your wing now, Albert," crowed Jess Callup the next morning, as the crew climbed off the crummy and began the hike up the ridge to the highest cold deck piles.

"Who are you referring to, Callup?" asked Delbert with sudden anger. Albert had never seen Delbert so feisty. "I ain't as old as you. I'm only forty-eight."

Callup whistled and smiled. "Didn't mean nothing by it, Delbert. Just joshing."

Albert quickly stepped in with instructions on the work for the day, which seemed to settle Delbert. But Albert knew that Delbert wasn't his only concern. The wind had begun blowing steadily from the west, racing up the ravine and across the now-barren ridge. With every gust, the skyline moved—whether it had a log dangling on the end, or it was simply returning the choker and bell to the cold deck pile. Albert studied the other crews to see how they were managing the gusts—but they were too far along the ridge for him to see.

"I'd take her from down here first," said Callup as Albert studied the pile carefully.

The comment caught Albert off guard.

"Why down here? The whole deck could go."

Callup flicked his eyebrows. "That's not likely, given this stack. But if we take it from the lower side first, you'll be less likely to pick up the wind. Jimmie What's His Name down in the donkey there can pull right down along the ground. Then we work our way into the pile. Maybe by then, the wind will have died down."

What Callup suggested made sense. It would reduce the likelihood of a danger from swinging logs. But it would also increase the chance that the men could get buried in the logs, thought Albert. The rest of the crew was silent, until one of the Carlson twins spoke: "Makes some sense to me, Albert," he offered, as he huddled his jacket closer around him.

Albert considered this. Then looked at Callup. "From the bottom it is," shouted Albert, as he gave the signal for the skyline to drop toward them. The men quickly began settling the blocks around the logs that Albert had pointed to. Once the logs had been secured, and everyone had stepped away, Albert gave the high sign, and the skyline began to whine.

A sudden gust made Albert turn into the wind. Somehow, it felt different. Snow? He looked off to the west, wondering what the gray clouds held. Or was it just rain? How long ago it seemed that the warm drafts of heat lifted the red tail hawks up and over the start of the scrawny trestle.

When Albert glanced back at the cold deck pile, a surge of heat rushed through his chest and face. The whole pile had broken loose and was rumbling down the slope. He shouted just as the wall of logs slammed into the steam donkey, half way down, sending pieces of metal in every direction.

Then he remembered Delbert. He had sent him down the hill for axes to lop off small branches on several of the logs in the pile. He couldn't see Delbert anywhere amidst the strewn logs and flattened donkey. As he cleared his way past several stumps, he finally came upon him—the screams mingling with the wind, then mixing with the emergency blasts from the steam whistle. Albert could see the brilliant red on both legs and the awful twisted feet.

"Oh God, Delbert," was all he could say when he reached him, but Delbert's face was ashen, a deathly blank look contradicted by the bloody screams. As he looked at Delbert's broken body, the only thought that came to him was that Delbert was not using words in his screams. Just saliva and blood, as Albert did the only thing he knew to do for a dying man—he bent over Delbert's body and cradled him gently in both arms.

## Chapter 42

Albert's decision was final.

After Bud Cole left him alone in the kitchen, Albert resolved never to move another log again. If it meant that he had to face the embarrassment of admitting that his mother was right, then he would face it. But the agonizing cries from Delbert, and the recognition that

Delbert was near death because Albert didn't have the fortitude to stick with his own intuition, convinced him that confronting embarrassment was much easier than sending men to their deaths—or near deaths.

He slept restlessly that night, awakening often to listen to the wind and reconsider. But he didn't change his mind. He got up and dressed. He refused to join in any of the bunkhouse chatter, aware that others were watching him. Instead, he busied himself with packing his duffle bag. No one inquired.

He climbed on the crummy to ride up the mountain so he could retrieve his heavy logging pants and lunch bucket. As soon as that was accomplished, he decided, he would take the first load of logs down the mountain. Down to Seakomish. Down to his house—to a different job. What it was, he didn't know. But it would not be logging.

The wind was cold. He wrapped his arms into his mackinaw and held tight. Maybe he was one of the lucky ones, he decided. Snow would come soon. Who knows then? Maybe they would all die.

"Tough break, but you'll recover." The voice was Jess Callup. Albert hadn't noticed him sitting on the opposite bench. The old leather face swam in a thick hood.

Albert ignored him. He turned to watch the blur of green race past. But Callup pressed. "Albert, there ain't no need for a logger to hang his head on account of a decision he made," said Callup. "You made the best decision you could. Nobody can gripe about that."

Albert turned to look into Callup's face—a friendly smile on top of the lined leather. He even smiled like Nariff, thought Albert. "I don't feel like going back over it, Jess," said Albert quickly. He turned back to the blur outside the crummy, feeling the machine lunge suddenly as the incline increased.

"I'll tell you what," said Callup quietly, turning to look each direction before he spoke. He dropped his voice as he leaned close. "I'll be happy to run things today, okay? Give you a little slack, you know—a little time to recover? We'll pretend you're running things, but I can help you with picking logs."

Albert searched for even the slightest recognition that Callup knew it was his own advice—Callup's strong recommendation against Albert's best judgment—that led to the accident the day before. And while Albert was willing to accept the fact that he'd made a mistake in overruling his own sense, he sought some indication that Callup knew all this. That, at the very least, Callup himself knew he shared the blame.

But Albert found nothing in the face. Just a smile, framed by a hood whose tatters along its sides flitted in the cold breeze. "You're saying you want to run my outfit today, because I don't know how?" Albert's voice was very low.

"Nothing of the type, goddamn it," said Callup. "Just that friends are supposed to help friends out of tight spots. I'll be happy to lend you a hand while you get a better sense of how to do riggingslinger work."

Albert snorted loudly. "You do know, Jess, that the reason Delbert got hurt is because I listened to you, don't you?"

"What the hell do you mean?"

"You gotta be joking."

Callup looked shocked. "You made the wrong pick from the pile, young man."

"The only wrong pick I made was to listen to you. I knew which one of those logs to take next, but I was a damn fool and listened to you. And there ain't no goddamn way I'm going to let you do anything else but fix the goddamn chokers, Callup."

Albert felt faces around him turn his way. The crummy had come to a stop. He grabbed his hat and climbed off quickly.

❄   ❄   ❄

For the next several days, Albert refused to think about anything other than the geometry of logs beneath him. The crazy crisscrosses of another cold deck pile. Albert pointed, and the choking crew scrambled to pull the logs out in the order he directed. Callup didn't argue, nor did he speak. He did the work that Albert ordered and quickly walked away during lunch and coffee breaks.

Harry Bachelder occasionally intervened to direct the crew to the next cold deck pile. Albert would nod, say little, and begin the trek up the hill. He was on the deck before any of the others and had selected the logs he would begin pulling first.

The weather had turned colder, with heavy gray clouds scraping across the tips of Three Sisters Ridge. While the crew was choking logs, Albert would stare off into the deep ravine below. How recent the scorching fire of mid-summer seemed. He studied the far ridge, which mostly lay broken, dotted by cold decks. And the link between the two—the trestle—now shouldering three or four loads a day, on their way down the mountain.

He searched the middle of the ravine for hawks that still might be residing into the late fall, but saw only occasional flakes of snow.

How many times had Petey told the story of the Indians and the snows and how the trappers were lost forever? How many times had Lightning Stevens made fun of him? But now, as Albert studied the low sky and felt the icy wind across his ears, he wondered.

Would the extra gear, the extra supplies, the snow blades on the front of the Shays be enough to get them out, he wondered? He had no idea. Or would there even be snow soon—it had held off so long already. But somewhere in the danger, somewhere in the sense of uncertainty, he felt a surprising calm.

For the first time in his life, Albert stopped wondering. The rhythm of the logs, the calculations in his head, the quick orders he snapped to the crew, and the wonder of seeing a reluctant winter fall upon the high mountains refreshed him. Even the stabbing cold, which he had come to hate for so long, gave him a sense of achievement. As the temperature dropped and the wind grew, and the sense of danger increased, he found a sense of calm rise within him.

The hawks had gone. The eagles had gone. The songbirds had long since departed. But for some reason—a reason he couldn't understand—Albert was still on the mountain.

## Chapter 43

Bud Cole felt a shiver run through his body as the cold, gray metal of the binoculars touched his face. From this vantage point, not far from where the Shay had crashed nearly six months ago, he could take in the entire Skybillings operation.

He traced each of the bents of the trestle, moving upward slowly from the rock ledge where it sat to the railroad track on top. He did this on each, stopping momentarily when one of the sentries came into view. Most had perched comfortably against the thick braces that ran parallel to the track well above. But a few stood silently on the rock ledge below. And one—following Bud's exact instructions—paced slowly from one end of the trestle to the other.

Yet this still wasn't good enough. Daily, he stopped at this spot and studied every brace, every bent, every crosspiece of the trestle. He wondered sometimes what he expected to find. Something unusual? Something out of place? He laughed gruffly—did he somehow expect to find ten pounds of dynamite neatly tied under the tracks? As he drew the glasses once again to his face, he had to admit that, yes, maybe that's exactly what he expected.

He went back to each of the faces of the sentries. Some were young men. Some older, stooped. All good loggers. He turned the glasses to look into the faces of several others—all he knew, all he trusted. Yet here he was, studying them secretly. Watching them stop, light cigarettes, look off absently in the distance, unzip a fly and turn away from the others. Would looking carefully into their faces yield something, he wondered? Perhaps give him a warning?

He took in a deep breath and felt the chill in the air. He swung the glasses past the trestle to take in the distant ridge. It resembled a beehive—no, more like many beehives. The cold deck piles—small triangles that dotted the ridge—were hubs of rapid movement. Men scrambled up and down, connecting chokers, then racing to the side. Logs roared upward instantly on the end of cables, dangled precariously above the triangles, before flopping violently onto rail cars. From this distance, there was no sound. But Bud could almost feel the rail cars shudder, spitting dirt, twigs, and leaves, when the logs landed.

Bud caught a glimpse of Harry Bachelder running one of the steam donkeys, jamming levers and guiding logs quickly onto the cars. Bud hadn't confided in Harry about the conversation with Witstrop— about who might be behind the sabotage. For some reason, it mattered less now. Bud only wanted to move the logs, to come as close as possible to beating whoever was after him.

His breath fogged the glasses, but he wiped them quickly and resumed his search of the ridge. The men were too far away for him to see the faces, though he could recognize most of them by their movements and dress: Valentine, standing with his hands on his hips on top of a cold deck; Lightning Stevens bending low to help hook a choker on another; Bucky Rudman pointing and gesturing to Bachelder about something next to the donkey.

As he watched them work, he felt a sense of France again—of watching the distant lines with the trenches in between. He'd wondered then, as a brigade of French and Brits scrambled between the barbed wire, who of them would survive. Whether either side could win. Whether only death and damage could be the result of such a treacherous venture. But he shook the memory and continued to search the ridgeline. He saw Little Boy and Conrad Bruel and Myles Norgren and several of the new men. Then, his glasses fell upon Albert—standing ramrod straight on top of a pile just below the spar tree.

Bud held the glasses as still as possible, and he squinted into them to try to get a clear look at the face, but the distance defeated him. Instead, he settled to watch the movements: Albert pointed and jumped, bending low to help guide chokers, then he backed away and pointed again to new logs when those secured to the choker slipped upward and away. Bud thought he could see several of the men laugh, then Albert slapped one on the shoulder. Was it Callup? Jess Callup?

Bud couldn't be sure. But as he watched, the men stopped abruptly and sat. It must be time for a coffee break, thought Bud, though he'd lost sense of the time. Callup offered Albert a cigarette, which Albert took into his mouth, cupped his hands around a match that Callup had struck, and after inhaling deeply, blew a foggy cloud upward. The others did the same. Several sat and opened flasks of hot coffee that seemed to boil upward in the cold air.

As Bud drew the binoculars from his eyes, he smiled. He didn't even know that Albert smoked.


## Chapter 44

The CIO didn't have a union hall. So Clare Ristall rented the meeting room behind the Methodist Church.

Lydia had assumed that if she got there a few minutes before eight, she could get in with little trouble. But the steps leading to the hall were jammed with men. Even as she approached, she detected something different. Something in the voices, in the rapid conversation. Someone spotted her and called out to the group, "Make way for Mrs. Weissler, boys," which brought several greetings as it opened a path up the steps and into the hall.

As she stepped through the door, she felt suddenly overwhelmed—a small room, filled to overflowing, melting in a pungent aroma of machine oil, perspiration, and the warm leather of caulk boots. For an instant, she felt like turning—turning from the moist heat and escaping into the cold Seakomish night. But she overruled her senses and scanned the faces, finding several she knew. She searched the crowd for Clare, finally finding him near the front.

He was leaning close to Sammons, who shook his head and then nodded. Clare leaned over him to greet several of the loggers, then finally spotted Lydia in the back of the room. Even in the midst of the confusion, thought Lydia, he's got a special smile. As he found her, his smiled flickered briefly, carrying a warmth in his eyes. Though she thought nobody saw it, she felt herself blush, even in the heat of the packed meeting hall.

Clare stood up and clapped his hands quickly. The conversation dropped, then came to a halt. "I got a story I want to start with," said Clare brightly. He surveyed the room with a broad smile. Something in that smile, thought Lydia, allowed this man to run a strike and run a campaign and still have energy left over. As he smiled, the room settled and seemed lost in the words. That there was a brutal strike underway, that Clare was the primary organizer, that many were suffering as a result seemed to be instantly swept away.

"It's a story about a logger—a religious logger." This brought an instant roar. Clare smiled while the laughter died. "He went to church every Sunday. Every Sunday." Clare surveyed the crowd, as if to test that he had all the attention. Lydia scanned the room and didn't see any side conversations. All eyes were turned to Clare Ristall.

"This logger was also a card player. And he got to thinking about whether there was card playing in heaven." Lydia chuckled along with several in the group. "So this logger went to his preacher, week after week, asking him to ask God if there was card playing in heaven."

Clare now turned his back to the room and began to pace, as if thinking about the story. Suddenly he turned back. "Well, after this logger pesters the preacher for all this time, the preacher finally comes to church one Sunday and says, 'My friend, I checked with God about your question, and I've got some good news and some bad news.'"

The men began to laugh more loudly. "The preacher said to this logger, 'The good news is that God says that there is card playing in heaven. The bad news is that he says you're all set to be the dealer next Tuesday night.'"

The men roared. Lydia noted that even Sammons smiled, along with a man next to him she didn't recognize. As the laughter rolled through the room, she again felt Clare's gaze upon her. He's glad I came, she thought. He wanted me to observe all this.

Clare's voice rose above the waning laughter. "Well, I've got some good news tonight and some bad news. Which do you want to hear first?"

"Good news, Clare," shouted a fat man sitting next to Lydia. She jumped at the loud voice, as several of the men directly in front of her turned and smiled.

"Good news it is then," said Clare quickly. He walked to a podium and took out his glasses. He inspected a sheaf of papers, then held one out directly in front of him. "Let me read this exactly to you. It's from a letter I received yesterday afternoon." Clare cleared his voice and read loudly.

"This is to inform you that our company board of directors voted this afternoon, unanimously, to recognize the Committee for Industrial Organization Chapter #22 as the sole organizing union for loggers in the Seakomish Valley. Signed, Tuttle B. Ashford."

Lydia felt the floorboards rock as the men jumped to their feet. Those in the row in front of her slapped each other's backs, several shook hands, while the thunderous noise in the room was punctuated with sharp whistles and hoots. For several minutes, all the men in the room stomped their boots in unison. They seemed to forget that Clare was in the room. The celebration was immediately followed by rapid conversation about when they would go back to work, how they were glad it was all over. Though she only knew a few of the men, she smiled at their relief. A long battle was over. Life was about to go back to normal.

Clare clapped his hands quickly again. He started speaking several times before the room grew quiet.

"Remember that I said there was some bad news, too." Clare's smile drew in the crowd again. "Remember the card-playing logger I told you about?" Soft laughter again. Nothing was going to dampen the excitement of the news about Ashford & Southern, Lydia decided.

"Here's the bad news." Clare studied each corner of the room, as if trying to pull each man individually into the conversation. "While we expected the rest of the valley to recognize the CIO as soon as Ashford & Southern did, it's clear that we were too optimistic. We've heard that while Cascade and Hartman Brothers have decided to do so, we've also learned that Deek Brown and Zollock & Sons have refused."

This brought a chorus of boos.

"We'll fight 'em, Clare," shouted a man from the middle of the room. He now stood on his chair and spoke to the rest of the men. "I say that we stick it out and close those bastards." This brought a chorus of support.

"Well, funny you should mention that," said Clare quickly. "We might just have to." Clare then went on to recall the meeting with Deek Brown and the arrival of Stearns from the AFL, and the confrontation along the track. This was the first most of the men had heard of it. Clare outlined the escape off the side of the crummy and through the notch in the ridge.

Sammons suddenly stood up. "The dirty bastards was in cahoots. They set an ambush. Lured us up to talk to Deek Brown himself, and once we was there, they closed the track." Lydia didn't like the looks of Sammons. He was just as Clare had described—a man who seemed incapable of honesty. Lydia shuddered at the details of the story, about how close Clare had come.

"So what do we do?" The man who had shouted from the middle of the room rose again and directed the question at Clare. "Do we go after them for ya?"

A young fellow wearing a torn shirt stood next to him. "A lot of us got families, Clare. We'd just as soon forget this whole thing and go back to work." This comment brought surprising silence in the room. The young man felt the silence, quickly turning around to see if he might be in any danger. Lydia suspected, however, that he spoke for more of the men than his look suggested.

"Here is the plan," said Clare quickly, once again commanding the room. "We'll obviously go back to work on Monday morning for Ashford & Southern and anybody else who agrees to recognize the CIO. But for anybody who doesn't, I propose that we continue to strike—we'll double the strike lines around each operation. And, this afternoon, I opened another line of credit at the bank so each of you who can't go back to work can draw a half-month's pay for groceries."

This brought a gasp—from Lydia, as well. She knew where the money must be coming from, but how long could Clare continue to finance a strike? As the men began to applaud and whistle again—she once more felt the sense of wanting to escape the room. The heat had risen even higher. She felt water running down her neck. But she drew in more of the moist air and willed herself to remain calm.

Clare raised his arms to still the crowd. "But I want to warn all of you—we can expect two things. First, we're going to get offers from some of these companies to accept all of our demands—except the most important one, which is that we are the sole representatives of the loggers in this valley. And to those kinds of offers I say, 'Hell no!'"

This brought a roar of approval. "You with me?" he shouted again. Another roar and thundering applause. "The other thing you can expect," shouted Clare, "is the kind of thing that Sammons and Fitzgerald and I ran into the other day. The AFL ain't gonna go down easy. They're gonna retaliate."

Lydia didn't know if it had been the story Sammons had told about the near escape from Deek Brown's operation, or Clare's ability to offer them strike pay, but she didn't detect even a hint of opposition to what Clare proposed. Family men, many with several children—following the worst business years of their lives—chanted that they would strike and battle the AFL.

Clare tamed the crowd long enough to ask for formal votes on each of his proposals—for strike pay, for continuing the strike, and for a vote of solidarity that no matter what the companies or the AFL proposed, the strike would not end until the companies recognized the CIO as the sole bargaining union. Each vote brought a resounding shout of approval. Even the young man who had voiced doubt earlier joined in.

"Then we are adjourned," shouted Clare with a smile. "Remember, you can get strike pay starting tomorrow at my office."

The room broke into waves of conversation and laughter. Lydia said hello to the men she recognized, but most were locked in excited discussion with one another. As she began making her way to the aisle, she studied the faces—brown and lined, some unshaven, most displaying stains where rivers of perspiration had run freely only a few hours before. But not one she looked at seemed fatigued, she decided. Perhaps the meeting had awakened them, given them new energy. Not one suggested a slight fear of the future, no indication of the risk in the strategy they just approved.

As she stepped into the aisle, Lydia felt the room tighten suddenly, as if the men outside had decided to rush in. She drew in her breath, but the surge continued. She grabbed for the chair in front of her—certain she was fainting—but the sound of crashing glasses and the frightened shouts of the men all around her told her that something else was happening.

In an instant she was on her knees, the backs of several men pushing hard against her face. She felt herself spin around, landing on sharp pieces of glass that tore at her hands. The room suddenly went black, then exploded in brilliant colors and screams.

She tried to crawl toward the door, but the path was blocked by flames that covered the floor. She turned to crawl toward the front of the room, but she felt only the suffocating heat that seared through her lungs. The smell and the pain were suddenly overwhelmed by the scissor-like arms she felt around her waist. She felt herself being lifted up violently, then cradled roughly in the darkness, as the shouts and the flames rose around her. Was she running? Was she flying? Her body jolted, as the pain in her ribs grew and an awful stench flowed across her face.

❊　❊　❊

Lydia looked up and saw Clare's face. He held her gently. She tried to speak, but he shook his head. "Stay still," he said softly. "We'll get you to the doctor right away."

Lydia struggled to sit up. She felt the coldness of the grass underneath her skirt. Several men lay nearby, moaning loudly. Several others simply stared into the darkness, while perhaps a hundred more milled around near them.

She leaned forward and caught a glimpse of the meeting hall, now fully engulfed in flame. Several men held fire hoses that shot arches of white against the brilliant blue and yellow. "What happened?" Her mouth felt numb from the smoke and the heat.

"AFL decided to let us know what they think of our decision," said Clare softly. He brushed hair from Lydia's face. "Sammons here got you out."

Lydia turned to Sammons, but he turned away. His dirty face flickered in the glow of the flames. She tried to find words, but nothing would come.

❊　❊　❊

Bud slipped the choker into the metal bell with a clank and jumped clear, just as the log shot upward. He squatted low to make sure the back end of the massive fir didn't clip him as it flew upward. Dirt pellets and shards of bark showered him with a pungent cloudburst.

"Done like a pro," said Jess Callup with a laugh. Bud had volunteered to fill in for one of Albert's crew who came down with the flu.

For two days, Bud had been Callup's partner. For two days, he'd been listening to advice about how to do the job. "You don't move too bad for management," added Callup, with a slap on Bud's back.

"I'll take that as a compliment." Bud stood and stretched. His arms ached. No matter how hard the bucking with Valentine's crew had been, Bud was reminded that choking hurt. Something in the bending and reaching. As he straightened his back, Bud noticed Albert standing near the top of the deck. A slight smile crossed Albert's face, but he turned away quickly as he moved further up the pile of logs laying against the bottom of the spar tree.

Bud's eyes now fell on the Shay roaring across the trestle. The locomotive seemed near full throttle—a solid column of steam rushing upward from the boiler. Bachelder had told both engineers never to exceed ten miles per hour. The trestle might start quaking in the middle. "If that happens," warned Bachelder, "It'll fold like an accordion."

But here came the damn Shay, roaring as if it were on open track. Bud didn't know whether it was going to make it across without plummeting into the ravine, but if it did, he was going to give the engineer hell.

He scampered down the pile of logs to meet the locomotive. But by the time it crossed the trestle and roared to a stop, Fergie had already jumped out and was running to meet him. The engineer pulled out a red handkerchief and mopped his cheeks. "There's been a bad fire down to Seakomish, Mr. Cole. The Methodist Meeting Hall burned."

This brought silence among the men, who had begun assembling behind Bud to witness the tongue-lashing.

"It burned clean to the ground, according to Sheriff Deets." Fergie's breath came in short gulps. "Sheriff said that the CIO boys was in there meeting. And a bunch of lugs from the AFL came up on 'em and firebombed the place. All kinds of people hurt."

Bud tried to hear the rest of what Fergie was saying, but the news threw the men into loud conversation. The meeting hall. Firebombed.

"A union battle? In Seakomish? I'll be goddamned," shouted Bucky Rudman. "What's this world come to, anyway? What do you AFL boys got to say for yourselves?" He turned to several of the men near him, but no one listened.

"Anybody hurt?" asked Lightning Stevens.

"A bunch, according to the sheriff," answered Fergie quickly. "And some of the townsfolk who just happened to be there." Bud saw the faces turn to one another. "Clare Ristall and his boys were running the thing."

"Did Clare get hurt?" The question came simultaneously from several of the men.

"Dunno. Sheriff didn't tell me. But he said the whole goddamn valley has blown up ever since."

Bud had tried to close the strike out of his mind. The conversation with Witstrop told him that his real enemy lay elsewhere. So he'd turned his attention to the only thing he thought he could do something about—move logs. But if violence was spreading, it could reach Skybillings as well, regardless of whether the company was one of the original targets.

The men prodded Fergie for more details. "All right, goddamn it, just hold your horses," he snapped quickly, opening a can of snoose and lifting a plug into his mouth.

"Goddamn it Fergie, what else did you hear," said Myles Norgren sharply.

Fergie stuck out a black tongue at Norgren, then cleared his throat. "They say that two bridges into the Ashford & Southern camps was dynamited, and a section of rail running to Zollock & Sons was torn up. Sheriff even said they had damn near a riot on Main Street when the fire department tried to clean up the mess at the meeting hall the next day. Hauled three boys to the clink in Everett over it."

"On Main Street in Seakomish?" Myles Norgren's voice was raspy.

"Where the hell else—Seattle?"

By this time, the crew on the entire hillside had stopped work and made their way down to the Shay.

Bucky Rudman pushed his way forward so he stood next to Fergie. He put his hand on the engineer's back, as if to nurse more information out of him. "Well who's behind it all, Fergie? What's the sheriff saying—the AFL boys did it, right?" With this, Bucky turned and smiled innocently to the group of men standing in a circle.

"Goddamn, Rudman, I don't know who was behind it all," said Fergie. "The sheriff said there's all kind of rumors flying. Some claim that the AFL boys are getting money from some of the big companies to battle Ashford & Southern and the CIO."

"That's wrong," snorted John Valentine suddenly. "Vicious rumors is all—just to discredit honest AFL men."

This brought several shouts of support, but Fergie held up his hands quickly. "Look, I'm just saying what I heard. The sheriff said that money was rumored to have changed hands—that's all." Fergie's eyes suddenly arched upward and a sly smile swept across his chubby face. "Of course, there's other stories circulating down there, too. Some say that the CIO itself might be behind the violence—launching attacks upon their own men to build support and convince outsiders that the AFL has gone violent."

This brought silence.

"The CIO doesn't have to attack its own men to build support," said Myles Norgren. "There's enough men who've had enough with the pissant AFL ways of representing us. We don't need to fake attacks to build support. The companies have built enough support for us on their own."

Several men cursed, some softly, others loudly, ripping the words out briskly, so that all could hear. Bud caught Harry Bachelder's eye, who shook his head and looked away. Lightning Stevens and Myles Norgren seemed caught up in the claims. Valentine, Conrad Bruel, Petey Hulst, and Bucky Rudman were locked in loud conversation, though Bud couldn't hear any of it over the other voices. Behind them, Bud's eye fell upon the ridgeline, with the patchwork cold deck piles silent in the darkening afternoon.

❄    ❄    ❄

Bud hurried to catch up to Petey Hulst as the crew climbed off the crummy, on their way to the mess hall. "Petey, don't I recall you telling a story a few years back about snow up here in Roosevelt Creek?"

The old man stopped abruptly. Even in the darkness of early evening, Bud thought he could distinguish the brilliant blue in Petey's eyes, which were locked on Bud. Petey studied Bud before he answered. "As a matter of fact, you probably do. Story about a crew of loggers—thinking they could put in a line along Roosevelt Creek, all the way up to Thunder Lake. Snow caught 'em. Almost killed 'em."

"How bad did it get?"

Petey continued to study him. "Well, there were different stories about that. Some said that they got trapped up here over the winter. No food. Some of 'em froze. But the others walked out healthy come spring time." A smile broke the line of sharp whiskers covering his face. "You figure it out."

Bud had heard the story, in different forms, since he first got to Seakomish. Some versions had it that the loggers stumbled back down along Roosevelt Creek when a Chinook wind arrived suddenly. They nearly drowned in the runoff. The more interesting version—the one that he'd heard repeated most often—concluded with several of them showing up in Seakomish come the first thaw in April, and several of them carrying the cleanly picked bones of their comrades in burlap sacks.

"You sure you want me telling that story?" asked Petey.

"That's the one." Bud sorted through the options for introducing Petey. "I've got several things I want to discuss with the men as soon as the pie goes on the table. One of them is how prepared we are for the weather—just in case it starts snowing. How about when I'm done, you sort of volunteer to tell the story about Roosevelt Creek Valley in winter?"

Petey rubbed his whiskers and spat onto the ground. As he did, Bud could see the deep fissures of skin that ran down his neck. Was Petey seventy? Eighty? Was there a chance that this was more than a legend to Petey? Was there a chance that Petey knew the story first hand?

"You think if I scare them they'll forget all this other foolishness? Is that it, Bud?"

"Either they'll forget it or they'll turn tail and all run like scared rabbits toward Seakomish."


**Chapter 45**

Zoe's food often stopped conversation. Hungry loggers often refused to talk when food like Zoe cooked was in front of them. But tonight was different, thought Bud as he watched them. The news about Seakomish, and the rumors about battles at other logging shows, overwhelmed even the corned beef hash that was always a favorite.

While Bud worked aggressively on his food, he listened closely to the conversation: Was there any truth to the rumors? How bad were the battles? Any chance anybody died? This comment usually made them pause. Death by falling limbs or broken cables was part of the job. But death by union violence was something different.

As soon as Zoe placed two pies on each table, Bud stood up and cleared his throat.

"I got two pieces of business to discuss tonight—and I'll be brief," said Bud, as the conversation died. It was replaced with the clanking of silverware on pie plates.

"I've decided to increase the number of sentries we've got around the camp and on the trestle. Nobody can predict if that trouble down in Seakomish and at the other camps will reach us, but we gotta be ready."

Bud waited for Zoe to finish delivering steaming pots of coffee to each table, before he continued. "So the first order of business is that I need additional volunteers for the trestle. We can handle the other sentry work through our normal rotation." Bud had established a system early in the summer, in which all men—except the youngest—stood two nights every week.

"Starting when?" called out Conrad Bruel from the back of the room.

"Starting tomorrow night," said Bud.

Several hands shot up. Without looking at the faces, he grabbed a piece of paper and began writing names, starting at the left. Rudman, Little Boy, Norgren, two men whose names he had to ask—Juarez and Reinslauer. Bud looked up to get the last name and met the gaze of Albert.

"Albert Weissler," said Albert clearly. Bud didn't write down the name for several seconds, as he looked into the face. Albert showed no emotion. His gaze was steady, patient, waiting for Bud to write down the name, which he did quickly.

"So do we shoot if we see 'em?" asked Bucky Rudman loudly. This brought nervous laughter.

"Most likely, there isn't going to be anybody to shoot at," said Bud quickly. "But each of you will get a shotgun, just in case." Bud looked quickly across the faces turned toward him. "Just let me warn you: I don't want anybody pulling any trigger until I tell you."

"What happens if they attack?"

Bud recognized the contradiction. He knew they needed guns. He knew there was a chance there would be an attack. But he hated the notion of scared loggers ready to shoot at anything that moved.

He drew a big sigh. "Look, let's just say that you better not pull any trigger until somebody is pointing a weapon at you and is about to fire. Got that, Bucky?"

"Got it, boss."

"Everybody understand?" Murmurs passed through the hall.

Bud put the clipboard down. "Now the second subject is snow. I want every man to understand what the plan is here." He explained that the snow blades would let the Shays clear the tracks. "They'll get us out unless it's really heavy."

Conversation rose again. "And what do we do if it's really heavy?" asked one of the new men.

"We stay right here until we have a chance to go out." Bud let this information settle for a moment. "We've got a load of extra food coming up from Seakomish tomorrow, extra fuel, and extra clothes— blankets, coats and such. And God knows we've got plenty of wood."

The room was nearly silent. "How bad does it get this high up?" asked Jess Callup finally.

Petey Hulst cleared his throat. "Some winters can get damned bad." Petey lit a match and drew it into the tobacco in his shiny pipe. When Bud stepped out the door, most of the men had shifted in their seats to face Petey, who sat by the wooden stove and began telling the legend of the snow in Roosevelt Creek.

❈    ❈    ❈

As soon as Bud stepped out of the mess hall, he could smell the change. Something in the wind—suddenly damp and cold. He walked along the edge of the lake, stopping at the end of the dock. The heaven above was a pincushion of twinkling light. No clouds yet, though he checked the sky directly above Crescent Peak. No, not even there.

Bud jammed his hands into his pockets and walked quickly past the bunkhouses and out to the depot, where the crummy stood silent. His boots dug loudly into the rock, echoing sharply in the crisp night. He didn't see the form move quickly from the right, but he could feel something different in the shape of the Hawthorne bushes that lined the track.

"Evening, Mr. Cole," said the voice crisply.

"Evening, Little Boy," said Bud.

"I bet you thought I'd gone to sleep out here."

"No, just came to report that you're on the trestle tomorrow night, according to your partner, Mr. Rudman." Bud had trouble seeing Little Boy's face, though the outline of the shotgun that he still held toward Bud was plain.

"Mind pointing that thing the other way?"

"Sorry." Little Boy paused as he stationed the butt of the shotgun at his feet. The thin stock paralleled his leg. "I'll be happy to help on the trestle."

"Thanks." Bud turned to go, then stopped. "Everything okay out here?" Little Boy nodded, but didn't answer.

"Just thought I'd check. Did Zoe pack your supper?"

"Yes sir. Already finished it." Little Boy didn't wait for more conversation. He slipped behind the bush again.

As Bud walked back to the bunkhouse, he stopped several times, peering upward at the sky. As he studied the sky, he heard the plaintive cries in the distance. First low, then insistent, and painful.

He laughed softly as he resumed walking to his bunkhouse. For the first few months he had worked in the woods, the old-timers claimed that the cries were those of a thousand dead loggers, still suffering the pain and torture of their last moments. Was I ever that young, he wondered, that I actually believed the winter cries of cougars were the sounds of ghost loggers?

He closed the door of his cabin and unlaced his boots. The bottle of brandy felt sticky to the touch, but rather than cleaning it off, Bud licked his fingers, then covered the bottom of a coffee cup with the amber liquid.

He dropped into the large chair behind his desk, then slowly opened the bottom drawer. Underneath a pile of books, he found a small object wrapped in a brown towel, then carefully set it onto the desk. As he finished the brandy in one swallow, he unfolded the towel and withdrew a pistol. With a swift motion, he opened the cartridge, snapped it quickly back, and dropped the pistol into the pocket of his mackinaw.

## Chapter 46

Lydia winced as the nurse unwrapped her hands. "Sorry, Mrs. Weissler, but I need to take a quick look." The woman was large, her fingers thick. Yet she unwrapped the hands carefully, gently unthreading the loose gauze, then cradling the hand in her lap as she pulled a brilliant white examination light closer.

"Probably another day or so and you can have these off," she said with a smile. "But I'm afraid that those legs are gonna keep you here a few more days."

Lydia groaned. "What I don't understand is what I gain from lying here," said Lydia sharply. "I could just as well be laying in my bed at home." She hadn't expected to get out immediately when the doctor reported the extent of the burns. But she hadn't expected a full week. On her back. Unable to read or write or even comb her own hair. And with each day, she knew her mood was becoming worse.

"Infection, young lady," said the nurse as she peered over half-glasses. "Infection sets into those burns and you'll lose not just those legs, but maybe your life." The woman smiled sweetly, as if the news would somehow cheer Lydia.

The days had been difficult for Lydia, but the nights dreadful. In the darkness, the doorway from the silent corridor seemed to fill with faces—Albert, then Clare, then students from her classes, even her long-dead husband—all speaking rapidly, often arguing with one another, until she would shout for order and find the doorway empty, the room silent. She would then lie for hours as her mind raced, focusing on each of the faces that had appeared in the doorway.

The turmoil that had suddenly beset Seakomish made things even worse. Gone was the sense of closeness that she'd always known in Seakomish, even during the worst of the Depression. In its place was tension and anger. She'd been visited by many friends and parents of students—but only those whose loyalties were with Clare Ristall and the CIO. Many friends—at least acquaintances she'd considered to be friends—did not appear. Not even after a week.

As she lay in bed, wide awake in the midnight stillness, wrestling with imagined conversations, she often found her thoughts returning to a photo that she had just framed. The afternoon of the CIO meeting she had hung it in the dining room, next to several photos of her and Albert and Liz. There wasn't anything particularly memorable about the photo. It was taken several Christmases earlier. The photo was of Lydia, holding Liz, with Albert leaning against her side.

But as she lay in the stillness of night, her mind kept seeing one thing—the furniture in the background. Not the children, not the Christmas tree, nor the array of presents, but the furniture. A worn leather armchair, a coffee table of bleached pine, and an old rug that covered the wood floors. She found herself burrowing into the details of every piece—where she and Fred had bought them. Then why they had. Then she went over every inch of each piece in her mind—she recalled the deep grooves that one of the kids, she couldn't remember which one, had scraped into the arm of the chair. Was it the right arm? No. The left. Then there was the coffee table, with its rings from hot coffee cups and water stains.

When she awoke in the mornings, she quickly returned to the photo. But not the details now, instead she struggled with why the photo occupied her so at all. There was nothing particularly interesting about it. Nothing noteworthy. But why couldn't she get it out of her mind, and why the furniture? Why did it come back?

"You look like you're in another world, young lady," said the nurse one morning, several days after she had been admitted. Lydia turned to see that the old woman was standing near the door, with Clare right behind.

"Hello, beautiful," said Clare warmly, as he rushed to the bed and gave her a peck on the cheek.

"Don't get close, I'm awful."

"The hell you are. Never looked better."

This brought a smile to Lydia's face. "That's supposed to be a compliment, I take it?"

Clare shrugged, as the nurse again examined the hands and nodded approvingly. When she had gone, Clare dropped a paper onto the bed.

"The Everett Chronicle finally says that the CIO has a legitimate issue with the owners," said Clare. "Can you believe it?"

Lydia sat up in bed, as she read the editorial. "That's wonderful, Clare. How'd you do that?"

"I didn't. When the batty publisher Meredith Cunningham heard about the AFL attacking our meeting the other night, she was outraged, I guess. She decided that what we'd been saying all along had something to it."

Clare abruptly stopped, his face a picture of shock. "My God, I'm sorry, darling. I came in here all full of myself without asking anything about how you're doing. Jesus."

"For goodness sake, I'm not dying. I've got some fussy old doctor who won't let me out, that's all."

"How are you feeling?" He stroked her arm gently.

"I'm fine. Little trouble in the middle of the night, but other than that okay. God, I wish I could get out of this cell."

"Oh yes, the arrangements...." Clare pulled a notebook from his pocket, and began ticking off all the arrangements he'd made for her so she could get help at home. "Mrs. Tilson from school will stay with you at night in case you need help, and the ladies from church will alternate in bringing over meals. And the librarian, Mrs. Whatsher name ?"

"Woolsey."

"Right. Mrs. Woolsey will help you organize your lessons at school until everything's working again."

Lydia felt herself smile as she studied Clare. His soft forehead was furrowed deeply as he concentrated on the list—he had now moved on to making sure the bills were paid, cleaning the house, getting her to school. You would never know that he's got a strike running, she thought—one that suddenly had turned violent. She studied him closely as he sat slumped in the chair, head down, eyes still on the list. He could have been a professor, she thought. He had the brains. He had the gift with people. He was quick on his feet. But here he was running a strike, running for the legislature, trying to keep his men in order, and worrying about who was going to get her to school.

He looked up suddenly, catching her intense gaze. "Are you trying to stare a hole through me?"

Lydia laughed. "No, just wondering what makes a fellow like you tick."

Clare suddenly jumped from the chair and nuzzled her cheek with a kiss. "A little piss and vinegar, a little shot of whisky, and an occasional roll in the hay," he said sweetly, with a sly smile.

Lydia held up her two hands, still wrapped in gauze. "And this sight, I'm sure, is very appealing."

"Actually," said Clare softly, "it's very arousing. You think they'd mind if we...." Clare suddenly reclined his chest across the side of the bed, as if he were crawling in.

"Clare!"

He laughed softly, a friendly, teasing laugh. "C'mon. I'd never do it. But it's sort of fun to think about, isn't it?"

The door opened, and the nurse walked in with a tray of food. This time, Sheriff Deets stood behind her.

"Hope you don't mind, young lady," said the nurse as she placed the tray on the table next to the bed. "The sheriff said he wanted to say hello."

Charlie Deets settled himself in a chair on the opposite side of the bed from where Clare sat and inquired about Lydia's condition. Though he listened politely and made small talk for several minutes, he abruptly changed the subject—leaving little doubt about the true purpose of his visit. The troublemakers who were arrested after the firebombing of the meeting hall had been released from the Everett jail, said Deets. A high-priced lawyer from Seattle had found some sort of technicality and gotten them out. He stopped by to make sure both Clare and Lydia knew about it.

"Where are they now?" asked Lydia.

"Dunno. They just disappeared." The nurse came in again to check on whether Lydia had finished lunch, but then exited swiftly when she heard the sheriff speaking. "As far as we could tell, somebody hired 'em to come in here and make trouble. They did their job, now they're gone."

Lydia studied Deets. "I don't understand, Sheriff. You mean they weren't local?"

"Not as far as we could tell. We overhead two of them talking when we hauled them up to Everett, and it was clear that somebody brought them in just to cause this trouble."

Charlie Deets leaned forward and looked at the tray of food next to Lydia's bed. "I hope you don't think this is forward, Lydia, but are you going to eat that pudding there?"

Lydia laughed and told him to help himself. When he had finished, he wiped his mouth carefully. "I always told the Missus—if she could just make food as good as you get in this hospital."

Lydia smiled and asked about Mrs. Deets. She was fine, said the sheriff. Finding it harder to move around due to arthritis in her legs, but otherwise okay, he said. She wanted to stop by to inquire about Lydia's condition, but couldn't navigate the stairs into the hospital. Lydia assured him that was fine, and asked him to pass along her greetings.

"I don't understand, Sheriff," said Clare suddenly. "You have decided that these men were from out of town?"

"From out of town, and at least a couple of them were Communists—trained in bomb-making and what-not. I learned that from a friend of mine who is a deputy in Everett. It was his job to keep an eye on them in the jail. He said they talked about the Party when they thought no one was listening."

Clare paced while Deets gave out the rest of the details. Three of the men had records of troublemaking in Portland and in Vancouver. And the deputy overheard them talking about more attacks in the coming days. "The way I see it, Clare, is that you have suddenly got yourself one hell of a battle on your hands," said Deets. "Which leads me to the other reason I dropped by. I want to personally ask you to come to the table with the AFL and the owners."

Clare quietly folded the newspaper he was holding and placed it on the table. His voice was quiet. "Charlie, what the hell are you talking about? Stop the strike?"

"That's exactly what I am talking about, Clare. This town is beginning to come apart. I've already put on three extra deputies, what with all the fist fights."

Clare's voice was still calm, but now angry. "I'm not going to discuss this, Charlie. We're not going to stop simply because the AFL bastards bring in a bunch of goons and throw fire bombs."

"We don't have proof it was the AFL," said Deets sharply.

The room was silent, except for the ticking of a clock above Lydia's bed. For the entire week she'd laid there, she hadn't heard it. But now it clanked loudly, numbering the seconds of the long silence. Finally Clare spoke—his voice thin. "What are you saying Charlie?"

"I'm not saying anything. I simply am reporting facts—we don't know who brought those bastards in. But whoever it was had a clear intent to kick the holy shit out of this town, and its people, for their own purpose. And the only way to stop that in my book is to get this damn strike behind us."

"You aren't implying that we had anything to do with it, are you?" asked Clare quickly. "That the CIO somehow was behind this?"

"I don't know."

Clare laughed derisively. "Oh come on, Charlie. The CIO hired outsiders, Commies, to come in here and attack our own meeting?"

"I said I don't know."

"Do you actually think that I would be a party to that?" Clare's voice continued to rise as he pointed at Lydia's hands. "Goddamn it, Charlie. You think I would have something to do with hurting the woman I love?"

Now Deets' face softened. "Of course not, Clare." He smiled at Lydia. "Of course not. But I am saying that I have talked to the owners. I have talked to the AFL. I have now talked to you—and I hear the same story from everyone: 'We didn't do it.'" Deets paused. "But I know that those hooligans were here. I know that twenty people were hurt. And I know that the ones who were released were talking about blowing up one of the rail lines to Everett."

"My God," said Clare.

"That's my point," continued Deets. "I've got to get an end to this damned thing before things get truly out of hand."

Clare sat quietly while Lydia questioned the sheriff about the details. He looked outside as the afternoon sun began breaking through the clouds. As Deets began to excuse himself, Clare returned to the conversation.

"I will make you this promise," said Clare. "I will make sure that the CIO puts all of its resources into the hunt for those characters. We'll help you find them, Charlie."

Deets smiled and nodded.

"And Charlie," said Clare as Deets began to close the door. "I'll do my damndest to bring this thing to a close quickly."

The sheriff nodded again but didn't answer. Once again, the old nurse swept into the room. She stopped when she saw the tray. "You didn't touch a thing, dearie." Her face looked stricken. "How are you ever going to recover?"

"I ate the pudding," said Lydia quickly.

The old woman looked at the empty pudding cup and let out a snort. "The sheriff ate that, dearie. He's the only one in the town who'll touch that stuff."

❄    ❄    ❄

Lydia expected Clare to explode as soon as the nurse walked out. But instead, he turned back to the list of tasks in preparation for Lydia's return home. "Both Liz and Shelley will help, of course," said Clare. "I've talked to both. Liz will do all the washing and Shelley will help. She's especially good with cooking. So she can help old Mrs. Whatsher name..."

"Woolsey."

"That's right." He seemed to study the last item. "Oh yeah. I almost forgot. Earl Talbert and his wife want to have you over for a little get together this coming Saturday night—just a few friends."

"A dinner? In the middle of all this?"

"All of what?"

"For God's sake, Clare, the sheriff just said that Communist flame throwers are being hired to disrupt your strike and you ask, 'What?'"

Clare waved his hand. "Oh that. I expected the AFL and the owners to pull a stunt like that a long time ago."

"So you aren't worried about it?"

"I didn't say I wasn't worried. I said that I expected it. As to worried, well, I think the key in all this is when Ashford & Southern decides to sign the contract with the CIO. When that happens, it's just a matter of time."

"And how many more Molotov cocktails, in the meantime?"

Clare's face broke into a broad grin. "I should've known that an English teacher would know the correct reference to Mr. Vladimir Molotov..."

"Forget the history lesson, Clare." Lydia's voice reflected the concern in her face.

Clare shrugged. "I personally doubt we'll see any more of those. I think that was a one-time effort—designed to do just what we saw a few minutes ago. It rattled a lot of people and"—he nodded toward Lydia's hands—"hurt a good many and made the powers-that-be like Charlie Deets try to force us to give in."

Lydia lay back on the bed. The glinting afternoon sun—so rare this deep into the autumn—filled the room with golden light, turning the stark room into a basket of yellow and tan. But it couldn't warm the feeling inside her. "Clare, I wish I were so positive." She sighed. "I've been through this before, you know."

He smiled softly as he came to the bedside, stroking her hair. "Lydia, I'm not in danger. Nothing is going to happen. We are going to have a happy life. We are going to get married. We are even going to prove to Albert that he should be happy about it."

Lydia groaned. "God, Albert. What'll he say when he hears about this," she said, raising her gauze-covered hands.

"I've sent word," said Clare quickly. "I wanted him to know so he could come home."

Lydia's voice sounded shrill, even to herself. "You did what?"

"I've sent word to the Skybillings crew that you were injured in the blast and..."

"Goddamn it, Clare, how could you? He's the last person I want to know."

Clare shook his head, a look of surprise mixing with the concern that he'd done something contrary to her wishes. "But I thought sure you'd want him here."

"For what? To tell me that I shouldn't associate with union organizers—that I shouldn't marry them?"

Lydia suddenly began to cry—loud sobs that shook her body. Clare held her, but the sobs continued. "What, sweetheart, what?"

Lydia held up her hands and looked at Clare as her cheeks shone in the late-day light. "Clare, can you imagine what he'll say when he learns I burned my hands?" Clare shook his head. The sudden burst of tears, the sobbing, the muffled speech had left him confused. He shook his head, as Lydia cleared her throat.

"Where's your literary wit suddenly gone, Clare?" Lydia's smile reflected no humor. "Don't you think Albert will find it somehow fitting that his mother burned her hands playing with something he thinks she shouldn't have touched anyway?"

Clare's shoulders slumped with the last statement. He held Lydia close, hoping that the sobs would not begin again.


## Chapter 47

Albert touched the wood at his feet with a wet finger. Torn to shreds, he thought, probably by one of the spikes. Somebody had probably tried to drive a spike into the beam, had hit a knot, then moved further down and tried again. Yet even in the pouring rain, the sharpness of the splinters somehow felt dry to his touch. Dry in the pounding rain, thought Albert. If only he could stay as dry as the damn wood on the trestle.

The first night of sentry duty wasn't bad—the sky was clear, with the moon so bright he could make out the half that hid in the shadow. But now, on the second night, the clouds had moved in and a cold wind had begun. Zoe had given all the sentries extra blankets—with a hole cut out for their heads—to wear under their ponchos, and a flask of hot coffee. But Albert now sat on the trestle feeling cold and wet.

Bud Cole had placed Bucky Rudman at the far end of the trestle; Albert in the middle, sitting directly on the tracks; and Little Boy at the near end. Three of the new men crawled down onto the crossbars. All of them carried flashlights with powerful beams that could be seen from a long distance. The plan was to signal each hour. The trestle was much too long for shouts to be heard, especially if the weather got bad.

And it had, suddenly, that afternoon—heavy, cold rain with growing wind that sent all of the men under their heavy ponchos.

Visibility was only a few feet in any direction. Albert could see the track at his feet, but nothing else.

As the rain increased, Albert had stopped pacing and settled onto the track, sitting between the two rails, his rear pressing against one, his feet against the other. He rearranged the poncho to stay as dry as possible, pressing it firmly between himself and the rails both in front and back. He slipped another poncho underneath himself to keep the water and wind from blowing upward through the railroad ties and crossbeams, thus creating a plastic cocoon. The only opening was a thin slit for his eyes and mouth, which he held tight against the rain. Every hour, he flashed his light toward Little Boy, who flashed back, and Bucky, who did the same.

Slowly, he felt warmth return to his legs. The thick rubber of the poncho also held heat, he discovered. He rested his arms on his knees, and looked out of the small slit. What was he supposed to see in a blinding rainstorm? He studied the distance, but it was pure blackness. He looked upward, to where he knew the tall firs stood at the rim of the canyon, but again, nothing. To the left and right, then downward—not even an outline.

For several minutes, his body felt as if it were floating. Why shouldn't he float?—he laughed to himself. He was on a trestle, in the middle of the air, hanging where the hawks of summer had hung. The thought of the summer hawks comforted him, as the warmth began creeping up his back, and his chin sank onto his arms, which curled even tighter around his knees.

Had the rain subsided? He couldn't tell. He opened his eyes for a moment, but again saw only black.

As his chin nuzzled into the warmth of his arms, he tried to remember—how long ago did he first see the hawks? May? Was he working for St. Bride? Albert laughed—he'd been here long enough that he couldn't remember when he started. He could still see St. Bride's face—ugly smile, stubby white whiskers, the drooping gray eyes, pot belly. The son of a bitch. Would it be too much to hope that, at this very moment, he was lying dead in a ditch somewhere?

Albert then saw another face next to St. Bride's. He thought he recognized it, but the fatigue was too great. He couldn't make it out. It was fat, like St. Bride's. It was fat—was it Delbert? But Delbert wasn't laughing, like normal. It was a sneer. At him? Before he could decide, Albert heard a terrible whining sound and screaming. His name. He thought it was his name. He could now see Delbert's face as he had just a few days before—the blood was pouring from Delbert's mouth, the teeth broken, and the scream. That awful gurgling sound.

"Stop!" shouted Albert. "Stop!" In an instant, the faces and the screams and all sounds were gone—snapped away by a gust of wind.

He lifted his chin and peered through the slot of the poncho—the rain now was battering the trestle like pellets. He stood, but slipped—the footing suddenly icy. He flicked his flashlight several times toward Little Boy, but the night was too black to see the response. He turned to look into the woods—but a blast of cold wind and pellets hit him. The rain had now turned to sleet and snow. Again he flashed the light, but still no answer.

Albert checked to make sure the flashlight was working, then tried again. Still nothing.

Wrapping the poncho tight around him and holding the flashlight as close to his body as possible, he set out toward Little Boy's end of the trestle. "If you don't get a response when you flash, start walking," Bud had said. For a moment, Albert hesitated. The wind howled. The trestle had turned icy. He tried not to think about the fact that he was walking on a narrow piece of wood standing above a deadly deep ravine.

But he knew he had little choice. Just step carefully, he told himself. You'll be alright. Keep the light focused between the tracks. If you walk there, you won't go over the side—even if you slip. But the wind came now in hard gusts, ripping at the poncho, then blasting it into billows from the bottom. Every step demanded complete concentration. He wrapped both hands around the flashlight, his elbows tight at his sides to keep the poncho under control.

"Little Boy!" shouted Albert. He guessed he was almost halfway to the end. "Hey, Little Boy! Everything alright?" The only answer was a blast of sleet. He bent low, and shouted again. But again, only sleet and snow.

Albert felt a flash of heat rush upward from his stomach and across his chest. He swung the beam of light around. Then around again. But no movement. He backed up several steps, shining the light just beyond where he'd stopped. As he did, the beam fell upon a hand lying across the track. The fingers, slender, delicate like a woman's, swam in a river of crimson, but were otherwise covered in sleet. They gripped the frozen rail, as if examining it closely, or perhaps trying to lift it gently, without disturbing anything around it.

"Little Boy," whispered Albert, as he bent down. The body lay along the right rail. A knife, in the center of a red circle, protruded from his back, just below the left shoulder. For several seconds, Albert held Little Boy, as if clinging to him might squeeze out the death. But a blast of wind caught him full force, and he dropped Little Boy as he clutched the nearest rail with both hands.

Albert tried to signal Bucky Rudman at the far end of the trestle. Once again, no signal returned.

Then, a low moan. From behind him. Albert swung around to find Little Boy on hands and knees.

"Jesus, Little Boy! You're alive!"

Little Boy moaned again, louder. The blood stain around the knife was now wider. Albert bent down, but couldn't see his face against the black night. "What can I do? How can I stop the bleeding?"

The voice was low, carried on ragged breath. "Bucky."

"Who did this, Little Boy?"

Little Boy cursed. A heavy sigh. "Find Bucky." The voice was slightly stronger.

Albert flashed the light again toward Bucky. Still no response. He turned back to Little Boy, who hadn't moved. Then he made his decision. He stood up, as much as he could in the driving sleet and snow, and started back toward Bucky's end of the trestle, which was now covered in white.

Why was he doing this? He should get off the trestle as fast as possible. Death awaited him on every side. He knew all of this.

Again he tried the flashlight. Again he shouted. He hunched down further, trying to keep his balance.

He continued forward for several minutes before he came upon what he knew he would find. The flashlight beam picked up the wide pool of blood in the deepening snow. At the edge of it lay Bucky, face-up across the tracks, a mask of red across his face. A deep purple gash ran across Bucky's throat.

Albert fell to his knees and vomited. His hands and legs shook, and gusts of stinging sleet could not cool the awful, suffocating heat that filled his chest and throat. He felt like he was about to fall, so he lay on his belly between the rails.

"Think. Think." He said the words out loud, his voice trembling. He studied the blackness, searching for any form, listening for any sound. But the only sound was the wind, the only movement was the stinging sleet that slapped his face. Little Boy was near death. Bucky was dead. There were three more Skybillings men underneath the trestle, but they were probably dead too. Or, if not, at least too far away to be of any help.

Whoever attacked Little Boy and Bucky must have started on the far ends of the trestle. But why hadn't they reached him? And where were they now? He tried to shake the questions from his mind because he knew he had a much bigger challenge—to get off the trestle, and back to the camp, or at least into the woods for cover. Whoever tried to kill Little Boy and Bucky must still be on the trestle, or underneath it.

The last thought lodged a ray of hope. Maybe the killers went down into the crossbeams for the other two sentries—that's why Albert was still alive. But if that were the case, it wouldn't take long before they would emerge on top again—and begin looking for him. Perhaps it was that thought, or the fear, he didn't know, but now he was running, ignoring the sleet, the icy surface, the blasts of wind. His mind saw only the end of the trestle and the protection of the woods beyond.

His flashlight and eyes now fell upon the blood where Little Boy had lain. But he was no longer there. "Oh my God!" shouted Albert. The thought that Little Boy had slipped over the edge, made him want to throw up again. Albert knew that Little Boy couldn't have made his way off the trestle any other way.

So he kept going. His footing often gave way, but every time he fell, it was between the tracks. As he ran, he held his body low, hoping that if somebody was on the trestle, the force might send him over the side.

Within perhaps a minute, he had reached the end of the trestle and nestled himself inside bushes at the end. He gulped breaths deeply, trying to listen to the woods around him. But still the pounding sleet and the howling wind prevailed. Now, it was added to by the roar of the firs overhead.

But at least he was off the trestle, he decided. Off the trestle and still alive. And hidden. For several minutes, he waited, gathering his breath and trying to think clearly.

The voices startled him. They were still well out on the trestle. Perhaps fifty feet away. As soon as he heard them, Albert leapt from the bushes and began running.

"Look up-ahead. Who the hell is that?" The voice was not far behind him, still out on the trestle.

"Jesus, I thought they were all dead," came another.

But Albert was already in a full sprint, too frightened to try to place the voices. He crossed the open area where the crummy unloaded men in the morning. Occasionally he slipped, landing alongside the track, but the voices seemed to be growing no closer. In fact, they'd stopped. He could see flashlight beams swinging wildly well behind him.

Albert willed himself to be calm. I know these woods, he told himself. I can slip into them at any point. They'll never find me. But he had to get to camp—to warn Bud, to get help. He raced passed the site of the Shay crash and rounded the corner where the ravine dropped straight away, then he looped back again for the long descent toward the camp. His feet crashed hard against the frozen gravel. But as he did, he saw several forms just ahead, standing on the tracks, holding lanterns that swayed in the wind.

He stopped instantly and considered dashing into the brush, but more men stepped from behind trees on either side. Perhaps eight men stood across the track, most holding lanterns. Two or three more on each side.

"Hello, Albert."

The voice was young, and strangely coarse, as if unaccustomed to speaking loudly in public. Yet Albert found something familiar in it. This was a voice he knew, a voice he'd worked with. But from this distance, he couldn't make out a face. Only a shadow, cast long in the driving sleet by the swaying lanterns.

"I said, 'Hello, Albert.'"

Albert stepped forward slowly as he searched the sides of the track for any possible route of escape. But the forest was black around him. A small stream raced beneath the track not far ahead, emerging in a torrent to his right. The lanterns now swung around him to the left and right so that they were nearly parallel with him.

For several seconds, Albert did not speak as he surveyed the scene: There were ten or eleven of them. Large men, hidden deep inside great coats that scraped the rails as they walked. None of the faces was visible, though the movement of the lanterns illuminated an occasional silhouette.

He felt himself shiver as the voice finally spoke again. "You remember when I asked you if you'd ever thought about killing a man,

Albert?" The question was followed by a fierce laugh. A slight movement of one of the lanterns cast light fully upon Conrad Bruel's face. Albert could see the ugly square smile, the fierce expression that contorted rage with the laughter. "I bet you didn't know that you were the one I was thinking about killing."

Albert studied the face and heard the words. But the pounding in his chest blocked any answer. He stared at the face, then into the darkened hoods of the others.

"What's wrong, Albert," said Conrad as he took a step closer and raised his arm. "Cat got your tongue?"

Albert suddenly felt an intense warmth well up inside him, followed by a snarl that hardly sounded like his own voice. "You're a sonofabitch, Conrad," shouted Albert into the driving sleet. "You aren't going to kill me. You don't have the balls."

This brought laughter from the group of men—a sound that Albert could identify only as a rumbling in the blowing snow. The lanterns swayed as they laughed.

"You don't understand, Albert," said Conrad, stepping even closer now. "We killed your friend Little Boy and his partner Rudman." Conrad's face was close now. Albert could feel his breath. "We had the balls, Albert. And you're next, because you had the bad luck of sentry duty on the wrong night."

Though Albert obviously knew both Little Boy and Bucky Rudman were dead, the report of it—perhaps its starkness, or the brutal way it was reported— brought such finality. Bucky Rudman dead on the trestle—his throat cut. Little Boy dead on the rocks at the bottom of the ravine.

Albert suddenly spit into Conrad's face. "How could you kill those guys?" snarled Albert. For a moment, the taller man remained motionless, as if not believing that the saliva hung on his cheek. Then he stepped back, his forehead furrowed deeply, as he wiped his face with a side of his hood.

In an instant, the confusion seemed to leave Conrad's face as he raised his rifle and leveled it directly at Albert's eyes. "Your problem, Albert, is that you never understood one thing," said Conrad softly. "Loggers ain't paid to think. They're paid to act—to do dirty jobs and collect dirty paychecks and fuck dirty women and..."

"Put the gun down, Conrad."

The voice came from behind Albert, but Albert didn't turn. The barrel of Conrad's rifle remained steady, only a few inches in front of Albert's eyes.

"I said to put the gun down, Conrad."

Slowly the barrel dropped. Albert took a deep breath. He'd forgotten the group of men pursuing him. He now turned to face them. As he did, he looked directly into the face of Clare Ristall.

For a moment, both men stared at each other in silence. Clare's face seemed caught between offering a friendly greeting—as if they'd run into each other in front of Walther's store—and turning away in horror. The face was set deep inside a black, wool hood, coated with sleet. One of the lanterns that was now behind Albert illuminated Clare's face fully.

"Albert," said Clare finally. The wind suddenly gusted, casting the lanterns violently back and forth. The effect was to flicker black and white shadows across Clare's face.

But Albert did not answer. He held the eyes tightly with his own, as if looking hard at Clare would give him the answers he needed.

Clare's voice rung out loudly, as he barked orders to the men behind him. Albert heard something about relighting lanterns that had gone out and something about when the crummy was supposed to meet them. But his mind was lost in the confusion of standing on an isolated track, in a blinding storm, high in the Cascades, and looking into the face of Clare Ristall.

"The crummy is s'posed to get here in about ten minutes," shouted one of the men from behind. Clare checked his watch, then turned back to Albert. The face now bore a look of sadness. If there was confusion on it before, it was now resolved.

"Clare, what in the hell is this all about?" asked Albert in a gasp. "What's going on? Why are you here?"

"We don't have time for questions or explanations, Albert," said Clare quickly. He fumbled with the lantern he held, as the wind suddenly gusted. Clare smiled as he looked up. "You hear that sound in the trees? Feel that sleet?" Clare now turned his face into the cutting wind. "That's the cover we've been waiting for, Albert. That and the confusion in the valley, of course." Clare now seemed the consummate businessman, the debater who seemed so confident from last summer at the fair. "We can get this business with Skybillings done, and we can get on with the important work ahead."

Albert listened to the words, he watched the mouth, he saw the eyes—but he could not fathom that this was Clare. Albert studied the men behind Clare, then turned around to see Conrad Bruel still holding the rifle. "Who are all these people, Clare? Is this some sort of union shit?"

This question brought loud laughter from the group of men around him. "Union shit!" laughed one of the men. "Just like you planned it, Clare."

"Shut up!" shouted Clare. "I will do the talking here." The man quickly turned away. Clare smiled as he turned back to Albert. "You have one choice, Albert. No—you have no choice, come to think of it. You can shut your mouth and take part of the prize, or you can, well, face the future that Conrad described a moment ago."

Albert laughed nervously. He studied Clare's face—now dominated by a friendly smile. This was the Clare from the backyard conversation last summer. The Clare Ristall who told him to get out of the woods. To find a different job.

"Are you saying you are going to kill me? You, Clare, you?" Albert laughed again, this time drawing his face close to Clare's. "I was right about you, wasn't I? I was right about how you weren't to be trusted. About how your union would always be more important than my mother or anything she cared about."

"She told me to come and get you."

"What? Who?"

"You knew she was hurt in the explosion in the meeting house, didn't you?" Clare's smile abruptly vanished as he asked the question.

"My mother? You're talking about my mother?"

"She's fine," said Clare, "in case you care. But she wanted me to come and tell you that it was alright for you to join with us...."

"Join you? You're a lying son of a bitch, Clare."

Albert sensed a sudden motion behind him. As he turned, a dark shape lunged from the bushes, arms outstretched, and slammed into Conrad and the two men standing beside him. The bodies crumbled, but Albert could see that Little Boy had already cut Conrad's throat wide open—and the knife that had been lodged deeply in Little Boy's back was now gone.

As others dove for Little Boy, Albert fell to the ground, then rolled into the stream that ran underneath the tracks. In an instant, he was on his feet, racing for the woods. The bloody melee startled the men so much that he was able to slip between them and get a head start.

They quickly recovered and began racing after him, but Albert had the advantage. He knew this streambed. The image in his mind was of the summer, as he wandered down a similar stream—trying to find a shortcut down the mountain to the camp. Was it that stream he now followed or a different one? He couldn't be sure, but he kept low to the water, to avoid the overhang of limbs that he recalled from summer. Several seconds later, he heard shouts as the men behind him got snarled in them.

Albert stayed low, then dropped to his hands and knees to hold onto the rocks as the stream began to break over the cliff. As he did, he felt his foot touch the shale that had engulfed him in summer. Without looking back, he leapt feet first onto the unsteady rock fragments that, once again, instantly turned into an avalanche.

❃   ❃   ❃

Had it been ten minutes? A half hour? Albert's only sense of time was the thin gray light of near-dawn. Zoe clanged the dinner bell as men poured from their cabins—some carrying guns, others axes and hammers—as they pulled on coats or boots; all racing for the Shay, which was already beginning to blow steam. And in the center of them—shouting orders—was Bud Cole.

As soon as Albert had stormed through Bud's cabin door and reported the events on the trestle, Bud had begun giving orders: Go tell Fergie to get the Shay ready. Start banging on each cabin door. Tell the men to arm themselves with whatever they can find. Then Bud stopped—as if he'd forgotten something—and tossed Albert the pistol that had been in his pocket.

"Here, you'll need this," said Bud. "I've got another."

Albert caught the gun. It felt heavier than Albert imagined a gun would feel.

"It may come in handy if you have another conversation with Clare Ristall," said Bud, as he pulled on his pants.

Albert laughed softly. Something in the look on Bud's face and the sound of his voice suggested that Bud hoped they would get a chance at Clare. Now Bud was racing toward the Shay—suspenders flapping, shirt unbuttoned, a rifle in each hand.

Within minutes, the Shay, with the crummy attached, was moving full speed. Lightning Stevens and Myles Norgren crawled onto the roof of the crummy, rifles pointed forward. Petey Hulst and Svenson the Swede positioned themselves at the sides, along with several other men—guns pointed outward. And Harry Bachelder made his way onto the platform of the Shay, alongside Bud and Fergie.

"Albert, get up here," shouted Bachelder over the roar. Albert scurried forward, a wall of dry heat enveloping him as he stepped into the cab and out of the wind.

"You right or left handed?" asked Bachelder, as Bud scanned the track ahead.

"Left," shouted Albert.

"Good." He pointed to the platform running along the left side of the cab. "Get ready with your pistol."

"C'mon Fergie, give it more power," shouted Bud to Ferguson.

"I can't go any faster without more steam, goddamn it!"

Bud and Bachelder began tossing more wood into the open furnace, as Ferguson opened the throttle further. Albert watched the trees race by as the light grew strong enough to make out the track ahead.

"Those bastards are long gone," shouted Ferguson to Bud. "Why the hell are we trying to tear the guts out of this Shay?"

Bud shook his head. "It ain't them I'm worried about, Fergie. It's the trestle."

Fergie turned full face to Bud. "We're headed for the trestle?"

"Damn right."

The old man shrugged his shoulders and began slowing the Shay to make the turn to the spur that would take them up the mountain. Albert studied the blank whiteness around them—the firs hung low with ice, the underbrush along the track seemed crisscrossed with white webs. He looked back into the crummy, wondering how Lightning and Norgren could lie on their stomachs so long on the icy roof. But he saw no sign of them. Only the others crouched along the edges, rifles ready.

Within seconds, the Shay had made the turn and was building speed for the race up the mountain. Occasionally, he heard Bud Cole shout for more, and Fergie curse in response, but Albert focused entirely on the track up ahead—as if trying to find the exact spot where he'd run into Conrad and Clare. But the only sight up the track was white.

Albert repositioned himself as they rounded one sweeping curve, resettled further forward on the Shay's narrow ledge, and looked out again. He peered hard into the distance, but this time, a black pinpoint appeared—where the two rails merged into one. As he studied it, he thought it might be an animal or rock which had lost its covering of frozen sleet. But it kept moving, and coming closer.

"Bud, look down the track!" shouted Albert, which drew all of the men to the windows in the cab. "It's a crummy—coming this way!"

The cloud of snow, along with steam rising, was the final proof. "Give it more throttle, Fergie!" shouted Bud.

Ferguson cursed. "If we go any faster, it'll be a head-on!" shouted the engineer.

"I said, more throttle, Fergie!" said Bud, as he positioned himself at the right window.

Albert felt his stomach tighten at the prospect of confronting Clare. He fingered the pistol, now feeling warm and comfortable in his hand. He let the safety out and stretched his hand forward—for the first time beginning to aim as the crummy was clearly visible.

"They've slowed down," shouted Bachelder. "They've spotted us, so they're trying to go back the other way."

Sure enough, the crummy had slowed and reversed directions. Though it was now moving in the same direction as the Shay, the Skybillings crew was gaining rapidly. Albert heard several sharp *pings* explode on the metal overhead, followed by shots from the Skybillings crew.

"Shoot at the metal in the back-end of the thing," shouted Bachelder to Norgren and Lightning. "We can blast through it—it's thin enough." This brought more shots from the Skybillings crew, but the crummy didn't slow.

In fact, it was now at full speed perhaps fifty yards ahead. Albert watched the track in the distance. They would soon reach the hairpin turn at the top of the mountain—where every morning he held his breath as the sharp drop on the other side came into view. How could either the crummy up ahead or the Skybillings Shay navigate the turn at such a speed?

"I've gotta slow her down, Bud," shouted Fergie. "The curves are coming up."

"Don't slow, goddamn it!"

Ferguson erupted. "You big dumb son of a bitch! Use your head. If I don't slow, we're going over into that fucking ravine as sure as I've got two balls and a pecker." With that, Albert felt the locomotive slow, as the crummy ahead suddenly lurched forward.

"Goddamn it!" shouted Bud.

As they slowed, Albert spotted a thick lump directly next to the right rail, covered in a garment of white, no evidence of blood or the deadly struggle. Should they slow or stop for it? Should he tell Bud?

Now Harry Bachelder was trying to reason with Bud. "Why the hell run such a risk, Bud? Those guys can't get away. There's no way out at the other end—just ice and snow. They'll freeze to death if they try to walk home."

Bud shook his head. "There ain't anybody craftier at moving around these mountains than Clare Ristall," shouted Bud. "Nobody. You let him get out of sight and he'll find his way through the snow and out of here somehow. We've got to get them."

The crummy entered the tight turn at nearly full speed, letting out a loud whine as metal bore down on metal. Albert could see the right wheels lift slightly as it took the turn, but the crummy stayed on the track. Once through the turn, it increased speed and shot through the hairpin turns where the Shay had crashed in the spring.

The Skybillings Shay was quick to follow. Though Fergie had cooled the steam slightly to make the sharp turn, he gave it a sharp boost of power when it came out. The old Shay seemed to shoot across the track where it usually plodded. And though the crummy was now out of sight, Albert had a clear sense that they were gaining ground on it.

As they rounded the final approach to the trestle, there it stood, right in front of them, perhaps fifty or sixty yards onto the trestle, just beyond its mid-point. It had come to a complete stop. Fergie jammed the brake on the Shay, but it was too late. The momentum of the locomotive carried it well onto the trestle. Albert felt the icy mist from the waterfalls that fell down the face of Three Sisters. Below, the open ravine yawned outward.

The pounding of the Skybillings engine finally slowed. And the locomotive, with the crummy in tow, came to a stop. Then near silence.

"My God, what's he doing?" asked Bachelder, as the whole crew watched Clare Ristall step onto the tracks, just in front of his crummy. He held something in his hand, but Albert couldn't tell what it was. He was waving his arms.

"Don't shoot!" shouted Clare. "If you do, we'll set off the dynamite." Bud shouted for his men to hold their fire.

"I want to talk to you, Bud Cole," shouted Clare. The breeze clipped his words.

Bud hesitated. But then he stepped out onto the Shay's metal ledge that ran just above the rails. "We got nothing to talk about, Clare. I was right about you all along."

Clare laughed loudly. Albert sensed no hint of hatred or desperation in the voice. "No, Bud. You didn't figure me out at all. You're as oblivious as you ever were."

Albert heard a safety unlatch overhead, but Bud waved again for all guns to be put down.

"Come on out, Cole—onto the trestle," shouted Clare. "Just you and me, Bud. Man to man." Clare motioned with his free arm.

Bud studied Clare closely for several seconds, then jumped onto the tracks and took several paces forward. He now stood directly in front of the steaming Shay—perhaps a hundred feet from Clare. The stiff wind rippled the pant legs of both men, as the mist coated them with ice.

"So what do you want, Clare?" Bud stood directly between the two tracks. "You know you and your boys can't get away."

The cold wind ruffled the hood that had been nestled on Clare's shoulders. A thin layer of ice lay across it.

"This has got an eerie kind of cops-and-robbers feel about it, doesn't it, Cole?" shouted Clare. He laughed loudly again. "A come-out-with-your-hands-up kind of thing, I guess."

Bud didn't answer. He studied the crummy behind Clare, trying to spot other members of his gang.

"There's no use looking for them, Bud," said Clare quickly. "They're gone—all of them. They crawled off—down your trestle before the Shay came around that last corner. They all got away."

Bud looked downward, between his feet, into the girders under the tracks, but didn't see anyone below. This again brought laughter from Clare.

"We could've surrounded you, you big dumb ox," said Clare as the wind began blowing more strongly. "We could've picked your boys off from the back, but I told them just to get the hell out. I told them I'd take care of it all myself." There was a pause now. "You do know that I'm something of a philanthropist, don't you Cole? It just seemed right for a guy like me to let my men get out alive, while the captain goes down with the ship."

"Clare, you're crazy."

"Crazy? Me?" This time the laughter was even louder, but then it died away quickly. "No, I'm not crazy, Cole. I'm the only logical one around here. I'm the only one who sees how goddamn foolish all of this is, and the only one who is willing to accept that simple fact and then put his energy to work for a worthy purpose—like trying to save men's lives, trying to make their lives better. I'm afraid that you're the crazy one, Bud—because you believe all this shit, and you want to succeed in it more than you want to do anything else in life. Isn't that right? Yet in the process of achieving that dream, you go about making the lot of man even more miserable than it is."

For several seconds, there was silence. Albert heard only the wind and the roar of the waterfalls against the mountain. Clare was silent, rigid against the white backdrop. Bud stood motionless, his gun at his side.

"So this is what all your union organizing comes down to, Clare?" shouted Bud. "It all comes down to blowing up a trestle? Trying to destroy a company? How does that save lives? You destroy men to save them?"

Clare seemed angry for the first time. "This has nothing to do with unions. The CIO isn't behind this—you understand me, Cole? You were wrong the day you came to my office. And you are dead wrong now." Clare paused as if surveying the entire scene—the trestle, Three Sisters, the Shay, and the two men who now stood opposite one another. "No, this has to do with decisions, Cole—with the brains to understand what those decisions mean, and the guts to own up to the consequences."

The two men now stood in silence, as if each was waiting for the other to act.

Finally, Clare spoke. "Here's my proposal, Cole," shouted Clare, with the smile again on his face. "If you let me go, I won't blow this little dream of yours to smithereens. I'll just disappear into that far ridge there." Clare turned and pointed into the white distance. "You'll never hear from me again, and you'll have your little company going gangbusters—everyone lived happily ever after," said Clare.

He stopped now, as if trying to fix the full measure of the man facing him on the tracks. "But if you decide to try to capture me or kill me," now Clare paused to hold up a small, metal plunger mechanism,

"I will drive this little baby home and this whole trestle, with you and your crew and your little dream, will go down in a ball of flames."

Albert sensed the other men in the crew beginning to look around—to sort through how far out they were on the trestle. Sure enough, the Shay was well beyond the edge of the ravine. Below them was air, hundreds of feet of it, then rocks. Any explosion would bring down the whole trestle. And there was no time to get back.

Bud slowly turned his head toward the Shay, then looked down, and back at Clare.

"Choices are hard aren't they, Cole?" Clare's voice had a sudden calm now. The laughter was gone. "Sometimes a man has to make a choice that has bad results, no matter how much he'd like to avoid them. I made my choice, Cole. Now it's your turn, my friend."

Suddenly, a shot rang out from the Skybillings cab and Clare Ristall doubled over. As he did, he lunged forward onto the plunger, which disappeared into the metal box at his feet.

Albert saw a brilliant flash and felt the trestle sway, then pitch violently in the middle as a mighty explosion tore away the section of track under Clare. The crummy that had stood behind him tilted slightly to the left, then fell into open air, twisting sharply before plummeting onto the rocks below. Albert could see Clare's body disappear underneath the pile of metal just as it smashed into the rock.

As it did, another explosion rocked the trestle—this one perhaps fifty yards beyond the first. Then another, and another, until the whole span, from in front of the Skybillings Shay to the distant edge of the ravine, was fully ablaze or had fallen into the gorge. The only section still standing was the one on which the Shay was sitting.

As soon as the trestle began to rumble, Albert had tried to get off of the Shay. But each time he tried, he'd been flung back. Now, he grabbed the ladder and worked his way down.

But as he finally landed on the trestle, he found that he no longer wanted to run away from the intense heat and destruction that spanned the width of the gorge. Something held him firmly in place—both feet planted firmly on the track bed as he hung onto the side of the Shay. He only wanted to look at the wreckage of the trestle—its twisted legs scattered on the rocks below, an occasional bent still standing, but fully aflame. The huge gap over the gorge again opened up, except for the short section of the trestle that still held the Shay.

As he peered into the glow of the burning trestle, he caught a glimpse of Bud Cole—standing just in front of the Shay, only a few feet from what was now open air, watching the orange flames beyond. A few feet behind him stood Harry Bachelder.

As the last piece of trestle at the far edge of the ravine collapsed, Harry walked up to Bud and put his arm around his shoulder. Against the white of the winter sleet and the orange billows of the explosions in the distance, the two men looked to Albert like a single, very small, silhouette.

# Book Four: Winter 1937

## Chapter 48

Charlie Deets laid the spoon carefully on the delicate china saucer and slurped the cinnamon-colored coffee. He held it in his mouth for a moment, as if sampling a fine wine, then swallowed quickly.

"The best part of being sheriff in Seakomish is that you can get the best food in town for free," said Deets. "But this here coffee is even better than our hospital stuff." Deets smiled broadly at Bertram Witstrop, who absently fingered the watch chain dangling from his vest.

"Fine, Sheriff. That's just fine," said Witstrop with a forced friendliness. He cleared his throat, but seemed suddenly at a loss for words. He turned to Bud Cole, who sat in a large wingback chair beside the tall windows lining Witstrop's office. Bud shrugged. Harry Bachelder—seated next to Witstrop at a long conference table—shook his head, then went back to studying the silhouette of the Olympic Mountains in the afternoon sun.

Witstrop started again. "Sheriff, you said you had a report for us?"

Deets seemed surprised by the voice. He looked at Witstrop quickly, then at the two other men. "Why, as a matter of fact, I sure do. Right here." Deets paused, then smiled. "What with this excellent coffee and enjoying this nice office of yours, Mr. Witstrop, I guess I got myself side-tracked." He opened up a small file.

How many weeks, Bud wondered, had he waited for this moment? How many nights had he awakened to the sound of the thunderous explosions and the scene of the trestle breaking into pieces? He'd tried to go back to the trestle—to study it, or crawl through the wreckage or, hell, maybe to just look at it—but by then the snows had closed Roosevelt Creek completely. He couldn't even get a mile out of Seakomish. Now, he fingered the tapestry of the wingback arm absently.

For a moment, just as Deets started reciting details, Bud wanted to get up and walk out. In fact, he cleared his throat loudly, preparing to excuse himself to the bathroom. All the eyes turned toward him, but he didn't move. His body sat heavily in the wingback. His boots clung firmly to the Persian carpet.

For the next fifteen minutes, Charlie Deets droned on, while Bud stared at the peaks of the distant mountains—as always, framed perfectly by Witstrop's windows. He listened to how the State inspectors had come out and sifted through the trestle just before the heavy snows hit. How the FBI had been called in. How Clare Ristall's books had been audited. When the sun finally broke through the clouds in the distance—casting deep red across Puget Sound and the tops of the Seattle buildings just below them—Bud heard the words that he had never wanted to hear.

"Clare Ristall's single target was Skybillings," said Deets. "He was taking money from Ashford & Southern to do their dirty work. And his biggest target in the Seakomish Valley was Skybillings."

Ashford & Southern, thought Bud. I'll be goddamned. The confrontation with Clare that day by the high school replayed in Bud's mind. What was it Clare had said? That Bud was just jealous; that he was afraid to admit that he had been in love with Lydia all these years. It was that line that had convinced Bud that he'd been wrong about Clare Ristall. At that point, he knew deep in his heart that it really wasn't the CIO that was after Skybillings.

How many times could a man be this wrong? He wished he had an answer.

Deets' voice interrupted. "The way the FBI pieced it together, along with the boys from the State, was this: Ashford & Southern's main goal was stopping Mr. Witstrop's company—Panama Northwest. Tuttle B. Ashford himself had decided that he was going to control all the Northwest logging and all the Northwest shipping. And Panama Northwest stood in his way."

Deets paused to look at Bud. "And Skybillings happened to be an agent of Panama Northwest—in Ashford's eyes. So they had to stop Skybillings—and a lot of other small logging companies like it in the State that were being funded by Panama Northwest. But Skybillings was the only one in the Seakomish Valley—and it was the first Clare was told to start with." Deets paused again. "So Nariff Olben, Little Boy Whittaker, and Bucky Rudman—and all those others—they died 'cause they were working for the wrong outfit."

Bud's eyes followed a ship moving gently past a low-slung ferry in the distance. The ship sat low in the water, loaded heavily with logs. He'd heard Deets' words, but they carried nothing new. Down deep, despite his questions, he'd known those facts for weeks now—lived with them, slept with them, woke up in a sweat with them. Men who worked for him were dead because of him.

The ship in the distance moved silently from where Bud sat. Its bow cut the water cleanly as it now moved well past the ferry. Were those logs from Skybillings perhaps, he wondered? Were they just now moving to the Orient? As he watched the ship disappear behind one of the buildings below him, the thought struck him: How terribly strange that he was sitting here. That he had even found Panama Northwest in the first place. That he had convinced them to give him money. If he'd just not decided to reopen Skybillings at all, there wouldn't have been a trestle, there wouldn't have been a battle with Clare Ristall, there wouldn't have been any of the destruction or the deaths.

"You still with us, Cole?" asked Witstrop.

Bud sat up in the chair and cleared his throat. "Sure. Just was trying to piece all of this together." He looked at Bachelder, whose face seemed narrower now, and Deets, and then began speaking as if his thoughts had focused only on the explanation. "So what you are saying, then, is that Clare Ristall was going after us because Ashford & Southern saw companies like us as Witstrop's best chance to keep them from gaining total control of the woods."

"Something like that," said Deets. "If Panama Northwest even got a toehold in the lumber market, they could prevent A&S from setting both lumber prices and shipping prices. And Skybillings was that toehold—at least in the Seakomish Valley. Course, there were plenty of other small logging shows up and down the Cascades—all of you the enemy in Ashford & Southern's eyes."

The room was silent again as the secretary tapped lightly on the door, then entered without waiting for approval. She carried another pot of coffee. "Just wonderful java, ma'am," said Deets quickly. The woman smiled, then closed the door quietly.

For the next several minutes, Bud listened intently as Deets listed the money involved. Ashford & Southern paid Clare $200,000 a year for several years. That allowed him to buy antiques and live lavishly.

"So he never really had money himself—his family, I mean?" asked Harry.

"Clare Ristall was poor as a church mouse," said Deets. "All his high living was from Ashford money."

"So the union was just a front—a cover for taking the money and doing A&S's dirty work."

Deets shook his head. "I wouldn't say that at all. From what we could tell—and the FBI did all this work—he spent most of his money on building his union. The antiques and paintings and all that stuff was just a little on the side."

Deets took a long sip. "No, it's my guess that Clare Ristall was a union man to his very soul. He believed in it, and he did everything he could to build it. And probably the most important thing of all is that he found a way to get the money to pay for it. As it happened, of course, it also required him to get in bed with the devil and to do the devil's dirty work here and there."

For several minutes, the men were silent. Witstrop paced in front of the windows, while Bud tried to sort through what Deets was saying. Deets waited.

Finally, Harry Bachelder spoke. "None of this makes any sense, Sheriff. Why the hell would Ashford & Southern pay a man to build a new, violent union right under their noses, just so they could hide a little dirty work on the side? They could've just hired a bunch of thugs to blow up our trestle."

Deets laughed. "What line of work are you in, Mr. Bachelder?"

"He's an engineer," snorted Witstrop quickly. The sharp tone drew a surprised look from both Bud and Harry, prompting Witstrop to add: "And a damn fine one." Bud had to laugh at the difference in attitude from the time that he and Harry had first paid Witstrop a visit.

"Well, you engineer folks are pretty logical I guess," said Deets. "But you can't forget the larceny and devious nature that can lie in the human soul. Ashford & Southern was scared as hell of the AFL—had been for years. Folks say the AFL strike of '35 didn't do much, but for Ashford & Southern, it brought home how powerful the union was in closing down business."

"So when a bunch of upstarts inside the AFL started making noise about breaking away, Tuttle Ashford saw his opening. He decided he could kill two birds with one stone—fund the upstarts so they could start tearing apart the AFL, then hide behind all the ruckus and diversion they created to go after the companies he needed to destroy."

Deets suddenly had a broad smile on his face, as if the clever strategy pleased even him. "You gotta respect the brains behind that. What better diversion could a man ask for than battles between the unions? Hell, the companies were just standing on the sidelines watching the unions beat the shit out of each other. So why should anybody suspect that Ashford & Southern was behind it all, and that they would have anything to do with blasting the shit out of companies like Skybillings?"

Deets continued. "And Ashford & Southern figured that if the little CIO actually got out of control down the road, they could squash it much more quickly than it could stop the AFL. So, A&S made a pact with the devil, too. In their case, it was the CIO and Clare Ristall—at least as far as the Seakomish Valley was concerned."

The room was silent again. The rays of the cold afternoon sun illuminated the walnut table in shades of yellow and orange. The oriental carpet seemed more red than blue. In the distance, the harbor moved silently—ferries and freighters gliding toward, then past, one another. A thin layer of snow was visible on the docks below.

There was a symmetry in this, thought Bud. In the ships out in the distance, in the rays hitting the room, a kind of symmetry that paralleled the events Deets was reporting. Ashford & Southern, Clare Ristall, Bertram Witstrop, Bud Cole—all had made their pacts, all had seized their moments, all had tried to attain the ends that were most important to them at the risk of others' lives and fortunes. And now Witstrop and Cole were still standing, though barely. Clare Ristall was dead. Tuttle Ashford presumably off to jail somewhere.

"So where does this leave us, Sheriff?" asked Witstrop suddenly. All of the other men quickly turned to him, as if the new voice added something crisp to the proceedings. "I believe a question of insurance is before us here."

Deets cleared his throat. "Right, yes. Well, I can certify that all of the events as I have outlined them actually happened, which is probably all that your insurance people really need. Except for one thing." Deets smiled quickly, as if embarrassed. "There is some confusion about how Clare Ristall actually died."

Witstrop's voice was more of a wail than a shout. "What in God's name can you be talking about? You said yourself that he fell off the trestle, under his own crummy. Christ, man, he set off a dynamite charge. Everybody saw him go!"

Deets shook his head. "I fully understand that, Mr. Witstrop. But what Clare's death has to do with it is this: If he was shot by one of the Skybillings' men, then in all likelihood the insurance company is going to say that Skybillings caused this loss, and they won't cover it."

"Jesus!" roared Witstrop. "The fucking maniac was holding dynamite!"

"No difference. The insurance company will want my word as to who shot Clare Ristall." Charlie Deets now lowered his face and looked at Bud Cole and Harry Bachelder. "I've never asked either of you boys this question before. But there it is."

Bud Cole had wondered about this very question himself in the weeks since the accident. As the snow closed the mountains, as Bud settled back into his two rooms in Seakomish, as he tried to reconstruct the facts—thinking through it all, day after day—this question kept coming back. Who fired the shot?

Whoever had fired had taken the risk that the whole trestle would go down, and all of them with it. Whoever had fired either didn't care about that fact or, for some reason, hadn't believed that Clare had wired the whole trestle. For that matter, whoever fired didn't believe, or didn't care, that the explosions could reach them. But then a new thought entered Bud's mind. Maybe somebody thought that the trestle was strong enough, or structured in such a way, that the explosions wouldn't reach the portion that the Skybillings Shay and crew were standing on. And, of course, that was exactly how it turned out.

Bud had asked each of the men on his crew if they knew where the shot came from. Each had said they didn't know.

Harry Bachelder spoke softly. "Anybody who shot Clare Ristall would have known that we'd all die if he pushed that plunger." He paused and looked around him. "As an engineer, I can guarantee that there is no way that the trestle could have been designed to prevent it." He looked quickly at Witstrop and Bud, whose face was without color, before turning back to Deets. "I was standing in the cab, Sheriff. I can guarantee that no shots were fired from our side. Clare pushed the plunger of his own free will. I saw it."

The room was again silent, as the rays of the sun fell behind the mountains. A gray twilight filled the office. As Charlie Deets studied each man in turn, his eyes stopped with Bachelder. He looked closely at him—and held him in his gaze for several seconds.

"So you're telling me then, that there were no shots fired by Skybillings?"

"That's right." Bachelder continued to look back at Deets.

Deets turned to Bud, who seemed about to say something, but

didn't. A door slammed in the distance, perhaps in an outer office. The noise punctuated the silence in the room.

"That correct, Bud?" asked Deets.

Bud looked directly into Deets' face. "That's right, Sheriff. No shots were fired from our side."

A flicker of a smile crossed Deets' face. "Well, if that's the truth, then. If no shots were fired." Here again he paused. "Then I'll accept it," said Deets. He hesitated for a moment, looked at each of the men once more, quickly signed a piece of paper, and closed the file.

# Epilogue: Spring 1938

Albert pulled the car into the driveway of his mother's house and held the door open for Julia Stevens, Lightning Stevens' oldest daughter. As soon as the snows had stopped all logging, Albert had moved to Seakomish and rented a room above Walther's store, where he worked part-time. He had also saved enough money to buy an old Ford that Lightning Stevens owned.

It was in the process of buying the car that Albert met Julia— brown eyes, long black hair, and friendly, with a dry wit. After buying the car, Albert had paid her a number of visits—and they'd even gone to the movies twice in Seattle.

They knocked loudly on the door, but no one answered. "Mother," shouted Albert as he opened it slightly. "It's me."

Lydia came rushing from the kitchen, wiping her hands on a white dish towel. "What a surprise, come in, please."

He gave his mother a warm hug and introduced Julia.

"This is who I've been telling you about, Mom. Julia works for the Everett Chronicle, in the research department," said Albert quickly. "Been there—how long?"

"Two years," said Julia. She swept her long hair out of her face as she answered. Lydia noticed that the beauty of the girl's mother came through clearly. Julia explained her job, the kinds of calls she had to make, and described her boss—the prickly woman publisher named Meredith Cunningham.

Lydia drew in a slight breath at the sound of the name. "Are you okay, Mrs. Weissler?" asked Julia quickly.

Lydia nodded. "It's nothing. Just too much coffee for breakfast, I guess."

Albert settled in the chair opposite his mother. "Julia says there is an opening up there," said Albert softly.

"For a beginning reporter," she added. "I think Albert would be great for it."

Lydia turned to face her son. His legs splayed outward in the narrow chair, his face tanned and leathery, his hands surprisingly strong and rough: one held a chocolate chip cookie, the other rubbed the slight, bristly growth of beard he was trying to start.

"The Chronicle is a good paper," said Lydia. "Very good."

Albert spoke rapidly. "Julia says she thinks she could put in a good word. If it all works out, the opening would start in two weeks." He paused now. "We were wondering if you had time to, well, go down to the diner and have coffee and pie, and we could tell you about it?"

Lydia smiled. She sat back. She held her son and this beautiful girl in a long gaze. She was about to speak when someone knocked on the door.

"Actually I'd love to, but I had"—she walked to the doorway and just before she opened it, she added—"Well, I promised a friend that I'd go to the church dinner tonight."

She swung the door open. Bud Cole stood in the doorway, wearing a white shirt with a tie still loose at the collar.

Lydia turned to Albert with a small smile. "You don't mind if I take a rain check, do you, Son?"

# Selected Bibliography

Although novels rarely provide bibliographies, I want to highlight some of the outstanding resources I found helpful in understanding the history of railroad logging and union unrest in the Pacific Northwest during the 1930s.

## Books

Andrews, Ralph W. *Heroes of the Western Woods*. New York, NY: E. P. Dutton & Company, Inc. 1960.

Bohn, Dave and Rodolfo Petschek. *Kinsey Photographer: Volume One, The Family Album & Other Early Work*. New York, NY: Black Dog & Leventhal Publishers, 1978.

Booth, Douglas E. *Valuing Nature: The Decline and Preservation of Old-Growth Forests*. Lanham, MD: Rowman & Littlefield, 1994.

Clark, Norman H. *Mill Town: A Social History of Everett, Washington, from Its Earliest Beginnings on the Shores of Puget Sound to the Tragic and Infamous Event Known as the Everett Massacre*. Seattle and London: University of Washington Press, 1970.

Clark, Norman H. *Washington: A Bicentennial History*. New York, NY: W.W. Horton & Company, Inc. 1976.

Drushka, Ken. *Working in the Woods: A History of Logging on the West Coast*, Madiera Park, BC, Canada: Harbour Publishing, 1992.

Foner, Philip S. *History of the Labor Movement in the United States*. Vol. 4. New York: International Publishers, 1997.

Galenson, Walter. *The CIO Challenge to the AFL: A History of the American Labor Movement, 1935-1941*. Cambridge, MA: Harvard University Press, 1960.

Hidy, Ralph W., Frank Ernest Hill, Allan Nevins. *Timber and Men: The Weyerhaeuser Story*, New York, NY: The Macmillan Company, 1963.

Holbrook, Stewart H. *Holy Old Mackinaw: A Natural History of the American Lumberjack*, New York, NY: The Macmillan Company, 1946.

Peterson, Florence. *American Labor Unions: What They Are and How They Work*. 2nd Rev. ed. New York: Harper & Row, 1963.

Schwantes, Carlos Arnaldo. *Hard Traveling: A Portrait of Work Life in the New Northwest*. Lincoln, NE: University of Nebraska Press, 1994.

Stolberg, Benjamin T. *The Story of the CIO*. New York: Viking Press, 1971.

Washington Writers' Program. *Washington: A Guide to the Evergreen State*. Portland, OR: Binfords & Mort, 1941.

Zieger, Robert H. *The CIO, 1935-1955*. Chapel Hill, NC: University of North Carolina Press, 1994

## Articles

Timothy Kilgren, "Harold Pritchett: Communism & the International Woodworkers of America," Seattle Civil Rights and Labor History Project, www.civilrights.washington.edu.

"Labor: Christmas Shutdown," *Time*, December 16, 1940.

Richard L. Neuberger, "Lusty Seattle, Still Pioneer at Heart: Port for the Klondike, It Draws Soldiers of Fortune Even as It Goes About the Business of Shipping and Lumbering and Getting in the News," *The New York Times*, February 7, 1937.

Richard L. Neuberger, "Labor War Stirs Northwest: Public There Views Battle as One for Supremacy between A.F. of L. and C.I.O.," *The New York Times*, May 23, 1937.

Richard L. Neuberger, "Labor Unrest Invades the Deep Forests: Loggers Unionize Their Lusty Calling in the Lonely Hills of the Far West," *The New York Times*, May 30, 1937.

Richard L. Neuberger, "Showdown is Near in Pacific Unions: Battle Looked for Between A.F. of L. and C.I.O., With Woodworkers Deciding," *The New York Times*, June 6, 1937.

Rod Palmquist, "Labor's Great War on the Seattle Waterfront: A History of the 1934 Longshore Strike," Waterfront Workers History Project, http://depts.washington.edu/dock/index.shtml

Gerald A. Rose, "The Westwood Lumber Strike," *Labor History* 13, no. 2 (1972): 171-199.

# Acknowledgements

To my patient, adorable, loving wife and daughter, thank you. Honestly, I never knew it would take that long.

Thank you to Helen Pettay for her masterful editing and ability to manage an author's frustrations as well as typos. Also, to Kathryn Froelich, you are a wonderful proofreader and so encouraging. Thank you.

Also, I must mention three people who were essential in keeping me going—they gave me encouragement when I was ready to quit: Jamese Rhoades, Paul Hemp, and, of course, my wife Barbara. And to Doug Smith and Jess Friedberg Smith, you don't know how much your encouragement meant.

Finally, thanks for the stories, Rube.

# About the Author

Ron Geigle was born and raised in the Pacific Northwest. He has spent most of his career in Washington, DC, working as a congressional aide and speech writer. In 1999, he founded the public relations firm Polidais. He is now completing a children's book, which will be published in 2014.

Made in the USA
San Bernardino, CA
29 March 2014